Praise for Patricia Davids and her novels

"A wonderful story…"
—*RT Book Reviews* on *The Farmer Next Door*

"Davids' deep understanding of Amish culture is evident in the compassionate characters and beautiful descriptions."
—*RT Book Reviews* on *A Home for Hannah*

"Davids' latest beautifully portrays the Amish belief that everything happens for a reason, which helps one focus on the most important things in life."
—*RT Book Reviews* on *The Christmas Quilt*

Praise for Kit Wilkinson and her novels

"[A]n engaging, well-paced tale."
—*RT Book Reviews* on *Lancaster County Target*

"This excellent story builds an intriguing mystery."
—*RT Book Reviews* on *Sabotage*

"Plenty of action, a heartwarming love story and a good mystery make this a compelling read."
—*RT Book Reviews* on *Protector's Honor*

After thirty-five years as a nurse, **Patricia Davids** hung up her stethoscope to become a full-time writer. She enjoys spending her free time visiting her grandchildren, doing some long-overdue yard work and traveling to research her story locations. She resides in Wichita, Kansas. Pat always enjoys hearing from her readers. You can visit her online at patriciadavids.com.

Kit Wilkinson is a former PhD student who once wrote discussions on the medieval feminine voice. She now prefers weaving stories of romance and redemption. Her first inspirational manuscript won a prestigious Golden Heart® Award. You can visit Kit at kitwilkinson.com or write to her at write@kitwilkinson.com.

USA TODAY Bestselling Author

PATRICIA DAVIDS

The Farmer Next Door

&

KIT WILKINSON

Lancaster County Target

H HARLEQUIN® LOVE INSPIRED®

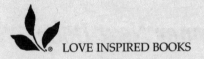

LOVE INSPIRED BOOKS

Recycling programs
for this product may
not exist in your area.

ISBN-13: 978-0-373-83892-9

The Farmer Next Door and Lancaster County Target

Copyright © 2016 by Harlequin Books S.A.

The publisher acknowledges the copyright holders
of the individual works as follows:

The Farmer Next Door
Copyright © 2011 by Patricia MacDonald

Lancaster County Target
Copyright © 2014 by Kit Wilkinson

www.Harlequin.com

Printed in U.S.A.

CONTENTS

THE FARMER NEXT DOOR

Patricia Davids

This book is dedicated with deep love
and affection to my mother, Joan,
a true wise-hearted woman.

And all the women that were wise hearted
did spin with their hands, and brought that
which they had spun, both of blue, and of
purple, and of scarlet, and of fine linen.
—*Exodus* 35:25

Chapter One

If the Amish farmer standing outside her screen door would smile, he'd be a nice-looking fellow—but he certainly wasn't smiling at the moment. His fierce scowl was a sharp reminder of all her life had been before— tense, fearful, pain-filled.

Faith Martin thrust aside her somber memories. She would not allow the past to follow her here. She had nothing to fear in this new community.

Still, the man at her door made an imposing figure blocking out much of the late afternoon sunlight streaming in behind him. His flat-topped straw hat sat squarely above his furrowed brow. That frown put a deep crease between his intelligent hazel eyes.

Above his reddish-brown beard, his full lips barely moved when he spoke. "*Goot* day, *Frau.* I am Adrian Lapp. I own the farm to the south."

His beard told her he was married. Amish men were clean-shaven until after they took a wife. He had his pale blue shirtsleeves rolled up exposing brawny, darkly tanned forearms folded tightly across his gray vest. A familiar, nauseous odor emanated from his clothes.

Faith's heart sank. It was clear he'd had a run-in

with one of her herd. What had he been doing with her animals?

She managed a polite nod. Common courtesy dictated she welcome him to her home. "I'm pleased to meet you, neighbor. I am Faith Martin. Do come in."

He made no move to enter. "Is your husband about?"

It seemed the farmer next door wasn't exactly the friendly sort. That was too bad. She had prayed it would be different here. "My husband passed away two years ago. It's just me. How may I help you?"

Her widowed status seemed to surprise him. "You're living here alone?"

"Ja." She brushed at the dust and cobwebs on her apron and tried to look like a woman who managed well by herself instead of one who'd bitten off far more than she could chew.

His scowl deepened. "Your creatures are loose in my fields. They are eating my beans."

Faith cringed inwardly. This was not the first impression she wanted to make in her new community. "I'm so sorry. I don't know how they could have gotten out."

"I tried to catch one of them by its halter, but it spat on me and ran off with the others into the cornfield."

She saw the green, speckled stain across the front shoulder of his shirt and vest. Alpaca spit, a combination of grass and digestive juices, was unpleasant but not harmful. What a shame this had to be her new neighbor's first introduction to her alpacas. They were normally docile, friendly animals.

Faith never tired of seeing their bright, inquisitive faces waiting for her each morning. Their sweet, gentle natures had helped her heal in both body and spirit over the past two years.

"The one wearing a halter is Myrtle. She's the expectant mother in the herd. You must have frightened her. They are leery of strangers."

"So I noticed," he answered drily.

"Spitting is their least endearing habit, but it will brush off when it dries." Faith's encouraging tone didn't lighten his scowl. Perhaps now wasn't the time to mention the smell would linger for a few days.

"What did you call them?"

"Alpacas. They're like llamas but they have very soft fleece, softer than any sheep. Originally, they come from South America. How many did you say were in your field?"

"I counted ten."

"Oh, no!" Fear blotted out any concern for her neighbor's shirt. If all of her animals were loose in unfamiliar country, it would be difficult, even impossible, to round them up before dark.

Her defenseless alpacas couldn't spend the night out in the open. Stray dogs or coyotes could easily bring down one of her half-grown crias, or they might wander onto the highway and be hit by a passing car. She couldn't afford the loss of even one animal. She had everything invested in this venture and much more than money riding on her success.

Please, Lord, let me recover them all safe and sound.

As much as she hated to be seen using her crutch, Faith grabbed it from behind the door. It was wrong to be vain about her handicap, but she couldn't help it. It was a personal battle she had yet to win.

The pickup truck that had crashed into their buggy two years ago had killed her husband and left her with a badly mangled leg. Doctors told her it would be a miracle if she ever walked again, but God had shown her mercy. After a long, difficult recovery she was able to get around with only her leg brace most of the time. But chasing down a herd of frisky alpacas required exertion and speed. Things she couldn't manage without added support.

She pushed open the screen door, forcing Adrian Lapp to take a step back. She didn't miss the way his eyes widened at the sight of her infirmity.

Let him stare. It wasn't something she could keep secret. She knew her crippled leg made her ugly and awkward, a person to be pitied, but she wouldn't let it be her weakness. Right now, the safety of her animals was the important thing, not her new neighbor's opinion of her. "Where did you see them last?"

"Disappearing into the cornfield beyond the orchard at the back of your property."

"I will need to get their halters and lead ropes from the barn." She left him standing on the porch as she made her way down the steps.

Adrian quickly caught up with her. "I'm sorry, I didn't know… I will take care of the animals for you. There is no need for you to go traipsing after them."

His offer was grudgingly given, but she sensed he meant well.

"I'm perfectly capable of catching them." She didn't want pity, and she wasn't about to leave her valuable livestock in the hands of a man who didn't even know what kind of animal they were.

Hobbling ahead of him across the weedy yard, she spoke over her shoulder. "Once I catch them, can you help me lead them home?"

"Of course."

Faith headed toward the small, dilapidated barn nestled between overgrown cedars some fifty yards from the house. In the harsh August sunlight it was easy to see the peeling paint, missing shingles and broken windowpanes on the building. The Amish were known for their neat and well-tended farmsteads. She had a lot of work ahead of her to get this place in shape.

She didn't know why her husband had never mentioned owning this property in Ohio or why he had chosen to leave it sitting vacant all these years, but finding out a month ago that she owned it couldn't have come at a better time.

She pulled open the barn door. Copper, her mare, whinnied a greeting. Faith spoke a few soft words to her as she gathered together the halters and lead ropes that were hanging on pegs inside the doorway.

Adrian took them from her without a word and slipped them over his shoulder. She was grateful for his help but wished he wasn't so dour about it. Why couldn't her alpacas have chosen to eat the beans of a cheerful neighbor? Maybe she didn't have any.

She led the way around the side of the barn to the pens at the rear. The gate panel that should have been wired closed had been pushed over, offering the curious alpacas an easy way out. Why hadn't she paid more attention when her hired help set up the portable pen and unloaded the animals? Now look what her carelessness had wrought.

Adrian removed the thin wire that had proven to be an ineffective deterrent. "Do you have a heavier gauge wire than this or some strong rope?"

"I'm sure there's something in the barn that will work."

"Then I should find it." He turned back toward the barn door.

Faith called after him. "Shouldn't we find my animals first and then worry about how to keep them in? It's getting late."

He didn't even glance in her direction. "It won't do any good to bring them back if they can just get out again."

She pressed her lips closed on a retort. She had learned the hard way not to argue with a man. Her husband had made sure she understood her opinions were not valued.

Leaving her new neighbor to rummage in the barn, Faith headed toward the rows of trees that stretched for a quarter of a mile to the back edge of her property, knowing he could easily overtake her. It was slow going through the thick grass, but at least she knew her alpacas would be well-fed through the summer and fall once she had her fences in place.

It didn't take long for Adrian to catch up with her. As she expected, his long legs made short work of the distance she had struggled to cover. A twinge of resentment rippled through her before she firmly reminded herself it didn't matter if someone could walk faster than she could. All that mattered was that she walk upon the path the Lord had chosen for her without complaint.

Adrian wasn't sure what to make of the woman charging ahead of him through the tangled grass of the old orchard. Her handicap clearly didn't slow her down much. He'd been curious about his new neighbors as soon as he'd spotted the moving van and large horse trailer inching up the rutted lane yesterday.

The farmstead had been deserted since he'd been a lad. It hurt his soul to see the good farm ground lying fallow and the peach orchard's fruit going to waste year after year. He could do so much with it if only he had the chance.

Even though he'd seen he had new neighbors, he hadn't gone to introduce himself. He didn't like meeting people or answering questions about his life. He liked being alone. He preferred to stay on his farm and work until he was bone-tired and weary enough to fall asleep as soon as his head hit the pillow at night.

Too tired even for dreams…or for nightmares.

He wouldn't be here today if Faith Martin had kept her animals penned up properly. This was costing him an afternoon of work that couldn't wait.

He glanced sideways at her. She was a tiny slip of a woman. She didn't look as if she could wrest this land and buildings back into shape by herself. A stiff wind could blow her away. Why, the top of her head barely reached his chin whiskers.

A white prayer *kapp* covering her chestnut-brown hair proclaimed her to be a member of the Plain faith, but he didn't recognize the pattern. Where had she come from?

She wore a long blue dress with a black apron and the same type of dark stockings and sturdy shoes that all the women in his family wore. As she walked beside him, the breeze fluttered the long ribbons of her *kapp* about her heart-shaped face, drawing his attention to the slope of her jaw and the slender curve of her neck. She was a pretty little thing with eyes bright blue as a robin's egg. She had long eyelashes and full pink lips.

Lips made for a man to kiss.

He tore his gaze away as heat rushed to his face. He had no business thinking such thoughts about a woman he barely knew. What was wrong with him? He'd not taken this much notice of a woman since his teenage years.

He used to look at Lovina that way, used to imagine what it would be like to kiss her. When they wed he discovered her kisses were even sweeter than he'd dreamed. After her death, he'd buried his heart with her and raised their son alone until...

So what was it about Faith Martin that stirred this sudden interest? He studied her covertly. She pressed her lips into a tight line as she concentrated on her footing. Did walking cause her pain?

Her eyes darted to his face, but she quickly looked away as if she were uncomfortable in his presence. Her glance held a wary edge that surprised him. Was she frightened of him?

He hadn't meant to scare her. He quickly grew ashamed for having done so. He wasn't used to interacting with new people. Everyone in his family and the community knew of his desire to live alone. He truly had no reason to be surly with this woman. Her alpacas hadn't actually damaged his crop.

He glanced at her again. How could he set this right? How could he bring back her smile?

Adrian abruptly refocused his attention to the task at hand. He had a corncrib to finish and more work waiting for him at home. He didn't have time to worry about making a stranger smile. He would help her gather her animals and then get back to his labors. A few moments later they reached the end of the orchard.

The fence that separated her land from his had fallen down long ago. Only a few rotting uprights remained to mark the boundary. Beyond it, his cornfield stood in tall, straight rows. There was no sign of her odd creatures. They could be anywhere by now.

Faith cupped her hands around her mouth and called out, "Myrtle, Candy, Baby Face. Supper time."

He listened for any sound in return but heard only

the rustle of the wind moving through the cornstalks. What did an alpaca sound like? Did they moo or bleat?

She took a step farther into the field. "Come, Socks. Come, Bandit."

Suddenly, a wooly white face appeared at the end of the row a few yards away. He heard Faith's sigh of relief.

"There's my good girl. Come, Socks." The animal emerged from the corn and began walking toward her with its head held high, alert but wary. It was butternut-brown in color with a white face and four white legs. Its head was covered with a thick pelt of fleece, but the long neck and body had been recently shorn, leaving the animal with an oddly naked appearance. It approached to within ten feet, but wouldn't come closer.

Faith glanced at Adrian. "Give me one of the halters and a lead rope and wait here."

He had no intention of venturing closer. Although the animal looked harmless, he still reeked of Myrtle's earlier disapproval.

Faith walked toward Socks with her hand out. The animal made a low humming sound, then ambled up to her and wrapped its long neck around her in a hug.

"Were you lost and scared? It's okay now. I know the way home." She crooned to it like a child as she slipped the halter on, then scratched behind the alpaca's ear.

A second animal stepped out of the corn. It already wore a halter. Adrian recognized it as the one that had spit on him. As soon as she caught sight of him, she turned back into the cornfield.

Faith led Socks to Adrian and handed him the lead rope. "Try not to scare her. If one gives an alarm cry, they may all scatter."

Faith took several halters and ropes from him and disappeared into his cornfield without another word.

Adrian found himself alone with the strangest animal he'd ever beheld.

He studied the creature's face. It was calmly studying him in return with large, liquid black eyes fringed with long black lashes. Besides doe-like eyes, Socks had a delicate muzzle with two protruding lower teeth. Her narrow, perked ears reminded him of a rabbit. Her round body was similar to a sheep, but she had long legs like a deer. Looking down, he saw two large, hooked toenails on each front foot that could have belonged to a giant bird.

When Socks tried to nibble his beard, he drew back abruptly, uncertain of her intentions. "I have orders not to scare you."

Socks hummed softly and didn't spit.

So far, so good.

Reaching out, Adrian scratched behind her ear as he'd seen Faith do. Socks closed her eyes and nuzzled into his hand. Her thick wool was as soft as anything he'd ever touched. He smiled at the sound of her hum. They might be odd-looking creatures, but they had a certain appeal. When they weren't spitting.

He ran a hand down her camel-like neck. She stood, patient and unconcerned. With his confidence in her temperament restored, he gave free rein to his curiosity. He wanted a closer look at her strange feet.

As soon as he grasped her leg, Socks lifted her foot as any well-trained horse would do. To his surprise, the bottoms of her feet were soft pads much like a dog's foot, not a hoof at all.

Straightening, he stroked her nose and chuckled. "It appears the Lord assembled you from leftover animal parts."

Socks looked past him and called softly. He turned

and saw another alpaca, this one black as night, emerge and look in his direction. Should he call out to Faith or would that scare the animal?

It looked more curious than frightened. He gave a gentle tug on the lead rope and walked with Socks toward her friend. He made a soft humming sound, hoping to soothe the animal and not frighten it into running away. Was he going to help Faith, or was he about to make things worse?

Tired, hot and discouraged, Faith emerged from the forest of corn thirty minutes later with only two of her alpacas in tow. The sun was touching the horizon. It would be dark within the hour. How would she find the others then? She would need dozens of people to comb this acreage properly in the dark.

It seemed she was destined to meet more of her neighbors tonight and not under the best of circumstances.

She had no doubt they would come to help. That was the Amish way. She would not be prideful. She would ask Adrian Lapp to gather a group to help in her search.

To her surprise, Adrian wasn't where she had left him. She glanced around, wondering if she had come out of the corn in the wrong place. No, this was the spot. Had he gone back to his own work? What kind of neighbor was he, anyway?

"I shouldn't be judgmental. Perhaps his work is as pressing as mine." As usual, Myrtle proved to be a good listener and followed obediently behind Faith.

"All I have to do is round up my missing animals, start a business and ready a dilapidated house to pass inspection in a week's time so I may become the guardian of my brother's child. I'm sure Mr. Lapp is equally as busy."

Tears pricked the backs of Faith's eyes as she struggled through the long grass. The past two years had been incredibly hard. First, there had been the terrible crash and her husband's death. She'd spent weeks in the hospital afterward. Her small savings had covered only a fraction of her medical bills. Thankfully, the congregation at her church had taken up a collection to pay the rest, but it left her little to live on. It had taken her more than a year to get back on solid financial ground.

Then, three months ago came word that her brother and his wife had been killed in a flash flood, leaving their five-year-old son an orphan. As the boy's only relative, she was willing and eager to take Kyle in. She'd been halfway through the maze of paperwork and home studies needed to approve his adoption when her landlord had informed her he had to sell the farm she'd been renting.

Her adoption plans fell apart. She couldn't take in a child when she was about to lose the roof over her head.

But in the midst of her despair, the Lord had delivered what seemed like a miracle. A delinquent property tax statement had arrived in the mail addressed to her husband. It was then that she'd learned she owned a house and farm in Ohio. She'd spent every penny she could scrape together to pay the bill and move.

She hadn't expected to find the place in such deplorable condition.

Was this God's way of telling her Kyle didn't belong with her? Did He want Isaac's child raised in the English world her brother had chosen instead of in her Amish faith?

Why would God see fit to give Isaac's child into her care when He had denied her children of her own?

She had no answers to the questions and doubts that

plagued her. It would be all too easy to sit down and bawl like a baby, but what would that fix? She sniffed back her tears and blinked hard, refusing to let them fall.

Tears hadn't made her husband a kind man. They wouldn't bring back her brother or undo any of the pain she had endured. They certainly wouldn't build fences for her alpacas, clean her house or make it a home for a lonely little boy.

She stopped to rest her aching leg and looked heavenward. "I know You never give us more than we can bear, but I could use Your strength right now. Help me, Lord. I beseech You."

As always, she felt the comfort of God's presence in her life whenever she turned to Him. She must not let her despair or her fears gain the upper hand. God was watching over her.

Had not the letter come in her hour of need telling her she owned this land? So what if it was going to take hard work to make it livable? She knew how to work. God would provide. She had faith in His mercy. Here in Ohio she had started Kyle's adoption process again. Now she had to prove to a new agency worker that she had a safe home and a stable income.

Which was exactly what she didn't have yet.

Drawing a deep breath, she started forward again. The time for tears was past. This was the new path the Lord had chosen for her. She had to believe it would be better than the life she'd left behind.

Chapter Two

When Faith emerged from the trees, she stopped short in surprise. Adrian Lapp stood beside her barn with all eight of her missing alpacas clustered around him in their pen. It seemed her prayers had been answered, and apparently her grumpy neighbor had a way with animals.

Not two minutes ago she had been piling unkind thoughts on his head.

Forgive me, Lord. I judged this man unfairly. I won't do it again.

Walking up to Adrian, she said, "I can't believe it. You found them."

"It was more like they found me."

Bandit stood close beside him, sniffing at his beard. He gently pushed the inquisitive black alpaca away and opened the gate so Faith could add her two to the herd. Adrian said, "I fixed the pen. They shouldn't get out again."

"Thank you. I was so worried I wouldn't be able to find them before dark. This move has been hard on all of them."

"And on you?"

Her gaze locked with his. Did she look like such a mess? She must. Embarrassment sent heat flooding to her face. Socks chose that moment to nibble at the rim of Adrian's straw hat. He pushed the alpaca gently aside. Faith concentrated on removing the halters from her pair.

"Where have you come from, Faith Martin? Surely not South America like your animals."

His interest seemed genuine. Some of her discomfort faded. "Originally, I'm from Indiana, but on this move I came from Missouri."

"That's a lot of miles."

It was, and many more than he knew. Her husband had been affected with a wanderlust that had taken them to twelve different communities in the ten years they'd been married. Faith was determined that this farm would be her final home. She wanted to put down roots, to become a true member of a community, things she'd never been able to do during her marriage.

Besides, she had to make a home for Kyle. A place where her brother's child could recover from the tragedy of losing his parents and grow into manhood. This was her last move. If it was God's will, she didn't plan to leave Hope Springs, Ohio, until He called her home.

"I'm grateful for your help, neighbor. I have fresh lemonade in the house. Can I offer you a glass?"

He opened the gate and slipped out, securing the panels with a quick twist of heavy wire, then double checking it to make sure it would hold. "*Nee.* I must get back to my work."

With her overture of friendship soundly rejected, she nodded and started toward the house.

He hesitated, then fell into step beside her. "What are your plans for this place?"

Oddly pleased by his interest, she said, "I want to enclose the orchard area with new fence. In the future I will divide it into separate pens so I can rotate where the alpacas graze. In spite of their behavior today, the fencing is really to keep predators out. My babies won't try to wander once they become accustomed to their new home. After that, I need to fix up the barn well enough to store winter hay for them." She walked slowly, more tired than she cared to admit.

"So my beans will be safe in the future?"

He hadn't really been interested in her plans, only in making sure his crops wouldn't be destroyed.

"*Ja,* as soon as I have the fences up. Of course, I will pay for any damages my animals caused."

"That won't be necessary. Do you plan to do all this work yourself?"

Faith paused and drew herself to her full height of five-foot-one. "I'm stronger than I look. I'm not afraid of hard work. With God's help I shall manage."

His eyes grew troubled. "I was going to offer the names of some young men who could use the work. That is why I asked. I did not mean to offend."

He had a gruff manner, but he was clearly sorry to have upset her.

Her defiance drained away, leaving her embarrassed. "I don't have the money to pay a hired man. Once I sell the yarns I am spinning, I will consider hiring someone."

"A light purse is nothing to be ashamed of."

"You're right, but I don't want people here to think I will be a burden on them."

"We would not think such a thing, Faith Martin. It would be un-Christian." There was a hint of rebuke in his words.

Amish families and communities supported all Amish widows and orphans. It was everyone's responsibility to care for them, but Faith needed to be able to take care of herself.

At her age and with her disability, she had no hope of marrying again. Even if such an offer came her way, she would never place her fate in the hands of another man. No, never again. The thought of doing so sent cold chills down her spine.

She looked up to see Adrian studying her intently. His frown had returned, but she wasn't frightened by it now. It was more bluff than substance.

He said, "If you find this farm is more than you can handle, I'll be happy to take it off your hands. For a fair price."

"I'm not interested in selling. I plan on staying here a long, long time."

"Then I pray you fare well among us, but do not forget my offer."

Faith watched as he strode away with long, easy strides. She saw a man at ease in his surroundings and at home on his own well-tended land. Not overly friendly, but not unfriendly. She found him…interesting. If his spouse was pleasant, they might prove to be good neighbors. She liked the idea of having someone close by to count on in an emergency.

She had turned down his offer to buy the place, but she sensed he didn't believe she could make a go of it on her own.

Why shouldn't he doubt her? She doubted herself. For years Mose had hammered into her head what a failure she was as a wife. She couldn't give him children. It was her fault all his business enterprises failed because she didn't work hard enough.

In her heart she knew he was wrong, but after a while it ceased to matter. She had simply accepted the unkind things he'd said and kept quiet.

But Mose was gone now, and she had to believe in herself again. This was the time and place to start.

Watching Adrian cross the field toward his farm, she wondered what it would be like to have a strong, handsome man like Adrian Lapp for a husband? She shook her head at her foolish musing.

A woman could not tell if a man would be a good husband by his looks. Mose had been a handsome fellow, but his good-looking face had hidden a mean nature at odds with the teachings of their Amish faith.

She forgave Mose for the good of her own soul. He was standing now before a just God, answering for his sins while she was free to live a quiet and humble life. It would be enough.

She wondered if other Amish wives suffered silently as she had done. She prayed it wasn't true. In her heart she wanted to believe in the gentle nature of men who professed submission to God in every aspect of their lives—but there was no way to be certain. Only God could see into the hearts of men.

Pushing aside the host of unhappy memories gathered during her marriage, Faith entered her new home determined to finish sweeping away years of debris and clutter, from the house and from her heart. She was ready for her new beginning.

"I heard someone has moved into the old Delker place. Do you know anything about it?" Ben Lapp handed the next set of boards up to Adrian who was perched on the top of the new corncrib.

Adrian knew there would be no end to his brother's curiosity. He might as well tell him everything he knew.

"*Ja,* I met her yesterday. Her name is Faith Martin. She is Amish and a widow."

"I don't suppose she has a pretty daughter or two?" Ben asked hopefully. At seventeen, Adrian's youngest brother was in the first year of his *rumspringa,* his running around time, and always on the lookout for new girls to impress.

Adrian hated to dash his hopes. "Sorry, but she said she was alone."

"Too bad. A pretty new face would be welcome in this area."

Adrian recalled Faith's soft blue eyes and the sweet curve of her lips. "She is pretty enough."

"Really?"

Adrian caught the sudden interest in Ben's tone and grinned. "Pretty enough for a woman in her thirties."

Ben's face fell. "She's an old woman, then."

"Do you consider me old? I'm but thirty-two."

Adrian tried not to smile as he watched the struggle taking place behind his baby brother's eyes. Finally, Ben said, "You're not so old."

"Not *so* old. That's good to know for I was thinking of getting a cane when I went to market."

The thought of a cane brought a sudden vision of Faith struggling through the long grass with her crutch. How was she doing today? And why was he thinking about her again?

Ben grinned. "Tell me more about the widow. What's she like?"

Determined, pretty, kind to her animals, wary, worried. A number of ways to describe his new neighbor darted through Adrian's mind, but they all sounded personal, as if he'd taken an interest in her. "She raises alpacas."

"Alpacas? Why?"

"She spins their fleece into yarn for sale."

"I remember grandmother Lapp sitting at her spinning wheel. It was fascinating to watch her nimble fingers at work even when she was very old."

"I remember that, too."

"I never understood how chunks of wool became strands of yarn. Whatever became of her spinning wheel?"

"I suppose it's in *Mamm*'s attic if one of our sisters doesn't have it."

"It's sad to think someone is living at the Delker farm now."

"Why do you say that?" Adrian hammered the last board in place.

"Because we could eat all the peaches we wanted from those trees. No one cared. Now, we'll have to get permission. Is the house still in decent shape?"

"From the outside it doesn't look too bad. I'm not sure about the inside." Maybe he should stop in again and see if there was something Faith needed done around the place. That would be neighborly.

Not that he was looking for an excuse to see her again. He wasn't. He grew annoyed that she kept intruding into his carefully ordered world.

Ben backed down the ladder. "Do you even remember the people who lived there before?"

Adrian followed him. "I remember an old *Englisch* woman yelling at our cousin Sarah and I when we were helping ourselves to some low-hanging fruit. I must have been ten. She scared the daylights out of us. I think she went to a nursing home not long after that. When she passed away, the place stayed vacant."

"Is the new owner a relative?"

"That I don't know."

"Didn't you try to buy the place a few years ago?"

"More than once. I got a name and address from the County Recorder's office and sent several letters over the years, but no one ever answered me. I even tried to buy it from her yesterday, but she wasn't interested in selling." He could still hear the determination in her voice when she turned him down.

Determination was one thing. A strong back was another. She'd need both to get that place in working order.

"It's odd that she'd show up after all this time. I wonder why?" Ben mused.

Gathering together his tools, Adrian started toward the house. He'd spent more than enough time thinking about Faith Martin. "It's none of our business."

"Not our business? Ha! Tell that to *Mamm*. She'll be wanting every little detail, and she'll have it by Sunday next or I'll eat my hat." Ben fell into step beside Adrian.

It irked Adrian that he couldn't get Faith off his mind. What was she doing? Were her alpacas safe? Was she having trouble putting up fences for them? It would be a big job for one woman alone.

Ben wrinkled his nose in disgust. "What's that smell?"

Adrian swiped at the shoulder of his vest. The dried juice had brushed off, but not the aroma. "Alpaca spit."

"That's nasty. I didn't know they spit."

"Only if you scare them."

"I'll avoid doing that."

"Me, too, from now on."

"Before I forget, *Mamm* wanted me to remind you to come to supper tomorrow night."

Alerted by the sudden uncomfortable tone in Ben's voice, Adrian stopped. "Why would I need reminding? I come to supper every Wednesday evening with the family."

"That's what I told her."

Adrian closed his eyes and sighed deeply. "Who is it this time?"

"Who is what?" Ben looked the picture of innocence. Adrian wasn't fooled.

Leveling a no-nonsense, tell-me-the-truth look at his brother, Adrian repeated himself. "Who is it this time?"

"Edna Hershberger," Ben admitted and flinched.

"Edna? She's at least fifteen years older than I am."

"Her cousin is visiting from Apple Creek. Her younger female cousin. I hear she's nice-looking."

"Why does Mother keep doing this?" Adrian started walking again. He wasn't interested in meeting marriageable women. He would never marry again. He had sworn that over his young wife's grave when he'd laid their son to rest beside her.

"Mother wants to see you happy."

"I am happy." The moment he said the words he knew they were a lie.

"No, you're not. You haven't been happy since Lovina and Gideon died."

The mention of his wife and son sent a sharp stab of pain through Adrian's chest. He bore wounds that would not heal. No one understood that. "I'd rather not talk about them."

"It's been three years since Gideon died, Adrian. It's been eight years since Lovina passed away."

"For me, it was yesterday."

God had taken away the people he loved, leaving Adrian an empty shell of a man. An empty shell could not love anyone, certainly not God, for He had stripped away the most important parts of Adrian's life.

Adrian went through the motions of his faith, but each day it became harder to repeat the platitudes that no longer held meaning for him. Disowning his Amish faith would only lead to being separated from his remaining family. For their sakes he kept his opinions about God to himself.

Ben laid a hand on Adrian's shoulder. "You can't blame *Mamm* for worrying about you."

Adrian met his brother's gaze. "Mother needs to accept that I won't marry again. You can tell her I've made other plans for tomorrow evening."

"What plans?" Ben called after him.

Adrian didn't answer him. Instead, he walked to the end of his lane and up the road for a quarter of a mile to where a small field of tombstones lay enclosed by a white wooden fence. A fence he painted each year to keep it looking nice.

He opened the gate and crossed the field to where an old cedar tree had been cut down. The stump made a perfect seat for him to sit and visit with his wife and son.

The breeze blew softly across the open field. Beyond the fence he saw fat black-and-white cattle grazing in a neighbor's pasture. Overhead the blue sky held a few white clouds that changed shape as they traveled on the wind. He took off his hat and looked down at the small tombstones that bore the names of his wife and child.

"It's another pretty day, isn't it, Lovina? I remember how much you enjoyed the summer evenings when the days stretch out so long. I miss sitting with you on the porch and watching the sun go down. I miss everything about both of you."

Tears filled his eyes as emotions clogged his throat. It took a minute before he could go on.

Clearing his throat, he said, "We've got a new neighbor. Her name is Faith Martin. I think you'd like her. You should see the strange animals she has. They spit. I think I like sheep better and you know how much I dislike them."

Clasping his hands together, he leaned forward with his elbows propped on his knees. "*Mamm* is at it again. She's trying to fix me up with a cousin of Edna Hershberger. I wish she would learn to leave well enough alone. I don't want anyone else. You will be my only wife in this life and in the next. If Gideon had lived, it might have been different."

The tears came back, forcing him to lift his head. "A boy needs a mother, but he's with you now. I know that makes you happy because it gives me comfort, too."

He sniffed once and wiped his eyes with the heels of his hands. "I'm not going over to *Mamm*'s for supper tomorrow. I'm sorry if that disappoints you. I've decided to go over to Faith Martin's. That place needs too much work for a woman alone to do it all. I can spare an hour or two in the morning and again at night. The days are long now," he added with a wry smile.

The memory of Faith declaring she wasn't afraid of work slipped into his mind. "She reminds me of you a little bit in the way her chin comes up when she's riled. She said an odd thing yesterday. She said she didn't want people here to think she would be a burden. It makes me wonder who made her feel that way in her last community."

Having said what he needed to say, he rose to his feet. "Enough about our neighbor. Give Gideon a kiss for me. I miss you, Lovey."

So much so it was hard to put into words. "Sometimes, I wake at night and I still reach for you. But you aren't there and it hurts all over again."

As he walked away, he wondered if Faith Martin woke in the night and reached for the husband who was gone.

Chapter Three

Faith woke to the sound of a persistent clanking coming from outside her house. Squinting, she could just make out the hands of the clock on her dresser. Six thirty-five.

Her eyes popped open wide. Six thirty-five! Panic sent her heart racing. Mose would be so angry when he discovered she'd slept late.

Throwing back the sheet, she sat up and stopped as every muscle in her body protested the quick movement. Had he beaten her again? What had she done wrong this time? She couldn't remember.

Swinging her feet off the mattress, she reached for her clothes. They weren't on a chair beside the bed. Looking around the strange room, she saw them hanging from a peg on the wall. Her panic dropped away like a stone from her chest. She drew a deep breath.

Mose might be gone, but his imprint remained in her life. In moments of mindless panic like this one. In nightmares that left her weak and shaking in the night.

Faith began to recite her morning prayers, letting the grace of God's presence wash away her fears and restore her peace.

Dear Lord, I give You thanks for this new day, for my new home and for the strength to face whatever may come my way. I know You are with me, always. Watch over Kyle and keep him safe. If it is Your will, Lord, let him join me here, soon. Amen.

A few years ago her morning prayers had been much simpler. *Please don't let me make Mose angry today.* Sometimes, she wondered if she would ever be truly free of him.

She stood and crossed to the open window. The sound of hammering started up again. It was coming from her orchard, but she couldn't see anyone. What was going on?

She dressed and set to work quickly brushing out her hip-length hair. When it was smooth, she parted it straight down the middle and began to make a tight roll of it along her hairline pulling all of it together and finally twisting the remainder into a tight bun, which she pinned at the back of her head. With her hair secure, she donned her *kapp* and pinned it in place. Outside, the clanking continued.

Sitting on the edge of the bed, she buckled on her leg brace, wincing as the padded bands came into contact with her chafed skin. She was paying for all the time she'd spent working and sweating the past few days. She needed to apply more salve to the reddened areas, but that would have to wait. Her priority was finding out what was going on outside.

After leaving the house, she limped to the barn to check on her animals. Copper dozed in her stall. The alpacas, all ten of them, as Faith quickly counted, stood or lay in their pen outside. Relieved, but with mounting curiosity, Faith made her way into the orchard.

A few yards from where she had stopped building the

fence the evening before, Adrian Lapp was pounding a steel fence post into the ground. He'd already added several stakes along the string she had laid out to mark the boundary of her pen.

What was he doing here? She hadn't asked for his help. As quickly as her objections surfaced, she swallowed them. Humility was the cornerstone of her Amish faith. Being humble also meant accepting help when help was offered.

Adrian hadn't seen her yet. She watched as he effortlessly drove in the stakes with a metal sleeve that fit over the top of each post. Compared to the heavy maul she had used to painstakingly pound each post into the ground, his tool made the job much easier. And he didn't even have to stand on the wooden box she had used just to reach the top of the six-foot-tall t-posts.

All right, he was strong and tall. It was a great combination when building fences, but that didn't mean she needed to stand here staring. She had half a mind to go back to the house and let him finish the row, but her conscience wouldn't let her. This was her property now. She was the one who needed to take care of it.

"Guder mariye," she called out in her native Pennsylvania Dutch, the German dialect spoken by the Amish. "You've done a lot of work while I was lazing abed. *Danki.*"

He stopped pounding, wiped the sweat from his brow with his shirtsleeve, and nodded in her direction. "Good morning to you, too. You have accomplished quite a bit here yourself."

His gaze swept across the posts that she'd put in yesterday, the yard she had mown into order with an old scythe and the fresh laundry waving on the clothesline she'd strung between two trees beside the house.

"I could have done more if I'd had a fence post driver such as you have there." She walked toward him to look at the tool.

"They aren't expensive. You can pick them up pretty cheap at farm auctions."

"I will keep that in mind."

It seemed to Faith that he wanted to say more, but instead, he returned to pounding the post he was working on until he'd sunk it another two feet into the ground.

"I appreciate your help, Mr. Lapp, but I can manage on my own. I'm sure you have plenty of work to attend to."

"Call me Adrian. I've got a few free hours today. Do you have a wire stretcher? I can put up the fencing after I get these posts in if you do."

"It's in the barn along with the rolls of woven fence wire I want to use. Are you sure you have time to do this? I hate to impose."

"I'll do the posts this morning and come back this evening to finish putting up the wire. Unless you object?" He grabbed another stake, measured off the distance with a few quick steps and began hammering the post into the ground.

"That will be fine." Other than taking care of her animals, she would have the whole day free to work on the house. Adrian's help was a blessing she hadn't anticipated.

Still, she had plenty to do to get the house ready for the social worker's arrival next Wednesday. Would God understand if she did a little extra work on Sunday? Sundays were days of rest and prayer and a time for visiting with friends and family even if there wasn't a service.

Since Amish church services were held every other

Sunday, she would have another week before she had to face the entire congregation. Would they all be as kind and helpful as her new neighbor? He had a gruff way about him, but his actions spoke loudly of a kind heart.

After watching Adrian work for a few more minutes, Faith realized there was nothing she could do to help him and she was wasting time. She left him to his work and returned to the house giving thanks to God for her neighbor's timely intervention.

Inside the house she applied salve to her chafed leg, then set about making breakfast and a pot of strong coffee. An hour later, just as she was pulling a pair of cinnamon coffee cakes from the oven, Adrian came to the screen door.

She fought back a smile. With the windows wide-open to the morning breeze, she had been sure the smell of her baking would reach him.

He said, "I finished the row of posts you had laid out."

She set the second hot pan on the stovetop. "Already? You've saved me a lot of work. *Danki.* Would you like some coffee?"

He hesitated, then said, "I would."

When he came inside, her kitchen instantly felt small and crowded. Unease skittered over her skin. She moved away to make more room between them.

He looked for a peg to hang his hat on, but there wasn't one. He settled for tossing it on the sideboard and took a seat at her table. When he wasn't looming over her, Faith could breathe better.

He motioned toward the wallpaper with its faded yellow flowers. "You will have a lot to do to make this a plain house."

"*Ja.* It will be a big task. Every room is wallpapered."

She tapped the floor with her foot. "This black-and-white linoleum will be fine but there is pink-and-white linoleum in the bathroom."

The colorful flooring and wallpaper would all have to be taken out. The Amish lived in simplicity, as they believed was God's will. They avoided loud colors and worldly things such as electricity in order to live separate from the world. Hopefully, the bishop in her new community would give her plenty of time to make over the house from English to Amish.

She would have the option of painting her walls blue, green or gray. The brightly patterned linoleum on the bathroom floor would have to go. She could leave the planks underneath bare or replace the linoleum with a simpler, more modest color. It was all on her list of things to be done. A list she was whittling down much too slowly.

She cut two pieces of coffee cake and carried one of them along with a cup of coffee to the table. Adrian accepted her offering with a nod of thanks. "The county will take down the electric lines leading to the house, but you will have to take down the ones leading to the barn."

"I know. At least the gas stove still works and I was able to have the propane tank filled before I arrived."

Fetching a cup of coffee and a piece of cake for herself, she said, "I've cooked on a wood-burning stove, but I'm not a good hand at it."

Adrian's look of sympathy said it all. She sat down at the table with a heavy sigh. "I take it the *Ordnung* of this church district doesn't allow propane cook stoves?"

"*Nee,* we do not. The stove must be wood-burning or coal-burning. But you may have a propane-powered refrigerator and washing machine."

The thought of chopping wood or hauling coal on top of her other chores was enough to dampen her spirits. She glanced sadly at the stove. It was old, but it worked well. She would hate to see it go.

It was always this way when she moved to a new community. Each Amish church district had their own rules about what they allowed and what they didn't. Each bishop in charge of a district often interpreted those rules differently.

She had lived in several communities that used tractors in the fields instead of horses. When they'd lived in Mifflin County, Pennsylvania, their church district permitted members to drive only yellow buggies, another place only gray ones. Here in Hope Springs the buggies were black.

She would have to make all new *kapps* for herself, too. The women of each district wore distinctive patterns. She would get around to that if, and only if, she met with the approval of this community and they voted to accept her as a new church member.

If they didn't accept her, she would have to look for another nearby district who would or live as an outsider. "I must meet with your bishop soon."

"Bishop Zook is a good man. He will help you learn your way among us."

"Is he a good preacher?" she asked, half in jest. Church services often lasted three or more hours.

"I've only fallen asleep twice during his sermons." Adrian didn't crack a smile, but she saw the twinkle of humor in his eyes. It surprised and delighted her.

"Then he must be *wunderbarr*. I'm looking forward to my first church Sunday already."

Adrian changed the subject. "Are you a relative of Mrs. Delker, the woman who used to own this place?"

"No, but Mose, my husband, was a grandchild of hers. I inherited this farm after he passed away. It's odd really, because he never once mentioned owning a farm in Ohio."

"I tried to buy it from him about five years ago."

"Did you? That must have been when we were raising chickens in Nebraska. Why did he say he wouldn't sell?"

They had certainly needed the money. The chicken houses had been another of her husband's failed business ventures. They'd left Nebraska owing money to everyone from the feed store to their landlord. Only Mose's last venture, buying her first four alpacas, had actually turned out well.

She never understood how her husband talked people into loaning him money for his wild ideas or how he could just pick up and walk away without looking back or even feeling badly for those who'd lost money because of him. Every time they moved, they left hard feelings behind.

Would this new community receive her into the church if they knew her husband had left debts unpaid all across the Midwest? She was sorry now that she had mentioned Nebraska to Adrian.

"Your husband didn't give a reason why he wouldn't sell. He never answered my letters."

She wanted to tell Adrian how lucky he was *not* to have done business with her husband, but she wouldn't speak ill of the dead. She rose and took her cup to the sink. "We moved around a lot. Perhaps your letters missed him."

"Perhaps. Do you find it hard to talk about him?" he asked quietly.

"Yes." She kept her back to Adrian. It was hard to

talk about Mose because there was so little she could say about him that was good.

"I understand."

The odd quality in his tone made her look at him closely. The pain in his eyes touched her heart. Why was he so sad?

He rose abruptly and crossed the room to pick up his hat. "I must be going."

"Wait a moment." She quickly wrapped the remaining coffee cake in a length of cheesecloth and added a small package wrapped in brown paper and string to the top. She held it out to him. He stared at her as if he didn't understand.

"It's a small token of my appreciation for all your hard work. A pair of socks made from my alpaca yarn. Please tell your wife that she is welcome to visit anytime. I'm sure she and your children will enjoy meeting my animals."

Adrian blinked back the sudden sting of tears. Gideon would have loved to have seen Faith's animals and Lovina would have liked this new neighbor with her determined ways. It was so unfair that their lives had been cut short. So unfair that he had to go on living without them.

"Is something wrong?" Faith inquired softly.

He took the packages from her. "My wife and son passed away."

"I'm so sorry. You must miss them very much."

Adrian met Faith's sympathetic gaze. Oddly, he found he wanted to talk about Lovina and Gideon. Somehow, he knew Faith would understand.

"I miss them every day. My son would have liked your alpacas. He had a way with animals, that boy did. He was always finding lost and hurt creatures and bringing them home for me to make well."

"Little boys believe their fathers can do anything."

"Too bad it isn't true."

He hadn't been able to save his wife or his son. That bitter truth haunted him day and night.

He blinked hard to clear his vision. Faith's face swam into view. She understood. He saw it in her eyes. It was more than sympathy and compassion. She had been in the same dark place that surrounded him.

"How old was your son when he died?" she asked.

"Four."

"You mustn't think me cruel, but four years is a gift. I wish I might have had four years, even four days, with my daughters."

"You've lost children, too?"

"Twin daughters who were stillborn. I always wondered if that was why Mose was never able to settle in one place. If we'd had a family, maybe things would have been different. Only God knows."

"I wanted at least six children. Lovina wanted a dozen or more. Gideon was the first and he was perfect."

Adrian couldn't believe he was talking to this woman about his family. He hadn't been able to talk to anyone about them since Gideon's death. Maybe it was because she'd known the same kind of tragedy that he felt she understood what he was going through. Maybe it was because Ben had brought the subject up yesterday.

Whatever the reason, Adrian suddenly decided not to bare more of his soul. Remembering was too painful.

He said, "The coffee cake is appreciated. I'll be back tonight to help finish your fence. I need my bean crop kept safe from your overgrown rabbits."

"Your help has been most welcome, neighbor."

He settled his hat on his head and walked outside into the summer sunshine. At the foot of her steps, he stopped and looked back. She stood framed in the doorway, her arms crossed, a faraway expression in her eyes. He wondered what she was thinking about.

Was she thinking about the children and husband she had lost or the work that needed to be done? Did she find it hard to go forward with her life? Somehow, he didn't think so.

Faith Martin was a remarkable woman.

The moment the thought occurred to him, he began walking, putting as much distance as he could between himself and his disturbing neighbor.

He'd come to Faith's home today to do his Christian duty by helping a neighbor, but he'd also been interested in seeing exactly what shape the place was in. The more he saw, the less he expected she would be able to manage it alone.

He might yet be able to buy the land. If he made some improvements for her, well, that would mean less work for him later.

Having a fence around the orchard was a good idea. Letting the alpacas graze down the overgrown grass would make it easier to mow later, or he could put sheep in to do the same job.

At the edge of his hay meadow, he stopped and glanced toward Faith's house once more. Helping her might turn out to be a good idea—from a business point of view. Not because he wanted to spend time in her company.

His wife might be gone, but he wouldn't be untrue to her. Lovina had been the one love of his life. He had no business thinking about spending time with another woman.

He had come to Faith's place to lend a hand. He hadn't been looking for sympathy or a shoulder to cry on. He hadn't planned on finding someone who could understand the pain he lived with. Yet, that was exactly what he'd found with Faith Martin.

Was that why he found her so attractive? His feelings toward her troubled and confused him.

He had already promised to help her. He wouldn't go back on his word. As promised, he would help her get her home in order as a good neighbor should, but he wouldn't spend any more time alone with her.

Chapter Four

It was shortly before noon on Saturday when Faith heard the sound of a horse and buggy approaching the house. She dropped the sponge she'd been using to wash grimy windows into her pail, dried her hands on her apron and waited to see who had come calling.

The buggy stopped in front of her gate, and three Amish women stepped out. They all carried large baskets over their arms.

"Guder mariye," called the oldest woman. She wore a bright, beaming smile of welcome. Behind her came a young woman with black hair and dark eyes followed by another woman with blond hair.

"Guder mariye," Faith replied. A faint flicker of happiness sparked inside of her. She was free to make new friends here—if they would have her. She wouldn't have to hide her bruised face or bear pitying looks from those who suspected her husband's cruelty.

The leader of the group stopped at the bottom of Faith's steps, adjusted her round wire spectacles on the bridge of her nose and switched her heavy basket to her other arm. "Welcome to Hope Springs. I am Nettie Sutter."

She indicated the dark-haired girl standing behind her. "This is my daughter-in-law, Katie."

"And I am Sarah Wyse," the blonde added. "My cousin is your neighbor to the south."

"Adrian?"

Sarah nodded. "When I heard he'd met you, I thought it best to rush over and assure you the rest of Hope Springs is more hospitable than Adrian is."

"He has been most kind and welcoming."

"He has?" Sarah exchanged astonished glances with her companions.

Faith swept a hand toward the front door. "Do come in, but please excuse the condition of the house."

"None of us can keep our houses free of dust in the summertime. With all the windows open to catch any breeze, the dust piles up before you know it."

Faith had more than a sprinkling of dust to contend with. She had twenty years worth of accumulation to haul out. She was thankful that she had made a coffee cake for herself while making one for Adrian that morning. At least she had something to offer her guests.

The women gathered around the kitchen table, each one setting her basket on it. Sarah opened the lid of the one she carried and began to pull out its contents. "We brought a few things to help you settle in and get this old house in order."

Out of her basket, Sarah brought cleaning supplies, plastic pails, pine cleaner, rags, sponges and brushes. "Where shall we start?"

Faith was speechless. She hadn't expected help from the community so soon.

Nettie picked up the pail and carried it to the sink. "I will finish these windows for you. Sarah, why don't you take a broom to the front porch and steps? Elam, Eli and his boys will be here to paint this evening."

"I'll get this food put away." Katie opened her basket and brought out two loaves of bread and a rhubarb pie with a gorgeous lattice crust just begging to be eaten. A second later she began unpacking mason jars filled with canned fruits and vegetables.

Faith was overwhelmed by their kindness. "*Danki.* This is far too much."

"No thanks are needed," Nettie assured her.

Perhaps not needed but gratefully given. Faith asked, "Who are Elam and Eli?"

Nettie smiled broadly. "Elam is my son and Katie's husband. Eli and his sons live down the road a piece. Our farm is a little ways beyond that toward Hope Springs."

"Where do you need me to start?" Katie asked, looking over the kitchen.

Faith took a second to gather her thoughts. "I've cleaned out one bedroom upstairs, but the others haven't been touched in years. If you want to start in one of them, that would be great. Sarah, perhaps you could help me drag the mattresses outside so I can beat the dust out of them."

Sarah held out her hand. "Lead the way."

The house quickly became a beehive of activity. Old bedding was taken out, walls and floors were scrubbed free of grime and rubbish was hauled out to the burn barrel. Everywhere inside the house, the crisp scent of pine cleaner filled the air. In one afternoon the women managed to do more inside the house than Faith had accomplished in four days on her own.

Her heirloom clock was striking five when the women gathered in the kitchen once more. Faith wiped her forehead with the back of her sleeve. "I don't know about you, but I've worked up an appetite. I believe I will sample this pie. Would anyone else care for a piece?"

Nettie smiled brightly. "I thought you'd never ask."

"Where are your plates?" Sarah was already moving toward the cabinets.

"To the left of the sink." Chuckling, Faith turned to Katie. "Would you like some?"

"Yes! I could eat the whole thing."

Nettie grinned. "That's because you are eating for two."

Faith endured a sharp stab of wistfulness but quickly recovered. "Congratulations. When is your baby due?"

"The last week of November."

"Is this your first?" Faith gathered forks for everyone and brought them to the table.

Katie shook her head. "It will be my second. We already have a little girl, so we're hoping for a boy."

Nettie sliced into the pie and slipped a piece onto the plate Sarah supplied. "Either will be fine with me as long as it is a healthy grandbaby."

Faith decided it was the perfect opening to share something about herself. "I am expecting a little boy soon."

Everyone's glances fell to her trim waist. She chuckled as she appeased their unspoken curiosity. "I'm hoping my nephew can come to live with me soon. That's why I have to get this house in some kind of order."

"Is he visiting for the summer?" Sarah asked. The women all took a seat at the table.

Sadness put a catch in Faith's voice. "*Nee,* he is not coming for a visit. I hope he will live with me until he is old enough to marry and have a family of his own.

My English brother and his wife were killed recently in a flash flood in Texas when their car was swept off the road. Fortunately, Kyle, their son, wasn't with them at the time. I'm all the family he has now."

Sarah reached across the table and laid a hand over Faith's. "I'm sorry for your loss. I lost my sister not long ago, so I understand your grief."

"*Danki.* I had not seen my brother for many years. He fell in love with an English girl and left our faith. I've never met his son. I'm trying to adopt him, but the process is painfully slow."

Nettie finished dishing out the pie and handed the plate to Faith. "It will be a hard change for him coming from an *Englisch* life to live in an Amish home."

"I am worried about that. What if he says he doesn't want to live here?"

Sarah gave Faith an incredulous look. "What little boy wouldn't love to live on a farm?"

"One who is used to television and video games." Faith was giving voice to one of her biggest fears. That Kyle would hate living with her.

"To worry about such things is to borrow trouble," Nettie chided. "God is bringing this child into your life. He knows what is best for all of us."

"You're right. I will put my trust in Him." Faith took a bite of her pie and savored the sweet tart flavor and tender, flaky crust. Nettie Sutter really knew how to make good pie.

"Tell us about yourself," Katie prompted. "I hear you have some unusual animals."

"I have ten alpacas. I raise them for their fleece. I spin it into yarns. Once I get this house in order, I will start looking for a place to sell my work."

Sarah brightened. "I work at a fabric store and we

sell many types of yarn. The store owner's name is Janet Mallory. You should speak to her."

"In Hope Springs?" Could it possibly be this easy to find a market for her work? Faith dared not get her hopes up.

"Yes, we are on Main Street, downtown. You can't miss it. It's called Needles and Pins. Janet is always looking for things made by the local Amish people to sell in her store. We get a fair amount of tourists in Hope Springs. Amish handmade items sell very well, although most of our yarn is bought by local Amish women for use at home."

Faith said, "I'm grateful for your suggestion. I will come in once I have my house in order."

Sarah leaned forward. "Is it true that your animal spit on Adrian? His brother Ben said he smelled as bad as a skunk."

Faith felt the heat rush to her cheeks. "Myrtle did spit on Adrian. I don't blame him for being upset."

Sarah laughed, a sweet light sound that made Faith smile, too. "I would have given anything to see Adrian lose his composure. What did he say?"

Faith crossed her arms over her chest and mimicked his deep stern voice. "Your creatures are eating my beans."

"*Ja,* that is just the way he talks." Sarah giggled again, then took another bite of her pie.

Faith couldn't let them think Adrian had been unkind. "He was upset, but he helped me catch them. Except for Myrtle, the others seem to like him. He's also been helping me build fences to keep them in."

Sarah sobered. "Adrian is coming over to help you build fences? That's interesting. He has stayed mainly to himself these past few years."

Faith's curiosity was piqued. Wanting to learn more about her stoic neighbor, she asked, "Why is that?"

Sarah glanced at the other women, then back to Faith. "Adrian's wife died shortly after their son was born. He raised the boy by himself. His son was his whole world. One afternoon, Adrian was walking home from his field that lies across the highway from his house. His son saw him coming and raced out to greet him. He ran right into the path of a car and was killed in front of Adrian."

Faith's heart twisted with pity knowing the pain he must have felt. "No parent should have to bury a child."

Nettie sighed heavily. "There is no greater sorrow. That is how we know God loves us. For He allowed His only son to die for our sins so that we may rejoice with Him in heaven for eternity."

From the tone of her voice and the sadness in her eyes, Faith knew that Nettie was speaking from first-hand experience. She said, "It is our solace to know they are waiting to greet us in heaven."

"Indeed it is," Nettie agreed.

Katie was the one to break the ensuing silence. "I have never seen an alpaca up close. May I take a look at yours?"

"Of course." Faith took pity on the expectant mother having to listen to such a somber conversation. Rising to her feet, she motioned for Katie to follow her. Nettie and Sarah deposited the dirty plates in the sink and quickly joined them.

Outside, they crossed the yard in a tight group. Nettie eyed the sad state of the barn. "You will need to find a strong husband to get this farm in shape. We have several bachelors in our church district who would make a good husband to you and a father to your nephew."

Quickly, Faith said, "I have no plans to marry again."

"Not even if the right fellow happens along?" Katie teased.

"I'm too old to remarry," Faith added firmly.

Nettie started laughing. "No, you aren't. I'm getting married in a few weeks. If I found someone at my age, you can, too. It is all up to God."

Katie asked Nettie a question about preparations for the upcoming nuptials, and the two women began an animated discussion.

Faith slowed her pace and hoped that would be the end of her part in the conversation, but Sarah shortened her stride and dropped back beside her. "Nettie is right. It's up to God."

"It is up to me, too. I see no need to marry again."

She felt Sarah's keen eyes studying her intently. Finally, Sarah said, "Your marriage wasn't a happy one? I understand. We won't speak of it again."

Faith could only wonder if Sarah's experience in marriage was the same.

As they rounded the barn, Faith saw her alpacas were all grazing except for Myrtle. She stood alone near the barn door. Faith called out to them. "Come here, babies. I have people who want to meet you."

They all raised their heads to look at her, but only Socks ventured close.

"Will they spit at us?" Katie asked.

"They only spit if they are startled. Sometimes they will spit at each other if they are annoyed, but for the most part they all get along."

"They are so cute," Katie gushed.

Faith had had the same reaction the first time she'd seen one. "They are wonderful animals. They are docile and they are quite smart."

"Which one spit on my cousin?" Sarah leaned her arms on the top of the gate.

Faith pointed. "That was Myrtle. She's the gray one standing by the barn door. She is expecting in a few weeks."

Katie started laughing. "I know just how she feels. Being pregnant makes me moody, too. Some days I feel like spitting at my husband. Poor Elam knows to stay out of my way when I get in a temper."

Nettie and Sarah joined in Katie's laughter. Myrtle moved as far away from the noise as she could get. She huddled by the corner of the barn and watched them all with a wary expression.

Faith felt a glimmer of hope begin to grow in her heart. She would enjoy having these women for friends. It seemed things were beginning to look up for her in this new place.

"Here you all are!"

Faith looked past Myrtle as a woman walked into view from around the corner of the barn. Myrtle took quick exception to the stranger coming só close. She spat and galloped to the far side of the pen, giving an alarm call that sent the entire herd milling in panic.

The middle-aged woman stood frozen with a shocked expression on her face as alpaca spit dripped from her chin.

Katie clasped her hands over her mouth. "Oh, no, not her."

"Who is it?" Faith asked, knowing full well she didn't want to hear the answer.

"The bishop's wife," Katie whispered.

"You should have seen the look on Esther Zook's face." Sarah started giggling again. "I'm sorry, I can't help it. It was the funniest thing. Poor Faith, I've never seen anyone so contrite."

Adrian, sitting in the corner of his living room, continued his pretense of reading the newspaper while he listened to his cousin regale his mother with her story. Sarah was a frequent visitor in his home. They had been close since they were children.

"What did you think of her?" his mother asked.

"Adrian's new neighbor or the bishop's wife?" Sarah began giggling again.

Glancing over top of the paper, Adrian saw his mother frown at Sarah's levity. "I meant Faith Martin."

Sarah shrugged. "She seems nice enough. She is certainly a hard worker."

His mother transferred her gaze to him. "It's a pity she is handicapped for there are several bachelors around who are on the lookout for a new wife."

Compelled to defend Faith, he said, "She walks with a barely noticeable limp. It isn't a handicap."

"I'm sure there is someone who is willing to overlook such a minor imperfection." She gave him a pointed stare.

He turned the page and ignored her broad hint. He wasn't on the lookout for a wife. His mother would eventually learn to accept that.

Sarah, a widow herself, rolled her eyes. "*Aenti* Linda, if you mean Toby Yoder and Ivan Stultz, I don't think they would mind a wife who walks with a limp. Not as long as she can cook and clean, mend clothes, run a farm and milk twenty cows twice a day while they spend their time gossiping at the feed store. Why, they would both be thrilled to have such a woman."

"You might be right," his mother admitted.

Adrian couldn't stay silent any longer. "Maybe she doesn't want to marry again. Did you think of that?"

"What woman doesn't want a husband and children of her own?" his mother countered.

"The love between a husband or wife doesn't die because one of them is with God. It lives on." He didn't care if she knew he was talking about himself.

Her gaze softened. "Of course not, but we can love more than one person."

I know. I loved a wife and a child and God took them both.

"Sarah hasn't remarried," he pointed out, keeping his painful thoughts to himself. His cousin ducked her head. Her smile vanished. He was sorry he'd brought the subject up. Sarah's husband had passed away from cancer over three years ago.

Glancing from Sarah back to Adrian, his mother gave him a fierce scowl. "Sarah has not closed her heart to love. It will find her again when God wills it. Hopefully, before she is too old to bear children."

He went back to his paper, knowing his mother would always have the last word.

Sarah said, "Faith doesn't have to worry about that. She already has a child on the way."

"What?" Adrian and his mother demanded together in shocked surprise.

Sarah couldn't keep a straight face. "She is adopting her brother's child."

"Well, that changes things a little," his mother mused. "Not all men want a wife and a child at the same time."

Sarah propped her elbows on the table. "Faith insists she won't marry again, and I believe she means it."

Linda waved aside her comment. "Nonsense. Once she has had the chance to meet a few of our fellows she'll change her mind. Let me think. Micah Beachy might be just the one. He's got a nice little farm over by Sugarcreek and he's never been married. I'll have to invite him over for a visit next month."

Intrigued by Sarah's comments, Adrian asked, "She specifically said she won't remarry? Does she intend to raise a child alone?"

Sarah turned in her seat to face Adrian. "*Ja.* What did you think of Faith when you met her?"

"I think she is going to have a hard time making a go of that farm. She doesn't have the money to hire help."

He understood Faith's reluctance to marry again. Suffering the pain of losing a spouse and child was more than anyone should have to bear. Loving someone meant risking that pain again. He wasn't willing to take that chance.

"The peaches in her orchard should be nearly ripe. If she sells her fruit, she'll be able to make some money, won't she?" Sarah asked.

Adrian shook his head. "The place is so overgrown, she'll have a hard time even getting to the fruit. Those trees haven't been pruned in twenty years. Most of them are so old they may not even bear fruit anymore. The peaches she does have will be small because no one thinned out the fruit when it was setting on."

"I told her to bring some of her yarns into Needles and Pins. I'm sure Janet will allow her to sell them there."

He turned the page of his paper. "It will take a lot of yarn to fix up that farm."

His mother left off cleaning the kitchen counter and began wiping down the table. "What kind of shape is the house in?"

Sarah brightened. "It's not too bad. I didn't see any

water damage inside, so the roof must still be sound. But it was so grimy. It took us hours to get the walls and floors clean. Elam Sutter, Eli Imhoff and his two sons managed to get the outside of the house painted but not the barn. I'm afraid it's in need of a few repairs first."

"More than a few," Adrian added, unable to stay out of the conversation.

His mother folded her arms over her ample bosom. "Then everyone will have their work cut out for them. It is clear our sister is in need. We cannot turn our backs on her."

Folding his paper and laying it aside for good, Adrian said, "Do you really think everyone will feel the same way? She isn't even a member of our church. Clearly, she didn't make a good impression on the bishop's wife."

His mother waved aside his objection. "Esther Zook will get over being made a laughingstock. She won't hold our new neighbor to blame for the actions of her animals. Esther knows her Christian duty, and when she forgets it, her husband will remind her."

Adrian exchanged glances with Sarah. She obviously wasn't in total agreement with his mother. She knew Esther Zook's opinion could sway many of the women in the community if she chose to rebuff Faith.

He rose to his feet. Grabbing his straw hat from the peg beside the front door, he slapped it on his head.

"Where are you going?" his mother asked.

"To see a woman about some peaches."

He left the house and headed for the hay meadow that separated his property from Faith's farm as fast as his feet could carry him. With him out of the way, his mother could finish fussing in his kitchen and talk about him freely. Not that his presence ever stopped her.

She meant well, he knew that. He appreciated that

she came by to cook and clean for him each week even though he didn't need her help. What he didn't like was her interference.

Twice he'd found Lovina's and Gideon's clothes had been packed away in a trunk in the attic. He never said a word to his mother. He simply put the clothes back into the bureau beside his own. He wasn't ready to let go.

Adrian's rapid steps slowed as he approached Faith's house. He wasn't sure exactly what he wanted to say to her. He wasn't even sure why he'd come. As he neared the front of her house, he saw she had moved her spinning wheel onto the front porch, probably to take advantage of the cooler evening breezes.

Her head was bent over the wheel as she concentrated on her task. With deft fingers, she pulled fleece from a bundle into long slender strands. Her feet pumped the pedals and made the wheel fly, spinning the fleece rapidly into yarn that wound around a pair of spindles.

It wasn't so much the art of her work that caught his attention. It was the look on her face. The worry and pain he'd seen before were gone, replaced by an expression of serenity. A sweet, soft smile curved her lips. He caught snatches of a song she was humming. So this was how Faith Martin looked when she was happy.

He couldn't bring himself to interrupt. Instead, he leaned on her rickety gate and simply enjoyed watching her work.

He had once wished to see her smile. He had no idea the sight could steal his breath away.

As much as he wished to let her work in peace, he had come here for a reason.

Chapter Five

❧

"You make that look easy."

Faith jerked upright, searching for the source of the voice that startled her. She relaxed when she caught sight of Adrian leaning against her front gate. What was he doing here this late in the day? Her fence was finished.

How long had he been watching her?

Did he disapprove of the song she'd been humming? Mose had always hated it when she'd sung or hummed.

Faith slowed her spinning wheel to a stop. It wasn't fair of her to compare Adrian to Mose. They were two very different men. Even from the small amount of time she'd spent with Adrian, she could see that. She had to learn to let go of the past.

She said, "It is easy when you find the right rhythm. What can I do for you this evening?"

"I have come with another proposition for you."

Disappointment stabbed her. He'd come to make another offer on her land. Was she foolhardy to hang on to her dream of a place of her own?

She gathered up her loose fleece and placed it back

in a blue plastic laundry basket. "I am still not interested in selling my land."

"What about your peaches?" He opened the gate and walked to the foot of her steps.

She shifted her basket to her good hip. "You want to buy peaches from me?"

"Not exactly. I'm willing to harvest your fruit and sell it for shares."

Faith pondered his surprising offer. She already had more work to do than she could possibly get done before Kyle arrived. That was, if the adoption when through. Selling peaches hadn't entered her mind. She had thought only of canning some for herself.

The extra income would be most welcome if Adrian was willing to do the work. "What share would you be asking?"

"I was thinking of a seventy/thirty split."

That was generous. "Seventy for me, thirty for you?"

He cracked a smile as he shook his head. "*Nee.* I would be doing the majority of the work."

Maybe so, but she wasn't going to *give* her produce away. "The fruit is all mine. If you will do fifty/fifty, I'll consider it."

"The crop will go to waste if I don't pick it for you. In that case, you'll get nothing."

He spoke the truth and she knew it. "Very well, sixty/forty and we have a deal."

Nodding once, he said, "*Goot.* We have a deal."

She expected him to leave, but he didn't. The heat of the day had waned. A cool breeze slipped past her cheeks and rustled through the leaves of the trees beside the house. For her, evenings were the best time of the day. She said, "I have some sweet tea made. Would you care for a glass?"

He hesitated. She thought he would refuse, but to her surprise, he said, "*Ja*. That would be nice."

"Let me put my fleece away and I'll be right back with some."

She hurried inside the house, feeling strangely light-hearted. When she came out again, he was sitting on the bottom step. After handing him the glass of tea, she awkwardly sank down on the step beside him. His hand shot toward her. She flinched away before she could stop herself.

He withdrew his hand slowly. The frown she was beginning to know so well settled on his face. He regarded her with a quizzical look in his eyes.

Faith stretched her bad leg out in front of her and tried to pretend nothing had happened. "I hope the tea is sweet enough."

"Does it hurt much?" he asked softly.

She rubbed her thigh and swallowed hard, uncomfortable with his sympathy. "Not as much as it used to."

"How did it happen? If you don't mind my asking?"

She didn't mind talking about the accident. It was talking about her marriage that she shied away from. "A pickup struck our buggy when we were on our way home from church."

Adrian took a sip of his tea, then stared out across the yard. "Is that how your husband died?"

"Mose was killed instantly." Faith stared into her glass as she relived those painful days.

"My son was struck and killed by a car. The English, they go so fast in their big machines. What in their lives makes them rush so?"

"It seems to me they are afraid they will miss something important."

"What was more important than my son's life?"

"Nothing." She wanted so much to reach out and comfort him. What would he think if she did? She tightened her grip on her glass.

After a moment of silence, Adrian shook off his somber mood. "I understand Myrtle met the bishop's wife today."

Faith pressed a hand to her cheek. "Please don't remind me. It was horrible."

"Sarah thought it was quite funny."

Faith cast him a sideways glance. "That was the worst part. Everyone was trying so hard not to laugh while I was stuttering my apologies."

"I'm sure you told her alpaca spit will brush off when it dries."

"Of course I did."

"Did you also mention how long the smell lingers?"

"I suggested she wash her clothes with baking soda to cut the odor as soon as she got home."

"I don't recall you giving me that information."

She tried to look innocent. "Didn't I?"

"*Nee.* I will assume you were too worried about your animals to pass along that important piece of advice."

"*Ja,* don't think for a minute it was because you were scowling so fiercely that the words flew out of my head."

"Did I frighten you that day?"

She shrugged. "A little."

"Are you frightened of me now?"

She knew he was referring to the way she had flinched from him a few moments ago. She stared down at the glass in her hand, avoiding his gaze. "You have been most helpful to me. I could not ask for a better neighbor."

It wasn't an answer to his question, but it was the

best she could do. He said nothing more. The sounds of cicadas rose and fell as they started their noisy evening songs. As abruptly as it started, their song stopped, and the silence stretched on for another awkward minute.

Faith racked her mind for something to say, but Adrian beat her to it. "I will go through your orchard on Wednesday and see if the fruit is ripe enough for picking."

"It's a mess. There are downed branches and dead trees all through it."

"We had a bad ice storm a few years back. I imagine most of the damage is from that. However, many of the trees are getting old. Peach trees only live about twenty years and these were planted at least that long ago."

"Do you know if they are freestone or clingstone peaches?"

A hint of a grin tugged at the corner of his lips. "The ones I snitched as a *kinder* were all freestone and extra sweet."

She smiled at his confession. It was easy to imagine him as a mischievous child. "*Goot*. Those are the best kind for selling at market."

Faith smoothed her skirt with one hand. It should have felt strange to be sitting beside Adrian and discussing the work that needed to be done on the farm, but it didn't. It felt comfortable. It was only when the conversation turned personal that she grew uncomfortable.

The shadows had grown long, and the cicadas resumed their evening serenade. Adrian finished his drink and rose to his feet. "It's getting late. I should go home."

Faith tried to stand but didn't quite make it. Embarrassed, she gathered herself to try again. Adrian stepped close and held out his hand to aid her.

Faith's heart began hammering so hard she was sure he could hear it. Fear made her mouth dry. Adrian wasn't Mose. She didn't have to be afraid anymore. They were brave words but hard to live by. She ignored his hand and pulled herself upright using the railing.

Adrian saw the change that came over Faith when he offered his hand. Was it pride that made her struggle to her feet alone? He didn't think so.

He saw the flash of fear in her eyes, although she hid it quickly. What reason would Faith Martin have to fear him?

He let his hand fall back against his side. If his presence was unwelcome, he would not force it upon her. "I will see you Wednesday, then."

She twisted her hands together as she avoided looking at him. "I may not be here. I'm taking my yarns into town. Your cousin Sarah was kind enough to invite me to bring my work into her shop. After that, I will be here, but I'm expecting the social worker from the adoption agency. I'm trying to adopt my brother's child."

Was that why she seemed so worried? Was she afraid her adoption wouldn't go through? He tried to picture her with a babe in her arms. She would make a good mother.

He said, "You don't need to be here while I survey your orchard. We can discuss what I find another time. I promise I won't eat up your profits."

She smiled halfheartedly at his humor. He wanted more. He wanted a real smile from her. "How are your beasts adjusting to their new home?"

"They seem quite happy in the pen you built for

them. Thank you for your help with that. They are grow-ing fat on the thick grass in the orchard."

"Will I disturb them working in there?"

"I do not think so. They may disturb you for they are quite curious. You're likely to find them underfoot and investigating everything you do."

He nodded toward the barn. "Has your expectant mother had her calf?"

"A baby alpaca is called a cria, not a calf." She re-laxed as she talked about her animals. The haunted look faded from her eyes.

"Cria." He rolled the unfamiliar word on his tongue. "Has Myrtle had her cria?"

"Not yet. I think it will be few more weeks before she becomes a mother again."

"This is not her first babe?"

"Bandit and Baby Face are both her offspring."

"You have chosen unusual names for your unusual creatures."

"My husband and I rented a farm from an English family when we lived in Missouri. I let their daughter name all the new babies."

"You will be able to name this one yourself."

She glanced shyly in his direction. "Perhaps I will give you the honor."

He stroked his beard as he considered her offer. "I could name it for its mother. *Shmakkich.*"

"Smelly? I will not call my new baby Smelly."

"Then you must find a better name yourself for that is my only suggestion." He handed her his empty glass.

She took it without hesitation. Her eyes crinkled with humor. "I did not think you would shirk from a diffi-cult task."

"A challenge, is it? Very well, I shall name it Stinky."

"*Nee.*" She shook her head.

"Foul Breath."

Faith giggled. "*Nee.* I will not call any creature Foul Breath. If that's the best you can do, it will remain nameless."

Her smile was back and Adrian was content. "I shall give it some more consideration. Good night, Faith Martin."

"*Guten nacht,* Adrian."

He started toward home but stopped a few yards away. Turning around, he called out, "What about Skunk?"

"*Nee!* That's the worst name ever."

"But what if it's black with a white stripe down its back?"

"Not even then. Be off with you, foolish fellow." She shooed him away with one hand, but she was smiling.

It wasn't until he was nearly home that he realized he was still smiling, too.

Faith guided Copper onto the highway and headed toward Hope Springs. The horse kept to a brisk trot, but it wasn't long before several cars were backed up behind Faith's buggy waiting to pass her on the next open stretch of road. The driver of the first car that went around her gave her a friendly wave. The second car drew alongside but didn't pass. When Faith glanced their way, she saw the passenger had the window rolled down and was aiming the camera in her direction.

Faith quickly turned her face away. No matter which Amish community she lived in, it was always the same. There were always a few tourists who just had to snap a photograph of an Amish person. They never seemed to realize it was rude.

The second car sped away, and Faith was free to

enjoy the green rolling countryside. It was easy to see how fertile the land was as she passed farm after farm with tall cornfields and fat cattle grazing near the roadside.

The outskirts of Hope Springs came into view after several miles. Faith had no trouble finding her way to the fabric store. She pulled Copper to a stop in the parking lot beside three other buggies.

As soon as she pushed open the front door of Needles and Pins, she was greeted with the scent of a floral and vanilla potpourri and the sound of chimes. The store was small, but it was crammed from floor to ceiling with bolts of fabric in every color. At the rear of the store a white-haired woman stood behind the counter. She looked up from her work and smiled in greeting.

"Welcome to Needles and Pins. Is there something I can help you with?"

Faith worked to quell the nervousness making her stomach queasy. She needed to find a market for her work as soon as possible. One of the things Kyle's social worker would be looking at was her financial situation. Faith needed proof that she earned enough to care for a child. Sending up a quick prayer, she said, "I'm looking for Janet."

"Then look no further. I'm she."

Faith approached the counter. After introducing herself, she opened her bag and pulled out a sample of her yarn. "Would you be interested in purchasing some hand-spun baby alpaca yarn?"

"I might be." Janet took the skein to examine closely.

"The black color is natural. It's from one of my crias."

Janet looked up in surprise. "You raise your own alpacas?"

"*Ja,* I have ten animals. Some are white, I have one black, several grays and two that are butternut-brown. I can die the wool for you if you have customers that want a particular color. It's very soft yarn and very strong." Faith forced herself to stop babbling.

Running her hand over the skein, Janet said, "I can see this is quality work, Mrs. Martin. I would be interested in buying all you have in black and dark gray. I'm not sure about the other colors. Perhaps I will take a few of them and see how they sell."

Faith struggled to hide her excitement. She had prayed to make a big sale today, and her prayers were being answered.

Janet continued, "If you are interested, I could post your yarn for sale on my website. I get a fair number of internet orders."

"That would be *goot, danki.*" This was better yet.

Faith sorted her yarns for Janet and pocketed the money with a happy heart. She was preparing to leave when Sarah came out from the back room. Smiling, Sarah came forward carrying several large bolts of powder-blue material. "Faith, how are you? Have you brought in your yarn?"

"*Ja.* Janet was kind enough to purchase several dozen skeins. If they sell well, she will buy more."

Sarah leaned close. "I will do my best to steer our customers toward them."

"I appreciate that."

"I have been instructed by Nettie Sutter to invite you to our widow's meeting on Friday night."

Such meetings were common in Amish communities where widows sought to remain active and productive members of the community even into old age.

Faith had been a member of such a group in her last church district.

As much as she wanted to say yes, Faith didn't have time to devote to social visits. "Perhaps I can join you when I've settled in."

"Fair enough. We are finishing two quilts that will be auctioned off next month. We help support an orphanage in Haiti with the money we raise and we give to the church to help our members who have medical bills and such. Several times a year we hold a large auction. Some of the women in our church have started a co-op to help members market and sell their work."

"I'm not much of a hand at quilting," Faith admitted.

"Don't worry, we will find something for you to do. We meet at the home of Naomi Wadler. Her daughter and son-in-law run the Wadler Inn and Shoofly Pie Café. You passed by it on your way in town. Naomi's home is behind the inn."

Faith remembered the Swiss-chalet-style inn at the edge of town. "What time are the meetings held?"

"Five o'clock."

"I look forward to the day I can meet with you."

"Wonderful. Have you decided to join our church?"

"I plan to ask the bishop about it soon."

"I must warn you that once you are accepted, you will be fair game as far as Adrian's mother is concerned."

Perplexed, Faith asked, "Why do I need a warning about his mother?"

"*Aenti* Linda fancies herself a matchmaker. Adrian and I are her only current failures. I admit she does have a knack for putting the right people together. You will provide her a new challenge. Hopefully, I can get a break from chance meetings and uncomfortable suppers at her house where I feel like a prize hen on display."

Faith shook her head. "She may matchmake all she wants. I have no intention of marrying again."

"That is exactly what Adrian says."

Faith began to rearrange the yarns left in her basket. "It is a shame he feels that way. He would make a good husband."

"He's a handsome fellow, I'll give him that."

"He's much more than that. He's kind and generous, strong and hardworking. He's everything a woman could desire in a mate."

As soon as she realized she was rambling, Faith looked up in embarrassment. Sarah stared back with a look of compassion on her face.

Faith wanted to sink through the floor. She hadn't realized how much she had come to admire Adrian or how much she wanted to be admired by him.

Sarah reached out and laid a hand on Faith's arm. "Adrian still grieves deeply for his wife and son. He says the love he holds in his heart for his first wife doesn't leave room for another. He speaks with conviction when he says he will never love again. A woman who sets her heart on my cousin is likely to find heartache instead."

Adrian started his assessment of Faith's orchard under the close supervision of her alpacas. The herd followed him everywhere, observing his activity with wide curious eyes. Their heads bobbed back and forth on their long necks as they tried to figure out what he was up to.

Before long, the group grew tired of simply watching him. They began a new game, bounding away, then racing back at him, dodging aside at the last second to avoid a collision. Soon, several mock battles broke out between the youngsters. They chased each other around the trees, kicking and knocking their long necks into one another. Socks and Baby Face reared up and began a boxing match as they hopped about on their rear legs.

Adrian chuckled at their antics. It was like being surrounded by five-foot-tall puppies. He began to understand Faith's attraction to them. They were adorable. Like their owner.

Only Myrtle refused to join the fun. She spit at those brave or foolish enough to encroach on her space. Adrian had no trouble staying away from her.

He finished his task and was letting himself out the gate to the orchard when he saw Faith returning. His spirits lifted instantly. She was sure to smile when he recounted her animals' antics.

She drew her horse to a stop beside the barn door. He held the mare's headstall as Faith descended from the buggy. "Did you sell all your yarn?" he asked.

She pulled a large hamper from the backseat. "Not all of it but a large portion. I hope you have some good news about my orchard."

"You have very curious animals prowling out there."

Her face filled with concern. "Did they give you trouble?"

"I was able to dodge their charges and most of the spit."

"I will wash your shirt if need be."

"*Nee,* I'm only teasing. You have about ten trees that should be cut down. They are too old and diseased to bear fruit. They can be cut up and stacked for firewood. They should dry out enough through the fall to burn well this winter."

Faith set her basket on the ground. "Should I replant more peach trees in their place?"

"If I were you, I'd diversify with some plum and apple trees. Since they flower at different times, you will be less likely to lose the entire crop if we get a late freeze in the spring.

Her eyebrows shot up. "So you think I will be here in the spring? Have you decided I can make a go of this place?"

"You have made a good start," he admitted.

"Only because you've done the majority of the outside work. Your help has been a godsend."

Adrian grew uncomfortable with her gratitude. He hadn't started out to help her earn a living. He'd had his own selfish reasons for doing the work needed. He had hoped she would sell her farm to him.

Did he still want her to leave?

No...and yes.

He hadn't once thought of Lovina all through this day. He'd thought only of what Faith would say, what would make her smile. Faith made him forget his pain.

He didn't want to feel this sense of wonder when she was near, but he did. Seeing her smile shouldn't make him happy, but it did.

Adrian turned away and started to unhitch the horse. Faith made him feel things he didn't want to feel. Things that had died in him when Lovina died.

Faith said, "I can manage. I'm sure you have your own work to see to."

"I've wasted the best part of the day here. I might as well stable your horse. It won't take that much longer." His voice sounded unnaturally harsh even to his own ears.

Faith took a step back and ducked her head. "I should

get these things up to the house. The social worker will be here soon."

As she hurried away, Adrian could've kicked himself for stripping the happiness from her eyes. Had he been wrapped up in his own grief so long that he'd forgotten how to be kind?

Chapter Six

Faith put her yarns and baskets away and worked up the courage to return to the barn. She had upset Adrian, but she didn't know how. Was it something she said? He'd done too much for her to let him go away angry.

She paused at the kitchen door, remembering Adrian as he had first appeared to her, dark and scowling. In spite of his fierce appearance, he'd been nothing but kind to her. She had come to care for him, to see him as a friend, yet she had scurried away from his displeasure like a sheep running from the wolf. Why was it still so hard to stand up for herself?

Because I'm afraid.

Was Adrian's kindness only an act or did her old fear make her suspect evil where it didn't exist? If she couldn't be sure, how could she do business with him, accept his help, allow him into her life?

Learning to trust again was harder than relearning to walk had been. Perhaps that was the reason God had brought her to this place. Because she had to begin somewhere. If this was her first test, she had failed miserably.

No, that wasn't true because she wanted to trust

Adrian. The real problem was that she no longer trusted her own judgment.

Dear Father in heaven, give me strength and wisdom. Let me not judge others lest I be judged in return. Help me to see the good in men and not suspect evil.

Bolstered by her prayer, Faith left the house, crossed the yard and pulled open the barn door. Adrian was busy forking hay into Copper's stall. He hadn't seen her return.

Unobserved, Faith took a moment to admire the way he made the work look easy. His strong arms and shoulders drove the fork deep into the hay and lifted a bundle with ease. Beneath the sweat-dampened shirt he wore, she could see the muscles tightening and rippling across his back. Her breath quickened as she realized she wasn't seeing him as a friend should. Embarrassed, she looked away.

He was a strong, handsome man, and he was proving himself to be a good friend and neighbor. That was all. She wouldn't let it be anything else.

He caught sight of her. "I'll be done in a minute."

He didn't seem angry now. She took a step closer. "I'm sorry I upset you earlier."

His eyes widened in surprise. "You did nothing to upset me. I'm the one who should be sorry. I let my ill humor ruin your day. That was wrong. The help I gave you was for selfish reasons. Please forgive me."

"You are forgiven. For what selfish reason have you worked here day in and day out?"

He hesitated, then sighed. "I thought if you couldn't make a go of this farm, I could buy it from you. The work that I've done here would have had to be done anyway when I took over."

"I see. Thank you for telling me this."

"I no longer think you will fail, Faith Martin. You have the will to succeed, and as you once told me, you aren't afraid of hard work."

A sound outside drew her attention. Faith's heart leaped into her throat when she saw the automobile pulling to a stop in front of her house. In the front seat she could see a woman surveying the property. "That must be Mrs. Taylor, Kyle's social worker. What do I do?"

Adrian came to stand beside her. Gently, he said, "Go and welcome her."

His simple reply made her realize how silly she was being. "Kyle was raised in an *Englisch* home. I'm worried that this *Englisch* woman won't think he belongs in an Amish home."

"You cannot discover the answers you seek by hiding here in the barn."

"Are you sure?"

"*Ja,* I'm pretty sure." He smiled and motioned her toward the door. "Go."

Gathering her courage, Faith walked out of the barn and toward the car, knowing this was the moment she had been dreading and praying for. She had had several letters from Mrs. Taylor, but she had no idea what to expect from the *Englisch* social worker.

The car door opened, and a tall, slender young woman got out. She wore a plum-colored suit and matching high-heeled shoes. Her hair was short and dark. It curled tightly against her skull. She held a briefcase in one hand.

Faith managed a smile. "*Velkumm.* Are you a Mrs. Taylor?"

"I'm afraid Mrs. Taylor no longer works for our agency. I'm Miss Watkins. Caroline Watkins. Are you Faith Miller?"

"Martin," Faith corrected her.

"My apologies." Caroline's gaze was fastened on Adrian standing by the barn. "Is that Mr. Martin?"

"No. That is my neighbor, Adrian Lapp. I am a widow. I thought you knew that."

"I'm sure it was in the file. I apologize if I sound unprepared. I've been swamped with work. Yours is my third home visit this week. Mrs. Taylor left on very short notice and I'm playing catch-up."

"Do come in the house." Faith gestured toward the front door.

Would her home pass inspection? Was it clean enough? Was it big enough? Would Faith pass as a prospective parent, or would this woman decide she didn't deserve her nephew? Worry gnawed at her insides. Exactly what would this home study entail?

Inside the house, Faith led the way to the living room. It was sparely furnished with a small sofa placed in front of a pair of tall windows. Two reading chairs flanked the couch. A small bookcase sat against the wall opposite the windows. Miss Watkins settled herself on the sofa while Faith perched on the edge of a chair facing her.

Miss Watkins must have seen the concern Faith was trying to conceal. "Please don't be nervous, Mrs. Martin. I'm here to make sure your home is a suitable, safe place for your nephew, not to pass judgment on your housekeeping or personal tastes."

"I am Kyle's only family. What could be more suitable than that?"

"I agree it is almost always best to place a child with a relative, but placing a child in a safe and loving home is our top priority, even if that means placing them with someone other than a blood relative."

The social worker searched through her papers. "First, I need to see two forms of identification. I have to make sure I'm talking to the right person. Confidentiality laws and all that, you know. Your driver's license and a Social Security card will be fine."

"I do not have such documents."

Miss Watkins frowned. "You don't have a Social Security card?"

"I do not. The Amish do not believe in Social Security. It is the responsibility of everyone to care for the sick and elderly. We do not depend upon the government to do that for us. I do have my birth certificate and my marriage license, if that will do?"

Faith rose from the chair and crossed to the small bookcase in the corner. She opened her Bible and took out several pieces of paper and handed them to the social worker.

"Under the circumstances, I think these will be fine. Today, I'd like to gather some information about your background, family life, child care expectations and about your parenting philosophy. I know you must be frustrated at having to repeat some of this process since you began your adoption in Missouri, but now that you are in Ohio, you will have to abide by Ohio law."

"I understand my move came at a bad time, but it couldn't be helped."

"I will do what I can to expedite your home study. A few things won't have to be repeated. Your background check and criminal search records have been forwarded to us by the Missouri authorities."

"I only wish to have Kyle with me as soon as possible. He has been with strangers for two months."

Miss Watkins opened a folder. "Kyle King is in foster care in Texas, is that right?"

Faith nodded.

"And you've not been to visit him, is that correct?"

"I've spoken to him on the phone several times and written letters to him twice a week, every week, but I've been unable to travel to Texas." It wasn't much, but it was all she could do for now.

"I will admit I know very little about the Amish, so please forgive my ignorance. You are the first Amish client I've worked with. I understand you do not use electricity."

"We do not."

"And you have no phone and no car."

"There is a phone shack at the end of the lane that I and my Amish neighbors may use. It is permitted for work and for emergencies. I have a horse and buggy for ordinary travel, but I may hire a driver if I must travel a long distance."

"I'll make a note of that. After our interview, I'll make a brief safety inspection of your home. Typically, this first visit lasts from three to four hours."

"Four hours?" Faith thought of all the work that she had waiting for her.

"Yes. Is that a problem?"

"*Nee,* of course not."

"If I can't gather all I need today I will schedule a follow-up visit. I don't see a statement from your doctor. Did you receive the paperwork we sent you?"

"I haven't had a chance to schedule an appointment."

Miss Watkins frowned. "Ohio law is very clear on this. In order to adopt a child, you must be in good health."

"I am. My limp is the result of an accident, not an illness. I'll take care of it this week." A doctor's visit was another expense Faith didn't need. The money from her yarn sales wouldn't go far.

"All right. Let's get started. Are there any other adults or children living in this home?"

"Nee."

"Do you have adequate room to house a child?"

"Ja, this house has four bedrooms upstairs, although I don't yet have a bed for Kyle."

Miss Watkins jotted down some notes. "I will have to see all the accommodations prior to his arrival. Do you suffer from any physical or mental illnesses?"

"Only the limp you see."

"What is the reason for your disability?"

"I was injured when a pickup struck our buggy. My husband was killed."

"I'm sorry for your loss."

"It was God's will." Faith couldn't pretend there was sorrow in her heart, for there was none. Only relief and guilt for not loving Mose as a wife should.

"Do you have a history of alcohol, drug or substance abuse, even if it did not result in an arrest?"

"Nee."

"Do you have a history of child abuse, even if it was not reported?"

"Nee."

"Do you have a history of domestic violence, even if it did not result in an arrest or conviction?"

Faith's heart jumped to her throat. Would Mose reach out from the grave and snatch away her only chance to raise a child? She couldn't let that happen.

Never again would she place herself, or Kyle, in such a situation. She answered carefully for she didn't want to lie. "I have never abused anyone nor have I been accused of such behavior."

"Have you ever been rejected for adoption or foster care?"

Faith relaxed. "I have not."

For the next several hours, Faith answered all the questions put to her. Finally, Miss Watkins said, "Why don't we take a break and you can show me the house."

"Of course. I have only recently moved in. There is still much work to be done."

"I understand. Let's start with the kitchen."

Faith led the way. Miss Watkins made notes as she walked. To Faith, it seemed that she took note of every flaw, every uneven floorboard and even the stains on the wall behind the stove. The house might not be perfect, but it was a roof over her head.

In the kitchen, Miss Watkins went straight to the refrigerator and opened the door. The shelves were bare except for a few staples—butter, eggs and some bacon. She turned to Faith. "You don't have much in the way of food here."

"I have only myself to cook for. I don't need much."

"Will feeding a growing boy be difficult for you?"

"Not at all. Come. I will show you the cellar." Faith took a lamp from inside the cupboard and lit the wick. Opening a door at the back of kitchen, Faith descended the steps, cautioning Miss Watkins to use the handrail.

Down in the cool, damp cellar, Faith raised her lamp to show shelves full of canned fruits, vegetables and meats. It had taken her two solid days to clean out the cellar, repair the shelves and stock them. "I brought most of this with me from my previous home in Missouri. Some of my new neighbors have brought more as gifts."

"Impressive. Can we go back upstairs now?"

Clearly, Miss Watkins didn't care to remain in a

small dark space. She frowned as she eyed the lamp Faith held. "I have some concern about the use of kerosene lamps around a small child."

"Amish children are all taught how to use lamps safely."

"Open flames are very dangerous. You will have to provide an alternate source of light."

"Would battery-powered lights be acceptable?"

"Absolutely."

"Then I shall purchase some." Faith smiled. More expenses.

After leaving the cellar, Faith gave the social worker a tour of the yard and outbuildings. Once again, Miss Watkins was scribbling furiously in her notebook. The alpaca herd came to the fence to observe the newcomer. Faith assured the social worker that they were not dangerous animals, but she gave Myrtle a wide berth. The rest of the herd remained well behaved, much to her relief.

Back in the house, Miss Watkins gathered together her papers. She closed her briefcase and handed Faith two additional pieces of paper. "I think that will do it for today. As far as paperwork goes, you will need to complete the health summary and you will need to have a fire safety inspection."

Was that a free service or was it something else she would have to pay for?

Miss Watkins held out her hand. "I will be back the same time next week. Hopefully, you will have everything completed by then."

Twisting her hands together, Faith asked, "What if I don't?"

"If there are deficiencies, it does not automatically

mean you can't adopt your nephew. It simply means that these are things we will have to work on."

As Faith watched the social worker drive away, she had no idea if she had passed inspection or not.

Why should they feel she deserved a child if God had not seen fit to answer her prayers for one? Simply because she was Kyle's aunt didn't mean she was the best person to raise him.

Glancing toward the orchard, she wondered if Adrian was still working out there or if he had gone home. An intense need to see him took hold of her.

Faith let herself through the gate behind the barn. Only Socks was grazing near the building. The rest of the herd had disappeared. Lifting her head, Socks ambled slowly in Faith's direction. When she reached Faith, she stopped and rubbed her head against Faith's side.

"What are you doing here all by yourself? Where is the rest of the herd?" Faith peered into the trees but couldn't see the animals. Giving Socks a quick pat, Faith headed deeper into the orchard.

She hadn't gone far when she spotted the rest of the group. They were clustered around a single tree and all gazing upward. A ladder stood propped against the trunk. She could just make out Adrian's legs halfway up the rungs.

She was startled when he called out, "How did it go?"

"I wish I knew."

A large, dead branch came crashing to the ground, sending the alpacas dashing in circles before they clustered again beside the ladder. Adrian descended from the tree. "How soon will you know if your nephew can live with you?"

"For all the hurry, hurry, hurry in *Englisch* lives,

their child placement process moves slowly. If all goes well, it may be two or three weeks."

"Where is he until then?"

"In a foster home."

"I'm sure they are taking good care of him."

"I pray so."

If the *Englisch* woman didn't find Faith acceptable, what would happen to Kyle? Was there someone else waiting and longing to adopt a child the way she was? Perhaps they deserved him more than she did.

She looked at Adrian. "Am I doing the right thing trying to bring an *Englisch* child here?"

"Why would you ask that?"

She crossed her arms and hugged herself as if she were cold. "Because in all the years I was married, God never saw fit to give me a child of my own."

Adrian heard the pain in Faith's voice. He saw the disappointment and loss in her eyes. He wanted to take her pain away, but he didn't know how. "Will you love this child?"

"I will."

"Then you are doing the right thing."

"If only I could be so sure. I must put my trust in God."

He said, *"And they that know thy name will put their trust in thee: for thou, LORD, hast not forsaken them that seek thee.* Psalm 9:10."

"You are so very right. He has not forsaken me."

Adrian wasn't sure why that particular Bible verse popped into his head. God had turned away from him. He had been forsaken. Faith, too, had suffered a great loss, and yet she still drew comfort and hope from God's word.

Why was her faith so strong when his was so weak?

Chapter Seven

On Sunday morning, Faith turned Copper off the highway and onto a farm lane two miles north of her home. At the edge of the road a homemade white sign with a black anvil painted on it said, "Horse Shoeing. Closed Wednesdays."

The church service was being held at the farm of Eli Imhoff, the local blacksmith, and the generous neighbor who, along with his sons, had painted the outside of her house.

Overhead, low gray clouds scuttled northward. The overcast sky was a welcome relief from the oppressive heat of the past few days, but the clouds were hanging on to any rain they held. Hopefully, any showers would remain at bay until after she was back home again.

At the other end of the long lane, Faith saw a two-story white house with a smaller *dawdy haus* built at a right angle from the main home. Both the grandfather house and the main house had pretty porches with white railings and wide steps. Three large birdhouses sat atop poles around the yard ringed with flower beds. Someday, her home would look like this.

Across an expanse of grass now crowded with buggies and groups of churchgoers stood a big red barn. In the corral, a pair of caramel-colored draft horses shared round hay bales with several dozen smaller horses. Copper whinnied a greeting. Several horses in the corral replied in kind.

A man came forward to take the reins from Faith. He tipped his black hat. "Good morning, *Frau.* I am Jonathan Dressler. I will take care of your horse." Although he looked Amish, he spoke in flawless English without a hint of the Pennsylvania Dutch accent she was accustomed to hearing.

"*Danki,* Jonathan." Faith stepped down from her vehicle and smoothed her skirt. Her stomach churned with nervous butterflies. More anxious than she cared to admit, she pulled a picnic hamper from beneath the front seat and stood rooted to the spot.

He pointed toward the farmhouse. "You may take your basket to the house. Karen Imhoff is in charge of the food today. It's nice to meet another newcomer to the community. Thanks to you, I'm no longer the new kid on the block."

"You are new here, too?"

"Yes. I guess I should say, *ja.*"

"You are *Englisch,* yet you dress plain."

"God has called me to live this simple life. Every day I give thanks that He led me to this place."

The smile on his handsome face was contagious. She asked, "Have you any advice to share with this newcomer?"

"The people of Hope Springs are wonderful, welcoming souls."

As they were speaking, another horse and buggy came trotting into the yard. She recognized Adrian at the reins. With him were an older man and woman, two younger women in their early twenties, and a teen-age boy.

Jonathan said, "I best get back to work, but I have to ask you one question. Did your alpaca really spit on the bishop's wife?"

Her shoulders slumped. "Has everyone heard of this?"

Jonathan chuckled. "It is not kind of me to say, but your alpaca sounds like a wonderful judge of character."

He laughed again as he unhitched Copper and led her to the corral.

Faith's heart sank to a new low. She would have to attend services several times in this church district before the congregation would be asked to accept her. Neither the bishop nor his wife was likely to want a new member who'd made Mrs. Zook a laughingstock.

Faith looked toward the house and saw the women from Adrian's buggy join a large group of women gathered on the porch. She recognized the bishop's wife standing among them. All eyes were turned in her direction.

She wanted to run home and hide.

"If I were you, I'd go in with my head up and smile as if nothing were wrong."

Faith glanced over her shoulder and saw Adrian unhooking his horse from the buggy. He wasn't looking at her, but she knew he was talking to her. There was no one else around.

He patted his horse's flank and spoke again, just as softly. "She will appear mean and petty if she snubs you when you are offering friendship, but if she senses fear, she won't have any trouble ignoring you. The other women will follow her lead."

"I should walk up to her and pretend my animal didn't spit in her face, is that what you suggest?"

"You have already apologized for that, haven't you?"

"More than once."

"Then it's over. Go, before they start to think you're *naerfich*."

She was nervous. But he was right, bless the man. His encouragement was exactly what she needed. Raising her chin, Faith limped forward and pasted a smile on her face.

As she approached the house, she nodded to Mrs. Zook. "Good morning. The Lord has blessed us with a fine morning, has He not? I look forward to hearing your husband's preaching for I hear God has graced him with a wonderful understanding of the Bible."

Mrs. Zook's smile wasn't overly warm, but at least she didn't cut Faith dead. She inclined her head slightly. "My husband speaks as God moves him. Joseph takes no credit for himself."

"That is as it should be. Where shall I put this?" Faith patted her basket, glad her voice wasn't shaking for her fingers were ice-cold.

A second woman spoke up. "Inside. Karen Imhoff will show you where she wants things."

Faith nodded her thanks, pulled open the front door and went inside with a huge sigh of relief. Behind her she heard the women's lowered voices begin to buzz. She knew they were discussing her. Unfortunately, she couldn't make out what they were saying.

Inside the kitchen, Faith was thrilled to see Nettie, Sarah and Katie at work arranging the food on the counters and long tables set up against the walls. Everything appeared ready for the meal the congregation would share after the service was finished.

A tall, slender woman came in from a back room with a box of glasses. She added them to the table where the plates were stacked. Her eyes lit with mischief when she spied Faith. She said, "Hello. I'm Karen Imhoff. You must be Faith Martin. I have been hearing so much about you."

Faith gave a quick glance around the room and saw Sarah and Katie trying to hide their grins. She looked back at Karen. "*Ja,* I am the one with the spitting alpaca."

Sarah and Katie dissolved into giggles. Nettie gave them both a stern look. The young women quickly pulled themselves together.

Karen said, "I hope you enjoy the service today. We are always glad to see new faces."

The front door opened and Jonathan stuck his head in. He said, "Everyone is here now."

Faith noticed the way his gaze rested on Karen. There was a softness in his eyes that bespoke great affection.

"*Danki,* Jonathan," Karen replied. "We will be there shortly." There was no mistaking the love that flowed between them.

What would it be like, Faith wondered, to love wholeheartedly and be loved in return?

Jonathan started to close the door but stopped as a little girl of about nine slipped beneath his arm and into the kitchen.

After he closed the door, Faith said, "Jonathan is a most unusual young man. I have never known an *Englisch* person to join our faith."

Smiling fondly, Katie folded her hands atop her bulging tummy. "You should have Karen tell you the whole story of how Jonathan came to be with us. It is the most romantic tale."

"I should tell it. I saw him first," the little girl declared. She was the spitting image of Karen and clearly not shy.

Karen laid a hand on the child's head. "You are forgetting your manners, Anna. This is Faith Martin. She is new to Hope Springs, and we must make her welcome. Faith, this is my sister, Anna."

Faith smiled at her. "I'm pleased to meet you, and I'm dying to hear the story."

Anna eagerly launched into her tale. "Just before Christmas, Karen was taking us to school. I looked out the buggy window and I saw a dead man in the ditch. Only, he wasn't dead. He was only hurt, but bad. God made him forget who he was, so we called him John. He stayed with us until God let him remember his name. And now he knows who he is and he wants to marry my sister."

Anna grinned broadly, Karen blushed rosy red and the rest of the women grinned.

Karen cleared her throat. "That about sums it up."

Nettie said, "It's almost time for the service to start. Girls, take Faith down to the barn. I'll be there shortly."

"I'll show you the way," Anna said as she bounced toward the door.

Outside, the solidly overcast sky gave way to intermittent sunshine. The women followed Anna to the far side of the barn where a sloping earthen ramp led to the barn's loft. The huge doors had been propped open to catch the cool morning breeze.

Inside, rows of wooden benches in the large hayloft were filled with worshipers, men on one side of a center aisle, women on the other, all waiting for the church service to begin. Faith took a place beside Sarah,

Karen and Katie. Anna wiggled her way in between Faith and Karen.

Glancing across the aisle to where the men sat, Faith caught Adrian's eye. He didn't smile, but he gave a slight nod to acknowledge her. He'd overheard her conversation with Mrs. Zook, and Faith had the feeling he approved. A moment later, Anna asked Faith a question, forcing her to look away from Adrian.

As everyone waited for the *Vorsinger* to begin leading the first hymn, Faith closed her eyes. This was a solemn time, a time to prepare her heart and soul to rejoice and give thanks to the living God. She listened intently, willing her soul to open to God's presence, preparing to hear His word.

She heard the rustle of fabric on wooden benches as people shifted on the hard seats. In the trees outside, birds sang cheerfully, as if praising the Lord with their own special voices. In the barn below, Faith heard the movement of horses and cattle in their stalls. The smell of alfalfa hay and barn dust filled the air. She drew a deep breath. Contentment filled her bones. This was where she wanted to be. This was where she had always belonged.

She remembered how nervous she'd been the morning she took her vows. At nineteen, she had been the youngest of the group preparing for baptism. In that final hour before the service, she had searched her heart, wondering if she was making the right decision. It was no easy thing to live Amish.

She knew she had made the right choice.

The song leader, a young man with a red beard, started the first hymn. More than a hundred voices took up the solemn, slow-paced cadence. There was no music, only the stirring sounds of many voices praising God. Two ministers, a deacon and the bishop took their places on benches facing the congregation.

When the first song ended, the congregation sat in silence waiting for the preaching to begin. For Faith, it was a joyful moment. This was her first service in her new district and it felt as if she had come home at last.

Adrian did his best to listen to the sermon being preached, but his eyes were drawn constantly to where Faith sat. At the moment, her eyes were closed. There was such a look of peace on her face that he envied her.

He had not known peace or comfort during services since his son was killed. As hard as he tried to find consolation in the words being spoken, all he felt was anger.

Anger at God for robbing him of those most precious to him.

If he had his way, he would have stopped coming to church, but to do so would only bring more heartache to his family. If he avoided services, he would soon find himself under the ban, shunned by those who loved him in the hopes that he would mend his ways.

His brothers and sisters, his mother and father, none of them understood the anger that filled his heart, so he kept it hidden. He went through the motions of his faith without any substance. His life, which had once been filled with daily prayers, was now filled with hollow silence. God knew Adrian Lapp had not forgiven Him.

Adrian glanced at Faith. Was she even better at pretending faith than he was, or had she discovered the secret of letting go of her anger and hurt?

Beside him Benjamin fidgeted. His brother was eager to see the preaching end so he could visit with the Stultz sisters. The pretty twins were nearly the same age as Adrian's little brother. They were always willing to share their sweet smiles and laughter with him. Benjamin would soon be of courting age.

Adrian no longer believed in asking God for favors, but he hoped Benjamin would be spared the kind of pain he had endured, if and when Ben chose a wife.

Three hours later, when the service came to an end, Benjamin practically leaped from his seat and rushed to join his friends outside. Adrian stayed behind to help convert the benches into tables for eating by stacking them together. As he worked, he visited with his friends and neighbors. He listened to his father catching up on who had a sick horse, how everyone's corn was doing and what they planned to sell or buy on market day.

As the groups moved out of the barn toward the house, Adrian kept an eye out for Faith. He wanted to see if she was fitting in with the women of the district. He'd seen how scared she was when she first arrived.

He'd offered his advice without thinking twice. It was strange how easily he read her face and demeanor. Stranger still was how often he found himself thinking about her. She was an unusual woman.

Since there wasn't enough room to feed everyone inside the house, the ordained and the eldest church members ate first at the tables set up for them inside. The rest of the congregation took turns getting their food and carrying it out to the barn.

When it was Adrian's turn, he saw Faith had joined Nettie, her daughters and several other women and was working alongside them in the kitchen.

He relaxed when he saw her at ease, visiting with Sarah and Katie Sutter, holding Katie's baby on one hip as easily as any seasoned mother. It was good to see her happy and smiling.

He caught Nettie Sutter's eye. She smiled and nodded

once. She was a good woman. She would do everything in her power to see that the women of the community welcomed Faith.

Adrian glanced away and caught Sarah studying him. She looked from him to Faith and then back again. Her grin widened. She beckoned him over. He immediately took his plate and went outside.

He finished his meal and was taking his plate back to the house when he saw Faith deep in conversation with Bishop Zook over on the front porch of the *dawdy haus.* Joseph motioned to Adrian. This time he had no choice but to obey.

The bishop smiled a broad welcome. "Adrian, I have been filling Faith in on our *Ordnung.* I suggested she refer to you if she has any doubts about changes to her home or business as you are closer than I."

Faith remained silent, but a rosy blush stained her cheeks.

"I will do what I can to help." He didn't need a new excuse to see Faith, but he accepted the responsibility. It was important that she be accepted in the community. To do that, she had to live within the rules of their church.

The bishop thumped Adrian on the back. "Bless you. I knew I could count on you. A few of the men are getting up a game of quoits. Will you join us?"

Similar to horseshoes but played with round metal rings, quoits was a game Adrian used to enjoy, but he rarely took part in such activities now. "I will go find Ben. He has the best aim in the family."

After passing the message to his brother, Adrian put Ben in charge of getting the family home. With his duty discharged, Adrian left early and walked the few miles back to his farm.

At the house, he took a sharp knife and cut two bunches of flowers from the garden. With a bouquet in each hand, he walked out to the small cemetery where Gideon and Lovina waited for him.

Kneeling between their graves, he placed his gift beneath each headstone. "I brought some daisies for you, Lovey. I remember how much you loved them. You always said they were the bright eyes of your flower beds. They've bloomed all summer for you."

He sat back on his heels. "We held church services at Eli Imhoff's place. That *Englisch* fellow is still attending. I didn't think Jonathan would stay but he has a plain way about him now. Our new neighbor was there, too."

Pausing, he considered what to say about Faith. "She smoothed things over with Esther Zook right nicely. Course, I gave her a hint on how to handle Esther. I hope that's okay. She's a smart one, that Faith is."

Suddenly, it didn't feel right to be talking to his wife about another woman. He rose and took his usual place on the cedar stump.

The silence pressed in on him. The wind tugged at his hat, and he settled it more firmly on his head.

"Gideon, you should see the crazy animals that live next door to us now. Alpacas. They're cute, but they spit on people and each other if they get annoyed. Faith has ten of them. The yarn she spins from their fleece is mighty soft. She gave me a pair of socks. The ones I'm wearing now, in fact."

He pulled up his pant leg and fingered the material. The warm softness reminded him of Faith's smile when he'd caught her humming as she worked her spinning wheel on her front porch.

Pushing thoughts of her out of his head, he said, "I'm

glad I'm not the fella who has to shear those beasties come spring. I'll bet he gets spit on a lot."

Adrian chuckled as he imagined anyone trying to clip the wool from Myrtle's neck.

The wind carried his mirth away. There was no answering laughter here. No one to share the joke with. Only two gray headstones among many in a field of green grass. Sadness settled in his chest, making it hard to breathe.

Adrian rose to his feet, shoved his hands in his pockets and started for home. It wasn't until he reached his lane that he realized he hadn't said goodbye.

On Monday afternoon Faith walked to the end of her lane and crossed the highway to the community phone. A small gray building not much bigger than a closet sat back from the road near a cluster of trees. A solar panel extended out from the south side of the roof. She could see through the window that it was unoccupied. She opened the door and stepped inside.

The shack held a phone, a small stool and a ledge for writing materials along with an answering machine blinking with two messages. She listened to them in case the agency had left a message for her, but they hadn't. Adrian had a message that his mower part was in, and Samuel Stultz had a new grandbaby over in Sugarcreek. It was a girl.

A local phone directory hung from a small chain at the side of the ledge. Picking it up, she searched for and found the number for the medical clinic in Hope Springs. She pulled a pencil and a piece of paper from her pocket to make note of the number for later. As she laid her pencil down, it rolled off the ledge and fell under her stool.

In the cramped space she couldn't reach it. She blew

out her breath in a huff of disgust, then awkwardly squatted down, bracing herself against the door. A second later the door opened and she tumbled out backward, landing in a heap at Adrian Lapp's feet.

"Faith, are you all right?" He immediately dropped to one knee beside her.

She looked up into his face filled with concern and could have died of embarrassment. "I'm fine, but my dignity is a little bruised."

He helped her to her feet. "I'm sorry. I didn't see you. What were you doing on the floor?"

His hands lingered on her arms. She could feel the warmth and strength of them through the thin fabric of her dress. He was so close. His masculine scent enveloped her, sending a wave of heat rushing to her face that had nothing to do with embarrassment or fear. She wasn't frightened of him. His touch was strong but gentle. She was frightened by how much she wanted to move closer, to step into the circle of his arms and rest there.

She took a step back. He slowly let her go, his hands slipping from her elbows to her wrists in a soft caress. She said, "I dropped my pencil."

"What?" He seemed as confused as she was by the tension that shimmered between them.

"I was trying to reach my pencil. I dropped it and it rolled under the chair." She brushed at the back of her dress. Her blood hummed from his nearness and the way his gaze lingered on her face. Suddenly, she saw an attractive man in the prime of his life. A single man.

She crossed her arms and looked down, hoping he wouldn't read this new and disturbing awareness in her eyes.

"No wonder I didn't see you." He stepped inside the building and retrieved her pencil.

He held it out and she took it gingerly, careful not to touch him. *"Danki."*

"I will let you finish your call."

"I'm only making a doctor's appointment. If you need the phone, you may use it now. I can wait."

His brow furrowed into sharp lines. "Are you sick?"

She was flattered by the concern etched on his face. *"Nee,* it is nothing like that. The adoption agency I'm using requires me to have a physical. I need to have a fire safety inspection of my home, too. Do you have any idea who I would call to see about that?"

"Michael Klein is our local fire chief. I'm one of the volunteer firemen. His number is in the book."

"Michael Klein. I will remember that. What would I do without you, Adrian? You have helped me at every turn."

"I have no doubt you would manage. Make your calls. I can wait."

He walked away to stand in the shade, giving her some privacy. She went back inside the phone booth, quickly placed her first call and was happy to find out the doctor's office could see her that afternoon.

The second call went smoothly, as well. The fire chief agreed to come by the following day and inspect her home. With her appointments made, she stepped outside. "I'm finished, Adrian."

He walked over, but instead of taking a seat inside the phone booth, he leaned against the doorjamb. "How is your adoption going?"

Faith struggled against the urge to linger here with Adrian and lost. She liked his company; she liked spending time with him.

"Things are going well, I think. The doctor can see me today and the fire chief can come tomorrow. The social worker did not run screaming from my house, although when we were in the cellar, I thought she might."

"You have not introduced her to Myrtle, have you?" There was a glint of humor in his eyes and in his voice.

Faith grinned. "*Nee,* I made sure Miss Watkins stayed away from her."

"That's *goot.* The bishop's wife and I are forgiving of such an insult, but an *Englisch* woman in her fancy suit might not be."

The clip-clop of a horse and buggy approaching made them look toward the highway. Samuel Stultz pulled to a stop. "Are you using the phone?"

Faith grinned for she already knew his good news. "You have a message, Samuel."

As he hurried to get down, Faith turned to Adrian. "I must be going. I will have to hurry if I am to find the clinic in time for my appointment. Poor old Copper isn't as fast as she once was."

"I need to take a harness into Rueben Beachy's shop for repairs. I go right by the clinic if you want to ride with me."

"That is very kind of you, but I have no idea how long I will be."

They moved aside to let Samuel use the booth.

Adrian said, "I have several other errands to run. I need to pick up some bushel baskets and the new blades for my sickle mower should be in."

"They are. I heard it on the message machine." She leaned closer. "And Samuel has a new grandbaby."

Adrian chuckled, "I'm glad my blades have come in. It will be time to put up hay in another few days and I must be ready."

"Is the work in my orchard taking up too much of your time?"

"*Nee,* I'm glad of the extra work. I don't mind waiting for you at the doctor's office as long as you don't mind waiting there if you are done ahead of me."

A ride into town seated beside Adrian was more appealing than it should have been. Should she accept? What was the harm in it? There was no need for both their horses to make the trip. "I accept your offer, gladly, and I won't mind waiting."

"*Goot.* I will be back with my wagon in half an hour."

"I will be ready."

Samuel stuck his head out the door, a wide grin on his face. "I have a granddaughter."

Faith laughed. "I know. Congratulations."

When she looked back, Adrian had already started toward his farm. Faith bid Samuel good day and hurried as fast as she could to her house.

Once there, she quickly freshened up. She changed her worn and stained everyday dress and apron for her best outfit. After patting down a few stray hairs, she decided she looked well enough to go into town. The blue of her good dress brought out the color of her eyes. Would Adrian notice? The thought brought her up short. Now, she was being foolish.

Her practical nature quickly reasserted itself. It wasn't that she wanted to impress Adrian. She merely wanted to look presentable when she met the doctor. Having rationalized choosing her best dress, she gave one last look in the mirror, pinched some color into her cheeks, put on her bonnet and went out to wait for Adrian with excitement simmering in her blood.

Chapter Eight

Adrian called himself every kind of fool as he drove his green farm wagon up to Faith's gate. He was about to give his nosy neighbors and his family food for speculation by driving the widow Martin into town. Knowing smiles and pointed questions would be coming his way for days. What had he been thinking?

Cousin Sarah would be sure to hear about this. She would make certain his mother knew before the day was out. He began lining up explanations in his head so he would have them ready. His mother was certain to drop by his house before nightfall.

He tugged at his beard as the source of his coming discomfort limped down the walk and crossed behind the wagon to the passenger's side. He glanced down at her as she prepared to step up into the wagon. Something of what he'd been thinking must have shown on his face.

A look of concern furrowed her brow. "Is something wrong?"

There was no point in ruining her afternoon with his glum thoughts. He extended his hand to help her in. "*Nee*. I've much on my mind. That's all."

She laid her hand in his without hesitation. He realized it was the first time she hadn't flinched away from him. A sense of satisfaction settled in the center of his chest.

Her hand was small and delicate in his grasp. His fist completely engulfed it. She was light as a feather when he pulled her up. She might be a tiny thing, but what she lacked in size she more than made up for in determination. He admired her tenacity. She had done a lot with her run-down inheritance. She was making the place into a home.

He turned the wagon around in the yard and set his gelding to a steady trot when they reached the highway. The drone of the tires on the payment, the clatter of the horse's hooves and the jangle of the harness were the only sounds for the first few minutes of the ride.

Adrian suddenly found himself tongue-tied. He hadn't spent time alone with a woman since his single days. What should he talk about? Or should he keep his mouth shut?

He glanced at Faith sitting straight as a board on the seat beside him. The wide brim of her black bonnet hid her face from his view. What was she thinking? Did she regret accepting his offer? Was she worried that gossips might link their names?

She spoke at last. "What is your horse called?"

"Wilbur."

"He has a fine gait."

Wilbur was a safe enough topic. "He was a racehorse in his younger days, but he was injured. His *Englisch* owner didn't want to waste money caring for him. You met Jonathan Dressler, didn't you?"

"The *Englisch* fellow who has become Amish?"

"*Ja.* He works for a group that takes in abandoned

and injured horses. He nurses them back to health and retrains them for riding or buggy work."

"I'll remember that. My Copper is getting old and slowing down. I will need a new horse in a few years."

"Perhaps you can teach your alpacas to pull your buggy."

She giggled and shot a grin his way. "Can you see how many tourists would want my picture if I did such a thing?"

"Not many once they met Myrtle."

Faith laughed outright. His discomfort evaporated as warmth spread though his body. She had a way of making him forget his troubles. He said, "You should laugh more often."

Their eyes met, and she quickly looked away. "How soon will our peaches be ripe?"

"Another two or three weeks."

"Will you sell them from a roadside stand or take them into the market in town?"

"To market unless you want to run the stand?"

"I've been thinking about it. Do we get enough traffic on this road to make it worthwhile?"

Adrian relaxed and started to enjoy the ride as Faith asked about his plans for the orchard. A few pointed questions from him set her to talking about her alpacas and her plans for expanding her spinning business. It wasn't long before the town of Hope Springs came into view. As far as Adrian was concerned, the ride was over all too soon.

He left her at the door to the medical clinic and quickly set about completing his own errands so she wouldn't have to wait when she was done seeing the doctor. With a jolt, he realized he was eager for the trip home.

Faith entered the Hope Springs Clinic, a modern one-story blond brick building, with a sense of dread. She had spent more than enough time in hospitals and doctors' offices over the past two years. What if they found something new wrong with her? What if they thought she wasn't strong enough to take care of a child?

Inside the building, she checked in with the elderly receptionist and took a seat in the crowded waiting room. When her name was called, she followed a young woman in a white lab coat down a short hallway and took a seat on the exam room table.

The young woman introduced herself. "I'm Amber Bradley. I'm Dr. White's office nurse and a nurse-midwife. Can you tell me what kind of problems you've been having?"

"None." Faith withdrew her papers from her bag. "I am adopting a child, but first, I must have a physical."

Amber's smile widened as she took the paperwork. "Congratulations. The doctor will be with you in a few minutes. We will need to get any previous medical records you have. I'll bring you the forms to sign so we can get them faxed to this office."

"I'm very healthy. I did not see a doctor until I was in an accident two years ago." Faith opened her mouth for the thermometer Amber extended.

"That doesn't surprise me. Many Amish go their entire lives without seeing a doctor. We see a fair number here because of Dr. White's reasonable rates. I tell him he's just plain cheap." Amber chuckled as she recorded the temperature reading, then wrapped a blood pressure cuff around Faith's arm.

The outside door opened, and a tall, silver-haired man walked in. "Good afternoon, Mrs. Martin. I'm Dr. Harold White. What can we do for you today?"

Faith again explained her situation. The doctor listened carefully, then took the forms from Amber. "This looks pretty straightforward. We'll get a chest X-ray, draw some blood and give you a complete physical while you are here today. My office will send you the results in a few days. Do we have your address?"

Faith recited it, and the doctor wrote it down. He said, "Isn't this the old Delker Orchard?"

"Ja."

Dr. White said, "That place has been empty for twenty years. I didn't know it was for sale."

"I inherited it when my husband passed away. He was the grandchild of the previous owner."

The doctor's eyebrows shot up. "He was that boy?"

Confused, Faith asked, "Did you know my husband?"

"I only met him once. I often wondered what happened to him. The whole thing was very hushed up at the time. Back then child abuse simply wasn't talked about."

Faith shook her head in denial. "You must be mistaken. He never spoke of such a thing."

"Was your husband's name Mose?"

"It was."

The doctor began counting to himself using his fingers, then said, "He would be forty-five years old if he were alive today."

She nodded. "He would."

"Did he have scars on both his wrists?"

"From where he was dragged by a runaway team of horses when he was small."

"I wish that were true. I'm not surprised he never spoke of it. Children who suffer such abuse often block it from their memory. His wrists were scarred from where he was tied up in his grandmother's basement. Apparently, he came to live with her when his parents both died of influenza. Old Mrs. Delker hated the Amish. Her only daughter ran away from home and wound up marrying an Amish fellow who left the faith for her."

"My husband said he was raised by his Amish grandparents after his parents passed away."

"Eventually, he was. I was called out to the farm when a utility worker reported he'd seen a boy chained in the cellar. The poor child was wearing only rags and he was thin as a rail. It was clear he'd been beaten and neglected. He hit and bit at anyone who came close to him."

Faith wrapped her arms around herself. "How terrible."

If only she had known. If only Mose had shared his pain instead of keeping it hidden all those years. Would their lives have been different? Surely they would have been.

Dr. White stared at the floor, as if watching that long-ago scene. "It was terrible. Eventually, the sheriff located his father's Amish parents and the boy was sent to live with them. Mrs. Delker spent some time in a mental hospital, but she came back within about six months. She was even more of a recluse afterward. She had a stroke and passed away ten years later."

Dr. White looked up, suddenly contrite. "I'm so sorry. I shouldn't go on like that. Sometimes we old people don't know when to stop reminiscing. The past can seem clearer than the present for us. This must be quite a shock for you."

"It explains a lot about my husband. He wasn't a happy man."

"I'm sorry to hear that. Let us talk of more cheerful things. You are adopting a child. That's wonderful. The sooner we get done here, the sooner that can happen. The first thing we need from you is a medical history." He became all business.

Faith answered what seemed like a hundred questions, had her X-ray taken and suffered through getting her blood drawn, but the whole time she kept seeing Mose's face. He had been a harsh man without peace in his life. She prayed he was at peace now.

When she left the doctor's office, she saw Adrian waiting for her. The sight of him lifted her spirits.

"Are you finished?" he asked.

"*Ja.* And you?" She climbed up onto the wagon seat.

"All done. Shall we head home?"

"Would you mind if we stopped at the fabric store? I need to see if I should bring in more yarn." She was in no hurry to return to the house that had seen such pain.

A fleeting look of reluctance flashed across Adrian's face. "*Ja,* we can stop at the fabric store."

"If it's too much trouble, I can wait," she offered, not wanting to upset him.

"It's no trouble at all," he drawled. Slapping the reins against Wilbur's rump, he set the black horse in motion.

When they reached Needles and Pins, Faith scrambled down from the bench seat. "I'll just be a minute."

A wry smile twisted his lips. "Take your time and say hello to Sarah for me. Tell her I'll be expecting *Mamm* this evening."

Faith wasn't quite sure what to make of his odd mood. He glanced toward the shop door as it opened and said, "Never mind. Here she comes now."

Faith turned around, expecting to see Sarah, but saw instead a short, gray-haired woman coming out of the shop. She stopped abruptly when she caught sight of Adrian, then smiled broadly.

"Hello, my son. What are you doing here?"

"I had some errands to run. *Mamm,* have you met Faith Martin?"

"I have not." His mother subjected Faith to intense scrutiny.

Faith was glad she'd taken the time to change her dress and put on her best bonnet. "I'm pleased to meet you, Mrs. Lapp. Your son has been wonderfully helpful to me. He has been the best neighbor anyone could ask for."

"Please call me Linda. It does a mother's heart good to hear such things about her son. I saw you briefly at the last church service, but I failed to introduce myself. I've been remiss in not welcoming you. Please forgive me."

"There is nothing to forgive. Excuse me, I must check to see if Janet needs more yarn from me. I won't be long, Adrian."

"No hurry," he replied.

Linda's grin widened. There was a distinctive twinkle in her eyes. "Your papa and I must stop by for a visit one of these evenings, Adrian. We have some catching up to do."

He knew where she was going and sought to cut her off. "Don't read more into this than there is. I'm helping out a neighbor. That's all."

Her smile faded. "It's time you put your grief away and took a close look at your life, my son. Many wonders of God are missed by a man who will not open his eyes."

As his mother walked away, Adrian mulled her

words. How did he put away his grief even if he wanted to? Did he want to?

His grief had become a high fence he used to hold others at bay. In spite of his efforts, and without meaning to, Faith Martin had made a hole in that fence. To close it back up meant pushing her out of his life. Was he willing to do that?

Even if he wanted to, he wasn't sure he could. There was something special about her, something more than her pretty face and expressive eyes. When he was with her…he felt alive for the first time in years.

True to her word, Faith was back in a few minutes. He glanced at her seated beside him as they rode homeward. She was unusually quiet. Her eyes held a faraway look, as if she were viewing something sad from her past.

Was she remembering trips she'd taken with her husband seated beside her? Had the doctor given her bad news? Did her leg hurt? Was she tired?

There were so many things he wanted to know about her, so many questions he wanted to ask, but he shied away from them because they might reveal the real question nagging at the back of his mind.

Did Faith enjoy being in his company as much as he enjoyed being with her?

The afternoon sun beat down on them as they traveled along. Faith untied her dark bonnet and laid it on the seat between them. He asked, "Are you warm?"

"A little."

Stupid question. Of course she was or she wouldn't have taken off her bonnet. Why did he revert to acting like a tongue-tied teenager around this woman?

They made the rest of the journey to her home in silence. When he pulled to a stop in front of her gate, she didn't get down but sat staring at the house like she'd never seen it before. She asked, "Did you know the woman who lived here before I came?"

"Vaguely."

"Was she evil?"

What a strange question. "I don't think so. She was old, and *ab im kopp*."

"Off in the head? Crazy?"

"Ja."

"She must have been," Faith whispered.

He covered her hand with his. "Is something wrong?"

She didn't look at him. Her eyes remained fixed on the house. He checked out the building but didn't see anything amiss. What was going on?

Gazing back at Faith, he studied her face intently. It was as if she couldn't see or hear him. He squeezed her fingers. "Faith, what's the matter?"

Her gaze slid to their hands and then to his face. She pulled away sharply and climbed down from the wagon, mumbling, "Goodbye."

Stunned by her abrupt departure, Adrian stared after her. Had he done something wrong? Had he upset her with something he said? Should he follow her and ask or leave her be?

The safe thing to do was to leave her be. He was becoming far too caught up in Faith Martin's life. He'd been neglecting his own work to help her, something he never did. This had to stop.

He turned the wagon and started for home. He'd only gone a hundred yards when he noticed her bonnet on the seat beside him.

Stopping the horse, he picked up the bonnet and held it in his hands. The dark fabric was warm from the sun. He lifted it to his face and breathed in. It held her scent.

He looked over his shoulder toward her house. Perhaps he was too caught up in her life, but he was ready to admit he was deeply drawn to Faith. He saw no way to free himself unless she turned him away.

Looping the reins over the brake handle, he jumped down from the wagon and strode toward her gate not knowing if he was simply returning her belonging or starting down a whole new path in his life.

When he reached the porch, he saw the front door stood open. He climbed the steps and called her name. She didn't answer. Pausing in the doorway, he started to call out again when a sound stopped him. Someone was crying.

"Faith?" He took a step inside. The muffled sounds of sobbing were coming from a doorway at the back of the kitchen. Hesitantly, he walked that way.

The second he realized the door led to the cellar, he rushed forward. Had she fallen? Was she injured? "Faith, is that you? Are you all right?"

It took a second for his eyes to adjust to the darkness below him. When they did, he could just make out her form at the bottom of the stairs. She sat huddled in a ball on the bottom riser with her arms around her knees. Her shoulders shook with sobs.

He descended quickly, stepping past her to crouch in front of her. He laid his hand gently on her shoulder. "Faith, did you fall? Are you hurt?"

She lifted her head and shook it in denial as she wiped the tears from her cheeks.

His heart began beating again with rapid erratic thuds. "You scared the life out of me. What's wrong?"

Words began pouring out of her. "If only I had known, I would have been a better wife. How could he keep such a thing locked away from me?"

"Faith, I don't understand."

"I married Mose because my parents were gone, my brother had left the faith and I had no one. I didn't love him as a wife should. I tried, but I couldn't, and I'm so ashamed." She buried her face in her hands.

This was way out of his depths. Faith needed another woman to talk to. Someone like his mother or Nettie, but he couldn't leave her weeping in the cellar.

No, that wasn't true. He could leave, but he didn't want to.

Adrian settled himself on the narrow step beside her. His hip brushed against hers. Her shoulder, where it touched his, spread warmth all down his arm. He wanted nothing more than to slip his arm around her and comfort her, but he knew it wouldn't be right. Such closeness between a man and a woman was for husbands and wives.

He had no idea what to say. He simply started talking. "I loved my wife dearly, but I can't remember her face. I try so hard to see her, but she isn't clear anymore. I'm ashamed of that. How can I forget the one I loved more than my own life?"

Faith sniffed and slanted a look his way. "You should not feel ashamed for that."

"Nor should you feel shame. We are only human."

Nodding, she looked away from him, staring into the dark corner of the room. "My husband was a cruel man. I think he tried not to be, but he couldn't help himself. I used to think it was my fault. I thought I couldn't make him happy because I didn't love him enough."

Adrian's breath froze in his chest. "He was cruel to you?"

She looked down at her hands and gave a tiny nod.

Was she saying what he thought she was saying? "Faith, did your husband beat you?"

She nodded again, as if words were beyond her.

His stomach contracted with disgust. No wonder she flinched from his touch. What kind of man could abuse someone as sweet and kind as Faith?

"No man has the right to be cruel to another in such a fashion. It was not your fault."

Scrubbing her face with her hands, she said, "I know."

She drew a deep breath and looked at Adrian. "My husband's grandmother lived here. Her daughter ran away with an Amish lad. When they died, Mose came back to stay with her."

"Are you sure? I don't remember a boy living here."

"Mose was twelve years older than I. You wouldn't have been old enough to know him, but, in truth, no one knew he was here. His grandmother kept him locked away in this cellar until the sheriff learned of it and took him away. Dr. White told me the whole sad story today."

"That's why you were so quiet on the way home."

"I kept thinking that I was the one person who should have loved him and I didn't. If I had, he might have shared this pain with me and been healed."

"You take too much onto yourself. Only God can know the hearts and minds of men. You would have helped your husband if you could. You have a kind heart, Faith Martin."

She shook her head in denial. "You are the one with the kind heart."

He gently cupped her face and turned it toward him. With the pad of his thumb, he brushed the tears from her cheeks. Her luminous, tear-filled eyes widened, and her lips parted.

She was so close, so warm, so vibrant, and yet so

vulnerable. He could kiss her—wanted to kiss her. He wanted to taste the sweetness of her soft lips, but something held him back.

Faith needed a friend now, not another complication. If he gave in to his desire it would change everything between them. She had given him a rare gift. Her trust. He didn't want to do anything to jeopardize that.

Faith closed her eyes and leaned into Adrian's hand, drawing strength from his gentle touch. If only she could hold on to this moment forever. She'd never felt so safe.

Why did this man make her wish for things that could never be? Long ago she'd given up the notion of having a happy marriage and children of her own. That wasn't God's plan for her. She accepted that.

And now this man had come into her life. A kind, sweet man who made her wish she still believed in a marriage with love between a husband and a wife. She cared for Adrian. Deeply.

As much as she wanted to hold on to this moment, she couldn't. She couldn't allow her growing feelings for Adrian to distract her. She had to think about Kyle. She had to focus on his adoption and on providing him with a safe, secure home.

She pulled away from Adrian. He withdrew his hand. The coolness of the cellar air made her shiver.

Pity filled his voice as he said, "Come upstairs, Faith. You cannot change what happened here. It is all in God's hands now."

Pity for her or for her husband?

She'd shared her darkest secret with Adrian. Did he think less of her for suffering in silence all those many years? Maybe she didn't want to know.

She struggled to her feet. "I didn't mean to burden you with my woes."

"They are no burden, Faith. Sharing your troubles makes them lighter."

She realized he was right. Her unhappy past didn't loom over her the way it once had. Her sense of relief left her light-headed. She started up the stairs. "You have work to do. You should go home."

"There's nothing that can't wait. Are you sure you're okay?"

"*Ja,* a stout cup of tea will fix me right up." She entered the kitchen and crossed to the sink. Her hands trembled as she reached for the teakettle. The room began spinning around her.

Adrian was beside her in an instant. His hand closed over hers as he gently took the kettle from her. "Let me do this. You sit down."

He took her by the elbow and led her to the table. Pulling out a chair, he held it while she sat, then he returned to the sink and began to fill the kettle.

She drew several deep breaths. "Adrian, you don't have to take care of me."

"If I don't, who will?" He carried the kettle to the stove. He turned on the burners and set the kettle over the flames, then started opening cabinets. "Where do you keep your tea?"

"In the green tin on the counter beside the refrigerator."

He found it and soon had a mug ready for the hot water. As he waited for the kettle to boil, he took a seat across the table from her.

She managed a small smile. "God is *goot* to give me a friend such as you. Are you so thoughtful of all your neighbors?"

"Only the ones with animals that spit on me."

She chuckled. "Poor man. What an impression we must have made on you. It's a wonder you ever came back."

"I reckon I came back because I didn't think you could make a go of this place. You proved me wrong."

Lacing her fingers together in front of her on the table, she said, "I've managed to hang on for a few weeks. That doesn't mean I can hang on forever. It doesn't mean the *Englisch* will think this is a good home for my nephew."

"What will happen if they don't let you adopt him?"

Faith closed her eyes. "I can't think such a thing. They *must* let him stay with me. I don't think I could bear it if they don't."

Adrian laid his hand over her clenched fingers. She opened her eyes to find him gazing at her with compassion and something else in his eyes. Longing.

Her heart began beating faster. He started to speak, but the shrill whistle of the kettle cut him off.

He pulled his hand away and rose to fix her tea. Whatever he had been about to say remained unsaid. After bringing her mug to the table, he muttered a goodbye and left abruptly. As the screen door banged shut behind him, Faith was left to wonder if she had imagined the closeness they had shared so briefly.

Chapter Nine

Two days after taking Faith into town, Adrian was cutting hay in the meadow when a car turned in his lane. It stopped on the road not far from him, and an *Englisch* lady got out. He drew his team to a halt. She approached but kept a wary eye on his horses. "Are you Mr. Adrian Lapp?"

"I am." He waited for her to state her business.

"I'm Caroline Watkins. I'm the social worker in charge of your neighbor's adoption application. I've just come from my second visit here, and Mrs. Martin has given me permission to speak with some of her neighbors. May I have a few minutes of your time?"

He wiped the sweat from his brow with his shirtsleeve and adjusted his hat. "A few. I must get my hay cut."

"I won't take long, I promise." She opened a leather folder and began to write in it.

Meg, the horse closest to her, stomped at a fly and shook her head. Miss Watkins stumbled back a step and looked ready to run to the safety of her car. Time was a wasting. Adrian said, "What questions have you?"

She gave an embarrassed smile but didn't come closer. "How long have you known Faith Martin?"

"Three weeks, I reckon."

"Is that all?"

"I met her the day after she arrived here."

Miss Watkins kept writing. "Are you aware of any reason why Mrs. Martin should not adopt a child?"

"Nee."

"Do you believe she can provide for a child?"

"I do, but it makes no difference if she can or not."

Miss Watkins's brows drew together in a frown. "Of course it makes a difference."

"An Amish parent does not need to worry about what will happen to his or her family if something tragic befalls them. All our widows and children are well cared for."

"By whom?"

It was clear this outsider didn't understand Amish ways. "Our church members will see that Faith and her child have food, clothing and a roof over their heads if ever they need such help."

"That's very admirable."

"It is the way God commands us to live."

"Have you seen Mrs. Martin interacting with children?"

He thought back to last Sunday. *"Ja."*

"Tell me about it."

"I saw her holding Katie Sutter's daughter, Rachel. She had the babe settled on her hip. It looked as if she had done it many times. I also saw her with Annie Imhoff. She is nine, I think. Faith gave her attention and directed her to help with the work as was right."

"What are your feelings about Faith's adoption plan?"

"It is a *goot* thing for her to take in her brother's child, or any child."

"How often do you see Mrs. Martin?"

"I've seen her almost daily since she arrived."

"And why is that?"

The question shocked him. Why had he found excuse after excuse to trek across the field to see her so often?

Wasn't it because he was happier when he was near her? Wasn't it because her smile drove away his loneliness?

Miss Watkins waited for his reply. He said, "Because she needs help and it is the neighborly thing to do."

"Describe her personal qualities and limitations."

At last an easy question. "She is hardworking. She is devout. Modest. She is kind to her animals."

Miss Watkins stopped writing and looked up. "And what about her limitations?"

A not-so-easy question. What could he say that wouldn't undermine her chances of adopting her nephew and yet was the truth? "She sometimes takes on more than she can handle."

"Do you see her physical handicap as a limitation?"

"You and I might see it as such, but she does not," he stated firmly.

"Can you describe her potential ability to parent?"

"She will make a fine mother." Of that he had no doubt.

Miss Watkins folded her notebook tight against her chest. "Will a child of a different faith be accepted in your community?"

He shouldn't be annoyed by her ignorance, but he was. "God loves all His children. How could we do any less? Faith's nephew will be raised to know and serve God, as all our children are. To become Amish is a choice, not a requirement. When he is old enough, he will make that decision for himself. I must get back to work now."

"Thank you for your time."

He clicked his tongue. "Get up, Meg. Go along, Mick."

The team began moving and set the sickle in motion. The clatter of the razor sharp blades drowned out the sound of Miss Watkins's car as she drove away.

It wasn't right that an outsider was the one to decide if Faith could adopt her nephew.

For the first time in many years, Adrian opened his heart and prayed. He prayed for God to smile on Faith and the child who needed her.

In the middle of the week, Faith purchased a used woodstove at a farm sale and had it installed in her home. She bid a sad goodbye to the propane stove but happily pocketed the money from its sale. Her first attempt to use her new stove resulted in a charred meal, but by the third day she had the hang of it again.

The fire chief's favorable inspection report arrived in the mail a week later, the same day her medical report came. Dr. White had found her in sound health. She mailed the reports along with mounds of paperwork to the adoption agency and waited for a reply.

The following week she opened her mail to find the news she had been waiting for.

Kyle was coming to stay with her...on a trial basis.

Finally!

Faith hugged the letter to her chest and twirled in a circle, nearly falling in the process.

When she was calm enough, she read the details again. There would be more follow-up visits by the agency after Kyle arrived, but if all went well, the adoption hearing was scheduled for the last Monday in September.

There could still be stumbling blocks, but Faith didn't care. Kyle was on his way. She was finally going to meet her brother's child.

As she waited impatiently on the porch the day he was to arrive, she worked at carding her fleece. The process of combing sections of hair over and over again between two brushes was a mindless task she could do as she watched the driveway. Each passing minute felt like an hour.

When Miss Watkins's car finally appeared, Faith dropped her work into a basket and walked toward her gate, her hands shaking with excitement. She had waited so long for this moment.

Caroline stopped her car and got out. Without a word, she opened the back door of the automobile. Faith smiled happily at the boy who emerged. With his flaming red hair and freckles, young Kyle was the spitting image of his father at the same age.

The anxiety Faith had been living with for weeks lifted away and vanished into the air like smoke. It took but a moment for love to form in her heart. This was her brother's son, and she would love him as she had his father. As she would love her own child.

"Welcome, Kyle. I am your *Aenti* Faith, and I am very pleased to meet you."

He looked ready to bolt back into the car. His green eyes held sadness and fear. The tragedy had left its mark on him. Faith could have wept for all he had endured. It would be up to her and God to see that Kyle's life was safe and happy from now on out.

Miss Watkins said, "Today is a very special day. It's Kyle's birthday. I didn't know if you knew that or not."

Faith grinned at Kyle. "I didn't know. Happy birthday, dearest. My goodness, you are six. We will have to get you enrolled in school right away if you are to start this fall."

She took a step closer and bent to his level. "I have a surprise for you. Someone else has arrived just this morning and I think he would like to meet you."

Kyle's gaze moved from her face to the house behind her. "Who is it?"

Faith straightened and crossed her arms. "Well, I don't know what to call him. He's down in the barn. Would you like to meet him?"

Kyle eyed the barn with uncertainty. "I guess."

"*Goot.* Come along. Miss Watkins, you are welcome to come, too." Faith nodded in that direction.

The social worker looked from the barn down to her high-heeled shoes. "I believe I'll wait in the house."

Faith extended her hand to Kyle but he didn't take it. She tried not to feel rejected. She knew she needed to give him time to warm up to her. She started toward the barn and glanced over her shoulder. Kyle followed.

Happiness warmed her heart. It had been a long time since she'd dared believe she could be this happy.

At the barn door, she waited for him to catch up. "Have you ever been to a farm before?"

He hooked his thumbs in the waistband of his jeans. "We stayed on a ranch once. The rancher was a friend of my mom's. They had a whole lotta cows and cowboys, too."

Faith smiled at his Southern drawl. He had lived his whole life in Texas and it showed.

She opened the door. "I don't have a cow yet, but we will have to get one soon so you can have fresh milk to drink. There are lots of things you will learn about living on a farm, but one of the most important things is to respect the animals."

A loud whinny came from inside. Kyle's eyes grew round. "You've got a horse?"

She grinned at the excitement in his voice. "It is your horse now, too."

"Can I see him?" His wariness gave way to tempered eagerness.

"It's a she. Our mare's name is Copper. You can see her in a minute. A horse is a very strong animal and can hurt you if you aren't careful. I want you to listen carefully to these two rules. Are you listening?"

He nodded.

"Never run behind a horse. Never. Always speak to them softly so that they know where you are. Can your repeat these rules for me?"

"I never run behind one and I speak softly so they know I'm there."

"That's right. Okay, come and meet Copper." Faith led the way down the narrow center aisle to the first stall on the right. Copper hung her head over the boards to investigate the newcomer.

Kyle took a step closer to Faith. "She's really big."

"Wait until you see my neighbor's draft horses. They are really, really big. They make poor Copper look like a pony beside them."

Kyle started to hold out his hand but snatched it back when Copper nibbled at it. "Does she bite?"

"She is looking for a treat. I just happen to have something she loves in my pocket. I will show you how to feed her."

Faith withdrew a kerchief from her pocket and opened it to reveal several apple slices. Taking one, she laid it in the center of Kyle's palm. "Keep your hand flat. You don't want her to think your fingers are the treats."

He bravely held up the slice. Copper daintily nibbled it up. Kyle wiped his hand on his jeans. "Her lips are soft but her chin whiskers tickle. Can I give her another one?"

"Of course."

He fed her two more apple bits and then grew brave enough to pet her nose. "Can you teach me how to ride her?"

"I can, but Copper is a buggy horse."

"Like the ones I saw on the highway coming here?"

"*Ja,* just like those. Come, I have some more animals for you to meet." She smiled at Kyle and wondered what Adrian would think of her *Englisch* nephew.

Leading the way to the back of the barn, Faith stopped beside the last stall. "This is who I want you to meet."

She pointed through the board to the farthest corner. Myrtle lay in the thick bed of hay Adrian had spread out for her. At her side, a coal-black cria lay beside her. He raised his long neck that still wobbled slightly and batted his thick eyelashes in their direction.

"Is that a camel?" Kyle climbed up the boards to get a better view. Faith was pleased to see his curiosity pushing aside his unease.

"It's an alpaca. Her name is Myrtle and that is her new son. He doesn't have a name yet. He was just born this morning."

"Sweet. Can I pet him?"

"As long as his mother doesn't object. Come, I will introduce you so that she knows you are a friend."

Faith opened the gate and stepped inside the pen. Her feet sank into the soft hay, making her stumble.

Myrtle shot to her feet in alarm. The cria struggled to its feet and ducked under his mother's body to hide on the other side of her legs.

"What's the matter with your leg?" Kyle had noticed her brace.

"I hurt it a long time ago and it didn't heal well so now I have to wear this brace."

"Does it hurt?"

"Sometimes, but not today."

Grasping the gate to steady herself, Faith spoke soothingly to Myrtle in Pennsylvania Dutch. When the new mother was calm, Faith crossed the pen carefully with Kyle at her side. Myrtle allowed them both to admire her baby, but the baby remained hidden behind his mother.

Kyle squatted down in the bedding and held out his hand. "Come here, little fella. I won't hurt you."

"Perhaps he wants a name first. What do you think we should call him? He's black as night. Shall we call him Midnight?"

"No, that's a girly name."

Feeling put in her girly place, Faith held back a chuckle. "All right, what would you like to call him?"

"I want to call him Shadow."

She considered it. "Shadow. I think that's a very good name for him."

By this time the cria had grown accustomed to their presence and ventured out from behind his mother. Kyle extended his hand. "Come here, Shadow."

Shadow approached slowly, wobbling as he walked. Barely bigger than a tomcat with impossibly long legs, he was still trying to learn to use them.

It was clear he was as curious about the boy as the boy was about him. Kyle inched forward and touched the baby alpaca's head. Shadow frisked away behind his mother but didn't stay there. He returned after a moment to investigate further.

Faith said, "Kyle, I think he likes you."

"I think so, too."

"Since you have chosen his name, would you like to be his owner?"

"Can I?" Kyle looked up with uncertainty in his eyes.

"There are many things you will have to learn in order to take good care of him. It will be hard work. Are you willing to do that?"

"Sure."

"I don't mean for one day. I mean every day."

"If you show me what to do."

Myrtle began stamping one foot and making huffing sounds. Faith said, "His mother says he has had enough playtime. We should let him rest."

"He's really neat. Thanks, Aunt Faith."

She held open the gate to let him out of the stall. "You're welcome, Kyle. Let's go back to the house. I'm sure Miss Watkins is wondering where we are."

When they reached the house, Kyle went in ahead of her. Miss Watkins sat at the kitchen table fanning herself with a sheet of paper. Faith said, "Kyle, why don't you go explore the house."

"Okay." He left the room.

Miss Watkins slid several sheets of paper toward Faith. "We have only two more documents to sign, Mrs. Martin. It won't take long. Now, you understand this is a temporary guardianship until the court hearing next month."

"*Ja,* I understand."

"Good. I'll be back to visit Kyle several times before the hearing and see how things are going for the two of you. Expect me at noon the day after tomorrow. These transitions don't always go smoothly, so be prepared for that."

"I will."

After Faith signed the papers waiting for her, she walked with Miss Watkins to the door. "Thank you for all your help."

"I'm just doing my job. The judge will consider my recommendations when making a decision about the adoption."

"Of course." Faith wanted to hug the woman. It was finally sinking in. Kyle was here. At long last, God had given her a child.

"Aunt Faith?"

She and Miss Watkins turned around. Faith asked, "What is it, Kyle?"

"Where's your TV?"

At the end of their first day together, Faith helped Kyle get ready for bed. The scared, lost look she'd seen on his face when he'd first arrived had returned.

Setting his suitcase on a chair beside the bed, she began putting his clothes into the lowest drawers of the dresser against the wall where small hands could reach them easily.

Her hand encountered something hard tucked in between his pajamas and T-shirts. When she pulled it out, she saw it was a photograph of her brother and his wife.

Faith let her hand drift over the glass as she studied her brother's face. He had changed a great deal in the twelve years that he'd been gone. A man looked back at her, not the boy she remembered. The woman with him had dark brown hair and green eyes, a stunning combination.

"That's my mom and dad." Kyle reached for the picture.

"You look just like him." She handed the forbidden image to the boy.

He kissed the picture and looked around the room. "I think I'll want this by the bed so I can see it when I open my eyes."

She didn't have the heart to tell him the photograph would have to be put away. He had lost too much already. She wouldn't take away this reminder of his parents. Not yet.

She patted his head. "On your bedside table will be fine for now."

Turning away, she opened his windows to dispel the room's stuffiness and to hide the tears that stung her eyes. When she had a grip on her raw emotions, she turned around. He was already under the covers.

"You will be too hot under all of this." She drew back the quilt and folded it to the foot of the bed, leaving him with just a sheet.

He looked around, then sat up in bed. "I need a fan to sleep with."

"I don't have one. The breeze from the windows will keep you cool."

He pointed at the lantern she had placed on the dresser. "Can I keep the light on?"

"If you leave it on all night the battery will go dead."

"Please? I don't like the dark."

"I reckon it'll be okay. I have more batteries."

Relief flickered in his eyes. He scooted down in bed and pulled the sheet up to his chin. His red hair and freckles stood out in stark relief against the white bedclothes. Once again she was reminded of his father.

She asked, "Do you want to say your prayers before you go to sleep?"

He pressed his lips together and shook his head. "I don't know any."

Surprised, she asked, "You don't? Did not your mother and father teach you your prayers?"

"I know one but I don't like it anymore."

"I'll tell you what. I will say my prayers and you can listen and add anything you want to say. How's that?"

He didn't consent, but he didn't object so Faith dropped awkwardly to her knees. Pain shot through her leg, but she ignored it. She folded her hands and bowed her head.

"Dear Father in heaven, Kyle and I give you thanks for the blessings You have shown us today. I'm so happy that he is here with me. Thank You for bringing him safely to my home."

"You could say thanks for giving me Shadow," Kyle whispered.

She nodded and closed her eyes. "Kyle and I both want to thank You for the gift of little Shadow. He brings us great joy with his playful ways."

She peeked at her nephew. "Anything else?"

He shook his head. Closing her eyes again, she said, "Bless us and help us to do Your will, Lord. Help us to live as You would have us live, humbly and simply, ever mindful of Your grace as we go about our daily tasks. Forgive us our sins as we forgive those who have sinned against us. Amen."

"Are you done?" he asked.

She smiled softly at him. "I'm done."

"Where are you going to sleep?" Worry crept back into his voice as she struggled to her feet.

Tucking the sheet around him, she said, "I will be right across the hall. If you need anything, just call out. Okay?"

"I guess. Can you leave the door open?"

"Certainly. Try to get some sleep."

"Am I going to stay here a long time?"

"I hope so, darling."

"Who decides if I stay or go to a another house? Do you?"

"It will be up to Miss Watkins and a judge to decide. If God wishes it, you will stay with me a long, long time." She bent down, kissed his brow and went to her own room.

Hours later she came awake with a jolt. Someone was screaming.

"Mommy! Mommy!"

Kyle! She shot out of bed, stumbling without her brace toward his room.

Chapter Ten

The door to Kyle's room stood open, but he wasn't in the bed. Frantic, Faith rushed in and searched the room. The lantern's battery was nearly depleted. It gave only a feeble, flickering light, but it was enough to let her see him huddled in the corner by the closet.

Some instinct made her approach him slowly. "Kyle, dearest, what's wrong?"

His eyes were open, but she knew he wasn't seeing her. He turned his head from side to side, sobbing. "Mommy? Mommy?"

Faith lowered herself to the floor. "Kyle, it's *Aenti* Faith. Can you hear me? Everything is all right. You've had a nightmare, that's all."

He sat with his arms around his knees. His little body trembled violently.

Faith moved closer. "It's all right, baby. It's all right. I'm here."

Suddenly, his eyes focused on her. He launched himself into her arms. Faith held him close, rocking him and stroking his hair as she murmured words of comfort.

He said, "I don't like it here. I want to go home."

"You are home, sweetheart. This is your new home, now."

He didn't answer, but slowly, his sobs died away. After a time, he fell asleep.

Faith sat holding him for a long time. Her heart bled for the pain he had endured in his young life. She could only pray that time and her love would heal his wounded soul.

When she was sure he was fast asleep, she struggled to her feet and carried him to his bed. After tucking him in, she lay down beside him in case he woke again and waited for the morning to come.

Miss Watkins would be back to check on him at noon tomorrow. If she learned how unhappy he was, would she take him away?

Late-morning sunshine glinted through the orchard canopy dappling the ground with dancing patterns of light and shadow as Adrian set to work harvesting the first of Faith's fruit. He hadn't been at it long when the hair at the back of his neck started to prickle.

Someone was watching him.

He lowered his fruit-picking pole to the ground. One of the alpacas, perhaps?

A quick check around showed he had Faith's orchard to himself. Shrugging off the feeling, he raised a long pole with a wire basket and a branch snipper on the end up into the branches of Faith's trees. As he worked, he transferred the peaches he'd plucked into a bushel basket at his feet. When he was finished gathering the fruit from one tree, he moved on to another. The feeling that he was being watched didn't leave.

As he emptied the pole basket into a larger one, a shower of leaves made him look up into the tree above him. The sight that greeted his eyes sent a slash of pain through his heart.

A red-haired, freckled-faced *kind* peered down through the leaves of a peach tree. The boy looked so much like his son that for a second he thought he was dreaming.

"Gideon?" He barely breathed the name.

The face disappeared back into the foliage. A small, disembodied voice asked, "Are you going to make me go away?"

The voice didn't belong to Gideon. This wasn't his son come back from the grave. Who was it? Adrian said, "Come down from there."

A few seconds later a pair of sneakers appeared. A boy lowered himself until he hung suspended from a branch with his shoes about three feet off the ground.

The kid shot Adrian a scowl. "Can I get a little help here?"

Adrian's racing heart slowed. Now that he had a better view of the boy, he could see the red hair and freckles were the only things that were similar to his son. This was an *Englisch* boy. He was several years older than Gideon had been. Stepping forward, Adrian grasped the boy's waist and lowered him to the ground.

"Thanks." The kid dusted his hands together, then cocked his head to the side as he studied Adrian. "Well?"

"Well what?"

"Are you going to take me away?"

"Nee."

"Are you going to be my new dad if the judge makes Aunt Faith my new mom?"

Realization dawned on Adrian. The boy was Faith's

nephew. He breathed a silent prayer of thanks that God had seen fit to bring her the child she longed for.

"I will not be your father. I'm a neighbor from down the road. I'm helping your *aenti* harvest her peaches."

"Oh. That's okay then. I didn't want a new dad. Aunt Faith is nice and all, but I want my real dad and mom to come back."

"They cannot come back from heaven."

Looking down, the boy kicked a fallen peach and sent it rolling through the grass. "Yeah, I know."

Adrian knew exactly what the boy was feeling. He said, "My name is Adrian Lapp. What is yours?"

"Howdy, Mr. Lapp. I'm Kyle King," the boy drawled.

"If you have nothing better to do, Kyle King, you can help me finish picking this fruit."

He didn't look enthused. "I don't know how. Do you have TV at your house?"

"*Nee,* it is *veldlich* and is *verboten.*"

"Huh?"

"It is a worldly thing and forbidden to us."

"How come you talk so funny?"

"Because I am Amish. How come you talk so funny?"

Kyle's solemn face cracked a tiny smile. "Because I'm a Texan."

"Ah. Do they have peaches in Texas?"

"I guess."

"But you have never picked peaches in Texas."

"Nope. We lived in Houston. Mom got our peaches from the grocery store."

"Houston, is that a big town?"

Kyle raised one eyebrow. "Are you kidding me?"

"*Nee,* I am not."

"What does *nee* mean?"

"It is Pennsylvania Dutch and it means no."

"Then why don't you just say no?"

"Because I am Amish and that is the language we speak."

"Oh. My aunt Faith is Amish, too. That's why she wears those funny dresses and that thing on her head."

"It is called a prayer *kapp*. It signifies her devotion to God."

"I'm not going to wear one 'cause I don't like God. He's mean."

"You must not say such a thing."

"It's true. My foster mom said God wanted my mom and dad with Him in heaven more than He wanted them to be here. That proves He isn't nice."

"I think she meant God *needed* them in heaven more than He needed them here."

Those were the same words Adrian's family and friends had used to try and comfort him, to help explain the inexplicable reasons why first his wife and then his son had been taken away. Like Kyle, Adrian found no comfort in the words.

The boy picked up a peach and threw it against a nearby tree, splattering the soft fruit against the rough bark. "I needed them more."

Faced with the impotent fury of this child, Adrian put aside his own feelings of bitterness and sought a way to help the boy. "You have a good arm, Kyle. Do you like baseball?"

"Sure. My dad was the coach of my team. He taught me everything about baseball. He was going to get me a new mitt when he picked me up after school, but he never came back. Why did God have to take him away?"

Adrian plucked a wormy peach from an overhead

branch and threw it. It smashed into bits against the same tree. "We cannot know God's reasons. We can only pray that one day we will see our loved ones again."

"Did your parents die, too?"

"No. God took my wife and my son to heaven."

Kyle chucked two peaches toward the hapless tree. Only one hit the target. He squinted up at Adrian. "So, do you hate God, too?"

Faith faced Miss Watkins across the kitchen table. This was the social worker's first visit to see how Kyle was adjusting to life on the farm. Faith had never been more nervous in her life. She wished Adrian were here. She could use his solid presence beside her to bolster her courage.

Caroline checked the contents of the refrigerator, made a few notes in her folder and asked, "How's it going?"

"As well as can be expected." Faith kept her hands still, trying not to fidget.

"Can you elaborate a little more?"

Faith wasn't sure what the woman wanted to know. "Kyle didn't have much of an appetite yesterday, but he ate a good breakfast this morning. He adores the alpacas, especially the baby. He misses his friends and his foster parents. We went to the phone booth yesterday evening and called his buddies, Tyrell and Dylan."

Should she mention Kyle woke in the night and was crying, or would that count against her?

"Did talking to the boys upset Kyle?"

"Maybe a little. It has to be hard being pulled from all he knew."

"Where is he now?"

"Upstairs in his room. Shall I get him?"

"We can go up together. I'd like to see his room now that he's settled."

Faith led the way up the narrow fight of stairs to the bedroom opposite hers. She opened the door to Kyle's room expecting to see him reading or coloring at his desk. He wasn't in the room. His bedroom window stood wide-open with the screen pushed out.

She rushed to the window. The porch roof beyond was empty. The limbs of the old oak beside the house overhung the porch offering an adventurous boy a way down to the ground.

"He's gone." Faith heard the panic in her voice as she turned to the social worker.

Miss Watkins said, "Maybe he came downstairs and we didn't notice."

It took only a few minutes to search the house and see he wasn't in it. Where could he be? Faith opened the front door and stepped onto the porch with Miss Watkins right behind her. Faith scanned the yard. At least Kyle wasn't lying unconscious on the ground beneath the tree.

"He's likely out in the barn with Shadow." She tried calling his name but got no answer.

Crossing to the barn, Faith pulled open the door and called him again. Still no answer.

Inside, she found Myrtle and Shadow lying together undisturbed. Copper dozed in her stall. Kyle wasn't in here. Faith's worry took flight like the pigeons fluttering in the rafters. Where could he be?

Caroline asked, "Did he talk about running away?"

"He hasn't run away. I'm sure he's playing nearby."

Why would he run away? Was she such a terrible parent that he couldn't bear to live with her?

Faith opened the back door of the barn and went out

into the alpaca's pen. They were milling about near the gate to the orchard and looking in that direction. The gate was closed. Faith knew she had left it open that morning so they could go out to graze.

She cupped her hand around her mouth and shouted for Kyle.

"He's with me!"

The booming voice from the orchard belonged to Adrian. Faith relaxed. Kyle was safe if he was with Adrian.

When the pair emerged from the trees, Faith crossed her arms and scowled at her nephew. "Did you climb out your bedroom window?"

"Yes."

"Why would you do such a thing? You could have fallen and been badly hurt."

He glanced from her to Miss Watkins. "I'm sorry. I won't do it again."

Miss Watkins dropped to his level. "Kyle, why did you sneak out of the house?"

He shrugged. "I don't know."

She laid a hand on his shoulder. "I understand that this is very difficult for you. If you aren't happy here, it's all right to tell me."

Faith held her breath. Would this woman take Kyle away from her so soon? They had barely gotten to know each other.

"It's okay. Sometimes it's boring, but it's okay." His voice wobbled.

Adrian said, "Idle hands are the devil's workshop. The boy needs work to occupy his mind. He can help me pick peaches if he is bored."

A quick frown crossed Caroline's face, but she didn't say anything to Adrian as she rose. Instead, she patted

Kyle's head. "I'll be back in a week to check on you. All right? You have your aunt call me if you need anything. Will you be okay until then?"

"I guess." He shoved his hands in the waistband of his jeans.

As Miss Watkins headed for her car, Faith turned to Kyle. "You may help Adrian gather fruit until lunchtime. I'll call you when it's ready."

Kyle ventured a small request. "Can we have burgers and French fries?"

As a reward for climbing out your window and scaring me half to death?

Faith put aside her fright and forgave the boy for his behavior. "I think I can manage that, but it won't be like the fast food you get from town. Adrian, would you care to join us?"

Would he accept? She didn't want to appear too eager for his company, but she had missed him the past several days.

"I reckon I can. My hay is cut and drying in the fields. I have no need to rush home."

"*Goot.* Kyle, you must do as Adrian says."

"I will." The boy's smile returned.

Adrian said, "There are some wooden boxes inside the barn door. Bring them out to the tree where we were working."

"You got it." Kyle took off at a jog.

Faith said, "It's kind of you to let him help."

"You look tired. Is everything all right?"

"Kyle has nightmares. I haven't been sleeping well, either."

"He's had it tough, poor tyke."

"When we unpacked his things, I saw he had a picture of his mother and father. He wanted it on his bedside table. I let him keep it." She chewed the corner of her lip. Would he think she had done the wrong thing by going against their Amish teachings? Photographs were considered graven images and thus banned from Amish homes.

"The boy is not Amish. He does not know our ways. Give him time to learn about the things we believe."

She nodded, pleased that Adrian's advice mirrored her own feelings.

He leaned close. "But don't tell the bishop's wife. You already have one strike in her book."

Faith held back a giggle as Kyle came through the barn, his arms filled with a tall stack of boxes. "Are these the ones you need?"

Adrian said, "*Ja,* those are the ones. Your *aenti* and I will earn a pretty penny if we can fill and sell this many boxes of peaches."

Kyle looked between them. "You should charge more than a penny."

Adrian laughed. "Your nephew has a head for business, Faith. Should we follow his advice?"

Pretending to consider it, she finally said, "I agree. I say we ask for a nickel."

Adrian ran his fingers down his chin whiskers. "Let's think big. We should ask for a dime."

Kyle scrunched up his face. "Are you making fun of me?"

Faith ruffled his hair. "Perhaps a little."

Kyle rolled his eyes. "Whatever."

Adrian said, "Come along. Our work is waiting."

Faith watched them walk away together with mixed emotions. Kyle would need the influence of a man in his life, someone to teach him how to earn a living and work the land. Was she wrong to hope that Adrian could fulfill that role? It was a lot to ask of a neighbor. Those were things a father should teach a son.

Adrian would make a great father. He was kind and patient. She'd never heard him utter an angry word. While she never intended to marry again, if she did, someone like Adrian would be the kind of husband she'd look for. Someone exactly like Adrian.

The idea of being his wife made her blush. She quickly dismissed it as a fantasy that could never come true. Adrian wouldn't marry again any more than she would. The love he held in his heart for his first wife didn't leave room for another.

Wishing things could be different was foolish. Daydreams about Adrian were a sure path to heartache. She knew that.

So why couldn't she put her foolish yearning away?

Chapter Eleven

Several days later, Faith rose at five o'clock. She dressed, brushed and rolled her hair, fastened on her *kapp* and went down to start a fire in the kitchen stove. Stacking kindling and newspaper inside the firebox, she put a match to it. When she was sure the fire was going, she closed the firebox door.

While the stove heated, she straightened up in the living room. Adrian would be over soon to start work in the orchard. She didn't want him to see her home in a state of disarray.

Grabbing her broom, she began sweeping the floors. Soon she would have to have the offending pink-and-white linoleum replaced. The bishop had generously given her eight months to convert the old *Englisch* house into an Amish home. A home for her and Kyle, where the ghosts of the past could be put to rest and their new lives could flourish. It wouldn't be easy, but it would be worth all her hard work.

She finished her floors, washed up and began making breakfast. At half-past five o'clock, Faith called to Kyle from the bottom of the stairs. "Kyle, time to get up. Breakfast is ready."

She had to call one more time before he appeared in the kitchen, his hair tousled and his eyes puffy with sleep. "What time is it?"

"Almost six o'clock, sleepyhead. We have a lot of work waiting for us."

"We do?" He sat at the table and yawned.

She loaded both their plates with pancakes and scrambled eggs and carried them to the table. "Adrian will be here soon to start picking peaches. You don't want to keep him waiting, do you?"

"No. Is Miss Watkins coming today?" Kyle folded his arms on the table and laid his head down.

"Not that I know of."

"Good."

Outside, a loud whinny came from the barn. Faith said, "Sounds like Copper is wanting her breakfast, too."

Kyle raised his head to squint at Faith. "Can I feed her?"

"*Ja*, but first eat before your eggs get cold." Faith sat beside him, bowed her head to say a quick silent prayer and then began eating.

"Can I feed Shadow, too?" Kyle forked in a mouthful of eggs.

"His mother will give Shadow all he needs for a few months yet, but we need to feed her."

"Okay. Then can I play on the swing Adrian made me yesterday?"

Adrian had turned a length of rope and a broad plank into a swing that now hung from the oak tree beside the porch. Faith said, "After all your chores are done."

"What chores?"

"We must feed the horse and turn her out to graze.

We must feed and water the chickens and gather their eggs."

"Then can I play?"

"Not until we feed the alpacas, clean up their pen, pick the debris out of their coats and let them out to graze."

"How long will that take?"

"It takes as long as it takes, Kyle."

It might sound like a lot of work to him now, but wait until next spring when there would be a garden to hoe and weeds to be pulled every day and all before he went to school. Faith smiled. Amish children did not have time to be bored.

Kyle finished his breakfast and waited impatiently for Faith to wash the dishes. When they were done, he dashed ahead of her to the barn. "Remember the rules," she called out.

He immediately slowed down. "Don't run behind a horse and always speak softly to let them know where you are."

"Very *goot*."

She passed Adrian's farm wagon sitting in the shade. The bed of the wagon was half full of boxes of peaches. The scent of the ripe fruit filled the still morning air. Today they would load the rest of the wagon and head into the farmer's market in Hope Springs where Faith hoped her fruit would fetch a good price.

She opened the barn door, and Kyle ducked under her arm to get inside ahead of her. He made a beeline for Shadow's stall. His little buddy rushed away to hide beneath his mother.

Faith showed Kyle how to measure and pour the feed into the troughs for the alpaca. While Myrtle was busy with her breakfast, Shadow ventured close to Kyle and allowed the boy to pet him.

Kyle's bright grin gladdened Faith's heart. She took a small rake and a shovel from their place on the wall and handed them to the boy.

He said, "What's this for?"

"To *redd-up* the stall. To clean it." She indicated the manure piles.

He wrinkled his nose. "Yuck!"

She folded her arms and scowled at him. "Shadow is your responsibility. You said you would take care of him. Do you want him to sleep on a messy floor?"

"No."

She held out the tools. He approached with lagging steps and took them from her. Faith had trouble holding back her laughter as he carefully raked the manure onto the flat shovel. He looked at her. "Now what?"

"I will fetch the wheelbarrow. When we have done everyone's stall we will empty it onto the pile behind the barn."

"We're keeping it? Why?"

"Because it will make very *goot* fertilizer for the orchards and gardens next spring."

It took most of an hour to feed all the animals and clean the stalls. To Faith's delight, Kyle didn't complain or shirk from the work. They let Myrtle and Shadow out into the pen. Shadow raced about in delight at finding himself outside.

Faith and Kyle were crossing back to the house when she saw Adrian striding toward them across the field. He was pulling a small wagon behind him.

He raised a hand and waved. Her heart flipped over with unexpected joy at the sight of him.

Kyle took off toward him. "Hi, Adrian. I cleaned

out the barn and fed all the animals and Shadow let me pet him."

Adrian grinned at Kyle. "Then you have done a man's work already this morning. You must be tired."

"No. Well, maybe a little."

"You deserve a rest." Adrian picked the boy up and balanced him on his shoulder. Kyle's squeal of fear quickly turned into giggles of delight.

Faith waited until the two of them caught up with her before falling into step beside them. Adrian immediately shortened his stride to match hers. Something Mose had never done.

She needed to stop comparing the two men in her mind. There was no comparison.

"Aunt Faith says we are going to town later. Are we?"

"We are. It is Market Day. Almost everyone goes to town on Market Day."

"Cool beans. Can you teach me to drive the horse?"

By this time they had reached the porch. Adrian swung Kyle down and deposited him on the steps. "Someday, but not today. We must take my team and they are too big for you to handle."

"I'm strong." Kyle flexed one arm and pushed up his sleeve to show his muscles.

Adrian whistled his appreciation. "We must put those muscles to work in the peach orchard. Are you ready?"

Kyle fisted his hands on his hips. "*Ja.* I'm ready."

Faith pressed her hand to her lips to hide her smile. "Spoken like a true Amishman."

Adrian folded his arms over his chest. "Grab a couple of boxes from the big wagon and put them in this one. We won't have to carry our peaches so far this way. Can you pull this out to the tree where we stopped working yesterday?"

"Sure." The boy took off at a run, the little wagon bouncing behind him.

Faith spoke softly to Adrian. "He has taken quite a liking to you. God was wise to bring you into his life."

"He is a fine boy. He reminds me of my son."

Faith laid a hand on Adrian's arm. "This must be very difficult for you."

Adrian waited for the pain of his son's loss to strike his heart, but it didn't. Instead, he recalled the way Gideon had always wanted to help, sometimes to the point of being in the way. Kyle had the same burning desire to prove his worth.

Adrian glanced at Faith's small hand on his arm. Her touch was warm and comforting. Was she right? Did God have a purpose for bringing him into Kyle's life?

For the past several years Adrian had thought only of what he had lost. He'd never once considered that God might use him as a gift to others.

He gazed into Faith's sympathetic eyes. "Kyle reminds me of Gideon, but he is not Gideon. I see in Kyle a boy with joys and pain, hopes and fears that are all his own. I'd like to think that they would have been friends. I know Lovina would have liked having you for a neighbor."

"I wish I could have known her."

"Me, too."

Adrian moved away from the comfort Faith offered. "We'd better get busy or we'll miss the start of the market."

"You're right. I need the best possible price for my fruit. My yarn is selling fairly well, but not well enough." They began walking toward the orchard.

"I've been thinking about that. Have you any items you'd like to sell at the market?"

"You mean things made from my yarn? I have several baby blankets and two dozen socks ready. Should I take them?"

"Many tourists come for the quilt auction that will be held this afternoon. They might buy your work."

She shook her head. "My plain socks hardly compare to the beautiful quilts they come to buy."

They reached the gate leading into the orchard. Kyle joined them carrying more boxes than he could safely manage. Shadow was prancing and bouncing beside him.

Adrian opened the gate for him. As usual, the curious alpacas came galloping up to investigate this new activity.

Kyle petted his little buddy. "I wish Shadow could come to town with us. I bet he'd like it."

Faith chuckled. "The tourists would stare at an alpaca riding in an Amish buggy, that's for sure."

Adrian stopped in his tracks. "They would, wouldn't they?"

Faith and Kyle walked on until they noticed he wasn't following. Faith stopped and looked back. "What's the matter?"

"Kyle and Shadow have given me an idea."

"We have?" Kyle looked perplexed.

"A very good idea. Faith, can you bring your spinning wheel to market and spin yarn while others are watching you?"

"*Ja.* What are you getting at?"

"Could we take Shadow to town with us?"

She shook her head. "He's only a few days old. It wouldn't be good for him to be separated from his mother for any length of time."

Adrian pondered the problems involved in his

scheme. "And Myrtle is known for her spitting skills. That wouldn't work."

Faith's eyes lit up. "You want to take one of the alpacas to market with us as an advertisement for my yarns."

"You said it yourself. People would stop and stare. They might also stop and buy. Which of your animals has the best temperament?"

"Socks," she said without hesitation. "She loves attention and she loves people."

He nodded. Socks was the least likely to spit on an unsuspecting customer. "Would she follow behind the wagon into town?"

Faith's face showed her growing excitement. "I don't see why not. She's halter trained."

He held up his hand. "What's wrong with this plan?"

Faith shrugged. "Nothing that I can see."

Adrian nodded slowly. "Kyle and I will get started on the peaches. You get together the things you'd like to sell."

He turned and scratched Socks between the ears. "Looks like you're going to town, girl. What do you think about that?"

Kyle ran ahead with the wagon into the orchard with Shadow hot on his heels.

Faith once again wore her best bonnet and Sunday dress as she sat on the high seat of Adrian's wagon. Kyle sat between them as excited as any six-year-old child on his way to a special treat. The boy had been awed into silence by the size of Adrian's draft horses but soon recovered his chatty nature.

As they approached Hope Springs, they met dozens of other Amish families all heading in the same direction. The influx of lumbering produce-laden wagons and buggies forced the traffic in town to drop to a crawl. The slow pace allowed many drivers and their passengers to gawk at Socks as she ambled along behind Adrian's wagon.

The alpaca didn't seem at all upset by the commotion going on around her. With her head held high, she surveyed the activity with wide, curious eyes.

Adrian turned off Main onto Lake Street. "The regular weekly markets are held every Friday afternoon in a large grassy area next to the lumberyard up ahead."

"Is it all produce?"

"You will find a wide range of fruits and vegetables sold here including certified organic produce. There will also be homemade baked goods, homemade jams, local honey, meat, eggs and cheeses. You can even find fresh-cut flowers as well as fresh and dried herbs and spices."

Faith could already see the striped canopies of numerous tents being set up. "I'm surprised at the size, given the fact that Hope Springs isn't that big of a town."

"This isn't a regular market day. This is our Summer Festival. It's held every year on the last day of August. The big draw this year is the Quilts of Hope charity quilt auction. My mother mentioned that they have over fifty quilts to sell."

Adrian maneuvered his wagon to a tent marked for fresh produce and fruit. With Faith's and Kyle's help, he began unloading the wagon and stacking their boxes of peaches in neat rows inside the tent. The work would have gone faster if not for the crowd of children and adults who quickly gathered around Socks. Faith answered numerous questions about her animal while helping Adrian and keeping an eye on Kyle.

When they had the wagon unloaded, Adrian parked

the wagon near a row of buggies and unhitched his team. He slipped off their bridles and put halters on the pair but left them in their harnesses. He turned to Faith. "Where would you like to set up your spinning wheel?"

"I wish I had a tent." The afternoon sun beating down on her head promised to make her demonstration hot work unless she could find some shade.

"*Ja,* we need to get one for you."

Faith liked the way he said "we," as if they would be doing this together again.

Kyle pulled at her sleeve. "Can I go look around?"

On one hand, she was as eager to explore all the tents and displays as Kyle was, but on the other hand, she didn't want Adrian to be stuck looking after Socks. The alpaca was her responsibility.

She put aside her childish desires and said, "Perhaps Adrian can show you around."

Kyle turned his pleading eyes toward Adrian. "Can you? Please?"

"I must stay with the wagon," he replied.

Faith wasn't about to let him miss out on a fun afternoon. "Socks belongs to me. I will stay with her. Please take Kyle and show him the sights."

A young man made his way though the crowd and straight to Socks. "So this is an alpaca! They are cute. Is this the one that spit on you and the bishop's wife?"

The resemblance between the two men was unmistakable. Faith wasn't surprised when Adrian said, "Faith, this is my *bruder* Ben."

Ben's grin lit up his face. He touched the brim of his straw hat. "I'm pleased to meet you, Faith Martin."

She bowed slightly. "I'm pleased to meet you, as well. Myrtle was the ill-mannered one. This is Socks. She likes people."

"May I pet her?" Ben asked.

Faith nodded. Ben reached out hesitantly and stroked his hand along Socks's jaw. She showed her appreciation by stepping close and wrapping her long neck around him in a hug.

From behind her, Faith heard a pair of girls' voices cooing in unison. "Isn't that sweet?"

The girls, identical twins, joined Ben in petting Socks. Adrian spoke to his brother. "Ben, would you mind watching Socks while Faith and I show Kyle around?"

Ben winked at Adrian. "Not a bit."

"Danki." Adrian looked to Faith and tipped his head toward the nearest tent. "Shall we?"

She nodded and reached for Kyle's hand. As she grasped it, he let out a hiss of pain. Startled, she let go. "Did I hurt you?"

He put his hands behind his back and shook his head. Adrian squatted to his level and said sternly, "Let me see."

Reluctantly, Kyle extended his hands. There were large blisters on both palms.

Faith sucked in a sharp breath knowing how painful they had to be. "Kyle, why didn't you tell me you'd hurt yourself?"

"I was afraid you would make me stay home."

She thought of all the raking and wheelbarrow pushing he'd done as well as the heavy boxes full of peaches he'd pulled through the orchard in the little wagon. Never once had he complained.

"Darling, you mustn't be afraid to tell me when something hurts. We need to find somewhere to wash these and put some bandages on them."

Ben said, "There's a first-aid tent near the front of the lumberyard."

Faith flashed him a grateful smile. "*Danki.* Come along, Kyle. We'll get you fixed up in no time."

She and Adrian guided him through the crowds to the tent run by the local firefighters. A kindly fireman rinsed Kyle's hands, applied an antiseptic cream and a large Band-Aid to each palm. When he was done, he gave Kyle a lollipop. "For being so brave."

Faith thanked him. He said, "No problem. If you go out behind this tent you'll see we are providing free pony rides to all the children attending the market today. Our police and fire departments are giving out snow cones and popcorn, too."

Kyle looked hopefully at Faith. "Can I ride a pony?"

He certainly deserved some fun after all the work he'd done. "You may."

They found the ride without difficulty. Kyle waited patiently until it was his turn. Adrian lifted him aboard a small white horse and stepped back beside Faith as he and several other Amish children went round and round on the plodding ponies.

Standing beside Adrian and watching Kyle enjoying himself, Faith had a glimpse of what her life might have been like if she had married the right man and been blessed with children of her own.

While she might never be a wife again, she now had a chance to raise a son. The thought was bittersweet.

After the ride came to an end, they walked on together exploring the various tents and booths until they came to the largest tent. Two sides of the tent had been rolled up to take advantage of the gusty breeze. Inside, dozens of beautifully crafted quilts hung from wooden frames meant to display them to full advantage.

The room was already crowded with *Englisch* men and women examining the quilts closely.

Faith was admiring a wedding ring quilt pattern done in cream, pinks and blues when she spotted Nettie Sutter, Adrian's mother and several other women conferring at a table near the back of the tent.

"Adrian, there's your mother."

"Where?"

She pointed. He quickly turned the other way and took her arm. "Let's go. I don't need any quilts."

Chapter Twelve

Adrian hoped to avoid his mother's too-sharp eyes but he should have known better. She had already seen them and was headed in their direction with Rebecca Beachy holding on to her arm. His mother's cheeks were rosy red from exertion. Wisps of her gray hair had escaped from beneath her *kapp*.

"Adrian, you are just what we need—a strong son to help me set up these tables. Hello, Faith." His mother's eyes darted between the two of them with intense speculation. No doubt she had already jumped to the wrong conclusion about his business association with Faith.

He said, "We've brought peaches to sell."

She winked at him. "What a clever excuse to bring Faith to our market. Faith, I'd like you to meet Rebecca Beachy. She and her aunt are neighbors of mine. Although Rebecca is blind, she stitches beautiful quilts."

Rebecca held out her hand. "My talent comes from God, it is not of my own making."

Faith stepped forward and took Rebecca's hand. "I'm pleased to meet you."

Rebecca tipped her head to the side. "And who else do you have with you?"

Adrian saw Kyle peeking from behind Faith's skirt.

Faith urged the boy forward. "This is my *Englisch* nephew, Kyle."

Kyle frowned up at her. "I'm not English, I'm from Texas."

Adrian's mother chuckled. "It's nice to meet you, Kyle from Texas."

"Have you had a pony ride yet?" Rebecca asked.

He nodded. "Aunt Faith says I can have a snow cone, too."

Rebecca grinned. "*Ach,* I love them. You must try the pineapple ones. They're the best."

"Adrian, can you spare a few minutes to help us?" his mother asked.

He looked over the number of visitors filing through the tent. This would be the best place for Faith to set up her wheel. "If I may ask a favor in return?"

Mamm nodded. "Of course."

"May Faith use one of your tables to sell her yarn?"

His mother grinned at Faith. "I don't see why not. The more, the merrier. Show Adrian where you want to set up."

Within a few minutes he'd set up the tables his mother needed and placed one for Faith near the open side so that Socks could be tethered out on the grass. His mother promised to keep an eye on Kyle while he and Faith returned to the wagon to collect Faith's spinning wheel and the yarns she had boxed up to sell.

They found the wagon surrounded by a dozen young Amish girls admiring Socks. Ben, seated casually on the tailgate of the wagon, was clearly enjoying the attention.

Faith and Adrian shared an amused glance before

Adrian stepped inside the circle of young women. "*Danki,* Ben, I'll take over now."

Standing up, Ben said, "I don't mind watching Faith's pet a little longer."

"If you want to be useful, little *bruder,* you can carry Faith's spinning wheel to the tent where the quilts are being auctioned."

"I can handle that if one of you girls can show me the way." Ben's charming smile gathered him several volunteers.

After Ben left, Adrian stacked together Faith's wares and carried the boxes while she led Socks through the maze of vendor stalls back to the quilt tent.

Adrian staked Socks's lead rope just outside the tent. The alpaca promptly lay down in the thick green grass.

Kyle was waiting for them with a snow cone in his hand. Adrian's mother sat beside him enjoying one, too.

Kyle held his out. "These are really good. You should get one, Aunt Faith."

Faith said, "I hope you thanked Mrs. Lapp."

"I did." He slurped at juice dripping over the paper holder.

Adrian's mother rose and came to stand beside Faith. "He's been well behaved. Is this one of your alpacas? They are cute."

She leaned closer, and Adrian heard her ask, "Is this the one that spit on the bishop's wife?"

Faith blushed a becoming shade of pink. "No."

He took pity on her and tried to distract his mother. "*Mamm,* do you need anything else?"

"Not that I can think of," she replied.

"Faith, can I do anything else for you?" he asked. He needed to get back to the produce and see that it sold for a decent price, but he didn't want to leave her side. He was happy when he was near her.

She smiled sweetly at him. "I will be fine, *danki*."

He turned to Kyle. "You must keep an eye on Socks while your *aenti* is busy and don't wander off without telling her."

"Okay." Kyle took his snow cone and went out to sit in the grass beside Socks. A number of people had already gathered to stare at the unusual creature. When they saw Kyle sit beside her, they pressed in for a closer look.

Faith, having arranged her yarns by color in small baskets on the table, sat down at the spinning wheel and began pumping the pedals that made it turn. Adrian stood back and watched to see how she would handle being on display along with her work. He didn't have long to wait.

A middle-aged *Englisch* woman with her husband stopped to watch Faith spin. She asked, "Is this all hand-made yarn?"

"*Ja,* from my own alpacas." She seemed so nervous. Adrian wondered if he'd made a mistake in suggesting the venture.

The man asked, "What type of dye do you use?"

Faith glanced to Adrian. He gave her a thumbs-up sign.

She turned back to the prospective buyers. "Alpacas come naturally in twenty color variations. I have white, fawn, brown, gray and black, with many shades in between. The fleece dyes beautifully if you'd like colors other than these natural shades."

Nettie Sutter stepped up to the table. "I've heard it's better than wool."

"Alpaca has a softness unlike any other natural fiber.

Most people find it doesn't itch like sheep's wool. It is also very lightweight and yet is warmer than wool. I have a receiving blanket made from white alpaca that you might be interested in for Katie's baby when it arrives." She indicated a box at the end of her table.

Adrian could see that the more Faith talked about her alpacas and her spinning, the more relaxed she became.

Nettie withdrew the blanket and gushed, "This is wonderfully soft. Feel it." She held the blanket out to the *Englisch* woman. She exclaimed over the quality, too. In a matter of minutes Faith made her first sale. Adrian turned to leave and found his mother at his side.

She said, "I like your new neighbor."

He scowled at her. "That's all Faith is. A neighbor. Nothing more."

A smug look settled over his mother's features. "Isn't that what I said?"

"What you say and what you mean are often two different things."

She patted his arm as if he were a child. "Now you sound like your father. Go and take care of your peaches. Don't worry. I will keep a close eye on your neighbor and her child. I think it's about time I got to know them better."

Chapter Thirteen

On Sunday morning Faith entered the home of Adam Troyer, the handyman in Hope Springs. His house had been chosen for the preaching service. Kyle was at her side.

She glanced down at him. It would be a long morning for a boy who wouldn't be able to understand the Pennsylvania Dutch preaching or the readings from the German Bible. How would he handle it? In the five days that he'd been with her he seemed to be adjusting well, but this might be stressful for him.

Sitting on a bench on the women's side of the aisle, she looked Kyle in the eyes. "You must sit on that side with the men today."

"But I want to stay with you."

"You are too old to sit with the women. I'll be right here. You must be quiet and respectful as we talked about last night. Amish children do not make a fuss, even when they are bored or tired."

"But I don't want to sit by myself," he whined.

"The boy can sit with me."

Faith glanced up to see Adrian standing beside them.

She couldn't control the rush of happiness that swept though her. Even Kyle's face brightened.

He said, "Hi, Adrian. I didn't know you were going to be here."

Faith nodded her appreciation for Adrian's offer to sit with Kyle. "*Danki,* Adrian."

His gaze settled on her face. Heat filled her face, and she knew she was blushing. She looked away determined to control the intense longing that took over whenever he was near.

No matter how often she told herself a match between them was impossible, her desire to spend time with Adrian grew stronger, not weaker.

Adrian placed his hand on Kyle's shoulder. "Come along. We must find our place."

He led the boy away and found a seat near the back of the room in case he had to take the boy outside. He wasn't sure how Kyle would act during the long, solemn service.

Amish children were taught from infancy to keep quiet during Sunday preaching. Amish mothers usually brought a bag of ready-to-eat cereal or snacks to help occupy the *kinder* who became restless. Adrian wished he'd thought of bringing something for Kyle.

Throughout the service, Adrian remained acutely aware of Faith across the room from him. There was a look of serenity on her face as she listened to the Word of God.

Her sweet voice blended well with the congregation when the hymns began. She sang almost as well as his cousin Sarah. Both women had received the gift of song from the Lord.

Adrian was no songbird. His wife used to joke that he couldn't carry a tune in a wooden bucket if his life depended on it. He joined the congregation for each and every hymn, but he kept his voice soft and low enough not to trouble his neighbors' ears.

To Adrian's relief, Kyle remained well behaved. During the second hymn, he stood on the bench to better view the hymnbook Adrian held. The pages contained only the words of each hymn in German. The melody itself had been passed down from generation to generation in an unchanging oral tradition that reached back hundreds of years.

During the second hour of preaching, Adrian noticed Kyle's head nodding as he struggled to stay awake. He wasn't the only one. Several of the elderly members and a few of the youngsters were having trouble, too. Adrian slipped his arm around Kyle's shoulders and pulled him against his side. Kyle soon dozed off.

From across the aisle, Faith caught Adrian's eye. Her soft smile encompassed both he and the boy. It was the kind of smile that made a man feel special. Made him want to earn more of them.

At the end of the service, Bishop Zook rose and faced the congregation. He read off the names of the young people who wished to be baptized into the faith two weeks from today. Adrian recognized all the names. He knew them and their families. He had watched them grow up. All of them were making the commitment after having experienced something of the outside world during their *rumspringa*. Like himself, most of them were ready to marry and start families of their own.

None of them had any idea of the heartaches that might await them.

Bishop Zook said, "And now I have one more matter to place before you. Our sister, Faith Martin, has come among us seeking to practice the faith of her fathers with piety and humility. She has asked to become a member of our congregation. As you know, this decision is not up to me alone. Therefore, I ask this question of all. Is there anyone who knows a just reason why this sister should not become one of us?"

Silence filled the meeting room. Adrian glanced at Faith. Her eyes were downcast as she awaited the verdict. The bishop's wife shifted in her seat but didn't stand up. No one spoke.

After a few moments, the bishop smiled broadly and said, "Come forward, Sister Faith. In the name of the Lord and the Church, I extend to you the hand of fellowship. Be ye a faithful member of our church."

Adrian relaxed. No one had spoken against her. Faith stood and walked to stand before the bishop. He took her hand, but because she was a woman, he then gave her hand to his wife who greeted her with a Holy Kiss upon her cheek.

Faith was now a member of their community and subject to all the rules of their faith. Adrian glanced at the boy sleeping against his side. She would have to raise Kyle in the ways of the faithful. It was a good life, and he was happy for the boy.

When the services came to an end a few minutes later, Adrian woke Kyle, and the two of them followed the other men outside. Kyle yawned and squinted up at Adrian. "I'm hungry."

"We'll eat soon."

Faith approached them. Happiness radiated from her face. She said, "Kyle, you were very well behaved today."

"I fell asleep," he admitted.

Her happy smile made her even prettier this morning. Adrian said, "Congratulations."

"*Danki.* Kyle, why don't you come with me now and let Adrian visit with his friends."

Other members of the church crowded around to offer their congratulations and welcome. Adrian stepped aside. It was her special day, and he was glad for her.

Because it was such a beautiful day, the meal was set up outdoors. The younger people soon had a volleyball net set up between two trees on the lawn. A dozen of the boys and girls quickly began a game. The cheering and laughter from both participants and onlookers filled the late-summer afternoon with joyous sounds. Faith sat on a blanket in the grass with Kyle beside her. They were cheering for the girls.

"She has the makings of a good mother, don't you think?"

Adrian looked over his shoulder to find his cousin Sarah observing him with interest. She'd always had an uncanny knack for knowing what he was thinking. He didn't pretend ignorance.

"She is good with the boy."

Sarah settled herself on the tailgate of the wagon beside him. "Faith tells me that you have been good for the boy, too."

"He reminds me of Gideon."

Sarah cocked her head to the side as she studied the boy. "A little maybe because of his red hair, but Kyle's hair is darker and curlier. Is she going to send him to our Amish school or to an *Englisch* one?"

"I don't know."

"You haven't asked her?"

"It's none of my business." He looked down to pretend he didn't care one way or the other.

"That's odd."

"What is?" he muttered.

"It's just that the two of you seem so close."

He slanted a glance her way. "What's that supposed to mean?"

"The two of you seem close, that's all. You've been working at her farm since the day she moved in. People notice."

"People should mind their own business."

"You know that's not going to happen. You're single. She's single. She's a member of our church district now. There's nothing wrong with courting her."

He drew back in shock. "Is that what you think I'm doing?"

"Me? No, of course not. I know you better than that."

Mollified, he said, "I should hope so."

"You're being kind, that's all."

"Exactly."

"What your mother or others think is beyond my control."

"Mother thinks I'm courting Faith? I will straighten her thinking out on the way home, today."

"Before you do that, let me ask you something. Has your mother invited any single women to your family dinners recently?"

He thought back over the past month and realized she hadn't. "No."

"See."

"See what?" He couldn't follow her reasoning.

"Kindness brings its own reward."

"Speak plain, Sarah. What are you hinting at?"

She patted his arm. "All I'm saying is that while you are being kind to your neighbor, your mother has stopped searching high and low for someone to catch your interest."

"That's not my reason for helping Faith."

"I'm not suggesting it is. You have a kind heart, and Faith needs all the help she can get until she has her yarn business up and running well."

"That's right."

"It would be okay if you did decide to court her."

He looked into Sarah's eyes. "I don't know if I can take that chance again."

She laid a hand on his arm. "You can, otherwise you will miss out on something special. Lovina wouldn't want you to waste your life grieving for her. You know that. She is happy with God in heaven. She wants you to be happy, too."

"What if something happens to Faith or to Kyle? How could I live through such a loss again?"

"Adrian, you can do one of two things. You can blame God for your misery or you can turn to Him and draw strength from His love. He is always there for us."

"You make it sound so easy. It isn't."

"Answer me this. Were you better off before you met Faith?"

"Nee."

"If you were given one and only one chance to kiss her, would you take it?"

He would take it in a heartbeat. *"Ja."*

"Then why are you turning down the chance to love her for a lifetime?"

He had no answer for Sarah, but she didn't seem to expect one. With a pat on his arm, she left to join Faith and Kyle on their quilt.

As was his custom, Adrian left the gathering early, went home and cut flowers from his garden. On his way to the cemetery, he pondered his feelings for Faith, what they meant and what he was willing to do about them. Did he have a chance to love her for a lifetime?

Was that really within his grasp? The thought excited and frightened him. What if he loved and lost her, too?

At his wife's graveside, he laid the new flowers over the dried husks of the old ones. He stared at her headstone, but he was at a loss for something to say.

Turning away, he took his usual seat and leaned forward with his elbows braced on his thighs. Suddenly, the words came pouring out. "I never meant it to happen, Lovey. I wasn't looking for someone to care about. In my whole life I never wanted to share my hopes and dreams with anyone but you."

Until now. Until Faith. He raised his face to the sky. "Is this wrong? How can it be wrong to care about such a good woman? Faith is a good woman, a strong woman, but she needs someone to take care of her and her boy."

And I need someone to care about me.

Wasn't that the truth he'd been hiding from?

Adrian closed his eyes. "I've been dead inside for a long time. Waking up is painful, Lovey. I'm not sure I can do it."

Chapter Fourteen

Faith sat at her kitchen table with her checkbook in front of her on Thursday morning. She'd been able to pay her outstanding bills with the money she'd made at the market and she still had money left over. Her small bank account was growing at last.

In her wildest dreams she hadn't imagined doing this well so quickly. She'd sold all the yarn she'd taken with her to the market and had taken orders for several dozen additional skeins plus eight of her white baby blankets. She would have to redouble her spinning and knitting efforts to keep up.

Adrian's mother had invited Faith to join their co-op group and display her handmade wares each week on market day. With the cool days of fall not far away, yarn for warm socks, sweaters and mittens were sure to be in high demand.

Kyle came running into the room. He stopped beside Faith to grab a leftover breakfast biscuit from a plate in the center of the table. "My room is clean."

"*Danki,* Kyle."

"Is Adrian coming over today?"

She missed Adrian's presence as much as Kyle did.

Maybe more. She'd gotten used to having him around. Some foolish part of her heart continued to hope that he'd come over with a new excuse to spend time with them, but it hadn't happened.

"I doubt it, dear. His work in the orchard is done. You will see him at the next preaching service."

"But that's another whole week away." Pieces of biscuit sprayed from his lips.

"Don't talk with your mouth full."

He swallowed. "I don't want to wait until church. Can't we go visit Adrian today?"

"No. Miss Watkins is coming today."

Faith hoped his sudden pout wasn't going to lead to a temper tantrum. "Why is *she* coming?" he demanded.

"It's her job to find out if you are happy here. Are you happy?"

Confusion clouded his eyes. "Can I go play with Shadow?"

A pang of disappointment stabbed her. Why couldn't he answer a simple question? "You may, but try not to get dirty."

He darted outside, letting the screen door bang shut behind him.

Was he unhappy living with her? He seemed to be adjusting well to this new way of life. She had been worried those first few nights, but he'd not had a nightmare for the past week.

Faith closed her eyes and took a deep breath. Her new life in Hope Springs was turning into a dream come true. Kyle was with her. The church community had welcomed her with open arms. Her business was off to a great start, and her share of the peach money had been an added bonus.

"Through you, Lord, all things are possible. I humbly give thanks for Your blessings."

Little more than a month ago she had arrived in Hope Springs with barely enough to support herself. Now, she had enough to support Kyle, too. An important step toward his permanent adoption. Would his social worker think it was enough? The Amish were frugal people. Faith didn't need a large sum of money to live comfortably. Could Caroline Watkins be made to understand that?

An hour later, the sound of a car pulling into the yard alerted Faith to Miss Watkins's arrival. Faith opened the door and waited as Caroline came up the steps. "Good morning, Miss Watkins. Do come in. How are you?"

Caroline said, "I'm fine. This shouldn't take long today. I'll make a quick tour of the house and then I'd like to talk to you and Kyle separately. Is that all right?"

"Certainly." Faith took a seat at the kitchen table and waited. She tried to ignore the nervous dread that started gnawing at the inside of her stomach. She knew there was nothing to fear, but she was afraid anyway. This woman had the power to remove Kyle from her home.

Ten agonizing minutes later, Caroline came back into the kitchen with smile on her lips. "Everything seems in order, Mrs. Martin. How are you getting along with Kyle?"

Faith let out the breath she'd been holding. "It's going well. He works hard and plays hard. We went to the Summer Festival in Hope Springs last week, and I think he really enjoyed himself."

"That's great to hear. Where is Kyle?"

"He's down in the barn playing with Shadow, the baby alpaca. The two of them have become fast friends.

Shadow is living up to his name for he follows Kyle around whenever the boy is near. Would you like me to go get him?"

"I'd rather talk to him alone." Caroline went out the door.

Faith began her preparations for making bread. Keeping busy was better than pacing the floor and wondering what was going on between Kyle and Miss Watkins. What if Kyle told her he didn't like it here? What if he complained that he had too much work to do? A dozen unhappy scenarios ran through Faith's mind. Her stomach rolled into a tight knot.

A few minutes later, Miss Watkins returned to the house. Faith dusted the flour off her hands, set her bread dough aside and turned around. "Are you finished already?"

Her worry knot doubled in size when she saw the green speckles on Miss Watkins's clothes. Myrtle had been at it again.

"I'm so sorry. I should have warned you about Myrtle." Faith wet a kitchen towel and handed it to Caroline.

Caroline wiped her face and brushed at her blouse. "Their spitting is a disgusting habit. I couldn't find Kyle. Where else might he be?"

"He said he was going to the barn."

"He isn't in the barn. I called but he didn't answer. He wasn't with the baby alpaca." She scrubbed at her shoulder.

"Perhaps he's in the orchard."

"Does he disappear like this often?"

"No, of course not." Faith rushed outside and began frantically calling for Kyle. She and the social worker made their way from one side of the orchard to the other without any sign of the boy.

When they arrived back at the house and saw Kyle hadn't returned, Faith said, "We should go to the neighbor's farm and see if he is there."

"Has he done that before?"

"No."

Miss Watkins pulled her cell phone from the pocket of her slacks. "Can you call them and see if he's there?"

"My neighbors are Amish. They have no phones."

Miss Watkins bit her lip, then opened her phone. "We are wasting valuable time. I'm going to notify the sheriff that we have a missing child."

Adrian lay on his back beneath his grain binder and loosened the last bolt holding the sickle blades in place. It came loose easily, and he lowered the bar to the ground. His cornfields would be ready to cut soon, and he needed to make sure his equipment was in good working order. Sharpening the sickle blades was his first priority.

"What ya doing?"

Adrian twisted his head around to see Kyle squatting beneath the equipment with him. "I'm getting my machinery ready to harvest corn. What are you doing?"

"I came to help you."

"You have, have you? Where is your *aenti* Faith?" Adrian wormed his way out from beneath his equipment with the long row of blades in hand. He looked eagerly toward the house, but he didn't see Faith anywhere.

He had stayed away from her the past few days because he knew if they came face-to-face, he wouldn't be able to hide his longing or his fears. He hadn't been ready for that. Was he ready now?

Kyle said, "She's at home with that mean social worker."

Faith wasn't here. Adrian tried not to let his disappointment show. He focused on Kyle. "You must not speak badly of others, Kyle. You must forgive them for the wrongs they do."

"Why?"

"Because that is what God commands us to do. Why do you say your social worker is mean?"

"'Cause social workers take kids away from their moms." Kyle glanced over his shoulder as if expecting to see one swooping down on him like a hawk.

"Where did you hear this?"

"Dylan and Tyrell told me."

The names weren't familiar. Adrian asked, "Who are they?"

"My friends in Texas. They were in foster care with me because a social worker took them away from their mom. They told me not to like Becky too much cause a social worker would come and take me away to a new place, and one did. Dylan and Tyrell had been in three foster homes so they knew it would happen and it did."

"Becky was your foster mother?"

Kyle nodded. "I liked her a lot."

Adrian sat on the steel tongue of his grain binder. "I'm sorry you were taken from someone you cared about, but I know that Faith loves you and she wants you to stay with her for a long time."

Kyle turned away from Adrian and patted the side of the machine. "What does this thing do?"

"This is a grain binder. It cuts cane or corn into bundles of livestock feed."

"How?"

Adrian understood Kyle's reluctance to talk about matters that troubled him. Wasn't he the same way?

Didn't he avoid talking about his family because it brought the pain back sharp as ever?

He said, "The machine is powered by this gasoline engine. My team pulls it through the field while I stand up here to guide them." He indicated a small platform at the front.

"Up here?" Kyle climbed the three metal ladder rungs and stood behind the slim railing that allowed the driver to lean against it and kept him from falling while he drove his team.

The boy grinned when he realized he was now taller than Adrian. He stretched his hands out pretending to hold the reins of a frisky team. "What do I do next?"

Adrian walked around to the side of the machine. "You guide your team along the corn rows. This sickle bar cuts the thick stalks about a foot off the ground. The reel lays them evenly onto this wide canvas belt. The belt feeds the stalks into a mechanism that gathers them together into a bundle, then wraps it with twine and knots it."

"Then what?"

"You must decide. See that lever in front of you?"

"Yup." Kyle reached beneath the safety rail to grasp a metal handle.

"Pull it back and the bundle is kicked out the side of the machine where it will lay in the field until I come back and stack them into tepee-style shocks."

"Why make a tepee out of them?"

These were things Adrian would have explained to his son if Gideon has lived. It was part of being a father, teaching the children how to farm and wrest a living from the land.

Kyle wouldn't have anyone to teach him unless Faith chose to remarry.

Would she remarry for the boy's sake? The thought didn't sit well with Adrian. What if the man she chose was unkind to her or to Kyle the way her first husband had been? He knew a few Amish husbands who believed they should rule their families with an iron fist.

"Why build tepees with them?" Kyle asked again.

"Because they shed water if you put the bundles together in an upright position. As they dry and shrink, it allows more air to flow around the inside of the bundles and they dry better. I put about twenty bundles into each shock."

"What if I push this lever forward?"

"Then the machine dumps the bundles onto a trailer that is pulled behind me, and my brother stacks them together so we can haul them to the barn."

"I wish I had a brother. That would be cool."

"It is sometimes, but sometimes they can be a pain in the neck."

Kyle climbed down from his post. "Can I see Meg and Mick?"

The boy had taken a liking to Adrian's team and had begged to ride one on the way home from market. Adrian hadn't allowed it then as they were on the highway, but he saw no harm in it now.

"*Ja,* they are in the barn."

"Can I ride one of them? They are like ten times bigger than the ponies at the fair."

Adrian thought of all the work he had to finish. Put side by side with Kyle's eager face, Adrian found only one conclusion. The work could wait.

In the barn, Adrian opened the door to Meg's stall and led her out to the small paddock. He hoisted Kyle to her broad back. She was so wide that the boy's feet stuck out straight instead of being able to grip her sides.

Adrian said, "Wrap your hand in her mane."

"Won't that hurt her?"

"*Nee,* it will not, but it might keep you from falling off."

Grasping the halter, Adrian led the mare around the paddock. She walked slowly and carefully, as if aware of the precious cargo she carried.

Kyle grinned from ear to ear. "I can see all the way to Texas from up here."

"How's the weather down that way?"

Shading his eyes with one hand, Kyle said, "Sunny and hot."

After the third time around the corral, Adrian stopped Meg and held his hands up to Kyle. "Come along. I have much work to do. I must sharpen my sickle and get my binder back together and Meg wants to have a good roll in the dust."

"Okay." Kyle reluctantly left his high perch. They walked back into the barn, leaving Meg in the pen where she promptly lay down, rolled onto her back and frolicked in the dust she raised.

As they passed her stall, Kyle looked at Adrian. "Do you want me to *redd-up* her stall?"

Tickled by Kyle's use of an Amish term, Adrian knew the boy would soon fit into their Amish ways and leave his *Englisch* past behind. He stared into Kyle's eyes and saw he was dying to please.

Adrian stroked his beard. "Reckon I could use a good stable hand now and again."

Puffing out his chest, Kyle asked, "Where's your wheelbarrow and your shovel?"

"I will get them for you."

When he returned with the requested tools and gave them to Kyle, Adrian leaned on the stall gate to watch the boy work. It took him a while, but he managed to rake up the mess and push the wheelbarrow back to Adrian.

Sighing heavily, Kyle said, "Alpacas are much easier to clean up after."

"They are not as big as Meg."

"No wonder Aunt Faith raises them instead of horses."

Adrian chuckled. "No wonder."

Kyle pulled at the Band-Aid on his palm. "It came loose."

Adrian bent down to see. He removed the bandages and looked at the angry red sores. "You should have told me they were hurting you."

"They don't hurt." Kyle put his hands behind his back.

"Lying is a sin, Kyle. I know you want to please and prove that you are a good helper, but Faith will have my hide if these get infected. Come up to the house and let's get them clean."

In the kitchen, Adrian gently washed Kyle's hands and patted them dry. He applied an antiseptic cream to them and wrapped a length of gauze around each palm. "Is that better?"

Kyle flexed his fingers. *"Ja."*

"I think I may have a pair of gloves you can wear over them." He rose and led the way to Gideon's room. Opening the door, he experienced the same catch in his chest that always hit him when he stepped over this threshold. The room looked the same as the day his son had left it.

On the blue-and-green quilt that covered the bed lay a baseball glove and a carved wooden horse. Gifts meant for a birthday that had never arrived. Crossing the room, Adrian pulled open a dresser drawer and retrieved a small pair of knit gloves.

"Try these on." He turned to hand them to Kyle and froze. Kyle was on his knees by the bed galloping the toy horse across the quilt.

He grinned up at Adrian. "This looks like Meg."

Adrian held back the shout that formed in his throat. *Leave that alone. It belongs to my son.*

He knew Kyle wouldn't understand. The boy meant no harm. He was simply doing what boys did—playing with a toy as it was meant to be played with.

Is this part of Your plan, Lord? Am I to see that I'm being greedy and selfish by hanging on to these things? Gideon would share his toys with this boy, I know he would. He had a kind heart like his mother.

Adrian forced a smile to his stiff lips. "I made it to look like Meg. I was going to make another one that looked like Mick."

"You made it? Cool beans." Kyle stared at the toy in awe.

"Would you like to have it?"

"Can I?" His eyes grew round.

"It is yours if you want it."

Kyle grinned. "Thanks. I mean, *danki.*"

"You're welcome. Now try these on." Adrian held out the gloves. They proved to be too small.

Knowing a pair of his would be much too large, Adrian said, "Try not to get dirty."

"That's what Aunt Faith tells me."

"Does it work?"

"Not so much."

Adrian smiled as he ruffled Kyle's hair and went outside to finish his work. He sharpened his blades while Kyle galloped little Meg across the workbench and jumped her over hammers and assorted tools. It felt good to have a child with him again.

He still missed his son, still wished it was Gideon with him, but he was able to enjoy Kyle's company and appreciate the boy for who he was.

Adrian was reattaching his sickle blades when the sound of a car coming up his lane drew his attention. He rose to his feet and saw the sheriff's white SUV roll to a stop in front of his house.

Adrian looked at Kyle seated on the ground beside him. "Does your aunt know you are here?"

The boy shrugged.

Adrian shook his head at his own thoughtlessness. "That is a question I should have asked an hour ago."

He held his hand out to Kyle. "Come. You have some explaining to do."

Reluctantly, Kyle rose and walked with Adrian toward the sheriff's vehicle. The passenger's door opened, and Faith rushed toward them, a look of intense relief on her face. In her hurry she stumbled and would have fallen if Adrian hadn't lunged forward to catch her.

He held her tight against his chest and breathed in the fresh scent of her hair. She fit perfectly against him. It felt so right to hold her this way. She looked up at him with wide, startled eyes. Eyes filled not with fear, but with the same breathless excitement she had awakened in him.

In that instant he knew she felt as he did. The next move was up to him. Did he dare risk his heart again?

Chapter Fifteen

Faith rested in the safety of Adrian's embrace, relishing the strength and gentleness with which he held her. Gazing up into his face, she saw his eyes darken.

Did he feel it too, this current between them that defied her logical, sensible mind?

How had it happened? How had she fallen in love with him?

He said softly, "Kyle is okay."

"I knew he would be if he was with you," she whispered. She and Kyle would always be safe if Adrian was with them. If only it could be this way forever. It couldn't. She knew that.

Adrian was still in love with his wife. She couldn't compete with a ghost.

Besides, she had to concentrate on Kyle. Finalizing his adoption had to be her top priority. Adding Adrian to the picture would only complicate and delay things.

Reluctantly, she left the comfort of Adrian's embrace and sank awkwardly to the ground beside Kyle. She gathered him close in a tight hug. "I was so worried when I couldn't find you."

He wrapped his arms around her neck and hugged

her back. Suddenly, he let go and stepped away. Faith saw he was looking at the sheriff and Miss Watkins as they approached.

Faith cupped his chin and turned his face toward her. "It's all right. You aren't in trouble."

The sheriff pushed his hat back with one finger. "Looks like the lost sheep has been found."

Miss Watkins clasped her hands together. "I am so sorry that we wasted your time, Sheriff Bradley."

"Don't be. I like a happy ending. I just wish all my calls were so easy."

Miss Watkins focused her attention on Kyle. "You frightened us very badly, Kyle. Why did you run away from home?"

"I didn't."

Faith accepted Adrian's hand as he helped her to her feet. She said, "Kyle, you must let me know when you are going to visit a friend or a neighbor."

"Okay."

Miss Watkins stepped forward with a sharp frown on her face. "What's wrong with your hands, Kyle?"

"I got some blisters. Adrian fixed me up. He gave me this horse." He held up the toy.

Glancing between the adults, Miss Watkins leaned down to Kyle's level. "How did you get blisters? Did you touch something hot?"

"No." He shrank away from her and toward Faith.

Faith said, "He got them cleaning out a stall and helping us with the peach crop."

Adrian spoke up. "He rubbed his bandages off cleaning one of my stalls. I washed his sores and redressed them. He'll be okay in a few days."

Holding out her hand, Miss Watkins asked, "May I see your blisters?"

Kyle buried his face in Faith's skirt and put his hands behind his back.

Turning his face up to hers, Faith smiled encouragingly at him. "Is it okay if I unwrap them?"

He held out his hands. Faith unwound the dressing from his right hand. Miss Watkins took a closer look, then said, "Okay. Kyle, why don't you go to the car with Sheriff Bradley. I bet he'll show you how the radio works."

The sheriff nodded toward his SUV. "Come on, Kyle. Would you like to turn on the flashing lights?"

Kyle glanced from Faith to Adrian. "Is it *verboten*?"

Faith exchanged an amused look with Adrian, then said, "It's not forbidden. It is okay for Amish boys to do such a thing."

Kyle followed the sheriff, but the worried expression lingered on his face.

Miss Watkins folded her arms. "I will be the first to admit that I'm not familiar with Amish ways, but to work a child of six until both his hands are covered in blisters is not acceptable."

Faith cringed before the social worker's anger. Fear stole her voice. Beside her, Adrian said, "The boy worked hard to prove that he belongs among us. We did not make him do this."

Caroline shook her head. "Be that as it may, I'm not convinced this is the best arrangement for Kyle."

"Please, don't take him away from me." Faith wanted to race to the car, grab her child and hold on to him so tightly that no one could take him from her. Adrian's hand settled on her shoulder holding her in place.

Caroline sighed heavily. "I don't want to take him away, Mrs. Martin, but I have to know that he's in a safe environment. I would be neglecting my job and Kyle's welfare if I placed him in a questionable home."

"I'll do anything you ask. Please, don't take him away," Faith pleaded.

"Ultimately that decision is up to a judge. I'm here to help make the adoption possible. I want you to re-think how much work a child of six should be doing. I'll be back to visit again next Friday. Before then, you will need to make a list of Kyle's chores. We can go over them together and see if we can agree on what's appropriate for his age."

"I can do that," Faith quickly assured her.

"Keep in mind that he's going to be in school. There will be even less time for him to do chores." She walked back to the sheriff's vehicle leaving Faith and Adrian alone.

Faith started to follow her, but Adrian caught her arm. "Faith, we need to talk."

"I can't. Not now."

His shoulders slumped in defeat. "All right. Go home and take care of your child."

She squeezed his hand. "Thank you, Adrian."

"For what?"

"For understanding." Faith left him and took a seat inside the sheriff's vehicle.

"Are you ready for your first day of school?"

Bright and early Monday morning Faith climbed into the buggy beside Kyle.

He hooked his thumbs through his new suspenders giving them a sour look. "Do I have to wear these? I look like a dork."

"You must dress plain now. All the boys will be wearing them."

"Are you sure?" He let them snap back against his chest.

"*Ja,* I'm sure. Do you like your hat?"

He raised his flat-topped straw hat with both hands and looked up at it. "It's okay. It's like the one Adrian wears."

"He wears suspenders, too."

"Yeah, he does, doesn't he?" That mollified him.

"Are you excited about school?"

He sat back and folded his arms over his chest. "No. Everyone's gonna think I'm stupid 'cause I can't speak Pennsylvania Dutch."

She folded her hands in her lap. "Kyle, you are learning our language just as the Amish children at school will be learning English. If you help them, they will help you and nobody will be stupid."

"Maybe." He didn't sound convinced.

Faith cupped his chin and raised his face so she could see his eyes. "I know this is hard for you, but school is not all bad. You will learn many good things. Do you like to play baseball?"

"Yes."

"Amish children also like baseball. When I was in school, we played it almost every day. Not in winter, of course. In the winter, we went sledding during recess."

"Really?" He looked at her with interest.

"Really."

"That sounds kinda cool."

She grinned. "It wasn't cool. It was downright cold." She poked his side making him giggle.

"Can I drive the buggy?" he asked.

"You may, but just to the end of the lane." Faith had no fear that Copper would bolt. The mare was well trained and placid. In fact, it was hard to get her into high gear anymore.

"Hold the reins like this." Faith demonstrated. Kyle was quick to copy her and soon had Copper moving down the lane. Faith sat ready to take the lines at the first sign of trouble. Thankfully, they reached the highway without incident.

"How'd I do?" he asked as he handed the reins back.

"Very well. You're a natural." She headed Copper down the road toward the schoolhouse a mile and a half away. After today Kyle would be walking, but she wanted to make sure he could find his way. Besides, the first day of school was special for any child, and she wanted to be a part of it.

When the building came into view, she said, "We're almost there."

Kyle slumped in his seat again. "Do I have to go? I feel sick."

She understood the anxiety he was feeling, but she knew he would soon make new friends. Faith had met earlier with his teacher, Leah Belier. A young Amish woman in her early twenties, Leah seemed devoted to students and to helping them learn. She had promised she would do her best to help Kyle adjust to his new surroundings.

Faith stopped the buggy on the sloping lawn of the one-room schoolhouse. Several other buggies were tied up alongside the building. Children were already at play on the swing set and the long wooden teeter-totter.

Faith sensed Kyle's interest, but he moved closer to her. Before she could convince him to get down, Leah came out of the schoolhouse door and waved to Faith.

Faith returned her greeting. Kyle buried his face in Faith's lap. "Can we go home, please?"

Leah was quick to assess the situation and approached the buggy. "You must be Kyle King. I'm so glad to meet you. I was hoping you could help me this morning."

Kyle eyed her with suspicion. "How?"

"I need a strong young boy to ring the bell for me."

Looking past her, Kyle assessed the situation. "I guess I could do that."

"Wonderful. Faith, would you like to sit in on class today?"

"I would."

After securing Copper to the hitching rail, Faith walked with Kyle to the school building where Leah waited for them. The teacher pointed to the bell rope hanging inside the doorway. "Give it a yank, Kyle. It's time to start our classes."

Gritting his teeth, Kyle pulled with all his might. The bell clanged loudly.

Leah clapped her hands. "Very good, Kyle. You're every bit as strong as you look. Now, I need someone to put pencils and papers on all the desks. Can you help with that?"

"Sure."

"*Danki*. That means thank you."

"I know."

"The papers and pencils are on the table behind my chair. The desk directly in front of mine belongs to you."

The other children began entering by twos and threes. Leah welcomed them all by their first names, asking after family members and previous students. It was clear she enjoyed her job.

Faith took a seat at the back of the room where several young mothers sat visiting with each other.

She stayed for the first hour of class, just long enough

to make sure Kyle was going to be okay. Leah kept all the students well in hand as she switched back and forth between English and Pennsylvania Dutch to make sure everyone understood her instructions.

After leaving the school, Faith drove home and set to work spinning another batch of yarns. Once they were done, she would take them into town after she picked up Kyle. She had a special treat in store for him.

By early afternoon, she had several dozen skeins ready to be dropped off at Needles and Pins. She hitched up Copper again and arrived at the schoolhouse just as the main door opened and a rush of children poured out.

Kyle, grinning from ear to ear, skidded to a halt beside her and held up a piece of paper. "I drew a picture of Shadow. Did you know we're the only people in Hope Springs who have alpacas?"

She grinned at his enthusiasm. "I suspected as much."

"Anna Imhoff and her brothers want to come over and see Shadow. Can they?"

"Perhaps tomorrow. Today, we must go into town and celebrate."

"Celebrate what?"

"Your first day at school. It's a big deal and it calls for a celebration."

"What kind of celebration?"

"I'm treating you to supper at the Shoofly Pie Café."

"Can we get pizza?"

"That sounds perfect."

"*Goot.* That means good in Pennsylvania Dutch. I learned it and some more words, too."

"I'm pleased to hear your day wasn't wasted. Did you make some new friends?"

"Anna Imhoff wants to be my friend, but she's a girl."

"Girls can be friends, too."

"Her brother, Noah, started teasing me 'cause I can't talk Amish. Anna got mad and scolded him."

"Then she sounds like a very good friend to have. Did everyone play baseball at recess?"

His mood went from happy to dejected. "Yeah, but no one picked me for their team."

"You are little yet. I'm sure you'll play many games when you're older."

"Maybe if I got a glove."

Leah approached the buggy. "He did well, Faith. He needs to work on his sums and his reading, but overall he's a bright, friendly boy."

"Wonderful." It was a relief to know that Kyle was fitting in. She had worried that the language barrier would make school unhappy for him.

Leah left to speak to other parents, and Faith turned Copper toward town. Once they reached Hope Springs, Faith dropped off her yarns at the fabric store and drove on to the Shoofly Pie Café.

She and Kyle entered the homey café and were instantly surrounded with the smell of baking bread, cinnamon and frying chicken. A young Amish girl came forward. "*Velkumm* to the Shoofly Pie café. My name is Melody. Would you like a table or a booth?"

"A booth," Kyle answered before Faith could say anything.

The waitress led them to one of the high-backed seats that lined the walls of the room. Faith slid into the nearest bench. Kyle scooted in opposite her and propped his elbows on the red Formica tabletop.

Suddenly, Kyle's eyes lit up. "It's Adrian."

The boy waved. Faith turned to see her neighbor entering the door. He raised a hand and waved back. He was carrying a small package wrapped in plain brown paper and tied with string.

He stopped beside their booth. Faith wished her heart would stop trying to gallop out of her chest each time he was near.

Kyle spoke up eagerly. "I went to school today."

Adrian grinned at him. "So I heard. How was it?"

"Pretty fun. I learned to count to ten in Amish and how to say please and thank you."

"Those are all good things to know." Adrian focused his gaze on Faith. "How have you been?"

Missing you madly. "Fine, and you?"

"Busy. I'll start cutting corn tomorrow if this nice weather holds."

She couldn't care less about the mundane details of his life. Just seeing his face brightened her day.

He asked, "May I join you?"

Surprised and delighted, she said, "Certainly."

Kyle scooted over to let him sit down. Adrian said, "I brought you a present, Kyle." He slid the package toward the boy.

"Why? It's not my birthday." Kyle tore open the wrapping to reveal a baseball mitt. It was too big for his hand, but he didn't seem to mind. "Cool. I've been wanting one like this forever."

Adrian smiled at him. "Happy first day of school."

Faith couldn't put her finger on it, but there was something different about Adrian today. He was more lighthearted, happier than she had seen him. She liked the change. She liked it a lot.

He met her gaze. "Every boy needs a good baseball glove."

She said, "You didn't need to spend money on Kyle. I could have gotten him one."

"It's an old glove I had lying around. I thought Kyle might put it to good use."

"I sure will. Now they won't pick me last." Kyle smacked his fist in the pocket.

Faith's heart warmed to see Kyle so excited and happy. She started to convey her thanks, but Adrian stopped her with a shake of his head. "It's nothing."

The look in his eyes said differently. Then it hit her. She reached across the table to lay her hand on Adrian's arm. "It was Gideon's glove, wasn't it?"

"It was, but now it is Kyle's." His glance settled on her nephew. It was easy to read the deep affection he had for the boy.

It was only when Adrian looked into her eyes that she became unsure of his feelings. He said, "I know Kyle's adoption is your main priority right now, but when that's over, I'd like to talk about the future."

Faith pulled her hand away. The future? What was he suggesting? Did he have more plans for the farm, or was he suggesting they could have a future together? Her heart raced as her breathing quickened. "The hearing is the last day of this month."

He winced. "That is a long time to wait."

"Then perhaps you should come over this evening if it's important." She bit the inside of her lip as she waited for his reply.

"It is important to me and I hope to you. *Ja,* I will come by later."

"I'm having pizza," Kyle announced.

Adrian tweaked the boy's nose. "Sounds good to me. I like pepperoni and extra cheese."

"Me, too." Kyle looked at Faith. "What kind do you like, Aunt Faith?"

"I'll have whatever the two of you are having."

Food was the furthest thing from her mind at the moment. What was on Adrian's mind that couldn't wait? Did she dare hope he returned her feelings of affection, or was she tricking herself into imagining what wasn't there?

"You're late getting back from town," Ben said, as he finished greasing the wheels of the grain binder and wiped his blackened fingers on a piece of cloth lying on top of the machine.

"I had supper at the café. Are you done already?" Adrian checked his brother's work and found it satisfactory.

"*Ja*. When will you start cutting?"

"I took a walk through the corn this morning. I think it will be ready by the end of the week, if it doesn't rain."

"*Dat* wants to start on our fields early tomorrow. We should be done in four or five days. When we're finished, I can come and give you a hand."

"I always appreciate your help with the farmwork." Could he trust Ben with an even more important task?

Adrian hooked his thumbs in his suspenders. He wasn't ready to reveal his intentions toward Faith to his family just yet. He wanted to know her feelings first. She had been adamant that she would not remarry. If those were her true feelings, he would respect them and never bring up the subject again.

He needed to speak to her alone, but he couldn't do that with Kyle listening in. Knowing the boy's penchant for turning up in the wrong place at the wrong time, Adrian didn't want to risk it.

The smart thing to do would have been to wait until the adoption was over or at least until the boy was in school tomorrow, but Adrian didn't want to wait another day to know if Faith cared for him as he'd grown to care for her.

Oh, he'd had every intention of waiting until the time was right…then she'd smiled at him in the café and laid her hand on his arm to comfort him. The understanding in her eyes had done something wonderful to his heart.

His carefully laid plans had flown out of his head, and he'd told her he would be over tonight.

Tonight! This was what he got for his impatience. He had to rely on his baby brother to help him secure time alone with Faith.

"Ben, I'm wondering if you could give me a hand with something this evening?"

"Sure. What do you need?"

Drawing a deep breath, Adrian forged ahead before he could change his mind. "I need someone to stay with Faith Martin's boy for an hour or so."

There was a long moment of silence, then Ben crossed his arms. "Why?"

"Because…because I need to speak to Faith, alone."

Ben grinned from ear to ear. "You're going courting."

Adrian closed his eyes. This had been another bad idea. What was wrong with him today? "I never said that."

"You don't have to say anything. It's written all over your face. The whole family has been wondering when you'd finally wise up. Wait until I tell *Mamm* she was right about you two."

"Please, don't. Not until I know how Faith feels."

Ben stepped forward and laid a hand on Adrian's shoulder. "She'd be a fool to turn you down and I don't think Faith Martin is anyone's fool."

"I pray you are right."

"Let me wash off this grease and then we can go. I won't keep you waiting to see your lady love." Ben walked away, chuckling to himself.

Adrian blew out a deep sigh of frustration. This was to be his punishment for involving his baby brother. Ben was never going to let him live this down, and he was never going to keep it a secret.

Twenty minutes later, the two men were driving toward Faith's house with Ben at the reins. Adrian's stomach churned with butterflies now that he was actually on his way. He rubbed his sweaty palms on his pant legs and tried to figure out what he was going to say.

Ben slipped his arm around Adrian's shoulder and gave him a brotherly hug. "Relax. She isn't going to bite your head off and I doubt she spits like an alpaca. You should drive her over toward the Stultz place and take the left fork just past their barn. The road winds up in a pretty little meadow beside Croft Creek."

"Where the old stone bridge has fallen down?"

Ben shot him a surprised look. "You know the place?"

"You don't think you're the first fellow to take a girl out there for a picnic, do you? *Dat* took *Mamm* there when he was courting her."

"No kidding? Our folks?" Ben looked as if he'd bitten a lemon.

It was Adrian's turn to laugh. "Love finds all sorts of people, little *bruder*. Every papa and granddad you see was once a young man with stealing a kiss on his mind."

"I reckon you're right." Ben pulled the horse to a stop in front of Faith's gate.

She and Kyle were both outside. Faith sat at her spinning wheel on the porch. Kyle was playing on the swing

Adrian had built for him. The moment Kyle caught sight of them, he jumped out of the swing and ran toward them.

"Howdy, Adrian. Howdy, Ben. What are you doing here?" He slowed to a walk when he drew near the horse.

Ben hopped out of the buggy. "I've come to see your alpaca herd up close."

"I'll show them to you. We've got a new cria. His name is Shadow and he belongs to me. Adrian gave me a baseball glove. Want to see it?"

"Sure. Maybe we can play some catch after we're done seeing your critters."

"Cool beans."

Ben gave Adrian a wave and walked toward the barn with the boy dancing beside him.

Adrian sat in the buggy as Faith came down the steps toward him. She looked so pretty this evening in a dark purple dress with an apron of the same color over it. His butterflies returned in full force. He nodded toward her. "Evening, Faith."

She paused behind her gate. "Hello again."

"It's a right nice evening, isn't it?" He tried not to fidget.

"Very nice."

"I was wondering if you might like to take a buggy ride?"

She glanced toward the barn. "I'm sure Kyle would enjoy that."

"Ben is going to stay here with Kyle until we get back."

"Oh." Her eyes widened.

Adrian held out his hand. "It will be just the two of us."

Faith hesitated. She wanted to go with him, but what

was she getting herself into? This wasn't going to be a farming discussion. She had sense enough to know that. Could he really want to be alone with her because he was ready to open his heart to another woman? To her?

Was she ready for another relationship?

There was only one way to find out. She pushed open the gate and took his hand to climb in his buggy.

When she was settled beside him, he clicked his tongue and slapped the reins to set Wilbur in motion.

At the highway, he turned south toward his farm but passed by his lane without stopping. She asked, "Where are we going?"

"Some place we can talk without being interrupted."

He turned off at the first dirt road to the Stultz place and then took the left fork just past their big white barn. The little-used road wound around the side of a hill and came out into a small meadow. A white-tailed doe grazing near the trees along the creek threw up her head and then bounded away in alarm.

Adrian drew his horse to a stop. "Will it bother you to walk a little way?"

"I'll be fine."

"It isn't far." He got out and helped her down. As his strong hands grasped her waist, she realized she didn't fear his touch. It didn't matter how strong Adrian was. He was always gentle.

Together, they walked side by side into the forest and down a faint path. She could hear the sound of the water splashing over rocks. The smell of damp earth and leaves mingled with the scent of pine needles crushed underfoot. A few yards later, they came to the remnants of an old stone bridge, an arch broken in the middle and covered by leafy vines. Just below it, a wide flat slab of stone jutted out over the creek. A single boulder made a perfect seat in the center of it.

"How pretty it is in here." Faith sat on the moss-covered stone. The coolness of the forest and the rushing water brought a welcome relief from the summer heat and the heat in her cheeks.

Adrian took a seat beside her. "This was one of my wife's favorite places."

There it was, the reminder that he still loved his wife. Faith's heart sank. She looked down at her hands clasped together in her lap. How foolish she'd been to think there could be something between them. "I can see why she liked it."

Adrian said, "I'm sorry. I didn't bring you here to talk about Lovina."

"I understand if you feel the need to talk about her. You must miss her very much." If nothing else, Faith could lend a sympathetic ear. If that eased his pain even a little, then she would be glad.

"I did miss her deeply for a very long time, but lately I haven't been thinking about her as much."

"Why is that?"

"Because I've been thinking about you."

Faith raised her face to look at him. "Me?"

"You have no idea what kind of effect you have on me, do you? You and your creatures upset my solitude, played havoc with my work, forced me to take a look at the way I…wasn't living. Until you came, I was only biding my time until I died, and I didn't even know it."

"I'm sorry." She didn't understand what he was trying to say.

He smiled at her. "Don't be sorry. Don't ever be sorry, Faith Martin."

He reached out and cupped her face in his hands.

"You and Kyle have brought joy to me when I never expected to have it again. I will never be able to thank God enough for bringing you here."

Before she could say anything, he bent his head and kissed her.

Startled, Faith pulled away. Adrian's hands still cupped her face. He stared into her eyes, waiting.

Waiting for her to say yes or no.

Oh, she wanted to say yes. She closed her eyes and leaned into his touch. Softly, his mouth covered hers again.

The sound of the rushing water faded away as Faith tentatively explored the texture of his lips against hers. Firm but gentle, warm and tender, his touch stirred her soul and sent the blood rushing through her veins. She had never been kissed like this. She didn't know it was possible for her heart to expand with such love and not burst.

When Adrian drew away, she kept her eyes closed, afraid she would see disappointment or regret on his face.

"Faith, look at me," he said softly.

"Nee."

"Why not?"

Old insecurities came rushing back to choke down her happiness. "You will say you're sorry. That this was a mistake."

"It was not a mistake. I will kiss you again if you need me to prove it."

Her eyes popped open. She couldn't believe this was happening.

He sat back. "I'm rushing you. That wasn't what I had in mind when I brought you here."

"Why did you bring me here?"

"To tell you that I care about you and about Kyle. To discover if you care about me. I know this is too soon, we've only known each other a short time. I know you have much on your mind and you are worried about Kyle's adoption, I know you have said you'd never marry again, but—is there a chance you could look with favor on me and allow me to court you?"

"Adrian, I don't know what to say."

"If you'd but nod, I'd take that as a *goot* sign."

She smiled at his teasing, even though she saw the seriousness in his eyes. How was it possible to feel so happy?

"*Ja,* Adrian Lapp, you may court me, but I warn you, I'm no prize."

"I will be the judge of that."

The word "judge" brought her back to earth with a thump. Would the adoption proceeding be put on hold if Miss Watkins or the agency learned of this? Would Adrian be subjected to the same scrutiny she had endured? It could take months. Now that the hearing was finally drawing near, she couldn't face another delay.

"Adrian, this must remain just between us until after Kyle's adoption is final."

"Why? Surely it could not hurt your case for the *Englisch* to know I stand ready to serve as Kyle's father."

She grasped his arm. "Perhaps not, but I can't take that chance. We must be friends until then and nothing more."

He covered her hand with his large warm one. "I will always be your friend. Do not look so worried, Faith. It is all in God's hands."

He was right. She relaxed and nodded. "I have faith in His grace. It will be fine."

Faith tried to retain her positive attitude as the week slowly rolled by. Miss Watkins's coming visit would be the last one before the official adoption hearing. Her recommendations would weigh heavily with the judge.

After supper on Thursday evening, Faith cleared the table and then sat down beside Kyle. He was coloring a page for his homework assignment. She said, "I have something important to talk about."

"What is it?" He exchanged a red crayon for a green one and began to work on the grass in his picture.

"Miss Watkins is coming tomorrow."

His small browed furrowed. "Why does she keep coming back?"

"Because she wants to make sure you have a safe place to live."

"I want to live here."

She planted a kiss on his brow. "I want you to live here, too. I love you."

He kept his mouth closed. He wasn't ready to say those words to her. Would he ever be? She went on as if nothing were wrong. "I want you to promise me that you'll stay close to the house tomorrow while Miss Watkins is here."

"Why?"

"We don't want her to think you don't like it here. That you'd rather live someplace else, do we?"

Confusion deepened his scowl. "I don't like it here a whole bunch."

Faith drew back in surprise. "You don't? I thought you were happy here. Is it school? Do you dislike your teacher, or is someone bullying you there?"

"School is okay. I don't want to talk about it." He gathered his paper and crayons and ran out of the room.

Faith stared after him in shock. Was she doing the wrong thing trying to raise him as Amish? Would he be happier in a home with *Englisch* parents? What should she do?

If only Adrian were here. She looked out the window toward his farm. What advice would he give? She hadn't seen him since he'd asked permission to court her. She wanted to believe it was God's plan for them to have a future together, but she was afraid to hope for such happiness.

It seemed as if she'd spent her entire life being afraid.

That night she went to bed but sleep proved elusive. She tossed and turned beneath the covers and prayed that she was doing the right thing.

When the morning finally came, she made breakfast and went out to do the chores. When she called Kyle down, her heart ached for him. His eyes were puffy, and he looked as if he hadn't slept any better than she had.

"Kyle, we should talk about what's bothering you."

"Nothing's bothering me. Can I have jelly on my toast?"

She set a jar of peach preserves on the table and waited until he helped himself. "Kyle, do you want to live somewhere else?"

He put down his toast without tasting it. "No."

"If you do, that's okay."

"Where else could I go?"

"I'm not sure, but there are a lot of people who would love to have a little boy like you."

"No, I can't go anywhere else. I have to stay and take care of Shadow. Shadow needs me. I'm his friend."

"All right. It's time to get ready for school. You'd better hurry. You don't want to be late."

She walked Kyle to the end of the lane and waited with him until the Imhoff children arrived. Faith bit her lip as she watched them walk down the road toward the school swinging their lunch coolers alongside.

When they were out of sight, she glanced toward Adrian's farm. She wanted to talk to him, to share her burden and her fears. Biting her thumbnail, she waged an internal war. Tell him or don't tell him? Before she could decide, she caught a glimpse of him driving his grain binder into the cornfield.

He had more than enough work to do. She didn't need to add to his troubles.

She opened her heart and began to pray. "Dear Lord, please let the social worker's visit go well. Let Kyle come to love me as I love him and to be content here among Your people. Give me the strength and wisdom to guide him throughout his life."

A car whizzed by, bringing her attention back to the present. She turned and walked toward the house. There was plenty of spinning to keep her busy until Kyle came home again. Praying while she was spinning was easy, too, and she had a lot of praying to do.

It was a few minutes before four o'clock when Miss Watkins arrived for her last visit. Faith put her spinning away and went out to greet her. After exchanging pleasantries, Miss Watkins got down to business. "Have you had a chance to make out a chore list for Kyle?"

"I have." Faith produced the paper hoping she had done as Miss Watkins wanted.

After reading it, the social worker looked at Faith. "Is he to clean stalls every day?"

"It is a chore most Amish children take care of at his age without a problem. I've limited it to just Myrtle's stall. Shadow is his animal, and he must take care of her."

"All right. That's a valid point." She reviewed the

rest of Faith's paper and said, "It seems like a lot of work for one boy."

"There is much work to be done around here and I can't do it all."

Caroline glanced at her watch. "I thought you said he normally gets home from school at four o'clock. It's four fifteen."

Faith rose to look out the window. The lane was empty. "He should be here any minute."

"I'm concerned that he doesn't have enough supervision on his way to and from school."

"Amish children walk to school. He doesn't walk alone. The Imhoff children walk with him."

The two women sat together in silence until another fifteen minutes had passed. Faith rose to her feet again as worry gnawed at her insides. She opened the door and walked out onto the porch. Had Kyle gone to Adrian's instead of coming home?

A splotch of red by the barn caught her eye. Kyle's lunch pail sat beside the barn door. She turned to Miss Watkins. "He's here. That's his lunch cooler by the barn door. He must have gone to do his chores first."

Faith walked down the steps and crossed the yard with Miss Watkins right behind her. As soon as Faith opened the door, she knew something was wrong. Myrtle was calling frantically for her baby as she rushed from one side of the stall to the other. Shadow was gone.

"Oh, Kyle. What have you done now?"

Miss Watkins came up behind Faith. "What's wrong?"

"Kyle has taken Shadow. I need to find Adrian."

Faith rushed out the back door of the barn and through the orchard to the cornfield where Adrian was working. His horses plodded along with their heads down as they pulled the large grain binder. The noise of the gasoline engine running the belt almost drowned out the clatter of the mower head as it sheered off corn-stalks as thick as her wrist with ease.

He was headed toward her, but he didn't see her. His attention was focused on the binder as it dumped out bundles of cornstalks and on keeping his horses travel-ing in a straight line. Faith hurried toward him know-ing he would help her find Kyle.

She stumbled several times as she crossed the rough ground. Where could Kyle have gone? Why had he run away again?

She was within fifty yards of Adrian when move-ment in the cornfield caught her eye. She crouched down to see better between the stalks. Was that Kyle hiding in the corn?

A scream erupted from Faith as she realized the dan-ger Kyle was in. Adrian didn't see him. The deadly blades of the binder would cut through a boy as easily as it did the tough corn.

She began to run, screaming at the top of her lungs to get Adrian's attention. Screaming at Kyle to get out of the way. She had to reach him. She tried to run faster, but her weak leg gave out and she fell.

Lying in the dirt, she screamed Kyle's name as tears blurred her vision.

Please, God, let them hear me. Please save my child!

Chapter Sixteen

Adrian wiped the sweat from his brow and braced his tired body against the rail at the front of his binder. His head pounded from the constant roar of the gas engine and the exhaust fumes that drifted toward him. As much work as he'd gotten done today, he knew the hard part was still ahead of him. Gathering the bundles of corn and stacking them together was a back-breaking chore.

He kept his eyes glued to the binder reel. For some reason, it occasionally threw out a bundle that wasn't tied. He felt the tension in his reins change, and he looked toward his team. It was then he saw Faith running toward him across the stubble field.

She was shouting and waving her arms, then she fell. He didn't know what was wrong, but he knew he had to reach her quickly. He slapped the reins against his horses' rumps and urged them to a faster pace. The bundles of corn fell off the conveyor belt and broke open on the ground.

Faith waved him back. He could hear her shouts now, but he couldn't make out what she was saying. Miss Watkins was running toward him, too.

Suddenly, a black blob darted out of the cornfield directly in front of his horses. They shied, and he pulled them back into line when he realized it was Shadow. In the next instant he heard Faith yelling Kyle's name, and he saw the boy step out directly in front of him.

"God, give me strength!" Adrian hauled back on the lines to stop his horses, kicked the shutoff switch on the engine to kill it and threw the lever that stopped the mower blades. The horses reared back at his rough handling. The noise of the machine died away to silence.

He kept his eyes shut as the vision of Gideon running in front of that car played out to its horrible end.

"Not again, God. Don't let me see him die. Please, don't let me see him die."

He heard Faith's voice first. She was sobbing. He opened his eyes and blinked to focus. Kyle stood barely six inches away from the blades.

Adrian tried but couldn't catch his breath. He collapsed onto the platform with his head spinning. By this time Faith had reached Kyle. She had him in her arms, holding him close. Shadow, frightened and lost, called pitifully for his mother.

Faith carried Kyle toward Adrian. She called out, "He's fine. Praise God, he's fine."

He waved her away. He didn't have the strength to stand. "Take him home."

God had given him a chance to redeem himself. He hadn't been able to save Gideon, but Kyle was alive. "Thank you, God."

Adrian gained his feet and turned his team toward home. He couldn't work any more today. Being afraid was part of being human, but shutting himself off from others hadn't lessened the pain of his son's loss. Like a knife left in a drawer unused, the edge stayed sharp. He vividly recalled every second of that terrible day.

Living meant using all his emotions. Living his faith meant trusting God to strengthen him in times of sorrow and of joy. He loved Faith and he loved Kyle, but was he strong enough to live each day knowing he could lose either one of them as he'd almost done today?

He wasn't sure.

Faith knocked at Adrian's door a few minutes before seven o'clock that night. She wiped away her tears as she waited for him to answer. She didn't know where to turn, so she had turned to the one constant in her life.

The door opened and Adrian stood before her, his face gray, his eyes sunken. He looked as if he'd aged ten years in one day. She probably looked worse.

His voice sounded raw when he asked, "How is he?"

She thought all her tears were done, but apparently she had more. They began to flow again. "They took him away, Adrian. The social worker thinks I can't provide a safe home for him and that his running away is proof that he's unhappy living Amish."

"Faith, I'm so sorry." He stepped out of the shadows and drew her into his arms.

"I don't know what to do," she wailed. Clinging to Adrian was like holding on to a rock in the middle of a raging river. She'd never needed anyone more than she needed him at this moment.

He led her into his kitchen and deposited her on a worn wooden chair. "Would you like some coffee?"

She missed his touch the moment he pulled away. "*Ja.* I'm sorry to come running to you with this, but I didn't know where else to go. I haven't even thanked you. Your quick reactions saved Kyle's life."

"We must thank God for little Shadow. I knew as soon as I saw him that Kyle couldn't be far away."

Adrian sat beside Faith and took her hand in his. "When I saw Kyle in danger I saw my son dying again, and I couldn't deal with that. I came home and lay on Gideon's bed. As my fright faded, I felt he was there with me. He was not. He's in a wonderful place where I can't go yet. I must remain here until God calls me. I realized my fear was part of being alive. You and Kyle have brought me back to life."

Tears choked her. Clearing her throat, Faith said, "I can't lose him, Adrian. I can't."

What she was about to say would put an end to anything between them. "If I move to town and live in an *Englisch* house with electricity and a telephone and enroll Kyle in the public school, they might let me keep him. To do that, I need money. You once told me if I couldn't manage the farm alone that you would buy it. Well, I want to sell it to you now."

The sadness in his eyes deepened. She couldn't bear to cause him pain, but if she had to choose between their happiness and Kyle, then it would be Kyle.

"Faith, do you know what you are saying? To do such things would go against the *ordnung*. It would put you outside of our faith. You would be shunned by everyone in the church. Your friends, my family. Can you really want this?"

She didn't, but what choice did she have? She was so confused and scared. "I don't know. I only know that I don't want to lose Kyle. Will you buy my farm?"

He sat back in his chair. "*Nee.* I will not. Do not turn your back on your faith at a time like this, I beg you. I did, and it was wrong. Grasp on to it, and it will become your strength. It took me long years to discover that, but I know it is true."

"You will not help me?"

"Not like this. Ask me anything, but I can not help you turn your back on God."

"You know what it is to lose a child." She couldn't believe what she was hearing. She'd been so sure she could depend on him.

"I know what it is to lose a child and I know what it is to find God."

The kettle on the stove began whistling. Faith rose to her feet. "I'm afraid I can't stay for coffee, after all. Good night, Adrian."

She had to get out of his house before she started weeping again. Tears would not fix this.

Adrian took the kettle off the stove and leaned against the counter with his mind whirling. Today, he'd finally come to realize God had already given him the strength he needed to face life's frailties and uncertainty. He'd come to believe that a single day loving Faith and Kyle was better than a lifetime of hiding from more pain.

Now, he was losing them both. Not by death, but by her choice.

He understood why, but that didn't ease his sense of betrayal or loss. Faith had made a vow before God and men to remain true to the Amish religion their ancestors had died to preserve and to live separate from the world. God commanded them that it must be so in 2 Corinthians 6:14

"Be not yoked with unbelievers. For what do righteousness and wickedness have in common? Or what fellowship can light have with darkness?"

This was a mistake Adrian could not let Faith make.

He took up his hat and headed for the door. He needed wiser counsel and he prayed Bishop Zook would be able to give it.

"Good luck in there today." Samson Carter, a white-haired man with a neatly trimmed white beard turned around in the front seat of his van to smile encouragingly at Faith.

"*Danki,* sir." She gathered courage before stepping outside.

He said, "I'll wait for you here."

"I have no idea how long this will take."

"Not to worry. I brought a book to read."

Mr. Carter ran a van service in Hope Springs. The retired railroad worker earned extra income by driving his Amish neighbors when they needed to travel farther than their buggies could comfortably carry them.

Faith got out of the vehicle in front of the county courthouse in Millersburg. She had just enough money left to pay Samson when he took her home.

Her farm was on the market, but until it sold she wouldn't have the money to rent a place in town. The extra money in her bank account had gone to pay the lawyer that was meeting her here today.

She glanced up at the courthouse. Three stories tall and built of time-mellowed stone, the building was capped with an elaborate clock tower that rose another story higher. A long flight of steps led up to the main doors on the second story. Narrow arched windows looked out over the well-manicured grounds and a monument to Civil War veterans.

As Faith stared at the building, her anxiety mounted. Behind which window would Kyle's fate be decided?

She remembered Adrian's words about holding on to her faith. Could she do it if it meant losing Kyle?

She closed her eyes. "May Your will be done here today, Lord. Grant me the strength to face the outcome, whatever it may be. Pour Your wisdom into the heart and mind of the judge that he may rule wisely."

Did God listen to the prayers of someone about to turn her back on her faith? When it came time to tell the judge she would leave the Amish world in order to adopt Kyle, could she break her most sacred vow? She closed her eyes and saw Adrian pleading with her not to make that choice.

Why had God put this test before her? Hadn't she suffered enough?

It took her a few minutes to climb the steps. Once inside, a friendly security guard directed her to the correct courtroom.

Mr. Reid, her attorney, waited for her in a chair outside the courtroom door.

He rose to his feet. His smile was polite. "Are you ready for this?"

Was she? Did she have the courage to speak up for herself and for Kyle? A second later, she remembered Adrian's advice at her very first church meeting.

If I were you, I'd go in with my head up and smile as if nothing were wrong.

It had been good advice that day. She would follow it again. Putting her shoulders back, she pasted a smile on her face and nodded. "It is in God's hands."

"Indeed it is. I will do most of the talking. You may answer any questions the judge directs at you. Have him repeat it if you don't understand."

"Will Kyle be here?"

"He won't be in the courtroom, but it's my under-standing that he will be nearby."

"Will I be able to see him if the judge rules against me?"

"Let's cross that bridge if we come to it. Are you ready to go in?"

Fear closed her throat. All she could do was nod.

Mr. Reid held the door open. The room beyond was paneled from floor to ceiling in rich dark wood. At the front, the judge's bench stood on a raised platform. A large round seal was centered on the wall behind it. Flanking the seal were two flags, the United States flag and the Ohio State flag.

It wasn't until she took a step inside the room that she realized she wasn't alone. The few dark wooden benches were filled with Amish elders. Around the out-side of the room, three deep, stood more Amish men and women waiting quietly, some with small children at their sides or in their arms.

Many of the faces she knew from her own church district, but there were many people who were unknown to her. Faith stood rooted to the spot. What were they all doing here? As she gazed about, one man stepped forward from the group and walked toward her.

Adrian.

Her heart turned over in her chest. Tears blurred her vision. When he said he wouldn't help she had been crushed. Why was he here now? Had these people come to denounce her?

She stiffened her spine. "Adrian, what are you doing here? Who are all these people?"

"These are your friends and your neighbors and the people you will do business with in the years to come. We are here to speak for you and for our way of life. The

Amish way is a *goot* way for Kyle to grow up. He may have been *Englisch* when he came among us, but he is Amish in his heart and so are you. The judge must understand this. You do not have to face this alone, Faith. We stand with you."

In that moment, Faith could not have loved him more. He had done this for her, gathered together people to speak on her behalf. *"Danki."*

"You are welcome, *liebschen.*"

The heat of a blush crept up her neck. "How can you call me dearest when you know I was ready to turn my back on our faith?"

He took her hand. "Because I must speak what is in my heart. Listen to God, Faith, and then speak what your heart says is right."

Mr. Reid spoke in Faith's ear. "We should take our places. It's almost time to begin."

Letting go of Adrian's hand was one of the hardest things she'd ever done in her life. He gave her fingers one last squeeze and then went back to his place beside Elam Sutter and Eli Imhoff.

Her attorney led her to a small table just behind the railing that separated the judge's bench from the rest of the courtroom. Caroline Watkins sat at an identical table on the opposite side of the aisle. She nodded politely to Mr. Reid but didn't speak as she opened her briefcase and pulled out several files.

Faith sank gratefully onto the chair Mr. Reid held out for her but had no time to gather her thoughts. The bailiff at the side of the bench called out, "All rise for the Honorable Judge Randolph Harbin presiding."

A small man with silver hair entered from the door behind the bench. He wore a dark suit and a bright green striped tie.

He paused for a second to survey the packed room in surprise before stepping up and taking a seat behind the bench. He beckoned to the bailiff, and the two men shared a brief whispered conversation.

When the judge was ready, he spoke to the entire room. "This is a hearing on the petition of Faith Martin to adopt the minor child, Kyle King. Is Mrs. Martin here?"

Her attorney rose to his feet. "She is, Your Honor."

"Very good. Miss Watkins, I understand you represent the child for the State of Ohio."

She rose also. "I do, Your Honor."

"Good, then let us proceed." The judge leaned back in his chair and clasped his hands together. "Mrs. Martin, it is my understanding that you wish to adopt Kyle King and that you are his only living relative. Tell me a little bit about your circumstances and your wish to adopt Kyle."

Faith's pulse hammered like a drum in her ears. She expected it to leap from her chest at any second. She glanced over her shoulder and saw Adrian standing with his arms crossed over his chest, just the way he had been standing the first time she'd seen him outside her door. He nodded once and lifted his thumb. He believed she could do this. She believed because he did.

She rose to her feet and faced the judge. "Your Honor, I am Kyle's aunt. His father was my only brother. I can't tell you how much Kyle reminds me of him. Every day he says something or does something, and I see my brother all over again. I loved my brother and I love his child. I love Kyle's smile and his sense of humor. I love the feel of his hand in mine when we cross the street together. I know he loves me, too. I would do anything for him."

"I see that you are Amish, as are the many people you have brought to support you."

Faith heard a voice say, "If I may speak, Your Honor?"

She turned to see Bishop Zook rise from a seat behind her.

The judge arched an eyebrow. "And you are?"

"I am Bishop Joseph Zook. Mrs. Martin did not ask us to come today. We heard that this good woman might lose custody of her nephew because she holds to our ways. We wish only the chance to say that our ways are not simple and backward as some may think."

"I am very familiar with the Amish and their ways. My grandfather was Amish but left the church. Had he not, chances are I would be a farmer or furniture maker and not a judge. You'll have your chance to speak after I've heard from everyone else. Thank you."

The bishop resumed his seat. Judge Harbin said, "Miss Watkins, you've investigated this case. I have read your report, but would you summarize your findings for the court, please?"

She looked at Faith sadly. "No matter how much I wish I could say having Kyle stay with his aunt would be in his best interest, I simply can't do it. Kyle's father left the Amish faith and chose to raise his son in the modern world. He had money put aside for his son's college education. If Kyle were to grow up with his aunt, he would only receive an eighth grade education."

The judge turned his pen end over end. "The ability of a parent to provide higher education is not a prerequisite for adoption. Are you sure you're not letting your personal feelings on the subject influence you?"

"I don't believe I am, Your Honor. My job is to do what's best for him. Kyle has had significant difficulty adjusting to an Amish home. They live without electricity, something he's never done before. He has run away at least three times that I know of. The last time put him in great danger. I feel an Amish farm environment is simply too dangerous for this young boy who has grown up without any experience around machinery and animals. Now, if Mrs. Martin would agree to move into town and enroll Kyle in the public school, I think he would be much happier. I also think it would make his adjustment to living with his aunt much easier. I would agree to a new trial period of six months if this were the case."

"I see. Mrs. Martin, would you be agreeable to such a move?"

These were the words Faith dreaded hearing. She could keep Kyle if she gave up her faith, or she could stay true to her faith and perhaps lose the child she loved.

Please, God, let this be the right decision.

She shook her head. "*Nee,* I would not. She wishes me to raise Kyle in an *Englisch* home with electricity so that he might have television and video games to play with. Yes, he is used to such things, but they do not make a home. A home is a place where a child is loved and raised to know and love God."

She studied the judge's face, but she could not tell what he was thinking. He began reading the documents before him, turning each page slowly. After a few minutes, he looked toward Bishop Zook. "Bishop, what is it that you would like to say to this court today?"

The bishop rose to his feet again. "I would ask that Adrian Lapp speak for us today."

Adrian came forward and stood beside the bishop. "I have come to know both Faith Martin and her nephew,

Kyle. It is true that Kyle has had a hard time adjusting, but it is not because he can't watch television. It's because he is afraid to love his aunt. He's afraid God will take her away as He did his parents."

Miss Watkins spoke up. "Your Honor, this man is not a child psychologist."

"But I am a man who knows about loss and about the fear of losing someone if I allowed myself to love again. I lost my wife and then my son when he was only four years old. But I lost more than my family. I lost my faith. I no longer trusted God. I was afraid to love again just as Kyle is afraid. But God brought Kyle into my life to show me how wrong I've been."

Adrian turned to Faith. "I see now that loving someone is never wrong, be it for a little while or for a lifetime."

She bit her lip to keep from crying.

He faced Miss Watkins. "By taking Kyle away from Faith, you are proving him right. Don't take away the person he is afraid to love. Let him come to know God's goodness and mercy. Let him find the strength to love again."

The judge laid his papers aside and rubbed his chin. "You speak very eloquently, Mr. Lapp. I appreciate your insight. Miss Watkins, would you have the boy brought to my chambers?"

She objected. "Your Honor, the child is barely six years old. He's far too young to know what is in his best interest."

"That's true, but that's not what I'm going to ask him about. Mrs. Martin, will you and your attorney join me in my chambers? Mr. Lapp, I'd like you there, as well."

"Yes, Your Honor." Mr. Reid gathered his papers together and closed his briefcase.

The bailiff called out, "All rise."

When the judge left the room, Faith turned to look at her attorney. "Is this a good thing?"

"I'm not sure, but let's not keep him waiting." Mr. Reid held out his hand, indicating Faith should precede him.

Chapter Seventeen

Together, Faith, Adrian and her attorney entered a spacious office situated just beyond the courtroom. The same dark paneling lined the walls except where floor-to-ceiling bookcases jutted out. They held hundreds of thick books bound in dark red, green and gray.

"I'll have you three sit over there." Judge Harbin indicated a group of brown leather chairs near the windows. He then proceeded to make himself comfortable on a matching leather sofa in the middle of the room. Before it sat a low coffee table. It held an elaborate chess set with figures carved from dark and light woods.

The door to the outside hallway opened, and Miss Watkins came in holding Kyle by the hand. Faith's heart contracted with joy at the sight of Kyle's face. She longed to race across the room and snatch him up in a fierce hug. She made herself sit still. When Kyle saw her, he tore away from Miss Watkins and launched himself into Faith's arms.

Tears blurred her vision. She whispered, "I have missed you terribly."

His voice shook as he said, "I'm sorry I ran away. I won't do it again."

Adrian laid a hand on Kyle's shoulder. "You are forgiven."

Faith stroked his hair. "I'm just happy you are safe."

Miss Watkins took the child by the hand and said, "Kyle, I have someone you need to meet. This is Judge Harbin and he has a few questions for you."

Faith and Kyle reluctantly released each other. She said, "Go and talk to the judge. I'll be right here."

"Promise?" There was such pleading in his eyes that it broke Faith's heart.

"I promise," she managed to whisper past the lump in her throat."

Kyle allowed Miss Watkins to lead him away. Adrian took Faith's hand and held it between his strong, warm fingers.

The judge patted the cushion beside him. "Have a seat, young man."

Kyle glanced at Faith. She nodded to tell him it was okay. The boy climbed on the sofa and propped his hands on his thighs. Miss Watkins took a seat near Faith.

The judge leaned toward Kyle. "My name is Randolph Harbin. These people have to call me Your Honor, but you can call me Randy. Kyle, do you know what a judge is?"

He pondered a second or two, then said, "A guy who sends people to jail?"

"Some judges do send people to jail, but I'm not that kind of judge. I'm the kind of judge who decides what's best for kids like you. Do you know how to play chess?"

Kyle shook his head.

"I guess you're a little young for that. How about checkers?"

The boy's eyes lit up as he nodded quickly and pointed toward the windows. "Adrian has been teaching me."

The judge swept the chess pieces from the board and set it between him and Kyle. From a drawer beneath the coffee table, he pulled out a stack of red and white disks and offered them both to the boy. "Tell me how you know Adrian."

After choosing the red pieces, Kyle began placing them on the board. "He's our neighbor. He's helping me become Amish so the boys at school will stop teasing me."

Judge Harbin slowly laid out his pieces. "Do they tease you a lot?"

"Not as much as they first did. Anna Imhoff gets mad at them if they do."

"And who is Anna?"

"She's my friend. She doesn't make fun of me because I can't speak Pennsylvania Dutch. She says her friend, Jonathan, can't speak it either and he's a grown-up. She's giving us both lessons. I can say a few things. Do you want to hear?"

"Sure."

"*Mamm* means mother. *Dat* means dad. *Grossmammi* is grandmother. *Velkumm* is welcome."

"I'm impressed with what you've learned so far. Has your aunt been helping you?"

"Lots."

"I imagine she's a very good cook. What kind of things do you like to eat?"

"Have you ever had shoofly pie? It's the best. Aunt Faith makes it for me twice a week."

"I like mine with a tall glass of milk."

"Me, too!" Faith smiled at the amazement in Kyle's voice. She squeezed Adrian's hand.

"Do you have a pet at your aunt's house?" the judge asked.

Kyle grinned and folded his arms over his chest. "Yes, but it's not a cat and it's not a dog. I bet you can't guess what it is."

"Is it a horse or a baby calf?"

"Nope. It's a baby alpaca. I bet you never would have guessed that."

"Never in a million years."

"A baby alpaca is called a cria. Mine is black. Aunt Faith let me name him Shadow. When we sell his fleece, I get to keep *all* the money."

"You sound as if you really love your aunt."

Kyle's shoulders slumped. He glanced from the judge to Faith, then down at his feet. In a tiny voice he said, "Not too much."

Faith pressed her fingers to her lips. Her heart ached for Kyle.

The judge moved a checker. "How much would be too much?"

"I don't know." His voice got smaller.

"You don't know or you don't want to tell me?"

"I don't want to tell you."

"Why not?"

"'Cause I don't want God to hear."

"You don't want God to hear that you love your aunt?"

Kyle held a finger to his lips. "Shh! If God thinks I love her, something bad will happen."

"What makes you say that?"

"Because I told Mommy and Daddy I loved them when they left me at school and then God took them away. God wanted them in heaven instead of with me. He's very mean."

"I'm sure it must seem that way to you, but He isn't."

"He's not?"

"No. In this job, I talk to God all the time."

"You do?"

"Absolutely. I need His help to make good decisions. Sometimes those decisions are very hard, but I believe His will guides me."

"Would you ask him to bring my parents back? I really miss them."

Faith squeezed Adrian's hand. Poor Kyle. He had suffered so much. She only wanted to hold him and make the hurt go away.

The judge shook his head. "I know you miss them, but they can't come back. They are watching over you. Right this very minute. God is watching over you, too."

"That's what Aunt Faith says."

"Kyle, God has His own way of arranging our lives. Things happen that we don't like, that frighten us and make us sad, but He loves us, just as your parents loved you. Now, since I talk to God all the time, is there anything you'd like me to tell Him?"

Kyle glanced toward Faith. She read the indecision and the longing in his eyes. He turned back to the judge. "Tell God I want to stay with Aunt Faith and not to take her away to heaven."

Judge Harbin patted Kyle's head, then said, "Miss

Watkins, would you take Kyle out to the courtroom and wait for me there? Counselor, you and Mrs. Martin may return to the courtroom, too."

"Yes, Your Honor."

"What does this mean?" Faith glanced at her attorney, but he simply shrugged.

Adrian helped her to her feet. "Be brave. It is in God's hands."

When everyone was assembled in the courtroom again, Judge Harbin motioned to Kyle. "Come up here, young man."

Hesitantly, Kyle walked up and stood beside the bench. Judge Harbin picked up his gavel. "Kyle, do you know what this is?"

"A hammer."

"It's called a gavel. It's a very powerful tool. If I say, 'order in the court' and bang this gavel, everyone has to be silent."

"Cool."

"It is way cool. Today, I'm going to let you use my gavel because this is a very special day. It's a day you will always remember. Today, we are going to change your name to Kyle King Martin. Do you know why?"

"Because you are going to let my aunt adopt me?"

"That's right. And when I say it, I want you to bang that gavel so that everyone knows it's official. Are you ready?"

Kyle nodded and took the gavel in his hand. Judge Harbin looked out over the courtroom. "I do hereby grant the petition of Faith Martin to adopt the minor child, Kyle King."

Grinning from ear to ear, Kyle smacked the gavel

down as hard as he could. The courtroom immediately erupted into cheers.

Late in the afternoon, Faith and Kyle got out of the van in front of her house. Samson carried Kyle's bag to the porch, congratulated Faith again and drove off. On the front steps of her home, holding Kyle's hand in hers, she raised her face to the sun and closed her eyes. Kyle was staying! Praise God for His goodness.

Kyle was hers.

The phrase echoed inside her mind in an endless refrain. She could scarcely believe it. Her prayers had been answered. She had regained her child and her faith all in one day.

When she opened her eyes, they were drawn across the fields to Adrian's farm. Much of the happiness in her heart was due to him. If Adrian had not gathered the church members together and spoken for Kyle, the day might have had a very different outcome. Love for Adrian warmed her soul.

Her thoughts were interrupted when another car came up the drive. To her surprise, she saw it was Miss Watkins. What was she doing here?

When Kyle saw the social worker get out of her car, he threw himself against Faith, wrapping his arms around her legs. "I get to stay, right? The judge said so."

Faith quickly sought to reassure him. "You will stay forever and ever."

He looked into her eyes. "Are you sure?"

"I am."

Looking to Miss Watkins and then back to Faith, he whispered, "You promise?"

She picked him up and kissed his cheek. "I promise."

Miss Watkins came forward. "I give you my word

that you can live here for as long as you want, Kyle. Just promise me you won't run away again."

"I won't. Not ever. Aunt Faith, can I go tell Shadow I'm staying?"

Faith lowered him to the ground. "Go tell all the animals."

He raced away to the barn. Faith pressed her hand to her lips to hold on to the joy that filled her to overflowing. To think she'd once wondered if she could love her brother's child as much as her own.

Miss Watkins cleared her throat. "I hope you realize that I only wanted what was best for Kyle."

"I know that."

"Would you mind if I stop in to see him from time to time? He's a remarkable young man." Tears sparkled in the depths of her eyes.

Faith grasped her hand. "You will always be welcome in our home."

"Thank you." Caroline returned to her car and drove away. When the dust settled, Faith saw Adrian walking across the field toward her.

How could one heart hold all the love she felt without bursting? It truly was one of God's miracles.

On the day they'd first met, she had wondered what it would be like to have a husband so strong and sure of his place in life. Would she have the chance to find out or had she ruined her chance at happiness by her willingness to put aside her religion?

She prayed he could forgive her.

She waited until Adrian reached her side. He took off his hat. "Faith Martin, I have something I wish to speak to you about."

He sounded so nervous. Had he to come to tell her

he wanted to call off their courting? His reaction at the courthouse had given her hope that he still cared for her. She said, "I'm listening.

"You have too much work to do to get this place ready before winter. You don't even have hay put up for your animals yet and your barn needs repairs."

"That is true." A lecture on her property wasn't what she had been expecting when she'd seen him coming.

"It will take the entire fall to get things ready."

"You're right. It will."

"I have hay and I have paint."

She crossed her arms. "Is there a point to this?"

He turned his hat around and around in his hands. "Your boy needs a man to help guide him on the path of the righteous."

"I agree. Bishop Zook has offered to help in just such a fashion."

"That is *goot*. You are not alone, Faith. There are people who will willingly help you carry your burdens."

"You mean like pruning my trees and shearing my alpacas?"

"*Ja,* those things, too."

It wasn't exactly the declaration of love she longed to hear. Maybe he had changed his mind. Did he see her as fickle and weak? Mose always said she was weak. Had he been right?

"Adrian!" Kyle's excited shout made them look toward the barn. The boy came running toward them at full speed. Adrian dropped to one knee as the boy raced into his arms.

Wrapping his arms around Adrian's neck, Kyle said, "I get to stay here forever and ever."

"That's something I was hoping to talk to you about."

Kyle drew back to look him in the face. "What do you mean?"

Adrian glanced up at Faith. "I reckon I should ask both of you since you're a pair now."

"Ask us what?" Kyle demanded.

Adrian rose to his feet still holding Kyle. "I never thought I would love anyone the way I loved my son and my wife. But, Faith, I love Kyle as much as I loved my own son, and I love you as much as any man can love a woman."

Faith heart began pounding in her chest as it swelled with happiness. She couldn't speak.

Kyle said, "Are you gonna get mushy with my Aunt Faith? Ben said you were gonna."

Adrian grew serious as he gazed into Faith's eyes. "I must have a chat with my brother, but in this case he was right. Faith, will you marry me and live as my wife for all the days God gives to us?"

She choked back her tears of joy. "I will."

She took a step closer and cupped his face with her hands. "I didn't believe love like this was possible, but now I know it is. We are truly blessed."

Adrian lowered Kyle to the ground and took Faith in his arms. His kiss was everything and more than she'd dreamed it would be. After a long breathless moment, he drew back and tucked her head beneath his chin. "Thank you for saying yes. Thank you for showing me my way back to God."

Kyle wrinkled his nose. "Does this mean we're going to live at your place?"

Adrian smiled at him. "If that's all right with you?"

"I reckon it is. Guess I'd better go tell Shadow we're

moving, after all." He took off and jogged toward the barn.

Adrian's eyes softened as he watched Kyle. "I can't believe I was so afraid of love and hid from it all this time."

"I was afraid, too, but you have shown me that a man can be kind even when he is upset. I learned to trust you, Adrian. That is something I was sure I would never do again. You've given me the one thing I need that no one else can give me."

"What is that?"

"Your love."

He smiled and pulled her close. "*Ja,* my heart holds all the love you will ever need."

She gazed into his eyes, happier than she could ever remember being.

He said, "I don't want to wait to marry you. I hope you weren't planning on a long courtship."

Unable to resist teasing him, she said, "I don't think we should rush into anything. It takes a long time to get to know a person well."

He nodded. "You're right. We should give ourselves two years."

"At least." She tried to keep a solemn face but failed. There was no way she could wait that long.

Pulling her close again, he whispered, "I'll be lucky to last a week. How soon can we get hitched?"

"With all the preparations I need to make…six months." When he was holding her close it sounded much too long to wait.

"My mother will help, and if I know her, she'll cut that time in half."

"If she can help arrange a wedding in three months, she is a worker with great talents."

"Then both of you should get along fine for you are one, too, my love."

When his lips closed over hers once more, Faith knew she'd found more than a home in Hope Springs. She'd found courage, a family and a love unlike anything she'd dreamed was possible.

* * * * *

LANCASTER COUNTY TARGET

Kit Wilkinson

To my lovely student, Emily Dingman.
What a pleasure to watch you mature into
such a fine young lady over the past three years.
Tu rends le monde si mieux—
you make the world better.
Always remember you make a difference.

Whatever your hand finds to do,
do it with all your might.
—*Ecclesiastes* 9:10

Chapter One

What is that doctor doing in here?

Abigail Miller's heart beat fast and hard as she stood, frozen, in the dark hospital corridor, watching a surgeon empty a large syringe of clear liquid into a patient's IV drip.

Why? What is he doing here? Alone with a patient in a closed-off part of the hospital?

Abby shook her head. It didn't make any sense.

Dressed in full scrubs with no ID badge that she could spot, the doctor's figure towered over the male patient who lay lifeless on the gurney. As large as the surgeon looked in the narrow corridor, the male patient looked small even on the hospital gurney—his olive skin pale, his head round and bald. He seemed so still.

Abby sucked in a quick breath and decided to backtrack without disturbing the doctor and patient. She wasn't comfortable confronting the tall, imposing surgeon herself, but something about the scene just didn't seem right. Perhaps she could find a security guard... She stepped backward and her shoe squeaked as it turned on the tiled floor.

"How did you get in here? This part of the hospital is

closed." The doctor spun toward her, his voice booming through the empty hallway. His cold, gray eyes flashed in the dim emergency lighting and chilled her like an arctic blast. The rest of him was hidden beneath a complete workup of surgical scrubs, including face mask, gloves and hat.

"I was just cutting through here. I do it almost every day." Abby forced her lips to move while her eyes stayed fixed on the surgeon. "I was on my way to Maternity. I hope that's not a problem."

"I don't understand how you got into this area." He advanced toward her, forcing her to take several steps back. "The entrances are supposed to be locked. This patient is highly contagious. This area is under restrictions. You shouldn't be here."

Contagious? Abby hadn't heard about any restrictions. Surely there would have been signs, announcements. The sense of something wrong grew stronger. Pulse rising, she skirted to the side of the large man and looked down at the patient's chart attached to the end of the gurney.

N. K. Hancock—TRANSFER.

In the dim lighting, that was all she could read, but she could see that the papers were solid white. If the patient were contagious, the chart would be marked with a prominent red stripe. Abby swallowed hard. Her heart drummed against her ribs. This doctor was lying—if he even was a doctor. She needed to find a security guard, stat. But first, she had to get away. She composed herself just enough to keep from sinking under the doctor's menacing glare and looming figure.

"I'm sorry, Dr...." Abby waited but he did not supply a name. With each syllable, she inched herself away from the man and his patient. "I didn't know we couldn't pass through. Again, I'm sorry to disturb you, Doctor. I'll just be on my way." She turned and headed for the stairwell.

"Oh, no, you don't." He was behind her in seconds. Over her. Around her like a giant spider. He grabbed the top of her arm and squeezed her flesh like a vise. His cold eyes flickered in the dim lighting.

She trembled and fought against him, but her struggles were in vain as the grip of his stubby, sausage-like fingertips dug deeper and deeper into her skin. He pulled her tight against his stout belly. She had no hope of breaking free.

Was this her just deserts after finally deciding she would not join the Amish church, defying the wishes of her father?

She'd gone to school to become a nurse, but she hadn't made her final decision about living the Plain life until recently. It had been time to put away one or the other and stop living on the fence. So last week, she'd laid aside her prayer *Kapp* and her frocks for good. She'd devote her life to nursing, delivering babies and helping others to stay healthy. But the choice had not come without a lot of pain, especially to her father, the *Ordnung* bishop.

Her father's words still rang through her head—a verse from the Psalms. *"If you stand in the counsel of the wicked, you will become wicked."*

Had she made the worst decision of her life? Right now, it certainly seemed that way. Tears filled Abby's eyes. Crazy, desperate thoughts swirled around in her mind. She continued to try to break free of the doctor's grip, but she could not come close to matching his strength. Her breathing came in short gasps. She would have yelled but there was no one to hear her.

"You've been exposed." The doctor's tone mocked her as he dragged her across the hallway. "I'll have to give you an injection, too."

"What?" *Is he mad?* "Please, stop. You're hurting me. Let me go."

With his free hand, he produced another full syringe from the pocket of his scrubs. The needle shook as it came at her. His fingers closed in tighter around her arm as he yanked her sleeve high, exposing the skin above his grip. The hot prick of the needle stabbed her and the drug burned like fire as it entered her bloodstream. "What? What did you just give me?"

The doctor yanked her to the end of the corridor and through the door to the stairwell, not seeming to care that he crashed the door frame's metal edge into Abby's forehead. The blow radiated across her skull. Nausea waved through her gut as the drug made her head light—too light. Her body began to collapse. She could feel her blood pressure fall…

Please, Lord, help me.

Finally, she felt his fingers release her. She slumped to the cold, tiled floor.

The empty stairwell spun around her. The strange doctor had vanished. With all her might, she tried to reach for her cell phone. It was in her back pocket. But the drug was hitting her full force now. Her hand shook uncontrollably and the device dropped from her fingers. Her eyelids closed as she groped the floor desperately for the phone. But it was no use. She was going under and there was nothing she could do to stop it.

Please, Lord…help…

Abby closed her eyes and the darkness overtook her.

* * *

"Code Blue. Code Blue. Paging Dr. Jamison. Room 307. Code Blue. Dr. Blake Jamison."

The announcement blared through the overhead speakers. Everyone in the operatory stopped what they were doing and looked at Blake.

Code Blue? How could there be a Code Blue? It signaled that one of his patients needed resuscitation, but that couldn't be true. He had taken on exactly three patients since transferring to Fairview Hospital. They'd been recovering well, awake, alert and resting as of two hours ago. This had to be a mistake.

"And clip." He opened his gloved hand and waited for the nurse to place the suturing instrument in his palm. With a delicate touch, he closed up the tiny incision, returned the instrument to the nurse and removed himself from the operating area. The surgical staff would have to finish the cleanup after his first surgery at Fairview Hospital of Lancaster County, Pennsylvania. Apparently, he had an emergency to look into.

"This way, Doctor." One of the nurses tugged at his sleeve, guiding him toward the doors. "Take the service elevator. It's faster. I'll show you."

A minute later, Blake entered a patient-recovery room where a crash team had assembled with a defibrillator. An unresponsive male patient, mid-to-late fifties, lay on the hospital bed. He was not one of the three patients Blake had seen earlier. Blake turned to the young nurse working near the monitors. "I'm Dr. Jamison. I was paged for a Code Blue, but this man is not my patient."

"Cardiac arrest," she said. "Started about fifteen minutes ago. Heart stopped soon after."

"But he's not my patient. I can't treat him. Hospital policy. It could lead to a lawsuit and an insurance nightmare."

She glanced back at the chart and pointed. "Your name is the only one on the chart."

"That's not possible."

She stared back at him with a go-ahead-and-look face.

Blake picked up the chart and thumbed through the pages. Unfortunately, the nurse was correct. His name was there. And what certainly looked like his signature. "I'm telling you this is a mistake. I've never seen this chart before. I've never seen this patient before. What kind of operation do you run here at Fairview?"

"This is no joke, Doctor. This man is in cardiac arrest and that chart says you're his doctor. I'm just the floor nurse. I have nothing to do with doctor assignments."

Blake stepped up to the bedside, opposite the working crash team, and put aside the chart. The nurse was right. He was wasting his breath getting upset with her. He'd have to speak to the appropriate people at the appropriate time—after he had done everything he could to treat the patient. "What's the history in a nutshell?"

"A nutshell is all we have," the nurse continued. "We have no idea. He came in this morning. A transfer patient from New York City. Some sort of insurance issue? Apparently, he's recovering from laparoscopic chole-cystectomy."

New York City? The place Blake had just escaped? Or tried to, at least.

He shook the spiraling thoughts of his parents' devastating plane crash out of his head. Today another man's life was on the line. He was a doctor. For the moment, that was all that really mattered. Forget insurance headaches. Forget his own personal grief and struggles to sort out his life.

"You're saying this man had gallstone surgery some-where else, was brought here and is now in cardiac ar-rest?"

She nodded.

"What medication has he been given? Does he have any known allergies?"

"I don't know. As you saw for yourself, there's not much in the chart and he only arrived an hour ago," the nurse said. "We can't seem to revive him. Hospital policy is to give it fifteen minutes. Should we call?"

"Not yet. Draw blood," Blake said. "I want a basic workup. And while we are waiting, continue efforts. I want to know more about what's going on."

The nurse took blood samples and scampered out of the room. The crash team continued to work.

"Stand by," one of the crew said. The other member prepared the electric plates to try to restart the patient's heart. "Three, two, one."

The man's body popped from the voltage. The moni-tor beeped once before the flatline signal returned. Wait and repeat. Blake glanced through the chart. He was still certain he'd never seen this paperwork before or the patient who went with it—Nicolas Hancock. The name was not familiar. But on the last page, there it was—*Dr. Blake Jamison.* With a likeness of his signature.

Clearly, someone had made a very big mistake and Blake intended to find out who was responsible.

After a few minutes, the nurse returned with the basic blood screen. She handed the report to him al-most breathless.

He read over the graphs and figures. Adrenaline levels were off the charts. That would certainly cause someone to go into cardiac arrest. "Any idea why his adrenaline would be so high?"

"No, sir."

Blake looked up at the IV drip. "Did you attach this?"

"No, sir. He arrived with the IV in place. But I did replace the fluids."

Blake tried to think of a scenario where a patient would have so much adrenaline in his body. The only explanation that came to mind was that he'd received a dose of epinephrine—a drug which could not be tested for, since the body already made it naturally. But a dose large enough to cause this sort of reaction was anything but natural.

This man's cardiac arrest was looking as if it had been induced. Blake shook his head. Something very strange was going on here, but there was one thing that was certain—Mr. Nicolas Hancock was dead.

"It's time to call," he said. "Time of death is twelve-oh-seven."

The nurse wrote down the hour.

"Is there a next of kin?" Blake would hardly know what to say to them.

"No, sir," the nurse answered, her tone softening a touch. "His file says to contact his lawyer in case of an emergency. I'll be glad to do that for you."

"Thank you." Blake rubbed his chin, deep in thought. This was not what he'd signed up for. He'd come to Lancaster County hoping for some peace to get past the loss of his parents, and to figure out what to do with the sudden discovery that he'd been adopted as a baby.

But he could hardly think with all this unorthodox nonsense at the hospital. If this had been an accident of some sort, then someone had really fouled up, medically speaking, with this patient. Blake wanted to know who and why. "I'm not signing a death certificate until I get some more information on this patient. This situation is—" Blake could not keep the strain of emotion from his voice "—unacceptable—medically, ethically and professionally unacceptable. Get the hospital administrator down here. Someone needs to look into this."

The nurse began to shut down the machines. "I'll inform Dr. Dodd."

Blake headed toward the door. He felt a dark cloud over him. The same one he'd had over him in NYC. He stopped in the doorway and turned back to the nurse. "So you changed the drip bag. But did you change the IV tubing?"

She shook her head. "No. The tubing was securely in place. I didn't see any reason to insert another IV needle into the patient."

"Then save the entire IV, tubing and all, in a hermetically sealed container. It's possible medications or a mixture of medications were administered prior to his arrival that caused the cardiac arrest. We have to cover ourselves legally in this day and time. Also, I'd like a copy of that chart. I want to find out how my name became associated with this patient."

"Of course, Doctor. Naturally."

Naturally? There was nothing natural about any of this. This was the twenty-first century. You didn't lose patients to gallstone surgery.

"Dr. Blake Jamison. Dr. Blake Jamison, please report to the E.R. as soon as possible. Please report to the E.R."

No way. This is not happening. Blake let out a deep sigh as he stepped back into the elevator. *At least it's not a Code Blue.*

"This way, Doctor. Follow me." Janice, a nurse assigned to assist him in the E.R. just the day before, held a grim expression. She led him to bay ten, where she stopped and flipped back a flimsy blue curtain.

"She's one of our nurses… Abigail Miller." Janice pulled him inside.

"I don't know her." Blake shook his head. A face that beautiful he definitely would have remembered. He drew closer. She was early twenties, pale with a long, golden braid flung across her shoulder. Her forehead had a nasty contusion. Her left arm sported a rough and fresh abrasion. "What happened to her?"

Janice shrugged. "The custodian found her like this in the stairwell off the third floor. Out cold. She hasn't even blinked."

"Pulse?"

"Rapid. BP low. This was found next to her." She handed him a large syringe.

Epinephrine, he read on the side label. Blake handed the syringe back to the nurse. With his other hand, he felt the woman's racing pulse at her neck. Her breathing was labored. Traumatic stress? "Get her on a monitor. Are you sure she was injected?"

Janice shook her head. "It was beside her. That's all I know."

"Is she known to have any severe allergies?"

Janice shook her head again. "No. She's never sick. Healthiest person I've ever met."

"You're sure nothing's broken? You moved her?"

This time Janice nodded. "Yes, Doctor. I'm sure the orderlies were very careful. No one would want to hurt Abigail."

Blake touched her cold cheek. "Miss Miller? Miss Miller? Wake up. I need you to tell me what happened."

On the outside, she lay there like Sleeping Beauty. On the inside, Blake knew that her body was fighting for its life. Janice rolled up the mobile heart monitor and began to put the sensors in place. As the cold nodes stuck to her skin, Abigail awoke with a start. She sat up, gasped for air and tried to reach for Janice. "It hurts. My chest. It hurts. I can't bre—"

The heart monitor sensors reacted with an alert.

Blake kept a firm hand on the woman's shoulder, pushing her back down to the bed. "Prep me a dose of Inderal, stat," he said. "She's going into cardiac arrest."

Just like Nicolas Hancock.

Chapter Two

Streams of blinding white light seeped under Abigail's heavy eyelids. Beeps and buzzes echoed in her ears. Everything around her whirled in a blurred circle. Fatigue. Nausea. Pain. Everywhere pain. Especially her head.

"Ugh." She lifted a sore arm only to touch a nice hard knot on the front of her head. *Ouch. What in the world? Where am I?*

She glanced around the small space. Heart monitor. Oxygen supply. Blood-pressure gauge. Blue hospital curtain wrapped around the small bed she lay in. *I'm in the Emergency Room!*

"Hello." A tall, sandy-haired man peered around the curtain at her, then stepped inside. He wore a white lab coat over a pressed blue oxford. His stethoscope and Fairview ID badge hung loosely around his opened collar.

"How are you feeling, Abigail?"

"I'm feeling a little confused." She looked down at her limp body in the hospital bed. "I don't remember how I got here.... I don't know you, Doctor, do I?"

"Nope. I'm new. Jamison. Blake Jamison."

"Nice to meet you, Dr. Jamison." Her mouth was dry and it hurt to try to sit up.

"Call me Blake. Please." He smiled. "And take it easy. You've had a pretty rough day. Don't worry if you aren't remembering everything just yet. You will."

Her head was foggy and thick, but she tried to focus. An IV drip fed into her left hand. The doctor—Blake—sat on a stool to her right. She was suddenly very aware of the fact that he was a handsome man, with a nice build and a kind face.

"So, why am I here?"

"I was sort of hoping you could tell me that. Maybe once your head clears up." He took her wrist in his hand. He studied her face as he counted her pulse. A strange and awkward sensation passed over Abby as his fingertips pressed her skin. She was unaccustomed to the touch of a man and especially that of a fancy *Englischer*.

"I didn't know Fairview was getting a new E.R. doctor. When did you start?"

"Well… I'm just here temporarily. I'm filling in for Dr. Finley."

"Oh, right. I remember now reading something about him teaching a course in one of the hospital newsletters. I didn't realize he would be away from the hospital for that. Do you often fill in for doctors on leave?"

"This is my first time. I have a private practice in New York. I'm just here for a change of scenery. Eight weeks. Then I'll go back." He released her arm. His lips pursed, as if he was thinking about something far away. "Seventy-two. Much better. You had me pretty scared there. Never a dull moment at this place."

He used his stethoscope and listened to her breathing and her heart. Then he whipped the instrument out from his ears and again rested it like an adornment around his neck. The light scent of musky cologne wafted over her.

"Did you say *never a dull moment?*" She tilted her head and glanced at him sideways. "I am still at Fairview Hospital, right?"

He chuckled and started to respond when an electronic device at his waist began to vibrate. "See what I mean?"

He took the phone into his hands, silenced it, read the message and returned it to his waist. "Not important. So, how's the head?"

"It's a little tender."

"I'll have Janice bring you some Tylenol. Drink lots of fluids. Get some more rest. I'll check back in another hour."

"Wait. I have questions. You can't leave yet." She wanted more information than that. "How did I get here? Where did this bruising come from? Why am I hooked up to a heart monitor? How long was I unconscious? And why?"

His phone began to buzz again. He clenched his jaw as he looked at the screen and silenced it. "Sorry. Friends back in New York who think I'm available 24/7. Not important. Again. And that's a lot of questions. I thought the doctor always asked the questions."

"You can't expect me to just lie here and not know what happened." She met his steady gaze.

"I might if I think that's what's best for you."

What? Who did this doctor think he was? Was he really not going to tell her anything? "At least tell me what day it is."

"It's Thursday," he said, following it up with the date.

"Thursday," she repeated. She leaned back into her pillow with a frown. It seemed that her memory was only missing most of one day. The damage could have been much worse…and yet it was troubling to think of those lost hours, especially given the injuries she'd sustained.

"You look upset." He stepped back inside the curtained area. "Worrying about your memory may only block it longer. Try to relax. Think about the things you did early this morning."

Abby shook her head. "Nothing. I don't remember a thing. Please, isn't there anything you can tell me about what happened? At least explain the heart monitor."

"Well, we aren't completely certain, but apparently, you took a hefty dose of epinephrine." His words were slow. His tone kind and compassionate. "Fortunately, you're strong and your body quickly absorbed much of the excess. We gave you something to calm your heart. It worked just the way it was supposed to—the monitor is just here as a precaution. You're going to be fine. There will be no long-term effects."

"Epinephrine?"

"Yes, it almost threw you into cardiac arrest."

"How? Why would I take epinephrine? That's crazy. Are you sure?" In a blink, Abby had a flash image of a shaking hand raising a needle to her arm. It was dark, like nighttime.

"You were found with an empty syringe, which we are pretty certain contained a killer amount of epinephrine before having a meeting with your arm."

"Wait a minute, what else? I—I…" She looked down at her bruised arm. Her pulse started to rise. Someone had held her. So tight. She remembered her arm had felt as if it might break. She also remembered a man so close she could feel his breath on her neck. Abby shivered.

"Someone gave me a shot. He was holding me around the arm. But where was I? And how did I get here?"

Blake's lips pressed together as he seemed to consider how much to tell her. He frowned. "The custodian found you on the third floor. He said you were out cold in the stairwell by that big hall that's being renovated. He's the one who brought you down. He saved your life. Now, look, you're getting too worked up. Try to rest. We can continue this conversation in a bit. You're very weak."

The third floor. Cold gray eyes. Abby could feel the tension rising in her, and it wasn't because of her condition. She locked eyes with the doctor. More images shot through her mind. *Gurney. Syringe. Eyes. Icy, fiery eyes.* She flung the sheet off her lap and swung her legs over the side of the bed. "I need to go back upstairs. Someone's in trouble. I wasn't the only one who was injected."

Blake placed a hand on her shoulder that gently but firmly kept her from moving. "Slow down, Abby. You could still be under the effects of the drugs."

"No. Really, I'm fine." She slipped from his reach and stood. Her legs felt like cooked spaghetti. Blake caught her as she leaned back for support.

"It will have to wait, Abby. You need to rest."

"I'll rest later." She pushed the doctor and his restraining arms away.

She didn't remember all the details of her attack, but she knew someone else had been in danger. She couldn't wait a minute longer—she might already be too late.

Blake could hardly believe the beautiful but provoking patient had talked him into letting her out of bed. Of course, when she'd plucked the IV from the back of her hand with a single yank, it was clear she was going to get up to the third floor with or without his approval. Since his shift had ended, he thought it best to accompany her. At least that way he could confine her to a wheelchair and keep an eye on her.

"Janice told me that you were raised Amish," Blake commented as he wheeled her into the elevator.

She nodded. "It's true."

"So why did you decide to stop being Amish? If you don't mind me asking?"

She laughed. "I don't mind you asking at all. But I wouldn't say that I stopped being Amish. I may not wear the clothes, but in here—" she touched her chest where her heart would be "—I will always be Amish. I didn't take vows to commit myself to the church because I wanted to continue nursing."

The elevator stopped at the third floor and Blake turned them toward the renovation area, taking in her words, which were more personal to him than she knew. "At the risk of sounding ignorant, I'm going to ask. Nursing isn't allowed?"

"No, it's not. It's *Hochmut*." Abby smiled and waved hellos to the few staff members they passed. "The Amish can have shops, build furniture or buildings, and farm. Professions that require higher degrees are not pursued."

"Hochmut?"

"Ja. Hochmut," she repeated with a teasing look, correcting his pronunciation.

"I don't speak Pennsylvania Dutch." Blake felt himself blush—her unfamiliar words were just another reminder of how little he knew of this place where he had come to find answers about himself.

"It means 'arrogance.' It's what comes with letting

the world in, with studying and learning more than needed. By going to school and becoming a nurse, I've become too much a part of the world. In many ways, I'm not worthy to take vows. But I have vowed in my own way to take care of people. My people. They need health care that they are comfortable with and I can provide that. I think I made the right decision. One day my family will understand. Some of them already do."

Blake tried to wrap his head around the Amish culture. After the letter his mother had left him, he'd researched anything and everything Amish. But now that he was there in Lancaster, he realized there was still so much to learn. And there was already one strike against him. Would his biological family think less of him for his medical profession?

"How about you?" She looked back at him with her bright blue eyes. "Why did you leave New York? And how did you pick Fairview Hospital of all places?"

Blake had a stock answer for that question. It was the one he'd given to everyone else who'd asked him, even his closest friends. No one knew the real reason he'd come to Lancaster. He'd told no one that he had recently found out that he'd been adopted, that he'd been born in Lancaster, not in New York City as he'd thought his entire life. He could hardly process the news himself, much less deliver it to others and expect them to understand. It was best to sort it out first. By himself. Yet he found himself on the verge of telling Abby the truth.

"Lots of reasons," he said in a low voice.

"Dr. Jamison. Dr. Jamison." The young nurse from Nicolas Hancock's room raced after him, waving a set of papers. "Here, Doctor. I called Mr. Hancock's lawyer, but I only spoke with a receptionist. She wouldn't let me through, nor would she tell me if there was a next of kin to notify."

"Thank you." Blake took the papers.

She glanced at the closed doors to the renovation area and easily guessed their intentions. "The renovation area has been locked up after what happened to you, Abby. But if you want to take a look, then we might have a key at the station." She started back in the direction she'd come. "I have your hermetically sealed IV and tubing, too, Doctor. Would you like to have that, too?"

"Yes, if you could bring the IV, too, I'd appreciate it."

Abby looked up at him. "Hancock? Did she say your patient's name was Hancock?"

"Yes. Nicolas Hancock." He handed Abby the chart so he could steer the wheelchair. "But he wasn't really my patient. Supposedly, he was a transfer. Somehow my name got on that chart. My signature, even—but I never laid eyes on him until I was paged for a Code Blue. I came right away but it was too late. The crash team tried and tried to resuscitate but he didn't make it."

Abigail stared down at the front page of the chart in her lap. "I've seen this before."

"Seen what?" Blake thought again about the fact that Hancock and Abby had had elevated adrenaline levels. Had that not been a coincidence?

"This chart. This name. This patient." Her eyes were wide.

"What? What do you mean? I thought you worked in Maternity."

Before she could answer, the young nurse returned with a set of keys to unlock the refinished wing. She opened the doors and handed Blake a small sealed plastic bag, which had *Hancock* printed across the side. He hung it on the back of the chair, thanked the nurse for her help and rolled Abby into the closed-off wing. The farther they got into the hallway, the more the blood had drained from Abby's face. He stopped the chair and walked in front of her. He took her arm and checked her pulse.

"Your heart is racing and you look really tired, Abby. This is too much. Let's go back down and rest. As you can see, the hallway is empty. There's no one else here."

"That doctor was *here*." Abby, white as snow, pushed him aside. She stood and began to move through the dim hallway. "He was here. In this hallway with that patient." She pointed at the chart. "He gave him an injection. Blake, I saw it. I wasn't supposed to, but I did. That's why he injected me, too."

"What doctor? What are you talking about?" Blake moved quickly around the wheelchair and put a hand under her shoulder to support her. He took the chart from her hands and tossed it back onto the wheelchair so he could take her hand. "I really think this is too much for you right now. Please sit back down. You're not really making a lot of sense."

"He tried to tell me that patient had a highly contagious disease, but I knew it wasn't true. There was no indication of it on his chart." Her pulse quickened as she pressed against him.

Blake didn't answer. She was already too worked up. He should never have let her talk him into this stupid excursion. "You need to be resting. Come on."

Abby continued, ignoring his efforts to make her return to the wheelchair. Her persistence was admirable, he supposed. But as a doctor, he had to object to the way she was putting herself at risk. But she would not stop. She continued down the hallway without his help.

"So how did he die?" She looked back at him.

"Cardiac arrest."

"Too much epinephrine?"

"Too much adrenaline. Yeah. Probably epinephrine. We saved the IV tubing—that's what's in the bag that the nurse brought to me. We might be able to get some idea of what the patient was given…but…" He caught up to her, trying to make sense of what she was saying. "Abby, are you saying you saw another doctor inject Hancock with medication? *Here?* Not in the patient's room?"

Click.

The doors behind them, the ones they'd come through, closed tight. The lock popped and the sound of it echoed down the dead, dark corridor. It was pitch-black.

Abby shuddered against Blake's supportive arm.

"Let's get you back. I think you've remembered enough for now." Blake started to redirect them the way that they'd come. "I'm sure someone will hear us if we knock."

But Abby pulled against him. "We are much closer to the stairwell. You said that's where the custodian found me, right?"

"Right." Blake shook his head, following behind her in the darkness. "Really, please, let me get you back to that wheelchair…. Are all Amish women this stubborn?"

"Most are much worse." She pushed open the door of the stairwell. There was some dim lighting.

"I'll keep that in mind in case I have any more Amish patients." Blake linked an arm gently under hers, supporting most of her weight. He led her carefully down the stairs. Shadows seemed to dance above them in the dim lighting. Twice she stopped and looked up.

"Do you...?" Were his eyes playing tricks on him? He could have sworn he saw someone above them. A shadow. A movement. Someone dressed in white.

"Yes," Abby said. "I see little..."

Blake frowned at her words. She was seeing it, too. He wasn't imagining them. A shadow passed over the wall beside them. "Lights? Shadows?"

She nodded. They continued a few more steps.

He tried to hurry her down to the ground floor. "I'm sure it's nothing. I guess our eyes are not adjusting to the bad lighting."

A loud clanging sounded overhead. Abby, startled by the sound, slipped on the next step. Blake helped straighten and steady her. He had to get her back to bed. She was about to collapse.

Clang. Metal against metal. Louder and louder. Something was falling. The sound echoed through the space, coming closer and closer.

He looked up, as did Abby, who was growing faint. He could feel her legs buckling. Blake wrapped himself around her and pushed them both under the cover of the second-floor landing. Something was coming down in a hurry and they had to move or get hit.

A magnificent crash sounded behind him.

A stainless-steel surgical tray landed in the very spot where they'd stood, complete with an assortment of sharp scalpels and other surgical instruments, which rattled down around them like a metal rainstorm.

Once the stairs were quiet, Blake lifted his hands to Abby's shoulders. "You okay?"

"No. I'm not." Her body trembled under his hands as she shook her head from side to side. "I think someone is trying to kill me."

Chapter Three

An hour later, Blake's thoughts were swimming as he sat with Abby and two policemen in a special conference room of the hospital. The more time they spent going over the particulars of the assault and the incident in the stairwell, the more confused he felt.

He shook his head. Nothing seemed to make sense these days. His parents' accident. The revelation of his adoption. His inheritance. His arrival in Lancaster to search for his birth parents. He couldn't even decide if he wanted to find his birth parents or not…and he might not have a choice. The search, after all, could very well lead to nothing.

Then again, it could change his life.

Blake wasn't sure which of those results he wanted. The future seemed so muddled. He wasn't used to that.

In any case, working on his search wouldn't be happening today. He wasn't even sure if he would be able to leave the hospital anytime soon. The more he and Abby repeated their stories to the police, the crazier and crazier the whole thing sounded. If it hadn't actually happened to him, he would not have believed it himself.

"And the name of the patient that died from cardiac

arrest?" Chief McClendon scratched his thinning red hair. He was tall and lean and looked like a man you did not want to cross.

"Hancock. Nicolas Hancock." Blake shook his head. "I had an extra copy of his transfer chart, but I left it on the wheelchair when we went to the stairwell, and—"

"Someone swiped it," Abby said. "That was right before the tray of scalpels came down on us."

"Right. By the time I got back up to the third floor to make another copy, the original chart was gone, too. And the bag containing the IV and tubing that I'd left with the wheelchair, as well." Blake felt his phone buzz yet again. A friend, a colleague, a lawyer from New York, no doubt. He silenced the phone.

"So no chart? And now it seems there's no body, either?" the chief repeated. "No evidence that the man was here at all, except for the testimony from you and the crash team, and the bruising and wounds inflicted on Miss Miller after the alleged injection took place."

"I did go to the morgue," Blake continued. "And no...there's no Nicolas Hancock. The autopsist said he'd never gotten the body. And now if you check in the hospital's electronic files, you cannot even find the name Nicolas Hancock in the system."

"But his name was there earlier?"

"Yes, I checked it this afternoon. Before Miss Miller woke up in the E.R. I couldn't figure out how I was assigned to this patient I'd never seen. I thought I might see another doctor's name in there."

"And did you?"

"No."

"Sorry, I'm late to the meeting." A small-framed, middle-aged doctor hurried into the room. He moved with sharp gestures as he made his way around the room and shook hands with everyone. "I'm Dr. Dodd. I'm the head administrator of Fairview Hospital and I'm just flabbergasted at the events that have happened here today. Has anyone called the media?"

"No," said Chief McClendon. "And that better not happen, either."

"Don't worry." Dr. Dodd pressed his dark-framed glasses up the bridge of his nose. "I'll see to it that it doesn't. Hancock's body is in autopsy. I'll make sure the findings are not released to the public. Dr. Jamison, in the interim, your actions today will be under review. I understand both of you will be taking a few days off. I've already made arrangements for that. Now, if you don't have anything else for me, I have another meeting to attend. Please let my custodial staff know when they can reopen the stairwell. Keeping it shut off is a safety violation, you know."

"You have the body?" Blake asked.

"Of course. It's in autopsy. But naturally, you won't see the report until it gets to me and the authorities."

"I guess I don't understand why I'm under review." Blake frowned. He really wished he'd been able to save that IV tubing and possibly prove that someone had caused Hancock's death. "Hancock was dead when I arrived to his room. I'd never seen him before that. The nurses can confirm this. Whatever happened to him—" he looked at Abby "—it happened before I saw him."

"No worries, Dr. Jamison." Dr. Dodd smiled. "It's just a formality. All part of the paperwork."

"You have his chart?"

"Of course we have his chart." Dodd looked annoyed.

"I'll need a copy of that," McClendon said. "Thank you."

"Is that all?"

McClendon nodded. Dr. Dodd scrambled out of the room as quickly as he'd come in.

"I guess you didn't look in the right places, Dr. Jamison," said McClendon. "Then again, you *are* new here."

Blake shook his head. He was new—he wasn't stupid. He knew how to look up files and find a body in a morgue. He'd even spoken to the autopsist. He didn't like the idea of this review. And he definitely didn't like Dr. Dodd. Something was fishy about this whole mess, and in situations like this, the administration usually looked for a scapegoat to blame. Blake had a sinking feeling Dodd meant for that scapegoat to be him.

McClendon tapped more notes into his tablet, then looked to his younger colleague. "Langer, head to the morgue. See what you can find out. Get that file. Then question the crash team and every nurse who came in contact with Nicolas Hancock. Even talk to the person who added his data to the hospital patient files. Somebody has to know something. Do not mention the word *murder* or either the doctor's or Abigail's names. I don't want any of this leaking out."

"Yes, sir." Langer, who was built like a pit bull and was probably just as feisty, spun away from the hospital conference room and headed to the elevators.

McClendon stowed his tablet inside his front jacket pocket. "This is a delicate situation. While we want to cover all of our bases, the person we are looking for could very well work in the hospital. This isn't the kind of person we want to cause to panic. That could make the situation more dangerous.

"Now, we know that Miss Miller was assaulted and drugged. If your Hancock and her Hancock are one and the same, then it sounds like you both could be in a lot of danger."

"We witnessed a murder, right?"

Abby's blunt assessment of the day's events hit Blake like a ton of bricks. Murder? *Unbelievable*—Abby had witnessed a murder. And to some extent so had he. Blake could hardly wrap his head around it all.

"Right," McClendon agreed. "From what Dr. Dodd said, it sounds like the two of you will have the next few days off. My advice is for you both to keep your distance from the hospital until we see what kind of information we can pull together."

He moved toward Blake and placed a card in his hand. "I'll be in touch. Make sure Miss Miller gets safely home." The chief tipped his head to Abigail, then left them alone in the conference room.

Blake stared after the chief for a long moment. What a day. He could barely take it all in. He was exhausted. And he could only imagine that Abby must be even more so, considering all the abuse her body had taken. Of course, if she'd just stayed in her bed in the E.R., some of the trouble could have been avoided.

He turned back to Miss Abigail Miller. Looked as if he was to give her a ride home. Frankly, he was glad to have the excuse to keep an eye on her a bit longer. She'd pushed herself too hard today and needed someone to make sure she went straight home and got some rest. Although as tough and stubborn as she was, she probably already had her own ideas about that.

He wouldn't admit to himself that he found the woman's ridiculous determination rather intriguing. Or that he found her pretty, too. Naturally pretty, not like many of the women he knew back in New York who spent a lot of money in order to look a certain way. Abby had smooth, creamy skin, huge blue eyes and a healthy glow, despite the lump on her head. And her energy— it was amazing. It drew everyone in—or at least, it drew him in.

Blake made a note to himself to be on his guard with Abby. Not only was she a patient, he had not come to Lancaster for romance. In fact, that was the *last* thing he needed in his life.

"I'm disappointed," she said. "I'd hoped there would be more they could do. And it all sounded so crazy as I was retelling what happened, you know?"

"Crazy but real. As real as whoever put those nasty bruises on you. Now that the body is in the morgue, I'm sure the investigation will move right along." Blake rubbed his hand through his hair. He didn't want to think about it anymore. He wanted dinner and a long, hot shower. "Let's get out of here."

"Am I allowed out of here?" She stood, too, a hopeful and wide-eyed expression on her face.

Blake smiled. "I already signed the release. But as I'm sure you already know, after a concussion you shouldn't spend the night alone. Someone has to be with you and wake you up at certain intervals during the night."

"Right." She let out a long sigh. "I guess I'll go to Eli's."

Was Eli a boyfriend? Abby definitely wasn't married. Everyone had been calling her *Miss* Miller. Blake shook his head. Why was he even thinking about that? "You shouldn't drive, either. You've had a lot of medication today."

She checked her watch and frowned. "Hmm…that's a problem. Janice has already gone home and most of my other friends and family drive buggies."

"I'm staying at the Willow Trace Bed-and-Breakfast. Are you headed in that direction?"

"Actually, that's not far from where my brother lives," she said. "Would you mind terribly?"

"Eli is your brother?" He lifted an eyebrow.

"Yes, and he drives a buggy, or I'd ask him to pick me up himself." She smiled. She had a fabulous smile. "He used to drive a Mustang, but now he's back to a buggy…. So, do I get a ride or what?"

"Oh, yes. Of course." Blake felt his face flood with heat. "I thought I already said that."

Abby collected her things from her nurse's locker and followed the new doctor to his car—one very expensive SUV.

Hochmut—that was what her father would say if he saw her in that fancy vehicle. Bishop Miller would shake his head and disapprove, just as he seemed to do of everything she decided these days. Her father didn't know how much his condemnation hurt—she wouldn't let it show. She couldn't.

Anyway, it would be silly not to take the ride from the doctor. He was headed in the same direction. And hopefully, her father would not be visiting when she arrived at her brother's.

Blake drove slowly out of the hospital parking lot. Almost immediately, they came up behind an Amish buggy. Abby sighed. Looked as if it might be a long, slow drive to Eli's.

"This highway is not a good one for passing," Abby said.

Blake was just about to reply when his phone rang. Again. It was almost nonstop—buzzing, ringing, vibrating. What could be so important?

"Sounds like someone needs to get in touch with you very badly," she said.

"Excuse me," he said to her, then answered the phone. "Hello…No, I can't…I'm not in the city….I don't know….You'll just have to figure it out….Not anytime soon….Okay…Bye."

He put the device away.

"I'm sorry. People back home keep forgetting I'm not in town. It's crazy. It's ringing all the time." He looked embarrassed or flustered or both. "In a few days it will slow down… I hope."

"So, getting away from all of that—is that one of your *reasons* for coming to Lancaster?" she asked. "Or are you interested in the countryside? The Amish? Horses and buggies? Avoiding a nightmare family you left behind?"

He laughed at her teasing. He was quite handsome when he smiled. Abby turned away as a strange rush of emotions shot through her.

"All of those things." He looked at his phone. "I guess some things are harder to get away from than others. But I don't have any family."

"Everyone has family."

"I don't."

She glanced over at him, waiting for an explanation.

"Only child. And my parents died recently."

Abby dropped her head. "I'm so sorry. I didn't mean to bring up something so—"

"No, no. It's fine. The accident was months ago," he said.

"I'm still very sorry." Abby turned and looked out the window. "Can I ask what kind of accident?"

"A plane crash." Blake relaxed his hands on the beautiful mahogany steering wheel. "You know, one of those little island-hopper planes. The computer inside malfunctioned. They hit a storm. It just happened. It wasn't anyone's fault."

"You must miss them terribly."

He smiled, but it was a sad, regretful sort of smile that touched Abby's heart at its core.

"So what else? You said you came to Lancaster for lots of reasons. So tell me a few. To get away from your phone and what else?"

"Well, the rest of it is a long story." He smiled at her again. "But *you,* you are doing remarkably well after all you've been through today."

"Thanks, but I feel like a wreck. A train wreck, actually. I can't wait to get to my brother's and collapse."

There was a moment of silence.

"So, another reason you came to Fairview?" she prodded him, not liking the silence. "Come on. It takes my mind off the assault."

"Okay, another reason… Actually, I was going to tell you earlier but then we started talking about… Never mind." He shook his head. "So another reason I came to Lancaster is to find something. I might have a family connection here I plan to look up."

"But I thought you didn't have any family."

"Well, I don't. I don't know these people. And it may be nothing. Really, forget I mentioned it." He changed the subject. "Did you need to stop by your own place? You must need to get some things? Some clothes? A toothbrush?"

"Oh, no. That's okay. I can borrow things from my sister-in-law." She hadn't thought about going by her place, but he was right. She really did need to at some point. Still, she didn't want to impose, nor did she want to take any longer than necessary to get to Eli's. She was still quite unsettled after the day's events.

"I really don't mind," he said.

He seemed sincere, so Abby decided to infringe on his kindness a bit further. The more she thought about it, if she didn't go by her house, then Eli would have to, and that would upset Hannah and get the night off to a bad start. "Actually, if you really wouldn't mind, it would give me a chance to check on Zoe, Chloe and Blue-jeans."

"Zoe, Chloe and Blue-jeans?" He shot her a furtive look.

"My two cats and my horse."

"You have a horse?"

"Yes, and a buggy, too. I couldn't decide if I wanted to sell it or not." Abby glanced at Blake. His big, chocolate eyes were soft and smiling. The rest of him was stiff and businesslike. At the hospital he'd been like that, too—two-sided. One very kind. The other standoffish. She wondered which message was the true Blake.

"I would love to ride in a horse and buggy," he said.

"Well, when I'm feeling better, I'd be happy to take you out in mine." Abby stopped as the words sank in. To an Amish man, an invitation like that would sound as if she was inviting him on a courting date. Fortunately, the doctor wasn't Amish and would take the invitation in the spirit it was given—as a friendly gesture and nothing more.

"Sounds like a plan," he said. "Thank you. And of course, you should check on your animals. You should have said so. You live on a farm? You must have some land if you have a horse, right? This is all new to me. I've lived my whole life in an apartment on the Upper East Side."

The upper east side of what? Am I supposed to know what he's talking about? "It's not a farm," she said. "I mean it is. But I don't farm anything. I run a clinic. I lease the land out to a real farmer.... Sorry. I'm rambling."

Following her directions, Blake maneuvered his way slowly around the buggy that they'd been stuck behind for the past quarter mile. A few minutes later, they pulled up in front of her home and clinic.

"I'll be quick." She hopped out of the car but paused when she saw how dark the house was. If it hadn't been for the headlights of Blake's car, they wouldn't have been able to see a thing.

"Is something wrong?" He parked in her semicircle driveway, leaving his headlights to shine over the front porch.

"I don't think so." She forced a smile and searched in her bag for the house key. A feeling of dread passed through her. She couldn't shake the feeling that something was wrong here, but she tried to ignore it. Likely it was nothing more than nerves—hardly surprising after the day she'd had. "I guess the sensors on my porch lights are broken? Those lights usually come on when it gets dark."

"Let me come up to the door with you, just to be safe. You weren't too steady on your feet earlier and shouldn't be stumbling around in the dark." He turned off the engine, but left his headlights on to shine over the front porch. "What a great house."

"Thanks." Abby fumbled with her key, taking what seemed like an interminably long time to unlock the door. Blake stood back as she went in and reached for the lights. Nothing happened as she flicked the light switch.

"Looks like the power is out." She headed across the dark space to a small hutch. She tried to turn on a small lamp. Nothing. "Yep, it must be the power. I have a flashlight in the bottom drawer here. Once we get to the kitchen, I can check the electrical panel. Just a second."

Abby rummaged through the drawers of the hutch. "I know that flashlight is—"

Blake's hand came down on her shoulder, giving her a chill.

"Shh," he whispered. "There's someone else in the house."

Abby swallowed hard as her hands finally landed around the flashlight she'd been looking for. Turning it on, she pointed it down the hallway in time to see a dark shadow flash across the entrance to her kitchen. Blake's hand swiftly eased the light from her hand.

"Stay here," he said before taking off toward the dark figure.

Abby wasn't about to stand there in the dark. She followed right behind him, feeling a cold blast of night air blow over her as she entered the kitchen. Blake flashed the light in every direction. The back door was wide-open. Whoever the intruder had been, he'd escaped without a sound.

Chapter Four

Abby rushed for the open door, but Blake grabbed her arm and pulled her back. After the day they'd had, he wasn't too sure running out into the darkness after the unknown was a good idea. Better to fix whatever had been done to the electricity. It would be much easier to spot the intruder with the floodlights on.

"I thought I told you to stay put."

"I didn't want to stay back there in the dark by my-self."

Blake couldn't argue with her reasoning, even though he was pretty certain he'd never met anyone as hard-headed as Abby Miller. In any case, he'd spotted her circuit-breaker panel a few feet from the door. The door to the panel had been opened as if someone had been making adjustments.

"Maybe the power wasn't off after all. Looks like someone's been messing with your breakers. Here, take this." He handed the flashlight to her. "Shine the light this way."

Blake opened the metal panel. As he'd suspected, the main breaker had been turned off. He flipped it back to the "on" position. Abby was right beside him, turning on both the inside and outside lights. The backyard lit up. Together they scanned the area from the back stoop. Blake saw open fields, a run-in shed and a horse grazing in a large paddock. No intruder.

"I guess we surprised whoever it was and he left."

"I hope so," Blake said. "But let's check the rest of the house anyway."

Room by room, Blake followed Abby through the house. Nothing looked out of order. When they reached the foyer again, Blake noticed an interior door that in the darkness he hadn't seen behind the front entrance. The sign on the door read Abigail Miller, R.N. and Certified Midwife, Consultation, Mondays and Wednesdays 12–4. "Impressive."

"Thanks. I went all-out when I designed the clinic. I wanted to bring the best to Willow Trace." She walked past him. "And this door was locked when I left for the hospital this morning. I'm certain of that."

Blake followed her into the clinic and saw that Abigail had built a state-of-the-art facility inside the old cottage. It had been thoughtfully and tastefully done and unlike the rest of the house, which had been so simple and plain, everything here spoke of modern medicine and technology. In its usual state, it was unquestionably very impressive. Right now, it looked like a disaster area. Abby gasped as she staggered forward. Broken glass crunched under her feet. The examining area had been trashed. Boxes of supplies had been strewn across the space. All the shelves had been stripped and their contents spilled all over the table, counters and flooring.

Tears streamed down her face. He could tell she was trying to wipe them away before he could see, but they wouldn't stop. "I'm sorry. I'm just so tired. And this is so unbelievable.... Two weeks ago, I decide that my calling is nursing, that I don't want to give it up. I told my family. My father. He's so upset with me. I had such a peace about it…but now? My wonderful clinic that I created just a few years ago has been ruined and I… don't know. I don't know what to do."

Blake knew she wasn't really talking to him, just venting aloud her frustration and fatigue. His heart felt heavy for her. He felt as if the very center of his life had been destroyed, too, when his parents died in that plane crash. He and Abby definitely had something in common—they were both struggling with their direction and their families.

He looked at her standing there sobbing. He had to do something. He couldn't just go on as if she were fine. She was a patient, after all. If a patient were crying, he would give them a hug, right?

Slowly, Blake put his arm around her shoulders and gave her a comforting squeeze. To his great astonishment, Abby turned into his chest and wept against his shoulder. Blake didn't know what to do. Keep hugging her? Push her back? He didn't move. But he couldn't help but catch the soft floral fragrance of her hair and her skin. After a moment, he unfroze himself, slid his hands to her shoulders and pushed her back.

Abigail's embarrassment was evident in her flushed cheeks and splotchy neck. "I'm sorry. I didn't mean to fall apart on you. I'm not usually this…this…"

"You have every right to fall apart." He grazed her cheek with the back of his hand. "I just thought we should call the police. Again."

He pulled out his cell phone and the card that Chief McClendon had passed to him only a few hours earlier. He dialed the number while trying to give Abby a reassuring smile. "Maybe later I can help you clean it up. It's not so bad. Right?"

Abby broke into a watery smile and chuckled. "Right. Not so bad."

As the phone line began to ring, Blake swallowed hard. Abby was like no one he'd ever met—such an odd mixture of independence and vulnerability, of determination and quick wits. He was going to have to be on his guard about more than this person who was after them, because if there was one thing in his life he did not need or have time for, it was romance.

"Abby, I can't believe you didn't send Chief McClendon here to tell me what happened to you today." Her big brother, Eli, paced his kitchen, pulling on his suspenders and shaking his head of thick blond hair as he walked.

"I was coming straight here." She could hardly speak from exhaustion. She couldn't stop shaking and her head throbbed terribly. "Blake was nice enough to swing by my house so that I could pick up some clothes and feed the animals, and that's when we walked in on whoever that was. Anyway, there was no point in telling you sooner. What could you do? There's nothing to do except try to get away from it all and wait for the police to catch the man responsible. And that's why I'm here."

Even though she still felt like a sitting duck. She'd thought being at her brother's would make her feel safe, but instead, she now worried that she and Blake had just brought danger with them.

"I don't know. There's got to be something we can do," Eli said. "Chief McClendon told you to lie low?"

"Not in those exact words." Blake spoke from the corner of the kitchen. Abby blushed at the sound of his voice. She'd hardly been able to look at him after she'd fallen apart at the clinic. Practically jumping into his arms. She wished he'd dropped her off and gone straight back to the bed-and-breakfast. But once Hannah heard they'd had nothing to eat, she wouldn't allow Blake to escape.

"Is McClendon still at your house?" Eli asked.

"I imagine so." Blake's brown eyes were soft again. Not hard and shocked like after the scene at the clinic. "There was an entire crew there, taking pictures and samples."

"That's good. Maybe they'll lift some prints." Eli continued to pace. He was making her dizzy.

"Relax, Eli." Abby gave him a hard stare. "You're not a detective anymore, remember?"

He ignored her. "Was anything missing from your house?"

"Nothing in the house—not that I noticed, anyway. But in the clinic. Most of my medicines were sabotaged. Opened. Slashed. Contaminated. And oddly they stole all my epi-packs."

"Epi-packs?"

Blake cleared his throat. "They're for people with severe allergies. Like an emergency kit. The EpiPen is a small dose of epinephrine, which prevents an allergy from sending someone into anaphylactic shock. They have saved a lot of parents trips to the hospitals and even saved lives. Epinephrine is the same drug that I believe was given to Abigail and to Mr. Hancock to send them into cardiac arrest."

"So too much of a good drug can kill?" Eli asked.

"Exactly," Blake said. "And epinephrine is not traceable like other drugs in the body because it is produced naturally."

"What's strange to me is that this person took the

epi-packs *after* he killed Hancock. What was the point of that?" Abby said. "And the amount of epinephrine he dosed me with was way more than what is in an epi-pack. Clearly, he has access to the drug on his own, so why steal my packs?"

"He's probably trying to scare you. Or throw off the investigation." Eli stroked his short beard. "It takes everyone's eyes off the hospital for a while. Maybe there is unfinished business there."

"Like killing patients in dark hallways?" Abby said.

"We must get ahead of this guy instead of behind him. The first attempt when he drugged you was serious. He was feeling powerful. But the stairwell and the break-in seem more like scare tactics. He's not as confident as he was and we should try to keep it that way."

"How do we get ahead of this person? We don't know who he is or where he is," Abby said.

Eli looked up at her with a hopeful expression. "You can describe him, right?"

"Not really." Abby shook her head. "He was wearing scrubs and a mask. I saw his eyes. That's about it."

"Well, the perpetrator could be anyone, not necessarily a doctor from the hospital. But if you have an idea of his size, his voice, skin color—with the computers the composite artists use now, you wouldn't believe how well they can narrow down a suspect list."

"Not tonight." Abby held up her hand. She couldn't take any more talk about the situation. Her brother meant well but he did not seem to understand what an ordeal she had been through.

Blake stepped forward. "I would have to agree. She needs rest."

Her brother turned to Blake, then back to her. Abby

hid a grin—another man having an opinion about her welfare had definitely thrown her brother off-kilter.

"Essa!" Hannah placed several plates in the center of the table and waved them all over. "Time to eat. Everyone to the table."

Eli led them in a prayer of thanksgiving. Abby could have listened to his words all night. Eli was a true man of God—he knew where his strength came from. And what kind of man was Blake? At the amen, she glanced at him. Were those tears in his eyes? She watched him wipe them away quickly as he dug into his dinner. This was one man she did not understand—he seemed to change more than the weather and she'd only known him for one day.

"Wow. This is wonderful." Blake had a faraway look in his eyes as he complimented her family on the house and the dinner.

"So, Blake…" Hannah started. "You're a doctor at Fairview?"

"Yes. Well, temporarily."

"And you're from New York?"

"Yes."

Eli slapped the table. "Didn't you say the patient Hancock was from New York, too?"

Abby nodded with a smile. Her brother could barely contain himself. He was concerned for her, but he was also reliving his work as a Philadelphia police detective. It was not too long ago he'd come home on a case to help Hannah find the men that had killed her stepdaughter. In the end, he'd decided to stay and leave his *Englischer* life behind, but his years of training and experience as a detective were still a part of him. He let out a long sigh. "I really need to talk to McClendon."

"Well, that's not happening tonight," Hannah said.

"No calls in the house. Let's just have a nice, relaxing dinner and worry about all of that tomorrow."

Blake's phone sounded almost simultaneously with Hannah's reminder of the no-cell-phones rule. Blake grabbed his phone from his pocket and silenced it. "Sorry. I'll just turn it off. I didn't even realize how much I'm on my phone until I came here. I guess back in New York, everyone is, so no one thinks anything about it. I think tomorrow I may just leave it in my hotel room."

"Well, not a bad idea, Dr. Jamison. We don't use them in this house." Hannah's tone was kind but firm.

"Don't feel bad," Eli said, teasing his wife. "She asked me to get rid of my gun. A cell phone is nothing."

Hannah waved away her husband's words. "Speaking of your life back in New York, Dr. Jamison...you're not married, are you?"

"No. I'm not." Hannah's tone had sounded a slight bit chastising. "Is that a problem?"

"Of course not," Abby said, glaring at Hannah so that she would not continue with the same topic. "It's just a common topic around here. With the Amish. Especially among the women."

Hannah looked indignant. "Oh, don't mind me. I'm just getting to know our guest. What brings you here to Willow Trace, Dr. Jamison?"

Blake had just shoved a large forkful of meat into his mouth and couldn't answer.

"Blake has family here, don't you, Blake?" Abby smiled. She'd purposely caught him off guard. Now he would have to answer what she'd been trying to figure out all day—why was Dr. Jamison at Fairview Hospital?

Blake swallowed down the lump of stew before he could answer. He'd almost rather talk about his pathetic love life than about why he was in Lancaster. "Maybe. I said that maybe I have a family connection in Lancaster."

There was clearly another question bubbling inside of Abigail, but a knock at the door sounded before she could get it out.

Eli excused himself from the table to get the door. Hannah hopped up to take care of the dishes. Blake and Abby tried to follow but Hannah stopped them.

"Go on into the other room." Hannah shooed them away like little flies. "Both of you. Sounds like we have visitors. I'll see to the kitchen. Go on. Go relax and visit. You've both done enough today."

Blake followed Abby into the living area, which, like the rest of the home, was tastefully but simply decorated. The walls were undecorated, simply painted a shade of light blue. All of the big windows were covered with green shades and simple white curtains. There were a few dim lamps set on handmade wooden tables. A sofa and several lightly upholstered chairs were placed about in an orderly circle.

Eli stoked the fire while his newly arrived guests sat together on the couch—a young couple holding a sleeping baby while their older child stood against his father. The boy stared wide-eyed at Blake and Abby as they entered the room.

"Mary!" Abigail rushed forward. She hugged the young mother and swept the sleeping child from her arms. "Little Levi. Oh, isn't he just beautiful? And, Stephen, you are so grown up—*sehr grose*."

The little boy straightened up from his position against his father, standing tall and proud.

"Jonathan and Mary, this is Blake Jamsion—a doctor at the hospital. Blake, this is the Zook family. Mary and I have been friends all our lives. Her parents own the bed-and-breakfast where you are staying."

Blake shook hands with the couple, admiring their Amish dress, which matched Eli's and Hannah's exactly—trousers, suspenders and simply cut shirts for the men, plain blue dresses and black aprons for the women. Little Stephen wore a miniature version of the grown men's clothing. He whispered something to his father, then took off out the front door.

"He likes to visit all of Eli's stock. We don't have the cattle Eli has here. He's fascinated by it," Jonathan explained. He had the same peculiar, square beard as Eli did, only around the jawline. No mustache. A strange and unique look. Blake couldn't remember seeing anything like it before.

Mary's hair, like Hannah's, was tucked up in a white *Kapp.* He glanced at Abigail and her long blond braid, maybe a little glad it wasn't hidden under a *Kapp.* He wondered what it might look like loose and free-flowing.

"We heard you had some trouble up at the hospital," Jonathan said.

"*Ja,* you could say that." Abby spun around with the tiny infant. "How did you hear?"

The couple explained how the news had spread from the hospital to another couple from the church to their neighbors. "We didn't know if Eli had heard, so we thought we should come over. We knew he'd want to know about his sister. We should have figured you'd be here telling him yourself."

"I'm glad you came. It's good to see you and the children. Just what I needed to get my mind off this afternoon."

Some conversation passed in Pennsylvania Dutch.

Blake sat back and listened to the lilting, rolling language. He didn't know if the talk was about him or the happenings at the hospital, but either way the language relaxed him. Called to him. Could it be that Amish blood ran through his veins? If he hadn't been put up for adoption, could he have grown up in a room like this instead of in a penthouse that overlooked Central Park?

"Well, at least you didn't go to the bishop." Abby broke back into English.

"Oh, but we did." Mary smiled. "We passed by there on the way here. He hadn't heard. He is very concerned. He would have been over to see you himself if he had not already had some other church business to attend to tonight. He assumed your brother would be looking after you as soon as he heard the news. But you should expect the bishop in the morning."

"Danki."

Even Blake could tell Abby was not happy about this news. She was not pleased that this bishop person knew her business.

"So, who is the bishop? Is he an elder of the church?" Blake asked.

Eli and Jonathan smiled at him. They looked at Abby. Everyone seemed to be holding back a laugh.

Except for Abigail. She turned, a sad frown under her big blue eyes. "The bishop is the leader of the *Ordnung*. The leader of the Amish church. He's also my father."

There was a second of silence over the room then the front door burst open like a bomb had blown it off its hinges. Little Stephen came running inside. He was pale and out of breath, and his hat was missing.

"What is it, Stephen?" his mother asked.

Her son ran into her arms, letting loose an onslaught of tears he'd bravely held back until that moment. He told his parents what had happened. Again, Blake couldn't understand the Amish language. But he watched as the rest of the people in the room reacted grimly to the boy's tale.

Whatever he said, it was not happy news. Several times they all looked at Abigail, who'd grown pale. As the boy finished, Abby put a hand to her head as if it ached worse than ever.

Eli stood and put a hand on his sister's shoulder. He nodded to Jonathan, and the two men headed for the door.

"Is something wrong? Can I help?" Blake stood with the other men.

Eli turned back, his expression bleak. "Someone is in the stable. He grabbed little Stephen and told him to go back to the house. He told him to tell Miss Miller that he is watching."

Chapter Five

Blake awoke early in his cozy bed at the bed-and-breakfast, his thoughts on Abby Miller and the string of strange events that occurred the day before. Someone had poisoned her and left her for dead on that empty third-floor wing of the hospital. That someone had already successfully killed Mr. Hancock, the transfer patient from New York, while manipulating the hospital's computer systems. Probably that same someone had dumped a tray of scalpels over their heads, broken into Abigail's clinic and sent a threatening message to her via a small Amish child, who'd been scared out of his wits.

Blake could not forget the horror on Abby's face as that child had told the others what had happened in the stable. She had looked beaten down. As her brother had pointed out later, that was most likely the man's intention—to beat her down until he caught up with her and eliminated her for catching him at the scene of the crime.

Eli and Jonathan had raced back to the barn after Stephen had returned, but whoever had spoken to the child had been long gone. Most strange was that the man had spoken Pennsylvania Dutch to the boy, realizing he was too young to understand English. This meant that whoever was after Abigail was close enough to the Plain folk to know their language. That narrowed down the list of suspects in Blake's mind. But Eli and McClendon had pointed out that it was very possible that more than one person was involved in all of this. Without a motive for the murder of Hancock, it was going to be very difficult to come up with an actual list of suspects. And how could they find a motive when there was no information about Hancock? He was a New Yorker with no known family or connections. Blake was afraid it would be a long time before the police got to the bottom of this affair, and that meant a long time before he and Abby could go back to the hospital.

Anyway, it was all so disturbing. Blake felt he was tied to these events in a way that went deeper than simply his name on Hancock's chart. But why, he couldn't say. It was probably nothing but silly conjecture on his part.

It was still early, but knowing he wouldn't sleep anymore with so much on his mind, Blake had a quick shower and shave. Then he dressed in jeans and an oxford before sitting down at the small corner desk where he'd plugged in his laptop. A hundred-plus emails loaded into his inbox. He had let them accumulate over the past three days while he'd been busy with his new job—now he had to deal with messages from his partners in his medical practice, from his friends in New York and from Natalie. The same people who kept texting and calling and needing him for this or that.

He had left New York without a lot of fanfare. None of his Manhattan friends knew the real reason he'd come to Willow Trace—not even Natalie, who had, at one time, been his fiancée. Things between them had ended before he lost his parents and found out the truth about his background, so not even she knew why he felt he needed to be here. And that was the way he wanted to keep it. For now. This was something he wanted to explore on his own.

Strange how it didn't bother him that he'd almost told Abby after only knowing her for a few hours. Just like he didn't care that she'd seen him shed a tear during the prayer. In New York, there had never been time or space to think over his real emotions, but here they seemed to surface without warning. Like his attraction to Abby. Something he'd have to keep a lid on. He was only in Lancaster to get away and explore his past. It was definitely temporary. He was not here to complicate his life with a romance. He had enough of those sorts of complications back home.

Blake closed his laptop and pushed it aside. With a trembling hand, he unfolded the beautifully penned sheet of linen stationery he kept in a folder in his laptop case. Mr. Pooler, his mother's lawyer, had given him the letter on his thirtieth birthday. Only two months after the accident.

Dearest son,
Happy birthday! If you are reading this letter, that means your father and I have left this world. Please know you have been our greatest gift during this life and nothing but a source of joy for us. But, as I think you suspected, I did not give birth to you. I could not have children and so your father and I adopted you. We never told you this simply because you never asked and we were perfectly content to keep you all to ourselves. How-

ever, we always agreed that we would tell you all
we know when you turned thirty. It is not much.
We only know that your parents were Amish and
lived in Willow Trace, Pennsylvania. They were
married and could not keep you for financial reasons.

The adoption was handled through a lawyer
by the name of Anthony Linton, Esquire, of Lancaster County. He can reveal the names if you so
desire. If you want to get in touch with your birth
parents, then we understand and fully support
your decision. Just know that no matter what, we
love you, and we're so very proud of you. Happy
birthday, dearest.
Your mother, Sarah

After six months, the letter still brought tears to
Blake's eyes. He refolded it and placed it back into the
file folder. This was the reason he'd come. But was he
ready to begin the search for his biological parents? He
wasn't sure. Without the encouragement from his own
mother, he might not have even ventured into Lancaster.
But after his visit last night to the Millers' home, Blake
decided to make that first step. He had a few hours before he was due to pick up Abby and head over to her
place to clean up the mess from the break-in. He didn't
have an appointment with the lawyer his mother had
mentioned. He hadn't had time to call, given his schedule at the hospital. But he didn't see the harm in driving
over to Linton's office and popping in.

An hour later, Blake drove through another section
of Lancaster, following the directions of his GPS to
Linton's law office. The area was extremely commer-
cialized in contrast to the quiet country appeal of Wil-

low Trace. He'd driven right into the thick of morning traffic. It was nothing compared to Manhattan and still he frowned. His easy, relaxing drive from the bed-and-breakfast to the hospital had already spoiled him.

It was a little after ten when he located the strand of connected offices. Linton's was sandwiched between a dentist and dermatologist. Blake parked his Land Rover at the end of the building and took a deep breath. Was it possible he'd know the names of his birth parents today? Did he even want to know them and meet them?

Blake's heart pounded against his rib cage. He took up a folder containing not only his mother's letter but also some other documentation of identification and a thorough inquiry, which his mother's lawyer had conducted, verifying Mr. Linton and the adoption. There was even a head shot of the lawyer himself. Blake steadied himself and entered the drab office.

"May I help you?" asked a woman seated at the front desk. She looked midfifties and had a motherly way to her. The rest of the reception area consisted of empty space and two empty armchairs. Behind her was another office. The light was on and Blake could hear a man's voice from within. But the door was pulled nearly closed, blocking anyone outside from looking in or hearing any of the conversation.

Blake approached the receptionist with his folder tucked under his arm. "Hello, I was hoping to speak with Mr. Linton."

"We don't take solicitors here." Her voice was kind but also firm.

"Oh, no. I'm not selling anything. I want to consult Mr. Linton about a legal matter."

The woman's fixed smile didn't change. "Mr. Linton

is not currently taking new clients. I'd be happy to furnish you with a list of alternative lawyers in the area."

Blake swallowed hard. Why was it so hard for him to just say why he was there? "I'm sorry. Let's start over.... I'm Dr. Blake Jamison. I'm from New York and I already have a lawyer. I'm here because I recently found out that I was adopted and that Mr. Linton handled the adoption. I have a letter and some documentation from my lawyer asking Mr. Linton to please release the names of my birth parents to me."

The woman was no longer smiling, but she wasn't dismissing him, either. She stood and motioned to one of the armchairs to her left. "Have a seat, Dr. Jamison. I'll be right back."

She disappeared through the door to the back office and closed it. This was it. Blake was going to learn the names of his real parents. He wiped his sweaty palms over the tops of his slacks and sat impatiently awaiting her return.

After a few minutes, the woman came back into the reception area, carefully closing the door to the office behind her. Her face was pale, but she once again pressed a practiced smile over her lips.

"It's just as I expected." She shook her head regretfully. "This has happened before. You have the wrong Mr. Linton. This Mr. Linton does not, nor has he ever, handled adoptions. I'm so sorry."

Blake's heart fell into his stomach. How could that be true? It wasn't. He'd researched Mr. Linton. His parents' lawyer had verified the information in the letter, as well. What was this woman hiding, and why?

Blake stood and faced the woman. There was deceit in her pale blue eyes. "I don't think I'm mistaken. I have documents here stating that Mr. Anthony Linton of this address is indeed the lawyer who handled my adoption thirty years ago."

He started to open the folder, but the woman waved away his documents.

"Perhaps if I could speak directly to Mr. Linton?" Blake asked.

"I'm afraid that's not possible." She turned back to her desk and took her seat. "Mr. Linton is not available. As I told you, he's not seeing new clients or taking new appointments."

Further discussion would clearly be useless. He would have to go about this a different way. Perhaps by contacting his parents' lawyer again.

"I'm sorry to trouble you." He turned toward the front doors, pulling his cell from his pocket. As he stepped out onto the sidewalk, a black BMW with New York plates peeled through the parking lot at Mach speed. The driver had a long, narrow face. His hair was silvery-white, cut close to the scalp, and he wore a dark suit.

It was Mr. Pooler—his mother's lawyer.

With his cell already in his hands, Blake found Pooler's number in his contacts and hit the call button. Something strange was going on here between the murder, his adoption and the scalpels down the stairs, and he was determined to get answers any way he could.

Abigail brushed and rebrushed her hair in a trance-like state. She had not slept well. Hannah had woken her up periodically as Dr. Jamison had instructed. Each time, the shock of waking had sent her into a panic. The terror was momentary, but the racing pulse and adrenaline rush were hard to recover from. As was the fact that she'd witnessed a murder and nearly been killed herself.

In her mind, everything was unbalanced and felt

strange, unfamiliar. Being at her brother's. Not being in an Amish frock. Not having to cover her head or hide her hair under a prayer *Kapp*. She had not realized how those simple things had given her comfort in the past. Her slender jeans and sweater set felt restrictive, clingy and showy. Her mind flashed through scenes from the day before—her attacker grabbing her in the hallway, walking into the trashed clinic and the feel of Blake's strong arms around her. Abby longed to feel comfortable again but she had a feeling that would be a long time coming.

She wished she had not asked Blake to drive her to the hospital to pick up her car. He did not help with the feeling-comfortable issue. For some reason, she couldn't get a read on him. And she didn't like that. One minute he was on the phone to New York, driving his fancy car and being the important new doctor in the E.R. The next minute he was looking at her with those soft brown eyes and holding her while she fell apart in the clinic. She didn't usually have so much trouble with figuring people out.

From the bedroom upstairs, she heard gravel churning under the tires of an automobile coming up the drive. Good. Blake was already there. He was early, which meant getting everything taken care of even faster. And more important, it meant she could avoid running into her father. She hurried down the stairs and onto the porch.

But it was not Blake in his large black Land Rover. It was a police car with Chief McClendon at the wheel and her brother beside him. Another small car—a silver sports car—drove directly behind them. Abby's head began to throb. Had something else happened? She wasn't sure she wanted to know.

Her brother and the chief got out of the car. From the small silver sports car emerged a woman, a brunette with short, spiky hair, looking as if she spent a lot of time at a gym. From her trunk, she loaded her arms with all sorts of equipment and headed toward the house.

They all walked up onto the porch together and paused in front of her.

"This is Carol Ruppert," Chief McClendon told her. "She's a composite artist from the FBI." Eli offered to help with her case, but she refused. "She's here to see if you can remember enough about your attacker to attempt an identification."

Abby could not stop her frown or her feelings of frustration toward Eli. He should not have gotten involved in this way. She had already brought danger to Eli's home, as was proven by the incident at the barn with poor little Stephen. But this? Bringing the police here? Right into their homes? *This* would really make her father upset. Not to mention the way it would draw attention to them. How had McClendon agreed to this? Especially after practically saying she should hide.

Abby wondered what Blake would have thought of all of this. She wondered if he was safe. She wondered what kind of family connection he had in Lancaster. And why did he seem so sad about it?

Eli was all smiles and optimism as he led everyone inside. Abby was all the more infuriated.

"Eli," she whispered, motioning him to hang back a ways from the other two. He leaned close to her at the kitchen door. She grabbed him by the arm. "Why did you bring them here? You shouldn't get involved in this. What will *Dat* say? Anyway, I didn't really see the man. Remember? Only his eyes."

"You need to quit worrying about *Dat*." Eli shook

his arm out of her grasp and placed them on her shoulders. "And worry more about staying alive. Somebody grabbed Stephen in my stable last night. You'd better believe I'm going to do something to find the person responsible."

Abby dropped her head. Eli was right. She had to do whatever she could to help catch this man who'd attacked her, murdered Mr. Hancock and scared poor little Stephen. "But the FBI?"

"They have the most sophisticated system."

Abby still frowned. "We couldn't have done this somewhere else?"

"Hey, I'll take care of *Dat*." Eli turned her toward the kitchen and led her in after the others.

Ms. Ruppert had already begun setting up her high-tech laptop with its very own digital sketchpad at the kitchen table. Abby had never seen anything like it.

She sat across from the woman and answered simple questions, which the artist seemed to have memorized. So many questions. There seemed to be no end to them. Hannah, who had been in her garden, returned and served coffee and pastries to everyone. Chief McClendon took advantage of any pause in the artist's inquiries to ask his own questions.

Abby had plenty of her own, as well.

"Your cats returned to the house soon after you left. One of my officers fed them," the chief said. "And other than the mess in your clinic and the missing epi-packs you reported, the house looked untouched. We didn't lift any prints. Whoever made that mess was wearing gloves. But he did leave footprints outside your back door. We made an impression of those. So far we can only say that he or she was wearing men's shoes and weighed about 170 to 180 pounds. Same sort of foot-prints in Eli's barn, too."

"Then there must be two men at work. There is no way that doctor at Fairview weighed 180. More like 220. He was a big man."

"What about at the hospital?" Eli asked. "Any news there?"

Before McClendon could respond, Ms. Ruppert beckoned everyone to her monitor. Abby's eyes grew wide. She could not believe how real the computer rendition looked. Everything on the screen was how she remembered it—his eyes and skin tone, even the way his face mask draped over his mouth and nose.

"That's amazing. But how can you match this to anything?"

"Well, the next step is all done by the computer. It will compare different chins and hair, et cetera, to the image. With each new combination, it runs searches through all the databases of online profiles."

"That must take forever."

"It's not a fast process, but it can be useful." Ms. Ruppert packed up her equipment as efficiently as she had assembled it and excused herself. Chief McClendon walked her out.

Abby went to the living room and looked out. She figured her father might be there at any moment and that did not bode well, especially with the chief's car in front of the house. She nearly jumped when she heard another car approaching. It was Blake. He passed Ms. Ruppert in the driveway, then joined McClendon on the steps. Abby could just overhear their words.

"Glad you're here, Jamison," McClendon said in his low baritone. "I've got Hancock's chart and the autopsy report, and frankly, I think you have some serious explaining to do."

Abby scooted away from the window. She hadn't meant to eavesdrop. But what was the chief talking about? Had Blake been hiding information? Was that why she couldn't get a read on him? Had he been untruthful?

Abby dropped her head. The disappointment slammed down on her like a lead weight.

Chapter Six

After the visit to Mr. Linton's office, Blake's mind had been reeling for the past hour. Had he really seen Pooler? Had his mind been playing tricks on him? It was hard to know which way was up.

Blake had left a voice-mail message for Pooler. He'd decided not to accuse him of being in Lancaster, but had spoken only of his difficulty in meeting with Linton. He'd taken a minute to calm down. During that moment he'd remembered that Linton, whom he'd seen a picture of when confirming his office address, and Pooler, his mother's lawyer, were both men in their late fifties with big tufts of gray hair—they would be easy to confuse driving by that quickly. Still pondering what he'd seen, he'd driven straight to the Millers' farm.

He was surprised to find Chief McClendon there. And even more surprised by his accusatory greeting.

"I've told you every single thing I know." Blake stood tall in front of the redheaded Lancaster chief of police. He had nothing to hide. He had done nothing wrong. Perhaps he hadn't shared one of the reasons he'd come to Lancaster, but that had nothing to do with Hancock or Abigail. It was personal—no one's business but his own.

The chief said nothing more on the porch but turned and went inside. Blake followed. Abigail stood with her back to the doorway of the kitchen. She was dressed in jeans and a sweater. Blake slowed his steps. That nurse's uniform she'd had on the day before had not done her justice. Her big blue eyes glanced back at him as she gave him a nervous half smile. For a second, his anxious thoughts melted away. But after taking a seat next to her at the table, a closer inspection of her face showed the tension around her eyes, reminding him why they were together. It occurred to him that she'd most likely slept worse than he had, and he had slept quite poorly.

She covered her cheek with a slender hand. "Eli brought a composite artist to the house. She just left. I was surprised what she was able to get from my limited descriptions. How was your morning?"

"Not very productive." Blake swallowed hard. He wanted to share with Abby about his family situation, but this was clearly not the time.

Eli took his seat next to his sister, and Chief McClendon cleared his throat. "We discovered why you weren't able to find the remains of Nicolas Hancock when you visited the morgue. The body was there the entire time, just with no identification. Dr. Dodd admitted later that there are some glitches in the records system at the hospital, which also explains why the electronic chart was unavailable when you tried to look at it. Final report from the autopsist agrees that this patient most likely died from an overdose of epinephrine."

Blake frowned. "But epinephrine wouldn't have been detectable through autopsy."

"No," the chief agreed. "That's not possible. But he ruled out other triggers to the cardiac arrest. The tubing of Mr. Hancock's IV, which you had the nurse save, showed up and was found to contain definite traces of epinephrine. This might not be enough evidence to convince a jury, but with what you both told me yesterday, it convinced me. And since the nursing staff can swear that you, Dr. Jamison, were in surgery at the time that Mr. Hancock was admitted and had never seen the patient before the Code Blue, your review has been closed. Of course, we need both of you to come to the morgue and identify that the body we have is indeed the one you saw yesterday. In the meantime, Lancaster County has officially opened a murder investigation for the death of Nicolas Hancock. Unfortunately, we've had trouble tracking down any information about him."

Abby's spine had gone rigid by midway through the chief's speech. Blake watched her fingers clench into a fist over the unfinished hardwood of the table. Abby was used to helping pregnant women and babies. He supposed the thought of traveling to the morgue did not appeal to her. Blake fought away the urge he had to comfort her and focused on the chief.

"What about Hancock's lawyer?" Eli asked. "Blake said that his information was on the chart."

"It's a phony. There's no lawyer—at least, not at that phone line. Just a bunch of numbers and a phony name someone keyed in."

"And who did key in all of that information at Fairview? Who placed my name with Hancock? I should never have been that man's doctor," Blake said.

"No one." McClendon shrugged. "Our computer experts tore that system apart. But they cannot find where, when or who keyed in Hancock's information and none of the data-entry personnel would own up to having done it."

"Anything else?" Blake asked, still waiting for Mc-Clendon's big accusation toward him.

The chief looked across the table at him. "Perhaps you would prefer to speak in private, Dr. Jamison?"

Blake shrugged. He felt Abby's eyes on him. He didn't like the tense expression on her face. No, he wasn't going to speak in private. He had nothing to do with Hancock. Of that he was certain. And he had nothing to hide from Abby or her family. "Thank you. But I don't see any reason for that."

"Good." The chief looked pleased, which gave Blake some relief. Maybe what he had to say wasn't so bad after all.

McClendon took out a file folder and placed it in the center of the table, opened it and spread the pages out. "This is Hancock's file. Here we see your name, Dr. Jamison. And your signature. Here is the lawyer's contact info. But this…this is the doctor who transferred Hancock to Fairview. Here are the insurance papers explaining the need for transfer. Everything is in order. Dr. Jamison, is there anything in the chart you'd like to explain to us?"

Blake clenched his teeth. He didn't like the way the chief was looking at him. He picked up the file and scanned through it. "There's more information here than what I saw yesterday. A complete workup of his surgery."

"Like I said, Dr. Dodd apologized for that. This is a complete and accurate file."

"Oh, and this!" Blake couldn't hide the surprise in his voice. "The name of the physician who transferred Hancock to Fairview." He reread the file in disbelief. He knew the name. He knew the name very well. "Dr.

Granger. He was a friend of my parents'. A very good friend, actually."

"I know, Dr. Jamison," the chief said. "On a hunch, since the patient and one of our key witnesses were both from New York, I ran some searches through newspaper articles to see if there was any connection between you and Hancock. I didn't find one—until I searched for ties between you and Hancock's doctor. Then the screen lit up with hits of articles and pictures of Dr. Granger and your parents at one society event after another. I also discovered that you're now worth a lot of money since the loss of your parents. I don't believe in coincidence. You just arrived and we have a murder in the hospital, which is connected back to someone you know in New York. Why don't you tell us exactly why you came to Lancaster so we can all get to the bottom of this?"

Blake nodded. "Right. I'd be glad to, actually. It's time everyone knew...."

"So, that's your family connection in Lancaster?" Abby said. "You're looking for your birth parents? That's kind of a big deal."

"Yes." Blake nodded. "After mulling it over for several months, I decided it's the right thing to do."

Abby stood, trying to think of how to respond. It was difficult to concentrate with everything she had on her mind. Hannah, her brother and Chief McClendon had already left the kitchen. Before leaving, the chief had given them an hour to get to the morgue and make the ID on Hancock's body. Abby was dreading that. She didn't want to look at a dead body. She didn't want to think about the man on the gurney, whom she'd seen murdered. It was enough that she saw him all the time in her mind. And his killer with his cold eyes.

So far, this was not the day she'd hoped for. The only thing that would make it worse would be running into her father. She did not have the energy or the heart for that.

"You don't approve of me looking for my birth parents, do you? What if I told you my mother believed that my parents were Amish?" Blake looked at her with his soft brown eyes. He wanted her approval. She wondered why. She hardly knew him.

"It's none of my business, Blake…but Amish? Are you sure?"

"Well, no. I'm not sure about any of it, except that I'm adopted. I only know what my mother said in her letter."

Abby had a million things she wanted to say, but she shook them off. It was truly none of her business. "Shall we go, then? I really want to get out of here before my father arrives."

"Sure." He looked disappointed that she didn't want to discuss his search for his birth parents.

"I'll just fetch my bag." She headed for the steps. "I'll meet you outside."

Abby grabbed her things and headed back to the living room. But she hadn't been fast enough. She slowed her descent as she saw *Dat* waiting at the bottom of the stairs. It was the first time she'd seen him since telling him about her decision not to join the church. It seemed in those two long weeks that he'd noticeably aged. The creases around his mouth and eyes were more pronounced. His hair thinner. His shoulders more rounded. Or was that her guilt making her see him in that way?

"Hello, *Dat*. How are you?"

The bishop took one look at her fitted jeans and sweater, letting out a disapproving huff as he ran his hands up and down his suspenders in an agitated motion. He readjusted his straw hat and tugged at his long, white beard.

"You should have tried all of this during your *Rumschpringe*. That's what run-around time is for. You were supposed to get all of this—" he motioned to her clothing "—out of your system. And now look what is happening. The outside world is crashing down around you, collapsing. And you are going down with it. I knew this would happen. And I knew how painful it would be to watch."

"You knew about what?"

"I can see the police car. I know what it means. I have heard the reports from the hospital and the Youngers. There has been a murder, and you have brought the killer into our world. What if that man had hurt that little boy?"

"And that would be my fault? I saw a doctor kill a patient. I am responsible for my own actions. Not for those of others. Isn't that what you always preach?" Abby had been completely wrong in thinking her father would be upset with Eli for bringing the police to the house. The bishop's anger was all directed at her. And if there was anything that made Abby down, it was disappointing her father. Even as she tried to defend herself and her actions, her head dropped.

"*Dat,* this is nothing. I was just in the wrong place at the wrong time. Chief McClendon will clear this all up in no time. You don't need to worry."

"Exactly. Wrong place. You do not belong there in that hospital. And now you are running around with this doctor?" He crossed his arms over his chest.

"I'm not running around with anyone. He saved my life, *Dat.* Twice. He's just giving me a ride back to the hospital so I can get my car." *And ID the man I saw murdered.* She decided to leave that part out.

"What do you know about this *Englischer?* He looks very worldly. I saw that fancy car of his."

Abby knew she was never going to win this discussion, not today, anyway. She might as well give up on it and talk about something productive. Her mind turned back to Blake's story.

She reached for her father's hand. He was a good man. A good father. A good bishop. He was wise, even if she felt he was a bit blinded when it came to looking at her situation. She took in a deep breath and smiled at him.

"What's that look for?" he asked. "I know that look. You're up to something. Abigail?"

If anyone would know about Amish adoptions, it would be her father. "*Dat,* let's not argue today. Let's just pray for everyone's safety and for a quick resolution to this situation and then we can pick this back up later. Okay?"

He grumbled but gave her hand a squeeze.

"So, I have a question for you. Have you ever heard of an Amish couple giving up a child for adoption?"

"Why do you ask this?" He frowned. "One of your patients wants to give up a child? This needs much prayer."

"So, it does happen?"

"There have been some times when a family could not keep a child. But always that child goes to another Amish family. Always. Why do you ask? I can see you are thinking something serious."

"No. Not really, *Dat,*" Abby said. "This has to do with the doctor. He was adopted and wants to find his birth parents. He thinks they might be Amish."

"See? You are attached to this doctor. I told you."
Her father's expression darkened. "No, this story of his
cannot be true. Amish do not give away children. We
take care of our own. You tell your doctor friend to go
back to his real home. He can only cause heartache here
if he tries to dig for fool's gold."

"That's what I thought, too." Abby smiled and patted her father on the shoulder. "See, *Dat?* We still agree
about most things. Don't worry about me."

"*Ach.* How can I not worry? My daughter. A car. A
job. Police. You should be married. Cooking. Taking
care of a family." With each word, his tone became increasingly aggravated. "What did I do wrong?"

"You didn't do anything wrong. You did everything
just right." Abby kissed his cheek and headed for the
door.

"Abigail." Her father's soft voice caused her to pause
in the doorway. "Promise me you will not get involved
with this *Englischer.* A New York man dies right after
a New York doctor comes to town? You agree that it
seems strange, *ja?* I do not believe in coincidences.
There is more to his involvement in this affair than
you think."

Abby swallowed hard, staring back at her father,
whose big, kind blue eyes were focused on her with all
the love of an adoring father. She'd already broken his
heart and she could barely stand how that felt to her.
She hadn't wanted her own decisions to cause pain to
her family. Had she only been selfish in doing what
she had done?

*It's not too late to change your mind about joining
the church,* his eyes seemed to say. She couldn't ease
that pain for him—but she could give him this promise.

"Do not worry about that. I can promise you with

every amount of certainty that I will never get involved—as you put it—with that *Englischer*." Abby kissed his cheek, then turned and fled through the door.

Blake shifted his weight in the driver's seat of his car. He couldn't get comfortable. Abby seemed strangely preoccupied and distant after her talk with her father. "You don't approve, do you?"

"Approve of what?"

"Of the reason I came to Lancaster. To look up my birth parents."

"I don't know what I think."

"You know I wanted to tell you yesterday," Blake said. He didn't like Abby so stiff and standoffish. He felt as if he needed to explain himself. He wanted her back the way she was. So confident and natural. She had totally clammed up and he didn't know why.

"Tell me what?"

"About being adopted. I just, well…with everything that happened… And the truth is, I hadn't told anyone yet. My friends back home wouldn't know what to say. I didn't tell any of them."

"Not sure I'd know what to say, either." Abby feigned a smile. "So, I do have a question, though…. Why did the chief say that you're worth a lot of money? I'm not sure I understand what that means or how it's relevant."

Was that what was bothering her? Not the adoption, but the money? That made sense and yet it hadn't even occurred to him. "My parents—my adoptive parents, the Jamisons—did very well. They both came from society families. Then professionally, they were high-paid doctors with an elite clientele. They made good investments. They started several charities and foundations. They left me in charge of all of them, which means I get to decide where all that money goes. A lot of people in New York were surprised about that."

"Well, who else would have been in charge of it?"

"Lawyers. My parents' partners in their medical practices—particularly for the medically related charities. There are several people who could have been left in charge of various organizations. Like Dr. Granger, even. The doctor whose name is on Hancock's file. He is very involved in one particular foundation that helps underprivileged children with operable birth defects. And there are others, too. It puts me in high demand. I feel really guilty saying this but it's awfully nice to get away."

"Is that why you get so many phone calls?"

"Yes, everyone needs me to get money. You might not have noticed but I left the phone in the car at your brother's. I didn't want to risk getting reprimanded by Hannah again."

Finally, he got a smile from her. "Do you enjoy all that work?"

"I don't know. My parents left it to me, so I feel like I need to do a good job. The charities help a lot of people. I don't want to see that fall apart. I have a responsibility to see it through."

"But do you like it? The work?"

Blake paused. "No one's ever asked me that. I don't know. I just do it. I guess I never thought about whether or not I liked it."

"Well, I love my work. I love being a nurse. I love my clinic." Abby relaxed a little, but then frowned again. He could see another question forming in her quick mind. "So why did you come here for so long? Aren't you needed back home? You could have searched for your relatives from New York. Right?"

Blake shrugged. That was a good question. But he wasn't ready to answer it. He didn't know the reason himself. "Seemed like I should do it myself, in person."

Abby sucked in a big breath.

"Are you nervous about the ID or do you have something to say?"

"Something to say." She laughed. "Guess I'm not too good at hiding my feelings."

"Say it," Blake said. "I really don't have anything to hide, despite how McClendon made it look. And I'm open to anything you want to tell me." As he spoke, he realized that that was the first time he'd ever said that to anyone.

"Well, okay, then…it's just that I don't see how your real parents could be Amish. You very well could have been born here in Lancaster. In Willow Trace even, but it's very unlikely that your parents are Amish."

He nodded, carefully watching her suspicious expressions. "You may be right, but my mother's letter says they were. You don't believe her?"

"I'm sure your mother told you what she knew. It's just that…"

"It's just that what?"

"Well, it's unlikely that an Amish couple would give up a child. Especially a son. Having sons means having farm help and labor for most families. Not to mention, every Amish church pools together an emergency fund that helps any families in need. We take care of our own. If an Amish family wanted to keep a child, everyone in the community would do anything they could to make that happen. And if that wasn't possible, they'd settle the baby with another Amish family."

He looked down, taking in her logic. "I didn't know that."

"And it's not merely that. It's also the impact your search might have on the people you're searching for."

"How do you mean?" Blake wanted to hear her thoughts. Having been raised Amish, she would have much more insight into the effects of his family connections.

"Well, can you imagine? You have the trauma of giving up a child and never thinking you'll see him again. If that child came back, it would bring up those emotions and hurt all over again. Not to mention the effect it would have on other family members. This isn't a small thing you are talking about. It's an event that would change many people's lives. Not just your own."

She touched his hand softly. The contact sent all sorts of feeling rushing through him. He thought of her words and her wisdom.

"This is important to you, isn't it?" Her voice was soft. "I'm sorry. It's really none of my business. I shouldn't have said anything. I didn't mean to upset you."

Blake swallowed hard, pulling his hand away from her. What if Abby was right? What if his one clue to track down his parents wasn't true? The thought left Blake feeling hollow inside. "It is important to me. I wasn't sure how I felt about it at first. But now that I'm here, I really want to know. I want to know if I'm from here."

He looked out the windshield at the beautiful rolling hills, the draping evergreens and the scattered farmhouses. It felt like home to him. A lifetime of living in the city and one trip to Lancaster and this—this rural countryside he'd never seen before felt like home. Either he was imagining the calm comfort he felt inside or this land was in his bones.

"What about McClendon's suspicions that your decision to come here started all this mess?"

Abby's direct question shook him from his daydreams of home and family. "Should I take it from your tone that it's now your suspicion, too?"

"Well, it does seem coincidental. Too coincidental. Your name mysteriously appearing on the chart? The former doctor being a friend of the family?"

What was she thinking? Blake lowered his brows. "You think I dosed Hancock? Or let him die?"

Abby looked at him as if he'd grown two heads. "No. Of course not. If I thought that I wouldn't be in this car with you. I'm just saying that… Well, I don't know what I'm saying. I just want to make sense of all of this. And it doesn't make sense, does it?"

Blake shook his head. "No, it doesn't. And I want to make sense of it, too."

He parked in front of the hospital in the convenient physicians' parking. They walked inside and headed down to the morgue. The pit-bull detective, Langer, was waiting for them.

"One at a time. And no commenting to each other in between viewings."

Abby went first. It didn't take but a couple of minutes and she was back out. She didn't even look at Blake as she passed. He followed Langer in. The autopsist stood by a table with a body lying on it, covered with a sheet. Langer nodded to the other doctor, who lifted back the sheet, revealing the face of the body. Short, bald, olive skin.

Blake nodded. "Yep. That's…that's Hancock."

Chapter Seven

You cannot serve both God and the world, Abigail. Her father's words echoed through her head. *What do you know about this* Englischer?

She glanced over at Blake. He was bent over her clinic floor, sweeping the last bit of glass into a dustpan. They had been working on her messy clinic ever since they'd left the morgue.

Her father had been right. She didn't know much about Dr. Blake Jamison. It seemed the more she learned about him the more confused it all became.

"Thanks for helping," she said. "I'm sure you have something else you'd rather be doing."

"Not really." Blake dumped the rest of the glass into the trash. "I'm glad to help. Like I said, it's nice to get my mind off things."

"So, what have you done in searching for your parents?"

He narrowed his eyes at her in a playful manner. "You sure you want to know?"

"I asked."

"Well, I went out early this morning to the lawyer's office—the lawyer who supposedly handled my adoption, according to my mother and the paperwork her lawyer compiled." Blake crossed his arms over his chest. She couldn't help but notice the muscular definition of his arms under his rolled-up sleeves, or the way his skin was sprinkled with freckles. "The receptionist really gave me the runaround. Told me I had the wrong lawyer. She wouldn't even let me speak to Mr. Linton. It was very strange."

"So, what now?"

"I can't imagine why, but I'm almost certain she was lying to me. So, I left a message for Mr. Pooler, my mother's lawyer back in New York, to see if there is anything he can do or suggest to me. I'm hoping he calls me back this afternoon."

"Well, don't be too discouraged even if he doesn't. There are other ways to find your birth parents."

Blake gave her a long, sideways look. "I thought you didn't approve of my quest. Now more questions and suggestions?"

"Well, if you don't want to hear it…" She started to walk away.

"No, no. I do. I value your opinion."

"You know, just because we are different and don't agree about this doesn't mean I can't be helpful." She finished arranging her supplies and leaned her weight over the counter, letting his compliment wash over her.

He leaned toward her. Was he flirting? She backed away, remembering her promise to her father. Even if she were attracted to Blake, which she wasn't, she would never go back on that promise. She'd broken her father's heart once. She wouldn't do it again. Anyway, it wasn't even an issue because she hardly even liked him and they had nothing in common. Nothing at all to worry about.

"Actually, while you were talking to your dad, Eli

told me that he could help me get into the town hall and gain access to the public birth records there." He stood back again as if suddenly aware that he'd entered her personal space. His freckled cheeks flushed. "I think I might take him up on that."

"Eli can be very resourceful when it comes to getting information." She motioned toward the kitchen. "I don't know about you, but I'm starving. Want to join me for a sandwich? It's the least I can do after all your help. I had no idea it would take so long."

"Sounds great."

She led him to the kitchen, where just the night before they'd seen an intruder.

"What can I do to help?"

Abby thought for a second, then headed to the refrigerator. "You can sit down and tell me what you like on your sandwich."

"The works." Blake pulled his cell phone from his back pocket and placed it on the kitchen table as he took a seat.

"Phone's been quiet today," Abby commented as she grabbed condiments, sliced honey ham, lettuce, pickles and tomatoes.

Almost as soon as the words were said, his cell began to vibrate on the table. Her eyes gravitated to the large image on its big touch screen—the very clear image of a lovely, sophisticated brunette. The name *Natalie* flashed across the top. Blake picked up the device quickly. Too quickly. "Oh, no. You spoke too soon. Excuse me."

"Of course." She turned back to the counter quickly, feeling as if she'd imposed on his privacy. Of course Blake had a girlfriend. What did she care?

She shook her head. She was only glad her father wasn't there.

* * *

"Hello." Why had he grabbed the phone so quickly and stepped out of the kitchen as if he'd needed serious privacy to talk to Natalie? He had no idea—he only wished he hadn't done it. Not that Abigail would care. She was not interested in him as anything more than a friend, but it still gave the wrong impression. It made it seem as if he had something to hide from her when in reality, she was the one person he felt completely comfortable telling the truth.

"Blake!" Natalie's voice was cheerful but guarded. "I—I was just going to leave you a message to remind you of the fund-raising gala next weekend. I hope you're still going to be my date."

"Look, Nat. I'm still in Pennsylvania and in the middle of something. I can't—"

"You're not canceling on me, are you?"

Yes, he wanted to say. But how could he miss the gala? It was a fund-raiser for one of his parents' charities. Didn't he owe it to their memory to attend? And anyway, it was still several days away. This mess with Hancock and the lawyer's strange behavior might be completely resolved by then. "Things here are a little up in the air—I don't know when I'll be getting back to town. I'll call you later. Can't talk right now. Goodbye, Natalie.

"I don't know why I walked out of the room to take that," he said as he reentered the kitchen.

"None of my business." Abby put their sandwiches on the table, turned and smiled at him. "Anyway, no one likes to blab in front of others on a cell phone."

Her nonchalant attitude stung. Clearly she couldn't have cared less about whom he was talking to on the phone.

Blake looked down hungrily at the food but waited as he noticed Abby did not eat.

"Would you mind if I said grace?"

"Of course not."

Abby bowed her head. "Dear Father, thank You for providing this meal for us. Thank You for Your hand upon us, which has kept us safe. Thank You for new friends and the blessing of a helping hand. Amen."

"Amen," he repeated. That was two days in a row now he had prayed, after so long a hiatus. The feeling it brought him was sharp and pricked right at his heart.

"Are you a praying man, Blake?"

"Why? Do I look awkward about it?" He tried to laugh as if his words were meant as a joke. Abby's face showed that her answer, if she had answered, would have been in the affirmative. "Yes, I am," he clarified. "It's just been a while."

"You should change that."

"I think I should change a lot of things in my life."

Blake felt as if he could talk to Abby about anything. He had the strongest urge to reach out and touch her long, silky hair. He wanted to know what it would feel like in his fingers. But he could see in her interactions with him that she did not feel that way about him. He needed to push away his silly and fruitless thoughts.

It was for the best that she wasn't interested in him as anything but a friend. The last thing he needed was to get attached to someone right now. His life was a wreck. He could barely handle things as they were. But then why did he feel so relaxed and content here and at the Millers' and working alongside Abby in the clinic?

"So you live here alone? No boyfriend? No husband?" he teased. "You said that was a common topic around here, so I thought I'd bring it up again."

His words caused her to blush. "No. I courted some here and there. Mostly Amish men. A few *Englischers*. Nothing serious. I'm not interested in marriage. I just want to run my clinic and help people. It's my calling in life and I feel God wants me to be 100 percent devoted to it. If I marry and have a family, I can't give 100 percent. But I haven't always been alone here. I did have a roommate for a while. A young girl from Philadelphia. She's at college now."

Not interested in marriage? Blake was stunned. And if he was really honest with himself, he was a little bit disappointed, too. He'd not thought of Abby as the career-driven type. But all the more reason to keep it professional between the two of them.

After they finished, Abby snatched up both the plates with a grin and headed to the sink.

"Let me help." His hand brushed against hers as she passed with the plates.

"You've done more than your fair share of cleaning up around here. And I have really appreciated it."

Blake started to respond but once again his cell phone vibrated. "It's Pooler, the lawyer. Do you mind?"

She shook her head and smiled.

The lawyer that looked so much like Linton.... Blake found himself wondering just how much he should share with Pooler. His gut seemed to tell him to trust the man as little as possible.

After a quick phone call, Blake came back into the kitchen with a look of hope on his face. "Can you believe my lawyer was able to get ahold of Mr. Linton and set up a real meeting for this afternoon? Apparently, the brush-off I got before was just because the receptionist doesn't take too kindly to walk-ins."

"That's good news for you." So why did Abby get a sinking feeling about Blake's plans? After all, it was none of her business. "So, just like that you could find out the names of your real parents? That must be a strange thought."

"Yes. Hard to believe, really." He smiled. "I have to take off, though. If I rush, I'll just make it. The office is all the way in Millersville."

"Well, you'd better get going. Thanks again for your help today, Blake. I guess I'll see you next time Mc-Clendon calls us together or at the hospital sometime." It felt strange to Abby to be saying goodbye to Blake after all the intensity of being with him over the past day and a half.

"Thanks for lunch." He started toward the front door and she followed him to see him out. "You should think about a security system."

"You sound like Eli." She laughed. "Truth is, I can't afford one. I don't charge most of my patients and I only work part-time at the hospital, so things are a little tight."

"You don't charge your patients?"

"Not money—not if they can't afford it. Sometimes they pay cash. If not, they pay me in other ways. Food, usually. I've gotten a few quilts. One couple whose twins I delivered brought me a pig."

"So, you buy all this medicine and these supplies out of your own pocket?" He looked incredulous, as if he'd never heard of such a thing.

"Haven't you ever worked at a free clinic? Or offered your services to the poor?"

"Well, yes, but only once or twice a year. Not every day. You are full of surprises, Abigail."

Abby wasn't sure if he meant it as a compliment or

if he found her way of life ludicrous. It was obvious he was rich and was used to a completely different way of life, but yesterday during the entire trauma, she'd thought him a little deeper than this. Perhaps he wasn't? Perhaps he was *Hochmut* through and through.

He stopped again at the door.

"Did you forget something?"

"Well, yes, I sort of forgot about being your doctor." He turned and looked at her head wound. "It's healing up really nicely but..."

"But what?"

"I have to advise against driving alone the day after you had a concussion."

Abby smiled. "But I already drove from the hospital to here."

"I know, but I was following you. I should follow you back to Eli's. You are staying there tonight, right?"

Abby nodded. "Quit worrying. You can't miss your appointment. Go on. I'll be fine. I'm only driving to Eli's and you know that's not too far."

Blake hesitated. "I don't know, Abby. You have been doing well, but you must be exhausted. I can reschedule my appointment. I'm not even sure if you should be alone. Not after all the things that have been happening."

"Bye, Blake." Abby practically pushed him out the door. Maybe it wasn't so smart to be alone. But she needed it. Her head was spinning, her feelings flying. She had patients to check on. And she had information she wanted to look up. She wanted Blake gone to be able to do it.

Clouds descended over the Lancaster skies as Blake drove back to the lawyer's office. Looked as if a big winter storm was blowing in or over. With all that was going on, he'd hardly thought to check the weather. A bad feeling chilled him as he reached the little village of Millersville. He still didn't feel right about leaving Abby alone. He should have followed her to her brother's. After all, she'd had a concussion the day before.

Meanwhile, he also kept thinking about what the others suspected—that his arrival in Lancaster had sparked this awful chain of events. He had come to Lancaster to find his birth parents—could his quest be connected to Hancock in some way?

And what about Dr. Granger? Blake hadn't heard from him in months, not since his parents' funeral. Dr. Granger had always been such a close friend of his parents'. Almost a part of the family. Blake assumed McClendon's detectives had made contact with him, but he could, too. He wanted to hear about the transfer and hopefully get some more information on the patient. Blake slid his cell from his pocket. At the next stoplight, he thumbed through his contacts and dialed Dr. Frank Granger.

"Dr. Granger's office. How may I direct your call?" A polite young voice sounded on the line.

"Hi. This is Blake Jamison. I'm a family friend of Dr. Granger's. I'd like to speak with him or leave a voice mail if I could."

There was a long hesitation before the receptionist said, "Dr. Granger is out on vacation this week. I'm taking messages but he will not return any calls until he is back in the States."

Blake swallowed hard. This was most unexpected. How could Granger have transferred a patient just yesterday if he were on vacation? "When did the doctor leave?"

"Over a week ago."

"And he returns soon?"

"He'll be back from St. Thomas midweek."

"Thank you. I'll call back."

Blake threw his phone aside as he turned his car into the same office-building strip he'd visited early that morning. He drove to the center of the parking lot and hit the brakes. There was the dental office that he'd seen on the left and there was the dermatologist's office to the right. But where Linton's office had been, there was nothing. The shades that had been in the windows and the sign with Linton's name—they were all gone. The office was empty, as if nothing had ever been there.

Blake parked his Land Rover in an empty space right in front. He hopped out of his car and raced up to the front door of the office. As he had expected, the rooms inside were empty. There was no reception desk. No large wing-backed chairs to wait in. Even the wall paintings were gone. There was nothing left but the carpet. So, how had Mr. Pooler just been on the phone with Linton not even an hour ago? It would have taken half the day to move out all of the fancy furnishings from inside the plush office—and it would have taken planning in advance to hire the movers. Yet there had been no signs of a planned move when he'd arrived earlier. It was as if the whole thing had been staged. But Linton couldn't have possibly known he was coming that morning. Only Pooler had known that….

Blake turned around, facing the parking lot. He blew out a long sigh of serious frustration. Maybe Abigail was right. Maybe searching for his birth parents was a bad idea. He'd certainly thought it would be a much easier endeavor than it had turned out to be thus far.

What should I do, Lord?

He raised his question hesitantly to the sky. Prayer had become awkward. How had that happened? A flake of snow flittered down from the sky as Blake looked out over the empty lot.

Zing. Something hot and fast and small grazed by his forehead. A second later the glass doors behind him shattered into a million bits that scattered over the sidewalk. Blake dropped to the ground, pressing his back flat against the grille of his car. That had been a bullet. Someone was shooting at him.

Chapter Eight

*W*hew. Abby closed the door behind Blake. She was glad for a moment to catch her breath and think on her own. She had told Hannah she'd be back at five o'clock. And she did need to return before Eli started to worry. She didn't want him calling Chief McClendon again. Or worse, her father.

She checked the time—she had just enough to feed the animals and call a few patients. First, Mrs. Brenneman. Abby dialed the number of the prepaid cell phone that she'd given to them. She often did that for her patients who owned oil-powered generators that could keep the phones charged when it was close to their due date. That way it would be easy for them to get in touch with her when it was time.

"Hello, Anna? This is Abigail Miller. I'm sorry I didn't get a chance to visit you yesterday."

"Ja." Anna's voice sounded over the line. "We have heard that you had an accident. Are you okay?"

"I'm fine. The real question is, how are you feeling?"

"I'm tired. A little pain in my side," she said. "It won't be long now."

"It's still a little early, Anna. How much work are you doing?"

"Not so much."

"None. No more work. You need at least one more week. Keep your phone close by at all times and call me right away if you have more pain."

"*Ja,* okay."

Abby was worried about Anna. She wasn't sure if the woman realized the dangers to the baby if he or she came too early. But it was hard to get an Amish woman to leave the chores for others to handle.

Next, she called Becka Esche. Her baby was also due anytime now, and it had been a rough pregnancy even though she was young and it was her second. Abby had insisted a few times that Becka see a doctor. But sometimes there was only so much Abby could convince her patients to do. Becka had delivered her first child in the hospital with an *Englisch* doctor. She'd lost the baby just hours after delivery, while she herself had developed a very dangerous condition called placenta accreta that nearly killed her. Now she and her husband, Jonas, wanted nothing to do with the hospital or any *Englisch* doctors. Abby could hardly blame them.

"Becka? This is Abigail. How are you feeling?"

"Ready to have this baby," she said. "I think it's almost time."

"Yes, it will be soon. Get lots of rest. Keep your phone close by."

Abby had other patients, of course. But none she needed to contact at the moment. That done, she fed her animals, collected her things and headed to Eli's. It was getting late, and as nice as it was to pretend everything was fine, she knew she needed to get back to the cover of her brother's home.

As she drove along the single-lane highway, Abby realized how tired she was. Blake had been right about her exhaustion. Tonight she would fix the chamomile tea that had a natural sleep aid in it. Then she would sleep like a baby. For now, she concentrated on the road. Thankfully, it was not a long drive, even if it was down a narrow, hilly, country highway.

After a few miles, a dark sedan with very bright headlights pulled up close to the back of her car. She checked her speed. It was fine. Some people were just so impatient. But there was nowhere to pass on this narrow road and no shoulder. The hurried driver behind her would just have to wait until she turned off at Eli's place. It wasn't far now.

But the car stuck to her like glue. The driver flashed his lights even brighter and swerved his car erratically from one side of the lane to the other. Abby accelerated to put some distance between them. She hated to go over the speed limit but she feared that the driver behind her might be intoxicated and dangerous.

The sedan kept right with her. Maybe he was even closer. Abby's heart began to pound. She wanted to pull off somewhere and let him pass. But there was nowhere to turn until she came to Eli's road. Thankfully, she was almost there. If only she had hands-free calling, she could notify the police about the reckless driving. But she didn't dare take her hands from the steering wheel or her eyes from the road. It was tough enough just concentrating on keeping ahead of the crazy driver behind her.

Something wet touched her windshield. Then another something. Abby's eyes darted up to the sky. It was snowing. Great. She tapped her brakes and turned on the wipers. The sedan seemed to have fallen back a bit.

Thank goodness! Abby let out a sigh of relief.

Finally, she was near the turnoff for Eli's place. The snow was really falling now. She slowed again and suddenly there was the black sedan. It had raced up behind her, accelerating as it approached. It was so close.

Then its front bumper struck the back of Abby's car.

The force of it thrust her head into the steering wheel. The pain under normal circumstances would have been excruciating, but for Abby, with her head still tender from her attack, the agony was nearly crippling. A warm trickle of blood dribbled down her cheek, distracting her as she tried to concentrate on the road.

She held her throbbing head up and gripped the steering wheel with all her might. The road before her seemed to split in two. Abby blinked hard and tried to force her eyes to focus. But it was no use. Panic raced through her veins. In her blurry peripheral vision, the dark sedan appeared to be beside her. But Abby did not trust her double vision and she dared not take her eyes from the road in front of her to look over and check.

If she could just make it another half mile, she would be at the turnoff for Eli's farm. But as the sound of metal on metal rang in her ears, she knew she wasn't going to make it to her brother's.

Abby fought the force of the sedan against her car as best she could, keeping her steering wheel to the left as the other car pushed her to the right. Her little Malibu was no match for the big sedan and it was only seconds before her tires were sliding into the deep ditch beside the road.

No. She definitely wasn't going to make it to Eli's.

Blake's instinct was to get up and run after whoever had fired that shot, but common sense told him he'd live longer if he stayed put. He looked both ways up and down the sidewalk, his back still pressed against the front of his car. His mind felt as scattered as the shards of glass spread around him. Why was someone shooting at *him?* Everyone had thought Abby was the target....

Abby! He'd left her alone. How stupid. He needed to get back to her as soon as possible. If someone was shooting at him, then who knew what was happening to her? His heart pounded. The shooter was behind him. Behind his car. But how far away? Blake didn't know but he would just have to risk exposing himself. He had to get into his car and head back to Abby's.

Blake stayed low and slipped back into the driver's side of his car. Starting up the car in a hurry, he floored the accelerator and raced out of the parking lot. He didn't look left or right. If the shooter was nearby, taking aim again, then so be it. He didn't care. He just had to get to Abby. He prayed he hadn't made a fatal mistake in leaving her alone.

The light snow seemed to have cleared the other drivers off the roads. He made good time back to her small cottage-clinic. But her car was already gone. Perhaps that was a good sign. He hoped that meant she was already safe at her brother's. Like she'd said earlier, it wasn't far. But he had to know for certain.

Blake pulled out his cell phone and dialed Abigail's number, which he'd programmed in earlier that morning. There was no answer. Perhaps she had the ringer off or just didn't feel like talking to him? Blake's gut told him that was not the case. Blake felt certain something was wrong. Or at least, he felt certain that he had to make sure she was all right. He would have to drive to Eli's and find out.

Blake continued on toward Eli's but much more

slowly—the snow was falling harder here. He passed a car that had slipped from the increasingly icy road. Thankfully, another Good Samaritan had stopped to help the stranded driver. The closer he got to Eli's, the heavier the snow seemed to be.

Just two more curves down the winding single-lane highway, past the Youngers' bed-and-breakfast and on to Eli's farm. When he knew he was close to the hidden turnoff, Blake scouted for the difficult-to-find gravel lane. At last he saw the drive and the mailbox that read E. Miller just ahead to the left of the road. He was moving at a snail's pace now and feeling his heart sink to his stomach as he realized that in the ditch across the street from Eli's mailbox was another stranded car.

It looked abandoned. Maybe the driver had already been picked up. Blake slowed his SUV, looking closely at the vehicle in the ditch. The car was a white Chevy Malibu.

It was Abby's car and she was still inside.

Oh, Lord, please, please let her be alive....

Chapter Nine

What had he done by leaving her alone?

It was immediately obvious that she had been attacked. The back bumper was dented and scratched, as was the driver's-side door. This was no accident—another vehicle had pushed her off the road. And the car hadn't been abandoned, either. Abby was still inside. Blake could just see the top of her head. She wasn't moving. A rush of frantic alarm hit him hard in the gut.

He threw his car into Park and raced across the street to the ditch. Based on the amount of snow on the car, she had not been there long. The engine was still hot and had melted everything touching the hood. Blake swiped the thin layer of flakes from the window so that he had a better view inside. Abby's body lay back against her seat. Her head was slumped forward in an awkward position. But he could see a mark across her forehead from the steering wheel. There was blood and dust from the air bag on her skin. "Abby!" He pulled at the door handle but it wouldn't open. "Abby! Wake up! Come on!"

Was she unconscious or was she…? Fear seized his body and mind. For a quick instant, he himself felt paralyzed. Then he rapped on the glass. Abby did not move. Blake knocked harder, then pounded on the glass with his fist. Abby did not respond.

Be alive! Please, God, let her be alive.

Blake searched the ditch. Just under and behind the car, he found a large stone. He stepped away from the backseat window and threw the stone like a cannon through the glass.

It cracked into a million pieces but did not shatter. Blake removed his jacket and covered his right hand. He picked up the stone again and pushed it through the weakest point in the break. Shards of glass scattered over the backseat. He reached inside, keeping the jacket around his arm to protect himself as he leaned forward and unlocked the driver's door.

Throwing the jacket aside, he opened Abby's door. His fingers went straight to the tender spot just under the neck as he felt for her pulse. Her body was warm, and with great relief, he detected the lightest rhythm of blood flow. He watched the rise and fall of her chest. She was alive.

Thank You, God...

Abby floated in a delightful dream. Cold air blew on her cheeks. Her hair was loose and flowing. Tiny icy dewdrops kissed her face and neck. It felt lovely. She drifted, flew, glided over a field of white tulips. The tall, handsome doctor stood at the edge of the flowers, watching her. He smiled and she laughed as a blast of cold air blew her nearer to him. His arms reached out and held her. They were warm and strong as he whispered to her. But she could not understand his words and then he was gone.

Darkness overcame her and she felt a hand on her

*arm. She turned back to see that a man in scrubs held
her. He was tall and round and breathed heavily, like
an old man. His eyes were gray and glassy. He pulled
down his surgical mask and whispered her name as if he
knew her well. Her arm ached. He pulled her back, then
thrust her forward. She hit something hard and sharp.
Her whole head filled with pain—incredible pain. If
she could just open her eyes again... But she could not.*

*The dream faded as the throbbing in her head in-
creased. She was sleepy and she longed to hear Blake's
voice again.*

Blake placed Abby gently into the backseat of his
car. He had not called 9-1-1. Abby had responded to his
touch with just enough movement to give him hope that
her injuries didn't require immediate paramedic care.
She had no broken bones. He'd checked for that. So
there really wasn't much point in an emergency crew
driving her on icy roads. Anyway, he was a doctor—and
a pretty good one. He would take care of her.

He drove slowly up the winding gravel drive, spot-
ting Eli near the front of the stables. Hearing the car,
Eli waved to him, the friendly greeting adding to the
guilt Blake felt at having allowed Abby to drive alone.
Eli would blame him, too. And Abby, too, once she
woke up.

"Abby's been in a car accident," Blake called to Eli
as he stepped out of his SUV.

Eli dropped what he was doing and ran over. "Where
is she?"

"Here." Blake motioned to his backseat. "I was wondering if you'd help me take her inside."

"*Ja,* of course. Or does she need to go to the hospital? She is so pale."

Blake looked over Abby again. He crouched down to lift her from his car. She stirred slightly for the first time, her eyelids fluttering. "I think she's coming to. If you'll allow me, I could examine her inside and we can make her comfortable. There is nothing broken that I can tell. And if the head swelling looks okay and she isn't bleeding too badly, I think the hospital can wait. It might be more dangerous driving in the storm."

Eli nodded. "Where was the accident?"

"Just in front of your drive. On the main road. Looked like another vehicle forced her off the road. We need to call Chief McClendon. There should be an investigation."

"And you were behind her?" Eli kept his eyes glued to his sister as Blake made his way with her across the porch and into the living room.

"No." Blake kneeled as he laid Abby carefully on the couch. He placed a pillow under her head and looked over her head wound again. He didn't want to tell Eli that he'd let her drive alone. *If only she would wake up...* "I need to wash my hands. Do you have better lighting?"

"Not really. With an oil-powered generator, which is the only power source allowed, we tend to use low-wattage bulbs. I can get a strong flashlight. We use those instead of the dangerous lanterns."

"What about ice? An ice pack would be good for her."

Eli pointed to the kitchen. "You can wash your hands there, as well. I'll stay with her and get the flashlight when you come back...but, Blake, I thought the two of you were together. I thought you weren't going to leave her alone."

"I had a meeting, so I let Abby drive over here by

herself." Blake explained exactly what had happened. "I wasn't thinking."

Eli touched Blake's shoulder in a brotherly way, but Blake could feel Eli's anger. He admired the man's ability to control his first reaction. Whether it was an Amish trait or just unique to Eli, it was something he needed to work on for himself.

"We will discuss this later," Eli said.

Blake nodded and handed him his cell phone. "You should also know that someone took a shot at me while I was in Millersville. When McClendon arrives, I'll fill you in on the details. I think your sister needs protection."

"Sounds like you both do," Eli said as he took the phone. Blake headed to the kitchen to clean his hands and get ice and try to calm his rattled nerves.

"I hit my head two days in a row? I can't believe it." Abby tried to sit up but immediately gave up the idea as a debilitating wave of pain traveled from her temples to the back of her skull and around again. "Ugh. Okay, I believe it."

"You should have taken some of the Motrin the doctor tried to give you." Hannah fluffed up the pillows behind her.

"Doctor?" She glanced at Eli, who'd been talking to her for the past twenty minutes, helping her remember the car accident with the big black sedan in the snow. "I thought that was Chief McClendon here with you."

"McClendon is here and your friend Dr. Jamison," Eli said. "Blake's the one who found your car in the ditch. You were unconscious. He brought you up to the house. He and the chief are outside at the end of the drive now, looking at the damage to your car."

"Here, have some of this tea you're always making us drink." Hannah passed her a warm mug.

"I had the strangest dream." Abby wrapped her hands around the cup, lifting the strong, familiar brew to her lips.

"I guess that's normal after a concussion. Was it about the accident?" Hannah asked.

"No, it was about flowers and—" *Blake* "—and... the man who attacked me."

"Do you think the man driving the car was the man who attacked you? The man from the hospital?"

"I don't know. I couldn't really see inside the car. Plus, I was mostly concentrating on trying to stay on the road.... So, what was Blake doing out here? I thought he was going to talk to some lawyer and then head back to the bed-and-breakfast."

"He did go to the lawyer's," Eli said. "And someone shot at him. So he came racing over here to make sure you were safe."

"What? Someone shot at him? As in, with a gun?" Abby's eyes went wide. "Is he okay?"

"Let her rest, Eli. She's tired and you're getting her all excited," Hannah said. "I've made enough food for everyone. We can talk about everything that's happened at dinner."

Abby didn't like the way Eli and Hannah were coddling her and she really didn't like the way they talked about Blake, almost as if he was a family member. Good grief. They hardly knew him. And maybe it had taken getting her head hit again but she'd decided that she didn't want to know him. She didn't like the weird way she felt around him. She didn't like that she'd gotten a little bit excited when Eli had said Blake had come to check on her. And she really didn't like when his phone rang and the display showed that beautiful women were calling him. Why did she even care about any of this? She shouldn't—it was as simple as that.

"Well, is he okay? You can at least tell me that...."

Not that she cared...much.

"He's fine."

Heavy footfalls sounded on the front porch. Eli went to the front door to let Blake and the chief back into the house. Abby wanted to blend away into the sofa cushions. She could only imagine how awful she must look after being in another accident. There was blood on her sweater. Her hair had fallen out of the tight braid and she ached from head to toe. She wanted quiet. She wanted safety. She wanted to go back to her life before Blake Jamison.

But despite her thoughts, McClendon and Blake tromped into the living room looking half-frozen as they brushed away the snow from their pant legs. Blake carried her overnight bag in his arms. "Here you go. Thought you might be needing this. I couldn't help noticing your laptop is in there. Do you have internet here? Does Hannah allow that?"

He smiled as he looked at her with his soft brown eyes. Ugh. She didn't want to smile back at him, but he made it pretty hard. It was difficult to will yourself not to like someone that you were naturally drawn to—and no matter how she sliced it, she was naturally attracted to Blake Jamison.

"No internet here. I have a wireless plan. An Air-Card." She put a finger over her lips to indicate it was her secret from Hannah.

But Hannah had overheard. She shook her head in disapproval before offering dinner to everyone.

McClendon declined. "Thank you, but I'll have to

be going. Lots of work for the police on a snowy day. Speaking of which, the tow truck will not be coming until tomorrow. He's got other jobs that can't wait. I hope you don't mind that I told him that this one could."

"Not at all." Abby forced herself into a sitting position, shutting her eyes against the excruciating pain in her head. "I don't think I'll be going anywhere anytime soon."

Blake mumbled something about not letting her go anywhere, then turned to Eli. "I don't want to impose, but I think I should stay to keep an eye on your sister tonight. After two blows to the head, there could be complications."

Eli gave a quick nod. "You're welcome to stay. Actually, in light of this unexpected storm, I could use your help getting the animals into the barn."

"Animals? Right. Of course. Be happy to help. Just need to call the Youngers at the bed-and-breakfast and let them know I'll be staying here." He pulled out his cell phone and followed Hannah and Eli into the kitchen, leaving Abby alone with the chief.

McClendon sat on a small wooden stool close to the sofa. "Are you up for giving me a quick statement?"

Abby gave a slight nod and recounted the accident. "Unlike yesterday, I remember it perfectly, right up until the moment the air bags inflated."

"Did you get a license number?"

"No. He was always behind me."

"Could you describe the driver?"

She shook her head. "Tinted windows and it was snowing. Plus, I was keeping my eyes on the road."

McClendon showed some dissatisfaction with her response. "There's something I don't quite get."

"What's that?"

"If you came straight from your house to your brother's after Dr. Jamison left for Millersville, then how is it that your car engine was still warm when he found you after going there and all the way back?"

"I didn't come straight here." Abby looked directly at the chief. "I made some phone calls first and saw to my animals."

"Miss Miller, I hardly need remind you that you were attacked inside the hospital yesterday. I thought you understood not to—"

"I'm not sure it would have made a difference. Someone shot at Blake. Seems like whoever it is can find us wherever we go—and *when*ever we go."

"What do you know about the shooting?"

"Nothing except that it happened, and Blake is fine. Aside from that, no one told me a thing."

"Not much to tell you," Blake said from the doorway. Apparently, he'd been listening in on their conversation. His voice gave her a start. "I went back to Linton's office. It had been cleared out since this morning. Not even a scrap of paper left behind. I turned around and a shot was fired just to the side of me. I thought of you and how if someone was attacking me, they might go after you next. I couldn't believe I'd listened to you and left you alone. I jumped back into the car and raced over. A little too late. I should have never left you at the clinic."

"I didn't give you much choice," Abby said.

"*Ach.* The truth." Eli reentered the living space, too. He shook his head at her, mocking her stubborn ways. "Come on, Blake. Need to get the babies inside."

"Babies?"

"Calves. Lambs, too."

"Ah."

They were dressed for the snow, ready to tackle the

evening chores. Abby wondered how Blake would manage. It was clear by the expression on his face that tending to animals was not something he was used to.

"So, Blake," Abby said as he and her brother headed to the front door, "since you've been shot at, what do you think about your involvement now? Still think it's all coincidence?"

Blake looked to McClendon. Perhaps they'd had a similar conversation outside.

He paused, then let out a long sigh. "It still doesn't fit together. It's hard to imagine that I brought this mess here. But I've never believed in coincidence."

Abby tried to nod, but her head wouldn't move as Blake's eyes seemed to have a fast hold on her. He stepped back into the room again.

"You should know, too, that I tried to call Dr. Granger on my way to Linton's office to ask him about transferring Hancock. His administrative assistant told me that he's been out of the country for the week. So there's no way he transferred Hancock. His name was probably put into Hancock's medical file the same way mine was—and I don't think any of us believe that was a coincidence."

Blake shook his head. "I still don't understand how any of it connects to my adoption or my choice to come here to look for my birth parents. Especially since, as I told you, no one knows about that except for you. And why would anyone kill over an adoption? So that makes me think of my parents' deaths and the inheritance. Then again, it could be none of those things."

"We are working on all those angles, Dr. Jamison." McClendon stood from the stool and walked toward the two men, though he continued to face Abby. "A killer is after both of you. Probably the very one who killed

Hancock. It's pretty likely he spotted you and the doctor at the hospital, followed you home and then here. And from the shooting and the timing of the car attack, it seems that there must be another person involved."

"And don't forget that one of them speaks Pennsylvania Dutch," Abby said.

McClendon nodded. "The FBI is considering all of this."

"The FBI?" Blake repeated.

"Sure. We have to involve the FBI—they are trying to identify Hancock. Taking fingerprints and running them as we speak."

Eli checked the clock on the wall and cleared his throat. "Night is coming. I've got to get out to the animals. McClendon, please keep us informed."

The chief nodded as Blake and Eli left the house. Then McClendon's face darkened and he straightened up and folded his arms over his chest. He lowered his voice. "Miss Miller, how well do you know Dr. Jamison?"

Abby swallowed hard and sank down into the plush cushions. "I don't. I don't know him at all. I just woke up in the E.R. yesterday and there he was. But since then, he's been very kind—even helping me tidy up my clinic. Why? Should I be concerned?"

McClendon looked toward the back of the house where the others had gone as if to ensure he had privacy to speak. "On a professional level? No. He's got an impeccable record as a doctor, a student. He's been to all the best schools, has worked in top hospitals—on paper, he's…he's flawless. On a personal level I guess that makes me a little nervous. I've known you and your brother for a long time. I just…well, I thought maybe

I saw something there between the two of you. I just want you to be cautious."

Something between the two of them? Abby could feel her face heating up like wildfire. Was it that obvious that she was a little bit attracted to him? Goodness. She was going to have to put on a better game face. She swallowed hard and willed away her blushing cheeks. "You think he brought this mess down here to Willow Trace, don't you?"

"I do. But… I also believe him when he says he doesn't know what's going on. Though I've been wrong before so… Anyway, I'm going to be checking all his connections, both personal and professional, on a deeper level. I'll let you know if I see any red flags. Just be more careful. Okay? No more driving alone."

"Of course. You're right."

"Good night, Miss Miller." He headed for the door. "Get some rest and know that I'll have a patrol car circling by."

"Eli won't like that. He still thinks he's a detective."

"Take care of yourself, Miss Miller. I'll check on you in the morning." He left through the front door. Abby heard the sound of his truck starting up and driving away.

With all the men out of the house and Hannah still in the kitchen, Abby slid down into the couch, closing her eyes. Her head ached terribly. Sleepiness must have fogged her thoughts because as she reviewed her conversation with McClendon, it was as if he'd been telling her not to get personally involved with Blake. She'd already decided that herself, and yet the chief's mention of doing more searches struck a chord. She really didn't know much about Blake at all. What harm would it do for her to run a few searches herself?

Abby thought about her laptop. It was sitting there a few feet away, waiting for her to look up Dr. Blake Jamison.

And while she was at it, she might look up a few other things, too.

Chapter Ten

Another twenty-minute nap and a good dose of her own healing tea and Abby felt like a new woman. She managed to get herself up from the couch, go upstairs and change out of her bloody clothing, then sit back down with her laptop. Her heart beat hard and steady as she connected to the internet with her AirCard and opened up the browser, unsure how much time she might have before the men returned or before Hannah guilted her into putting the computer away.

First, she typed in *Blake Jamison, Doctor, New York City.* Pages of links popped up—his practice, his doctors' associations, awards, special programs, the foundation and charities he'd mentioned, then articles and articles and articles about Blake, his parents and more. Abby couldn't believe it. Blake was a New York socialite. Like royalty, his whole life was online—photographed and documented by glossy, high-end, who's-who magazines. Abby didn't know where to start reading.

As quickly as she could, Abby skimmed articles about Blake's parents, their charities and huge fancy events. She knew his family was wealthy, but not to this extent.

Blake was the CEO and director of many of these organizations. Some of the articles spoke of his travels around the world to help the needy. On and on, Abby grew dizzy trying to take it all in. No wonder so many people were calling him. He was a big deal. And now she knew why McClendon, like her father, had warned her to be cautious.

She also knew that despite what she'd been telling herself, she did like the doctor. She liked him a lot.

Because if she didn't, seeing this whole other life of his wouldn't have made her feel so hopeless.

After all the charity-event links, Abby saw a page of Google images of Blake. Wow. There was one of him on a yacht. Another showed him shushing down ski slopes. Helping needy children in third-world countries. At a ribbon-cutting ceremony for the opening of a new clinic for the underprivileged. Although this discovery made her aware of the great differences in their social standing, seeing Blake at work and play and knowing how modest he'd been about it all only made him more attractive. Go figure. Abby sighed.

Her cursor stopped over an image of him in a gorgeous tux. In the photo, he was stepping out of a stretch limousine with a beautiful brunette wrapped around his arm—the same lovely woman who had called him at lunch. The caption read "Uptown power couple Blake Jamison and Natalie Jenkins. Sources say he has already been to Tiffany's and is just waiting for the perfect setting to pop the big question."

What? Blake was engaged? He might have mentioned that. No wonder he took the call in the other room. Abby quickly sloughed away her sappy sentiments when looking at the other articles. She had no right to think such things about another woman's fiancé. Now she only wondered what else Blake Jamison was hiding.

With a grunt, she aimed her finger down at the mouse, ready to close the search.

But she didn't. There was something that kept catching her eye. And somehow it seemed as if it might be important. Almost every single image of Blake had the same owner imprint across it—Daveux.

She wasn't sure if that meant Daveux owned the photo or took the photo or what. Sheltered in her Willow Trace upbringing, Abby knew next to nothing about the photojournalism business. But the consistency there sparked her interest. She enlarged one of the pictures so that she could read the whole name glossed over the image. Phillipe Daveux.

There was a link to his website. She clicked it.

Lots and lots of celebrity shots. Pages of fabulous, dazzling photos. Abby recognized some of the faces. Others were unfamiliar to her. Blake had his very own section of images by Daveux. Obviously, this photographer knew a lot about Blake and his family. Under many of the photos were links to articles that Daveux had written. Most of the articles had been published in a magazine called *New York Ways*.

Abby shrugged. She'd never heard of that, either. Blake lived in a whole other world from her—a world where people followed him around and took pictures of him and wrote articles; a world where he owned over ten different businesses and was responsible for other people's jobs; a world where he was engaged to a beautiful woman named Natalie; a world where Abby would never belong....

Blake matched Eli's long strides across the rolling pasture leading to the barn. The bleating flock of sheep looked nearly invisible against the hillside, blanketed in snow. Some of the small, fluffy animals skittered toward the barn as they approached.

"No one was expecting this weather," Eli said, "including the animals. They look ready to get inside and get warm and dry."

"So, what's the procedure?"

"Well, if you will just slide open the barn doors and stand in the aisle at the second gate, I'll herd them in. With you blocking the back of the aisle, they'll file into the first holding pen. Make sure that gate is open. It should be."

"I think I can do that." Blake headed to the great barn door. He slid it to the left and walked inside the large structure. The air was warm and surprisingly dry. The second gate was open, so Blake positioned himself just a step farther down the long aisle. Seconds later, he heard a rumbling of hooves. He turned just in time to watch the first of the little critters race into the dry, straw-filled pen. Eli brought up the end of the line, giving one or two of the more reluctant ones a little push on the rear.

"Lock the gate," Eli instructed after he chased them into the pen.

Blake shut and pinned the gate. Eli smiled as he hopped effortlessly over the high railing and touched Blake's shoulder. "Cows next."

Following Eli's lead, Blake helped repeat a similar but slightly more challenging process with the small herd of cattle. Soon the barn was filled with the animals' warmth and smells and sounds. Blake found himself smiling at the sight—it looked like a Norman

Rockwell Christmas card, only it was the month of April.

"Wow. That was kind of fun." Blake laughed, then paused to take an awkwardly long step over a pile of manure. "I guess you can tell I haven't been around many farm animals."

"We'll make a farmer of you yet." Eli patted him on the back.

They stepped outside, and Blake took in a long, deep breath of the fresh, snow-filled air. "I have to admit that it's extremely pleasant here. I like it much more than I'd anticipated."

Eli nodded. "I missed this place—the smells, the sounds, the people—every day when I lived in Phila- delphia. Don't get me wrong, I'm glad I was a cop for ten years. But now I'm so glad I'm home."

The word *home* stung Blake's ears. "Home. I feel like I don't have one right now. I suppose that's why I'm here. Without my parents, New York suddenly didn't feel like home anymore."

Eli's expression grew dim. "After dinner last night, Abigail told us about your loss. I'm very sorry. My *dat* and I have our issues—as you saw this morning—but I can't imagine losing him. Nor my *mamm*." He looked back dreamily toward the house. "Nor Hannah."

Blake swallowed hard. Eli's words tightened the band of ever-present loneliness that strangled his heart. "Thank you. It was difficult to make the decision to leave so much in limbo back home to be here. But in the end, it felt like the right thing to do. I only wish it were going a little smoother."

"You are having difficulties with your search? I didn't know that," Eli said. "As I said last night, I will be happy to help you in any way I can. I did used to be a detective."

Blake smiled at Eli's humor. He wondered how one sibling could be so intense and the other so seemingly laid-back. "Actually, it looks like the lawyer I was hoping to get information through is unavailable. I'll have to call back the man in New York who helped me with the contact here and see if he knows anything. But I suppose my next move would be to comb through public birth records. Not sure how that works…and I'm surprised you want to help. Your sister doesn't really approve of my plan to find my birth parents."

"I think my sister likes to claim opinions on many subjects that she has little experience with." Eli lifted his eyebrows playfully.

"What else should I know about your sister?" Blake laughed.

"Too much to tell you between here and the house." Eli laughed with him. "But in all seriousness, I can hook you up with the Lancaster Public Records. If you know specifically which township, that would save you a lot of time."

"According to the file my mother passed on to me, the transaction was signed in Millersville. The document doesn't reveal the names of my birth parents, but it does state that Willow Trace was their town of residence," Blake shared in a tentative voice.

"Okay, then. The old Hall of Records. I'll take you there on Monday."

"That would be great."

"If you don't mind, I might look into this lawyer that you went to see. If an office was there and then moved, all within one day, someone had to see it happen. Let's look into that." Eli stopped alongside the whitewashed four-board fence. He stretched his arms over the top rail and leaned back. Looking out over his land, his expression was a mixture of deep thought and curiosity. "Too many strange things are happening. We need to figure out how this is all connected."

Blake stood against the wooden fence next to Eli, watching the heavy snow tumble through the air. So many thoughts scrambled through his head. "I've been wondering, too, if..."

A dark figure flashed between trees in the distance. Blake turned to Eli. "Did you see that?"

Eli followed the direction of Blake's gaze across the rolling pastures and into the distance. It wasn't difficult to detect the dark movement against the sea of white snow that lay before them.

"I did." Abby's brother sprang into motion. "Come on. I think we can catch him. It might just be one of the teen boys who live nearby, but no one should be passing through here this time of night. Especially in this weather."

Blake fell in behind Eli as they tromped through the snow over the adjacent pasture and toward the dark figure. Their target moved away, but not nearly at the pace Eli could maintain. Blake struggled to keep up with Abby's brother as they climbed a steep hill. But a better view of the dark figure made him forget the burning lactic acid in his thighs. The dark figure was certainly dressed as an Amish man—short, dark wool coat, black trousers and black brimmed hat—but he was no teenager. He was a man, and judging by the white hair peeking out from under the brim of his black hat, an older man.

"Do you recognize him?" Blake asked.

"No," Eli said over his shoulder. "But he's no teenager. I don't know who he is."

That it was a stranger seemed to alarm Eli even more for he somehow increased his already frantic pace. The man picked up his own pace, running toward the nearby woods.

Blake and Eli reached the edge of the woods where the man had disappeared. The forest was thick but Blake could just make out the lumber mill situated on the other side. The two men forged their way through the woods, following the set of fresh footprints that cut between the scattered birch trees toward the mill. The old wooden structure loomed as a daunting figure against the late-evening sky.

Blake and Eli came to a screeching halt at the edge of the woods as a large black sedan blazed around the corner of the building. It raced along the side of the mill—heading straight for them.

The two men scrambled back into the cover of the trees as the vehicle swung at them, just missing the closest trunk. Blake noted that the grille of the car was badly dinged and the passenger side was scratched and dented. The car flew past them, screeching its wheels as it slowed to take a left out onto the highway that ran in front of the mill.

Blake ran after the car to the edge of the road, watching as it disappeared behind the next hill. "I think that was the car that hit Abby. Did you see the dents along the side?"

"Yeah. I did." Eli stopped beside him. "But I didn't get the license-plate numbers. The car was moving so fast. Did you see anything?"

"No. But I'm thinking it must have been the man in the woods that we were following."

"I'm sure it was, even though he was dressed Amish."

"I think first we should go back and check on the ladies. We've been gone for a long time. I'm starting to think that we should never have left."

Chapter Eleven

"You must be feeling better." The strain in Blake's face had lessened considerably since he and her brother had entered the house. They'd explained about the strange man in Amish clothing and the black car at the mill. Hannah and Eli had gone into the kitchen to put dinner on the table, insisting that Abby stay in the sitting room and entertain their guest.

Abby suspected that her brother had taken quite a liking to Blake and was aiming to get them to know each other better by leaving them alone. If he'd seen the pictures of Blake in a tux with a beautiful brunette on his arm and knew what Abby did about his money and fiancée and celebrity status, she was pretty sure he would change his mind about getting all chummy.

"Yes, much better." She had resumed her seat on the couch that she'd occupied most of the evening. Blake sat across from her in the most uncomfortable but closest chair to her spot. His nearness made her a bit uneasy. Or maybe it was the way he fiddled with the wool hat Eli had lent him. He'd made a job of staring at it and twirling it between his fingers. He only lacked a pair of black trousers and suspenders and he would have passed for a member of the *Ordnung.*

"I can't believe the guy that ran you off the road was right there," Blake said, startling her out of her thoughts. "So close. And we couldn't do anything to stop him."

"Was he tall and heavyset with cold, gray eyes?"

Blake looked up with a start. "No, in fact, he was quite the opposite. Well, we weren't close enough to see his eyes, but he had a slight frame. He was fast. And so is your brother."

Abby smiled. "Eli may not have caught him this time, but he won't give up. Persistence is one of my brother's greatest flaws—and virtues." Thinking back over what she'd learned earlier that evening, she realized that that quality could also be used to describe the photojournalist who so diligently captured every event in Blake's life. "Hey...does the name Daveux mean anything to you?" *How about Natalie?*

Blake scratched his head and looked pensive. But before he offered an answer, Abby's cell phone chimed. She pulled the phone from her pocket and read the screen. "It's one of the prepaid numbers. Must be a patient."

He nodded.

"Hello?"

"Abigail. *Doomla*—hurry." The Pennsylvania Dutch sounded a bit anxious. "It's time. Anna is going to have her baby tonight."

"*Ja,* Mr. Brenneman, rest easy. How far apart are the contractions?"

"Two minutes."

Two minutes? That meant the baby was coming very soon. With all the snow, would they even make it? She had to try. Abby stood and headed for the stairs so she could grab her things from the upstairs bedroom. "I'll be there as soon as I can," she promised before hanging up the phone.

"What? Where are you going?" Blake asked. "You're not in any shape to go anywhere."

"I forgot. I don't even have a car." Abby stopped at the edge of the stairs, completely ignoring Blake's comment. "I guess I can take Eli's horse and buggy. That will take forever, though."

"Are you not listening to me?" Blake stood and headed toward her. "You can't go anywhere. You've been in a serious accident."

"I have a patient with a baby to deliver." She started up the stairs. She would need her coat and her car keys to open the trunk.

"I'll go. I can deliver a baby. Or they can go to the hospital." He grabbed her elbow before she passed the third step. "You have to stay here."

Abby swung around, not realizing how close he stood behind her. Their faces were inches apart. She looked away and brushed her hair off her shoulder. "I appreciate your concern, but I have to go and you can't do anything to stop me."

"Time for dinner." Eli entered the room, eyeing them curiously. "What's the matter?"

Abby explained the situation. "Anna shouldn't deliver for another week or so. I have to be there."

"They should call an ambulance," Blake said. "Or I could go."

"Not going to happen." Abby couldn't keep the frustration from her voice. Blake was wasting time arguing with her.

"Abby is right, Blake," Eli said quickly. "The Brennemans will not be comfortable with anyone but her. They won't call an ambulance, either. But you should take her. Go together. It's not far. You should be fine in Blake's car. If not, you can ride a horse or get as close as you can and walk the rest of the way."

Abby froze on the step as her brother told them what to do and how to do it. He was turning into the proverbial Amish head of the family. The only thing lacking was a houseful of children, and judging by the new snugness in the waistline of Hannah's frock, it wouldn't be long before the first one joined their home.

Abby was just grateful that this time, the patriarch was on her side. She smiled and turned to Blake. "He's right. I have to go. But if you would drive I would be very grateful."

"Yes, this plan I can live with." He grabbed his coat from the back of the chair and waited for her at the front door.

In less than three minutes, the two of them were out the door, in Blake's car and halfway down the snowy drive.

"Stop at the ditch with my car. I have to get my medical kit."

Blake drove carefully through the snow, which, thankfully, had all but stopped falling. Blake threw the car into Park just across from her Malibu. "I'll get it. In the trunk?"

"Yes. Thank you." Abby handed him the keys, then watched him cross the street, grab her equipment and return. He climbed back in behind the wheel and passed her things to her.

"Thanks. And thanks for taking me. It's not far to the Brennemans'. Just turn left here and go about a mile down the main street. It's within a little cluster of homes on the right."

"It's my pleasure." Blake drove on, turning onto the main road. "You know, that name you mentioned just before the phone call seemed really familiar but I can't quite put my finger on it. What was it again? Devero? Is that someone at the hospital?"

Abby swallowed hard at the reminder of the distance between them. "Daveux. He's a celebrity photojournalist in New York. You didn't tell me you were a celebrity."

"What? I'm not." Blake frowned, with an air of confusion about his face.

"I looked you up on Google. You are. And so were your parents. I read about all the good things all of you have done."

"That doesn't make me a celebrity."

"A photojournalist has a whole page of his website devoted to you. That sounds like celebrity status to me."

"Well, it's not." Blake shook his head. "Listen, Abby. I'm a doctor. Not a celebrity. And yes, my parents gave a lot of money away and they liked all of that attention. But I don't. So there—there's another reason I left New York. And so what? What's this all got to do with anything?"

"I don't feel like you've been honest with me about who you are. You're a socialite. Isn't that what you call it?"

"My parents were socialites. Not me. You say things with such certainty, but you are not right about everything. And you really aren't right about me. Sometimes I think you repeat your conviction about becoming a nurse because really deep down inside you wonder if you should have given it up and done what your father wanted. You're no different than I am. Neither of us can figure out what's ahead."

Abby could hardly take Blake's painfully true words. Not even her own brother had dared to say those things to her. She swallowed hard and sucked in a difficult breath.

"And why were you investigating me on Google?"

"I felt like I wanted to…" She could feel his disapproving gaze on her. Ugh. Why did she even care? Why was she listening to a word he said? Wasn't he engaged? Perhaps she should mention that she saw his fiancée in the pictures. *Probably not.* Abby shook her head. She was being ridiculous. She had to get all these silly, petty thoughts out of her head and concentrate on what was important. "I don't know. I thought I might find something that would help us figure out why people are trying to kill us."

He dropped his head.

"Turn right here." She pointed to the small, gray stone cottage to the right. He had her so flustered with all of this talk that she'd almost missed the turnoff. "So, have you ever even delivered a baby?"

"I had a rotation through Obstetrics." Blake managed a weak smile as he parked the car. "Does that mean I get to assist?"

"If Anna and Benjamin are comfortable with you," she said, turning toward him as she opened the car door. "I don't see why not."

Blake's eyes met hers. He reached over and took hold of her hand. He leaned close to her and her pulse doubled in speed.

"Abigail, I am who I say I am. I haven't hidden anything from you. I'm nothing more than a doctor from New York who just found out he was adopted. That's it. I'm certainly nothing special. And if this mess we've gotten into has anything to do with me or my parents or any part of my life in New York, I promise you I don't know how or why. You have to believe me."

Abby held her breath. His hand on hers and his pleading brown eyes had her feeling so uncertain. After a long moment, she managed to nod. "Let's get inside."

Despite Abby's expectations, the labor was not fast. A long evening stretched into an even longer night and Abby couldn't have been more thankful for Blake's presence. Her head and body needed too much rest for her to have handled the delivery alone. The Brennemans were charmed by Blake's humble and helpful demeanor. The baby came slowly, but he was healthy—small, but strong and able to breathe. For that, Abby stopped and thanked God.

By morning, a screaming Gideon Brenneman was ruling the roost while Anna was resting in her room. The sun was out and melting the unexpected snow more quickly than it had fallen. By 8:00 a.m., she and Blake said their goodbyes and were about to head back to her brother's.

"I don't think I've ever enjoyed being a doctor more than I did in these past few hours." Blake opened his car door for her. "Thank you."

His soft brown eyes caught her again. *A woman could get lost in those eyes.* But she wouldn't. There was nothing for her there. They were from different worlds. She'd known it before, but seeing those pictures of him on the internet had really driven the reality of that home. The beautiful, sophisticated woman who had called Blake just the day before—*that* was the type of woman who needed to be with a man like Blake. They lived in a world she did not belong to and never would.

"I'm glad you were there. I couldn't have handled it alone. I'm exhausted."

"You must be." He closed her door and drove her to her brother's. "Get some rest. I'll see you Monday."

Abby was glad he wasn't coming inside. "What's Monday?"

"Eli is taking me to the Hall of Records so that I can go through the birth records."

What? Why was her brother getting so involved in Blake's personal business? Especially concerning this adoption. Abby held in her shocked reaction. She thanked Blake again, then scrambled up the front porch and went straight to the guest room. She would confront Eli later, after a few hours of rest.

Abby lay down, closed her eyes and fell into a fitful sleep.

"I can't thank you enough for letting me look through these files, Mrs. Betts." Blake tucked the folder of documents under his left arm and surveyed the crowded filing room. It was stuffed with floor-to-ceiling cabinets with drawers and drawers of birth records.

A sole computer station had been set up in the far corner.

"Of course, we had all the records converted to electronic files years ago. They can be accessed from any government computers if you know the right codes. This station will give you direct access to Lancaster County."

Blake laughed. "It's just like the hospitals. Everything is electronic, but no one throws away the paperwork, just in case."

"I'm going out for lunch. If you find what you need, you can print or make copies over there." She pointed to a large Xerox machine next to the computer station. "Please lock the front door if you leave before I get back."

"Are you sure? I can come back later if this is inconvenient." Blake made the offer more out of politeness than sincerity. He had little time before he was needed back at the hospital. Dr. Dodd, the head administrator at Fairview, had been less than happy that he'd taken off the past couple of days, regardless of it being a firm request directly from the chief of police.

"I'm completely sure. This is all public record and if Eli trusts you, then so do I."

"Thank you."

Mrs. Betts left the small documents room, closing a thick metal door behind her. The air felt instantly still, as if the administrative assistant had sucked all of it away with her. The old documents gave the room a dank, unpleasant odor. Hopefully, his search would be fast. Blake was not much for tight, closed-in spaces with no windows.

He sat down at the one computer station, placing his own file folder—the one with the letter from his mother—on the small desk. He waved the mouse, and the screen lit up with a typical search page. He typed in his birth year, month and day, and hit Enter.

A swirling circle popped up. *Loading. Loading. Loading.* He sat back in the old office chair. What did he hope to accomplish through this search? Maybe a doctor's name. He wasn't sure. It was quite possible that his Amish birth parents didn't even use a doctor for the delivery. He doubted that thirty years ago many of them did. He'd learned a few nights ago from Abby that not too many now did, either.

The wheel continued to swirl around the screen. *Abby.* She'd been on Blake's mind ever since he'd dropped her at her brother's after the all-night delivery—a night that he would never forget. It was the first time in a long time that his work, his medicine, felt good—felt as if it made a difference.

It was the way he'd wanted his work to be—the way his mom and dad had always talked about their mission trips. And being there with Abigail, watching her work, had made it even more special. At least to him, it had felt special. He wasn't so sure she'd thought so. Then again, she'd been so tired she'd hardly been able to talk. And she was so mad at him about the internet articles and all that other nonsense in his life back home. He had to admit he didn't miss it, any of it, not one bit.

He'd hoped to see her today. He'd thought she'd still be with Eli that morning, but she wasn't. Her friend Janice from the hospital had picked her up and taken her to get a rental car while hers was in the shop. As soon as he finished at the Hall of Records he planned to call her.

The screen had gone dark. He wiggled the mouse. The screen relit.

No data for date provided.

Of course. He threw his hands in the air. That would have been too easy.

Think. Think. Think.

Blake returned to the search screen. He typed in the same information for year and month but left the day blank. This time the swirling wheel lasted only a few seconds before turning up three-hundred-plus entries.

Blake's heart leaped as he scrolled down the list of surnames. Jamison, of course, was not going to be there. However, it wasn't too difficult to spot some of the Amish surnames. But still there were so many. He needed to refine his search.

Male births.

The three hundred entries dropped to less than one hundred and twenty. Now he might thin these out by location.

Willow Trace.

He was down to twenty. Blake smiled. That number he could manage. Blake began to read through each file, paying particular attention to the ones with Amish surnames. Most of those listed Dr. Miles as the doctor. There were none from the day that he'd always known as his birthday, so Blake double-checked the four records that were nearest that date. All of those listed Dr. Miles. He printed those records. He was pretty certain that Eli or even Abigail might be able to tell him if they knew these families. Maybe it would lead to something. Maybe it wouldn't. Talking to this Dr. Miles might be worth a try, as well.

Blake collected his things and stood from the computer station when he heard footsteps passing in the hallway outside the door. Mrs. Betts must have returned from lunch, although that seemed a bit quick, he thought as he checked his watch.

"Mrs. Betts?"

There was no answer. She probably couldn't hear him through that thick door. Oh, well. He'd see her on the way out, which was exactly where he was headed.

But as he passed through the maze of filing cabinets, he happened to see that he was standing right by the files containing his own birth year. He paused. Why not take a peek?

He rolled open the drawer and pulled out the thick file for November of that year, his birth month. Just eyeballing it, his guess was the file had a lot more than three hundred records. Suddenly, he forgot all about leaving. *What if some of the records didn't make it into the computer?* Blake shook his head. The files would have been entered from microfiche years ago, read by an electronic laser or something of that sort to get everything computerized…. How could they have missed anything?

Still, out of curiosity, he sat back at the desk, opened the folder and began to turn through the records. The task proved more interesting than he'd imagined. On the computer, there had been no births in Willow Trace on his birth date. But in this folder, there were three. All male. All delivered by Dr. Miles. One listed John and Jane Doe as birth parents.

Blake grabbed the file with a shaking hand. He made a quick copy, replaced the folder and headed to the door. As soon as he could, he would find this Dr. Miles and hope he could lead him to the truth. It was something. And it gave him hope.

Blake turned the large metal handle of the thick door. He was more than ready to get out of that tiny closet of a room. But the handle wouldn't budge. Blake shook the handle and tried again.

"Mrs. Betts?" Had she locked him inside accidentally? If Blake hadn't felt claustrophobic before, he sure did now. "Mrs. Betts?"

He shook the door again.

Nothing.

He put his file folder to the side and studied the door handle. Oddly, it looked as though it locked from the inside. Blake turned the button lock one way and then the other but it was no use.

He was locked inside.

Blake pulled his cell phone from his pocket. Except it wasn't in his pocket. He'd left it inside the car.

Of course…his new habit inspired by Hannah Miller.

Blake made his way back through the maze of file folders to the computer station. He hoped there was a phone there.

Chapter Twelve

A bby spent her morning rushing from here to there in the rental car she'd picked up, stopping at the hospital, her home, the body shop and at the police station for a quick conversation with Chief McClendon. According to him, a Detective Day of the FBI had taken over the investigation of Hancock's murder and would be in touch with her if necessary. At this point all he knew was that they were focusing on identifying Hancock and trying to make connections in New York City. McClendon warned her that both she and Dr. Jamison might have FBI tails. He'd also asked her to pass on the information to Dr. Jamison, which she had reluctantly agreed to do.

Truth was she wanted to avoid Blake as much as possible. She didn't like the way she felt around him. He was too rich and cool and confident. She was plain and awkward and unsophisticated. She didn't like how he'd just come to town to serve his own curiosity about his birth parents. What if he created a wake of heartache behind him? Had he even thought about that?

There was more, too. She didn't like the way he looked at her with those chocolate-brown eyes—the way he had that whole night when he'd helped with the delivery. Of course, she couldn't help but admire his skills as a doctor. He'd been amazing. Hard to believe he was the same man in all those internet pictures. How could he be? Abby shook her head. She didn't know and it didn't matter. Blake was all wrong for her and all wrong *about* her. She knew exactly what she wanted and it had nothing to do with him. She just had to deliver this message and then she could leave Blake to his own affairs.

Abby pulled up in front of the Hall of Records. Blake's Land Rover was parked in front. She knew Eli had arranged for him to have access to the Lancaster birth records.

A wave of unease fell over Abby as she parked next to Blake's car. The building looked abandoned. There were no other cars in front. This was a small operation, a satellite office to the main town hall, run by a skeleton staff.

This won't take but a second, she thought, leaving her handbag in the car. She pushed open the double doors leading inside.

"Yoo-hoo," she called out.

The front desk sat empty. It was dead quiet. Abby turned her head, peering around the room. Nothing much in the small room but a few chairs and a reception desk. Behind the desk was a hallway leading to the other offices. She glanced back through the glass window of the front doors, feeling more and more uneasy. The parking lot was still empty but at least across the street was a mini-mart, which had a few customers. Seeing busy people nearby should have reassured her a bit, but it didn't.

Oh, Abby, you're being silly. Just find Blake and get this over and done.

Abby followed the narrow hallway toward the center of the building. "Blake?"

"Abigail?" his voice answered back from the far end of the hall.

"Yes, it's Abby." She looked around. "Where are you?"

"I'm in here. Locked in here. I can't get this door open." A big metal door at the end of the hallway shook. "I wanted to call you, but I left my cell phone in the car."

Abby smiled. No wonder he sounded panicked. He'd locked himself in the filing room. "Hold on. I'll be right there."

She tried the doorknob. *Click.* It opened easily.

"Wow." Blake came out of the room, looking flushed and out of breath. "I do not like being enclosed in small spaces. Thank you. That was so creepy. How long have you been in the building?"

"Not even a minute. Why?"

"I don't know." He shrugged. "I thought I heard someone walking down the hallway a few minutes ago."

"It wasn't me." Abby shivered. "Actually, there isn't another car in the parking lot. No one around. I was feeling pretty creepy coming in this empty old building. Where's the receptionist?"

"She went to lunch."

"And just left you alone here?"

"She said she trusted any friend of Eli's." He tugged at her arm and pulled her inside the filing room. His coloring was normal again and he looked almost giddy with excitement. "Come here. Look."

"Blake? You really want to go back into that room?" she teased.

"Good point." He propped the door open with a wedge. "Now it's safe. I want to show you what I found."

"Your parents?" She followed him into the stuffy room to where he stopped at a table that held an open file folder.

"No. Adoption records are sealed for the most part. I didn't really expect to find that. But I didn't expect to find this, either."

Blake spread out several file copies that he'd made. Each of them was a birth close to the same date. Abby recognized a few of the family names—Amish names. Blake pointed to the line that indicated the attending physician. "Look. All of these families used the same doctor."

"Dr. Nathan Miles," Abby read with a frown. "I've never heard of him."

"Well, this was thirty years ago—he could have retired or passed away by now." Blake pulled out the last photocopy and showed it to Abby. "But I think he may have delivered me—I mean this could be me. Same birth date. Same doctor. Jane and John Doe parents."

"Amazing. Now you can look for this doctor. Right?" She forced a smile for him even though she still had a bad feeling about his search.

"Yes. I could even talk to these other families who were having babies at the same time with the same doctor, too. They might remember who else was expecting at the same time."

Abby shook her head.

"What? You don't like that idea, either?"

"You can try, Blake. But Amish families are not going to talk to you as freely as you might think."

He smiled and touched his hand to her chin, looking as if he'd conquered the world. "That's why you're going to go with me and help."

She locked eyes with him—his chocolate eyes that sucked her in and made her forget about everything else in the world. Did he feel that when he looked at her? He had to feel something—she could see it in his face as he leaned toward her, his gaze on her mouth.

"I've never met anyone like you, Abby. You—"

Whooph.

Abby and Blake pulled apart as a flash of light glowed at them from the hallway.

"What was that?" Blake tossed the file papers down and raced toward the hallway.

Abby followed but stopped short behind him as she felt the heat coming from the corridor.

"The only exit is on fire." Blake turned to her. "There's no way out."

Abby tried to lunge past him.

"Stay back, Abby. There's some sort of accelerator on that. It's spreading fast." He pulled her back behind him into the filing room.

Flames lined the hallway to the front office. They flew higher and hotter, inching closer to the end of the hallway and the room they were now trapped in.

"Please tell me there's a phone in here." Abby looked at him anxiously.

"I'm not sure. I was going to check earlier, but then you showed up." Blake headed back to the computer station. "If there is one, I think it would be back here."

"Or we could use the computer to contact someone," Abby suggested, following him back.

Blake located the small office phone plugged in behind the computer. He lifted the receiver to his ear. "It's dead."

Abby was already beside him trying the computer. "No internet. It's probably all connected."

"Someone has trapped us in here for good." Blake looked around at the walls and the ceiling. "Should we close the metal door? Maybe it's fireproof."

Blake crossed the room.

Abby was right beside him. She stopped him from closing the door. "If you shut that then we are definitely locked in here."

He looked down the hallway at the hungry flames, already halfway to the filing room, devouring the old dry wood. "We're already locked in."

Blake scratched his head. What could they do? They had to do something. If they didn't, they'd be sitting ducks.

Just as someone had planned for them to be.

Blake looked around the room again—and then he looked up. The drop ceiling was low and tiled. The rooms might be connected through the ceiling duct-work. If the fire was contained to the hallway, perhaps they could maneuver around it and make their way to the front of the building.

"I've got an idea." Blake hopped up on top of the closest filing cabinet. Being a good six foot two, he merely needed to rest on his knees on the top of the metal structure and he had access to the tiles above.

"Good thinking." Abby was already hopping up onto the adjacent filing cabinet.

Together they lifted away the closest overhead tile and peered up through the space. The air was hotter there but not yet as smoky—the flames from the hall-way had just begun to reach the height of the ceiling.

"I can crawl across that beam." Abby started to lift herself into the ceiling structure.

"Maybe not." He grabbed her arm just as the framework began to bend under her weight. "Those flames are going to eat through the ceiling tiles like termites on wood. But at least we can see that the front of the building is clear. We could get out if we could just find a way to get there."

Abby pointed down. "How about that?"

Blake followed her gaze to the lower side wall. There was a small space between two filing cabinets and behind it was an air return.

Blake nodded. They both hopped down to the floor and inspected the screen.

"We need a screwdriver," Abby said.

Blake took an ink pen from his pocket and ripped the clip from the front of it. Holding only the small, flat part of the clip, he maneuvered it into the screw head. It took both hands to hold it in place but slowly he was able to loosen the bolts and remove the return cover.

"Look. It goes down under the building." Blake pointed behind the grate. Just the sight of the downward ductwork caused hope to return to his smoke-filled head. He grabbed Abby's shoulders and kissed her out of sheer joy. "We can get out."

Abby smiled, though she looked a little puzzled by his quick peck on the lips. She might have been blushing, but then again, the red in her face could have been from the ever-building heat that encircled them. Closer and closer.

Blake reached into the return with both arms and yanked the ductwork away from the wall. Just as he had hoped, the large metal cylinder-shaped tubing dropped away and cold, musty air flowed over them from under the building.

"You first." He smiled at Abby, who looked as relieved as he felt. She slid over to the gigantic hole in the wall that he'd created.

"Crawl to a vent and push your way out. I'll be right behind you."

Blake grabbed hold of Abby's arms and was helping her to get her legs down under the building when she squirmed one hand loose from him. "Your files. Go grab your files."

Blake smiled. He stood and reached over to the desk area where he'd spread out his findings to show Abby before the fire had started. He scooped them up, tucked them under his arm and slid down under the building after Abby.

Chapter Thirteen

Abby's arms and hands clutched deeply into the cold, wet, gravelly muck under the old Hall of Records auxiliary building. It was wonderful to breathe in the damp, smoke-free air, but her lungs were still full of fumes, and she coughed continually as she groped along the floor.

Where to go?

Abby turned around on all fours. The hallway's flames had eaten through that area of the building. From the underside, it looked like a great bluish-orange ball of lava churning in midair. The fire was spreading out to all four sides of the building. They would have to stick to the edge of the stone foundation to make their way out...if there *was* a way out.

Blake dropped down beside her. In the orange glow, she could see his sooty cheeks and his dirt-coated hands. He had to crouch even lower than she did to fit under the flooring. But he seemed to have his bearings as he touched her elbow and motioned to the back wall. He scurried along first and she followed. It was slow moving as the dirt floor seemed to rise up, leaving less and less space for their bodies.

"We're almost there. I see the vent. It's just ahead." Blake looked back at her. Probably heard her gasping and coughing even through the rumbling roar of the flames. "You okay?"

Abby was nodding when the unmistakable sound of splitting wood cracked overhead. Abby scooted back instinctively, while Blake moved forward. There was a terrible ripping sound as the beam just over them began to split.

"Get back!" Blake yelled.

Abby was already scrambling as quickly as she could on her hands and knees until she hit the edge of the stone foundation. As quickly as the beam split, flames licked around it from the center outward, racing from the start of the wood all the way to the end, which had fallen between them, leaving her and Blake divided by a wall of fire. And the only way out was on his side of the beam.

Abby fought her tears—they would do her no good here.

It was no use. Blake could not get around the fallen burning beam, which separated him from Abigail. He couldn't even see her or hear her, but he knew that she had been forced into the far back-left corner of the building's foundation. It was shallow there and with fire blocking her, there would not be much oxygen for long.

This was all his fault. His stupid quest to find his birth parents. If he hadn't been at the Hall of Records looking up birth records, they wouldn't have gotten caught in this fire.

Or was this just a continuation of the attacks by the man from the hospital, still after Abigail? It was hard to know. It was all starting to blur together for Blake.

And anyway, what difference did it make? Right now what mattered was saving Abigail. If only he knew how.

Blake turned reluctantly away from the fallen beam and Abigail and slid the next few feet to the panel of the foundation vent.

"Please do not be locked," he prayed aloud.

Blake pressed on the wood panel, and much to his relief, it punched out of the cut frame with great ease.

The opening wasn't large but it was large enough. Blake began to squeeze through the small hole. Sunlight. Fresh air. Cold, fresh air. And voices.

"Here he is!"

In seconds, two firefighters had him under the arms and cleared him from the foundation of the old building. As soon as Blake was on his feet, someone draped a huge blanket around him. Slowly, his vision readjusted from being inside the dark crawl space.

With a cough, he grabbed the arm of the closest firefighter. "Abby's in the corner. Blocked. You have to get her out."

One of the two firefighters grabbed a sledgehammer from the truck and went running to the spot Blake had indicated. The far-left corner of the building.

"Are you sure she's here?" he asked. "There's not much clearance."

"A beam fell down the center of the crawl space when we were heading for the vent. It closed her in. She has to be here." *If she hasn't already been burned or asphyxiated...* He couldn't stand to think of what might have happened to her.

"We'll have to cut out the mortar and take the stones out one by one. Otherwise we could do more damage than good," said the other firefighter.

Blake was ready to grab the hammer and have a go

at the wall himself. The building was already collapsing. They were wasting precious seconds.

The firefighter with the hammer fixed his stance on the uneven ground and began knocking at the bricks hard enough to crumble some of the mortar. A couple of stones broke loose and fell to the ground.

"We're coming in through the corner," yelled the other worker. "Cover your head."

Blake doubted she could hear them. Even if she could, he doubted there was much she could do to get out of the way. If she was even conscious...

"There can't be much air left in there. Hurry!" Blake yelled.

A second hit of the hammer knocked a small three-inch hole at the edge of the corner. Blake stood back, anxious and panicked, but also amazed at the careful approach of the two workers. With another stone held at an angle, the firefighter was able to hit down at the foundation instead of inward. The stonework crumbled under the next few blows. Once the opening was about a foot wide, the other worker lay prostrate on the grass and reached into the dark space under the building.

Blake fell to his knees when he saw Abigail's arms and hands wrapped around those of the firefighter's as he pulled her from under the building. Covered in soot and dirt, the worker slid her out facedown onto the grass. Blake moved in to help, but the hand of an EMT pulled him back.

"You need medical attention," the EMT said.

Blake shook the man off. "I'm fine. I'm a doctor. I'm fine."

His focus was completely on Abby, scanning her head to toe, looking for any sign of life. *Please be okay. Lord, she has to be okay.*

Finally, he detected the expansion of her lungs. She was breathing.

Thank You, Lord. Thank You.

Following the EMTs as they strapped her to the gurney, he watched her eyes flicker. He wanted to cry for joy. He may have only known Abigail Miller for a few days, but it was long enough to know that the world was a better place with her in it.

Thank You, Lord, he thought again as he aligned himself alongside the EMTs and offered his assistance, much more politely than the manner in which he'd refused theirs.

She had two third-degree burns on her right forearm and was blue in the lips and face from lack of oxygen. Her eyes flickered as he helped attach the oxygen mask. Once that was situated, Blake took a close look at her pupils and the contusions made on the front and back of her head earlier in the week.

A cold compress to her burns caused her to awaken with a start.

She patted his arm with her left hand as he wiped away some of the dirt and debris from her cheeks. She was so beautiful, he thought, even like this, even plain and dirty and beat-up. She was so strong—like his mother.

Her fingers wrapped around his hand and pulled at him. He bent over her. "Just relax, Abby. They're going to take you to the hospital. You need treatment on those burns. I'll go with you."

"I'm so sorry," she whispered. "I'm so sorry."

Blake shook his head. She was sorry? More like he was sorry. This was all his fault—him and his stupid idea to find his birth parents, an idea that he was pretty certain he would let go of after this. In fact, maybe it was time for him to get back to New York. He looked at Abby and those feelings she inspired in him stirred again. Yes, for more reasons than one, he needed to get back to New York.

"I couldn't save all of the documents," she whispered. "I tried, but I couldn't reach them. I'm so sorry. I know how much that meant to you. I'm so sorry, Blake."

With her left hand, Abby slid a square of folded papers from under the corner of her blouse. She had tucked them away for him. More guilt weighed at Blake's conscience. What if McClendon was right and all of this mess that was happening was his fault? He should never have come to Lancaster.

Blake climbed into the ambulance and sat beside Abigail, ready for the ride to the hospital. His left hand kept hold of Abby's and in his right he had the few documents she'd saved for him—the letter from his mother, the anonymous birth record on his birthday and three more birth records from the same year with Jane and John Doe listed as parents, all delivered by the same Dr. Nathan Miles.

Blake took in a deep breath and exhaled slowly, thinking about where he should be and what he should be doing. Why had he come down to Lancaster? More and more, he was thinking that Abby might be right. The search for his birth parents might only cause grief and pain, not to himself but to the very people connected to him. Nothing good was going to come out of his selfish quest. He could see that now—he just wished he'd realized it before he'd hurt Abigail. He swallowed hard as he looked at her burns and watched her drag in each breath of air. Blake had some serious thinking to do.

He turned his head and glanced out the back windows as the ambulance slowly pulled away from the burning building. The fire was getting under control but it had already done its damage. The roof was gone and the entire center frame of the old structure was now cinders. Only some of the brick-and-stone outer structure remained—it was a pretty safe assumption that no documents were left in that document room.

In the distance, Blake saw a group of Amish and *Englisch* onlookers watching the firefighters at work.

And while he couldn't be 100 percent sure, it looked to Blake as if off to the side of that group stood the same Amish-dressed man that he and Eli had seen in the woods the night before.

Abby never thought she'd be tired of hospitals, but she was—at least, she was tired of being a patient. Thankfully, she wasn't going to have to stay the night. The burns on her right arm were terribly painful, but the treatments done in the burn center and some pain medication had gotten them under control. She couldn't wait to get home and get cleaned up…that was, if Chief McClendon would let her go. She supposed she would find out soon enough. She'd been told he was sending two detectives to come talk to Blake and her in the hospital conference room.

She hoped Blake would return to the conference room soon. He had stayed with Abby until Dr. Dodd, the hospital administrator, had called him away for a meeting. Abby could only imagine that it had something to do with the whole crazy ordeal that seemed to be going on around them. But she wanted him there to clarify the events of the fire and those leading up to it when the police arrived.

"Miss Miller?"

"Yes?" Abby turned to a familiar face. It was the same detective who'd come to the hospital the other day with McClendon. "Oh, hello, Detective. Come on in and have a seat. Dr. Jamison should be back at any moment."

A tall brunette stood just behind him. "This is Agent Linda Day from the FBI. She's working this case and I'm her local liaison."

"Please, don't get up," Agent Day said. "I know you've had a rough week. You've certainly been keeping me busy."

The two officers took seats across from her.

"We have a few updates for you and then we want to hear about what happened at the Hall of Records today." Agent Day placed a tiny recording device on the table between them, then she opened up a leather notebook and took out a pen, ready to review and take notes.

"Sorry I'm late." Blake appeared at the door.

After introductions, Blake gave a quick rundown of exactly what had happened at the Hall of Records. Abby was surprised how much she had remembered accurately.

"Remarkable that you two escaped." Agent Day shook her head in disbelief. "According to the chief fire inspector, the inside hallway was the first to burn, the definite point of origin. Whoever set the fire used strong accelerants to draw the fire toward the document room, which, as you know, had only one exit. You were good and trapped. Everyone working the case is very impressed with your escape route."

"Except that it almost killed Abigail," Blake said. She could still hear the guilt in his voice.

"You might have both died if you hadn't gone into the crawl space," Agent Day replied. "You should be thankful, not critical."

Blake dropped his head. He seemed even more agitated since his return from meeting with Dr. Dodd.

"I heard you say that you have updates." Abby wanted to wrap up the meeting and get home. She wasn't sure if she could even take in any more information or warnings of danger. Exhaustion had set in days ago. Now even her fumes needed refueling. Soot and dirt covered every inch of her body. She needed a long, hot bath and an even hotter cup of tea.

"Yes." Agent Day turned to a different page in her notes. "Since this is my first meeting with you, I'm not sure where to start. I have no idea how much McClendon shared with you."

"Just tell us everything." Blake sighed.

Abby stiffened. Blake's presence both comforted her and disturbed her. She felt as if since their introduction in the E.R. a few days ago, they'd been together almost nonstop—and now that she thought about it, it had been nothing but nonstop trouble.

"Right," Agent Day said. "Well, then, here are the facts—Nicolas Hancock entered Fairview Hospital on Friday. He was given a lethal dose of epinephrine and died subsequently from cardiac arrest. We know virtually nothing about Mr. Hancock, except that he was a patient of a Dr. Granger, who is a family friend of Dr. Jamison's. Other than that, his contact information is bogus. His prints don't match anything in any of the databases, so he's not a criminal that we know of. Still, a man who uses an alias tends to raise eyebrows. The FBI has subpoenaed the medical records from Dr. Granger but we have so far been unable to identify Mr. Hancock. This is a problem because without knowing the victim, it's hard to put a finger on motive and therefore difficult to narrow in on possible suspects. We don't know how Hancock got to Fair-view or who admitted him. Possibly it was the killer Miss Miller saw.

"Then Miss Miller was attacked at approximately the same time and suffered similar symptoms as Hancock. Miss Miller's home was broken into and her work space was vandalized. The next day, Miss Miller was side-swiped and rear-ended on the way to her brother's by a black sedan, which was later spotted at Miller's Mill. Shortly before, Dr. Jamison was shot at while trying to connect with Mr. Linton. Today, the two of you were locked in the Hall of Records auxiliary building, from which you barely escaped when it went up in flames. The last two events are directly linked to Dr. Jamison's search for his birth parents. We think it's safe to assume that these events have all been sparked by Dr. Jamison's stay in Lancaster."

"So, the biggest missing piece is who Hancock is and why someone wanted him dead?" Abby asked.

"Yes. That and how Dr. Jamison's adoption is linked to Hancock's murder. If someone just wanted Dr. Jamison out of Lancaster, then we don't think they would go to such extreme measures."

"It seems to me that's exactly what they want. And you may change your mind after you see this." Blake paused as he pulled a magazine from his lap. He opened it to a double-page spread in the front.

"What is it?" Abby felt her heart beat faster as she stood to better view the fancy magazine with its high-gloss pages. The section was titled *Updates*. Across the two pages were various pictures of men and women Abby assumed were New York socialites. Each picture was accompanied by a short paragraph explaining some sort of business deal or life event concerning each of the young men. One of the pictures was of Blake.

Abby read aloud.

"Not quite following in his parents' footsteps, Dr. Blake Jamison loses his first patient to a simple procedure while on a pro bono sabbatical in Lancaster County. Rumors have it that the cause is substance abuse. Speculations have been made that Dr. Jamison will not wield a scalpel much longer, either here or in the quaint countryside of PA.

"But this is ridiculous!" Abby said. "That patient was never in your care until after his cardiac arrest. By that point, he was beyond saving."

"It doesn't matter. Dr. Dodd has asked me to leave Fairview."

Chapter Fourteen

"Yes, Natalie." Blake held his cell phone about three inches from his ear. Natalie was so excited that the volume of her voice had increased enough to be heard by everyone in the small coffeehouse. "I can hear you. I just can't understand what you're saying."

"Saturday. The gala. Pick me up at six."

"Yeah, about that." Blake sighed. "I don't think—"

"You promised, Blake. You're making a toast and introducing the keynote speaker. You have to be there."

Guilt slinked around Blake's neck. Natalie was right. He'd agreed to this over a month ago. But that was before the murder and the bad publicity in the *New York Ways* magazine—and meeting Abigail. Still, he had to go back home. After talking with Agent Day, it seemed best for him to give up his search, leave the hospital, try to get that damaging article retracted and just get back to his regular life.

"You haven't seen this month's copy of *NYW,* have you?" Blake asked.

"*NYW?* No. No one has. It doesn't come out until next week. Why? Did you finally agree to do that cover story?"

Next week? Then how did Dr. Dodd have a copy of it already? "No, never mind. Look, Natalie. You're right. I should be there for the gala. I hope I *can* be there. Let me see if I can get things squared away down here by the end of the week. I'll talk to you in a couple of days."

He hung up. Well, that was interesting. Maybe he could get the story retracted before it actually hit the stands. Was that possible? He was afraid to hope.

Blake gulped down his last bit of espresso. It was no longer hot, but he wanted the shot of caffeine to keep him going. What were the chances of things getting wrapped up by the end of the week? Slim to none. Every time he hoped to get answers about what was going on, instead there only seemed to be new questions to add to the equation.

In fact, he could hardly keep track of all the questions. He wished his mother were still there to talk to. She always helped him to reason out things, especially when he had tough choices to make.

Blake left a generous tip for the waitress and slipped out of the coffeehouse. He drove to the bed-and-breakfast, ready to change into something a little nicer as Abby was meeting him there for dinner. Blake had not invited her. The Youngers, the owners of the bed-and-breakfast, had heard about the fire and insisted that they both come for a big dinner on the house.

Blake changed into khakis and a freshly starched oxford. Then he straightened up his room, caught up on email and sat down with the documents that Abby had saved from the Hall of Records fire.

Dr. Nathan Miles. Blake went back to his laptop and searched for the name on Google.

Ob-gyn. New York City.

What a surprise. In fact, Dr. Miles's practice was located at 73rd on the Upper East Side, just a few blocks from Blake's apartment.

Blake also looked up the *New York Ways* website. Natalie had been right, of course. This month's issue wasn't due out for a week. So, where had Dr. Dodd gotten his copy?

Blake studied the other birth notices, the ones with different dates but also with the Jane and John Doe mother and father listings. Could all five of those babies have been given up for adoption? Blake didn't know much about adoption rates, but he doubted that in a township as small as Willow Trace there were more than two or three a year. Not five in a three-week span, especially given what Abby had told him of how rare adoption was in the Amish community that made up much of the town.

Blake ran his hands through his hair. Nothing made sense. The only constant here was that everything seemed to point back to New York.

His hotel line rang. It was Mrs. Younger announcing Abby's arrival.

Blake put away the papers and shut down his laptop. He scurried down the steps but put on the brakes as he entered the dining room. His mouth went dry and his feet froze to the floor.

There was only one guest seated, facing him in the center of the room. She wore a knee-length pencil skirt with a fitted blouse. Her long blond hair was smoothed out and loose, falling over both shoulders and waving over the left half of her face. Blake thought his heart might leap from his chest. She was so beautiful.

"Wow, Abigail," he said. "Your—your hair... You should wear it down more often. It's incredible."

Her large blue eyes looked up at him with an awe-inspiring hypnotic effect. "Thank you. I haven't worn it this way since my *Rumschpringe* days. I felt so icky after that fire, I thought…why not dress up and look nice for a change? You know what I mean?"

Blake nodded. His hand missed the back of his chair as he reached to pull it out and take a seat.

"I hope you're okay with me coming to dinner." There was a natural blush on her cheeks. "It was so nice of the Youngers. They are a great couple."

Okay? He was more than okay. Abigail was already beautiful in the jeans and sweaters she wore, but with a skirt and blouse and her hair down, she would have given any runway model a run for her money.

"I'm glad you're here for dinner." Blake forced his eyes to his water glass, which he grabbed and nearly drained trying to relieve his dry mouth. "There are a few things I wanted to discuss with you."

One glance back into her mesmerizing blue eyes and he wasn't sure if he would be able to remember a single one of them. Blake shook his head. What was happening to him? Or had already happened…

"Me, too." Abigail swept her long hair behind her shoulder. It felt strange wearing it down. What would her father say?

She knew what the bishop would say…but he'd be wrong. She hadn't dressed this way to impress Blake. She'd done it because she'd spent too much time in the past few days covered in dirt or blood or both. The bed-and-breakfast had a nice restaurant, which made for a good excuse for dressing up—and this was the only fancy outfit she owned.

She looked down at the bandages that covered the burns on her arm. The pain was steady but bearable.

Still, it fatigued her. She doubted very much that she would need to take the sleep aid the hospital had recommended.

"Well, there you are, Dr. Jamison." Mrs. Younger bounced into the room with a basket of hot yeast rolls, which she placed in the center of the table. "You can't keep a woman this special waiting. But I'm sure you already knew that."

Abby's cheeks were warm with a deep blush. She'd always liked the Youngers. Easy, no-nonsense Amish.

"Pop and I are very happy to take care of you both tonight," she continued. "It's going to be a special evening. Just sit back and enjoy. You don't even have to order. Pop already decided what the menu would be. First up is a bowl of hot Amish Church Soup. I'll be right back with that and some sweet tea. You must be starved after the rough time you've had these past few days."

Abby agreed. She was starved. And being in a fancy restaurant seemed to help put some distance between her and what had happened that afternoon.

"She's right. It has been a rough couple of days."

Blake nodded his agreement. "Yes, I was afraid you'd be too tired for this."

"What I'm too tired for is to cook for myself."

"Good point. So, how well do you know the Youngers? I really like them. They seem a bit different than your family, though—you know, in the way they are Amish."

"I went to school with their two daughters. You met Mary the other night. So I know them fairly well, but they belong to a different *Ordnung.* It's a little more modern than the one my family belongs to. And running the bed-and-breakfast and having *Englisch* guests all of the time…well, the Youngers have to be pretty in tune with everything on the outside. That makes them better hosts."

"They're the best. I'm really glad I decided to stay here." He looked down at her arms. "How much pain are you in?"

"It's okay. A steady, stinging burn, but nothing a good night's sleep won't fix."

"That was a close call. Your third one this week. Do you really think you'll be able to sleep well?"

"I hope so. I have a plan and I was hoping you'd be a part of it."

He smiled. "A plan? I like that. Let's hear it."

"Okay." Abby took a deep breath. "I hardly know where to start…." She smiled. "It has been a rough few days in more ways than one. And I'm ready to change all of that around. Like Eli has said from the beginning. We need to get ahead of this guy. I know this will surprise you but I've changed my mind about you finding your birth parents. I think you *should* find them. And I want to help. You said the very first day we met, when this whole thing started, that you didn't believe in coincidence. I don't, either."

Blake's dark chocolate eyes softened as she spoke. "You're right. I'm surprised."

"Wait. There's more." Abby held up a hand. "I also want to get you reinstated at Fairview. And I think I know how to do that. What Dr. Dodd did today is completely unfair. He can't get away with it."

Mrs. Younger brought in the steaming soup and placed it before them. *"Guten appetiten."*

"Smells delicious," Blake said.

"It's Pop's Church Soup. He says it cures any ailment." She smiled. "Enjoy."

A few minutes of silence ensued as they plunged into their soup—steaming hot and loaded with richly stewed vegetables.

Blake put down his spoon and wiped his mouth with the cloth napkin. "I appreciate your sympathy. I agree about the situation. It doesn't seem too fair. But I don't know what can be done about it, unless we call a jury of peers. I don't want to do that. You saw the magazine today. After that hit to my reputation, I have to keep a low profile. Anyway, Abby, I was going to tell you… I have decided to give up my search. It's gotten too dangerous. I have to go back to New York and take care of this article. Our foundations can't afford this bad publicity. You can't imagine what a mess it will start in New York if the wrong people get ahold of the information—it could ruin a lot of good organizations that my parents started. I really don't want that. You were right. My search is selfish and could bring a lot of pain to a lot of people. It already has."

Abby couldn't believe Blake had changed his mind. She had to talk him into continuing the search. It was the best way to get to the bottom of things. "What about the rest of the investigation? I think you must be close to finding your parents. You shouldn't give up now."

"I can't believe your change of heart." He looked truly bewildered. "I don't even know what to say." He swallowed hard. "It's been nothing but trouble since I came here. The fact that everything is tied back to New York, or seems to be, is what really has me convinced that I need to let it all go before someone else gets hurt."

"But that would only resolve half the problem." Abby sat tall in her chair. "You're forgetting that we witnessed a murder. Should we let the killer go free? And don't you care about getting reinstated? This is your career.

I know you care about medicine. I saw you the other night helping Mrs. Brenneman. You are a great doctor."

"Thanks. I guess I hadn't had a chance for that to really sink in yet. I should call Dr. Dodd first thing in the morning. I was so stunned by that article, I didn't know how to respond. Speaking of which, I found out this afternoon that that article—the one I showed you and Agent Day—well, it hasn't been released yet. A friend of mine in New York said that magazine doesn't come out for another week. So how did Dr. Dodd get hold of a copy?"

Abby pressed her lips together. "That is strange. Can you keep it from coming out?"

"Maybe, but I'd need to get back to New York." He reached across the table and stroked her hand. "I wish things were different."

Abby knew what that meant. She pulled her hand away. Things weren't different, no matter what they might wish. Blake was engaged—and he was not her type, anyway. She could never understand the world he was from, much less be a part of it. "You're right. You should go back to New York."

He blinked hard. "I thought you just said I should stay and keep searching."

"I think you should do both. Go up to New York. Talk to Dr. Granger. Fix things at the magazine. And find some answers." Abigail focused her gaze on him, careful to remove any single romantic suggestion. "You said yourself, everything leads back to New York."

"And Dr. Miles."

"Dr. Miles?"

"Yes, the doctor whose name is on all those birth records. The ones you were so careful to save for me in the fire. Did you know that you also saved a letter from my mother? It's the last thing I have from her. You have no idea how much that letter means to me."

Abby could feel his eyes on her again. He did feel that connection between them, even though it could never amount to anything.

"I was going through those papers just a few minutes ago," Blake continued. "When I looked up Dr. Miles online, I found that he practices medicine in New York."

"That's just one more reason to go."

"Come with me."

"What? I can't go to New York."

"Here we are." Mrs. Younger bounced into the room again carrying a large tray. "Miller's Homemade Chicken Potpie. It's made from scratch, and all the ingredients are local and Amish grown."

"Miller? As in Abigail Miller?" Blake looked over at her.

Mrs. Younger explained as she placed the plates on the table with pride. "Oh, yes, it's the best recipe there is. I had to beg for it, but Abigail's mother finally relented after I told her that we didn't want our tourists going away not knowing who started the chicken potpie. Of course, Abby and her mother make it best, but I hope you'll both find this a close second. In any case, it's the best comfort food in the world."

"I don't know about you," Abby said after Mrs. Younger had left them alone, "but I could use a little comfort."

"No kidding." Blake smiled before digging into his pie. "Wow. That's the best chicken potpie I've ever had. And you can make it better? I think I'd like to try that."

Abby blushed and looked away. It had been so long since she'd cooked with her mother. So long since she'd thought about caring for someone in that way. There was something intimate and loving about making food for the people you cared for. Blake's comments forced up a longing in her that she'd put away years ago when she'd decided to become a nurse.

Abby forced down a bite of the chicken pie. It was full of familiar home-cooked flavors but they gave her no comfort just now. She had to help Blake, because that was the only way this whole ordeal would end. He was really starting to get under her skin and it scared her. She did not want to feel this way. And she certainly didn't want to feel this way about someone like Blake.

"I don't really cook anymore," she said. "But I could give you the recipe. Maybe you could have your private chef make it for you."

Blake laughed at her teasing tone. "Seriously. It's not like that. No private chef for me."

"So you cook?"

"I eat out." He smiled. "Come to New York with me tomorrow. We've been in this whole ordeal together, it doesn't seem right if I go alone, especially if I end up getting some answers from Dr. Miles. You deserve to be the first to know."

"Dr. Jamison, I'm so sorry. We're both so sorry." Mr. and Mrs. Younger raced into the dining room half-breathless. "I must have left the back doors open. I can't believe it."

Abby put down her fork. "What is it? You both look pale as sheets."

"I was just going in to give you fresh towels for the night and turn down your bed…." Mrs. Younger shook her head. "You're so meticulously neat. I knew you couldn't have left your room like that."

"Someone's been in my room?" Blake stood.

Mr. and Mrs. Younger both looked down, nodding their heads nervously.

"It's terrible." Mrs. Younger looked as if she might cry. "They've ruined everything. I'm so sorry."

Chapter Fifteen

Blake stood at the doorway of his hotel room and scanned the wreckage. Every word the Youngers had said was true. Clothes had been strewn everywhere. Anything and everything of value had been taken— his watch, his computer, and the precious file containing the newly found birth records and the letter from his mother.

Chief McClendon and Detective Langer shook their heads as they surveyed the space. As with the hospital, Abby's car wreck and the break-in at her clinic, the FBI investigative team, headed by Agent Day, took pictures and asked lots of questions.

Blake was not just tired this evening; this event had made him angry.

"How can we end this?" he heard Abby murmuring to one of the agents. He couldn't have agreed more. And he realized that everything she'd been saying at dinner was right. He needed to go to New York to see if they could connect the dots. At least it was worth a try.

He pulled Detective Langer aside and told him that he planned to go to the city in the morning and that he hoped Abby would go with him. Langer explained that he or someone from the FBI might accompany them. He would look into it and get back to Blake as soon as possible. In any case, they weren't to go anywhere for the night. Langer and Day wanted them both to stay at the bed-and-breakfast.

"It's safe to have you in one place, where we can be certain you're protected," Agent Day explained. "The Youngers have rooms for each of you. One of the FBI agents is going to take one of the other rooms. You should both sleep well."

Abby wrapped her arms around her chest. He supposed it was to stop her shivering. She looked on the verge of tears. She was clearly not happy about having to stay the night there. "You'll have to get word to my brother. He's expecting me."

"Should I tell him you're going to New York tomorrow?" Langer asked her.

Her eyes shot a surprised look to Blake and he nodded. "You were right. I thought we could go up for the day…talk to Granger and Miles and someone at the magazine. Maybe we'll learn something."

Abby nodded to Langer. Blake was glad. He wanted her to be with him when he talked to the people in New York. Somehow he felt it would be helpful—or maybe he just liked the idea of her being by his side. Although tonight, she looked so weak and frail—she was not the spunky woman who was just having a nice dinner with him. Part of him wanted to put an arm around her and pull her close. It was getting harder for him to look at her and not feel the strong pull of the attraction and admiration for her that had developed over the past few days.

Ignoring those feelings, as he knew he had to do,

Blake took hold of her hurt arm and lifted one of the bandages. "I need to change this dressing. Come on."

She looked up at him with her dark blue eyes, which began to smile back at him. "I'm sorry about all your things getting stolen. Especially the letter from your mother."

The understanding in her words touched him deeply and caused a lump to form in his throat. He had to look away as he swallowed it down and led her away to tend to her burn.

"Is this truly your first trip to the city?" Blake asked as he steered his Land Rover through the Holland Tunnel into Manhattan.

"First time out of Pennsylvania." Abby couldn't believe she'd slept almost the entire way to New York. But at least she was feeling better. The lump on her head was gone. The burns on her arms had stopped hurting. Her energy was returning. "I've been to Philly once but other than that I haven't been outside of Lancaster. I guess that's hard for you to imagine. You've been all over the world."

Blake shrugged and grinned at her. He looked well rested and extremely handsome in a pair of gray dress slacks with a yellow oxford. She liked how he rolled the sleeves up, making it easy to see the strong muscles of his forearms.

"What about high school and college? You must have left home for that."

"But I didn't go far. I was homeschooled with a Mennonite family that lives close to my parents. My dad gave me until I was twenty for education, which was very generous. So I finished high school at sixteen and commuted to a small college. I was a registered nurse by age nineteen."

"That's impressive," Blake said. "And it's great your parents gave you and your brother choices and opportunities."

"I think now my *dat* wishes he hadn't. He thinks he failed as a father—as an Amish father, that is."

"It's ironic, actually, that my parents weren't as liberal with me as yours were with you and your brother. I wasn't given choices. I had to have what they thought was the best whether it was what I wanted or not."

There was sadness not bitterness in his voice.

"Do you think that you would have chosen differently?"

"I don't know. I hadn't really thought about it until they died. It was then I realized that I had everything. Always, I've had everything—and yet, no peace."

"We find our peace in God," Abby said.

"That I know, thanks to my nanny. She made sure I understood the love of God. I do get that, Abby." Blake pressed his lips together. "I have spiritual peace. I just don't always like who I am, what I do, where I live, my friends."

Abby didn't have time to consider his words too much as they drove down an elegant street lined with designer shops and fancy restaurants.

"This is the Upper East Side. I grew up here."

"You don't like this?" she asked rhetorically. "Really?"

Such beautiful homes and stylish apartment buildings. Even the well-dressed and coiffed pedestrians looked as if they'd come straight out of a magazine—a magazine like the one Blake had shown her the other day. Abby grew more and more uncomfortable by the minute. "I guess I see what you mean by having the best. Poor you...."

"I know. That's why I've never said to anyone what I just said to you. I should be nothing but grateful. And I am. But I sometimes wonder what I would have been or what I would have done if I had made more of my own choices. That's all. I'm not ungrateful. Or disappointed. I just want to find that peace inside again and know I'm exactly where God wants me to be."

There was a struggle in his expression Abby had never seen before. Blake wasn't merely looking for his birth parents. He was looking for himself. He just didn't know it yet.

"Dr. Granger's office is just around the corner. We'll park here. I called ahead to let them know I'd be coming in today."

"Is this your office here?"

"No, but my apartment is. I thought we'd park here and take cabs." Blake turned down an alley and stopped in front of a hidden garage door. He pressed a button on his dash and the door disappeared slowly into the wall. Inside was underground parking. An armed guard sat in a small glassed-in office. He looked up and waved to Blake, who smiled back and drove straight to a corner spot, crowned with a sign on the wall that read Dr. Jamison in large black letters. Almost every other spot was occupied—occupied by cars that Abby knew cost more than she could earn in two years.

Blake gave a half laugh. "Funny. It feels like I've been away for ages. Not a week."

He turned off the car and looked over at her. He reached across the console and touched her forearm. "Thank you."

"For what?" She slid her arm away and glanced in

another direction. He had no idea how uncomfortable he made her.

He smiled. "I don't know. For being here. For being you."

She looked back at him. "I just want us both to be able to get on with our lives."

"Abby, are you ever afraid you're going to let everyone down?"

"Sure. All the time. And I have. Look at my father. I couldn't have let him any more down if I'd tried."

"Do you think you'll go back to what he wants for you? Get married? Be what your father thinks you should be?" His eyes were warm like chocolate and the meaning behind his question went beyond her conflict with her father. He was asking her what she saw for her future. Would it be Amish? Or *Englisch?*

She shook her head, filled with sad emotions. She didn't want to care about Blake the way she was starting to. Nothing could be more stupid. But he felt it, too. She could see it in his eyes. She had to put an end to his hope once and for all.

"No. I won't go back. And I won't get married. I'll keep living the life I have now—the one I've chosen. That's where I belong. But I hope one day my father will want me just the way I am."

There was silence as she followed Blake out of the parking garage and down 73rd Street.

"Dr. Granger, thank you so much for taking the time to see us this morning on such short notice." Blake shook the elderly doctor's hand and introduced him to Abigail.

"Your parents were such dear friends to Stella and me. You know you are welcome anytime." He motioned for them to take a seat in the chairs on the other side of his desk. "Would you like a coffee or tea?"

After they declined, he excused his assistant and took a seat in a big leather chair behind his desk. "How can I help you, Blake? Miss Miller?"

Blake first explained about his sabbatical to Lancaster, which Dr. Granger had little reaction to. "Abigail and I both saw this patient and his paperwork. His name was Hancock, Nicolas Hancock. His file indicated that he'd been your patient at Norcross Hospital before being transferred to Fairview. Then Mr. Hancock died, and some…irregularities were found in his information. Enough to make the police believe he might have a different identity completely. It's put me in a bit of a situation with Fairview. I thought if you had any particular information you could pass on about him, it might be helpful."

Dr. Granger leaned forward, his expression flat as he made a steeple with his fingertips over the desk in front of him. "A police detective was here just a few days ago, asking similar questions. I'll have to tell you the same thing I told him. Any client information is privileged, as you both know. I can't divulge anything to any of you. I'm very sorry."

"I don't think that confidentiality applies here." Blake was ready for his response, even though he'd hoped to hear a different one. "You were his physician and so was I, according to the transfer chart. Any information you pass on to me is a consultation over a common patient. That is completely legal."

Dr. Granger frowned. He sat upright and shifted his weight, again clearly thinking over his answer before speaking. He raised a hand and pressed a speaker button on his phone. "Mrs. Timmons, could you please bring me the Nicolas Hancock file?"

Almost instantly, Mrs. Timmons rushed in with a thin patient file. She passed it over the desk to Dr. Granger. He opened it, looked inside and closed it again before smiling at Mrs. Timmons. "Thank you. Please close the door on your way out."

Mrs. Timmons left the room and Dr. Granger passed over the file to Blake. "I'll let you thumb through it. I'm afraid I can't give you a copy without consulting my lawyer. I'm sorry, Blake. I wish I could be more forthcoming, especially to you, but as you know with malpractice suits running rampant, I just can't be too cautious."

"I understand. I appreciate this." Blake reached a nervous hand over and took the file. He opened it and began to scan the first page.

"Well, then… I hope that helps you both. Now if you'll excuse me, I have patients waiting. Please take your time. Mrs. Timmons will see you out and you can leave the folder with her." He shook Blake's hand as he passed on his way out of the office. "A pleasure to see you again, Blake. I hope this situation at Fairview is resolved quickly. Miss Miller, lovely to meet you."

"Dr. Granger?" Blake stood and turned to the door. The old friend of his parents' looked back over his shoulder. "Did my parents ever tell you that I was adopted?"

Dr. Granger stopped fast. His shoulders rose up as he took in a quick breath. He turned his head back slowly. He was still smiling but the expression was different than it had been earlier. "No. I didn't know that. In fact, I find that hard to believe. How did you find out about this?"

"My mother told me."

"Well…as I said, that surprises me, Blake." Granger was frowning now. "If I were you, I'd be careful who I shared that with."

"Oh, I am, Doctor. I am very careful." Blake watched Granger leave the room. Then he tossed the Hancock file on the desk and turned to Abby. "Come on. Let's go."

"Don't you want to read the file?"

"No, it's a phony. Dr. Granger was lying about almost everything."

Chapter Sixteen

"How do you know he was lying?" Abby asked as they sped along in a cab toward the magazine office. She didn't question for a moment whether Blake was right or not. She hadn't liked Dr. Granger. There was something slightly snaky about his expressions. And she didn't appreciate how he'd added that ominous warning to Blake after he inquired about the adoption.

"It was obvious that he was lying about not knowing I was adopted. Dr. Granger used to work with my mother. How could he not have known? All of a sudden his colleague has a baby and was never pregnant?"

"So why lie about it to you now that you already know?"

Blake shrugged. "I can't imagine why he was lying at all. Just like I can't imagine why he would go to all the trouble to create a phony Hancock folder. It was so generic—and the specifics were dead wrong. Said the man was six feet tall and had blond hair."

"He was bald and maybe five foot eight."

"Exactly."

"It's like he was expecting us or expecting the detective to return with a warrant for the file." Abby sighed.

"Maybe the visit to the magazine publishing offices will be more productive."

"I'm not so sure that this visit wasn't advantageous. The clock has been ticking ever since we saw Hancock and now it's ticking double-time. I think we are closing in on things. Just one little missing piece will have it all make sense."

"Or one big piece," Abby said with a teasing tone.

"Yes. And here we are. This is what they call midtown."

Abby could hardly believe the size of the buildings. It hurt her neck to look up at them. They exited the cab and stood together in front of the giant publishing company.

"Wow. You know, you can't really fathom how so many people can be on one little island until you get here and see it for yourself. Are you sure Langer is still behind us? I don't see how he can keep up with all this traffic and people. It's amazing."

"He's right there." Blake nodded his head in the direction of the other side of the street. The Lancaster detective was leaning against a park bench with a newspaper rolled up under his arm—his eyes on the two of them.

Blake opened the front doors of the fifty-plus-story building on Avenue of the Americas. "*New York Ways* offices are on the twenty-eighth floor."

After passing through a tight security check, a bellman ushered them up to the magazine offices and helped to buzz them inside. Blake told the receptionist who he was and that he wanted to see the managing editor, Mitchell Bain.

For ten minutes, Abby and Blake pretended to look through back issues. As fate would have it, Abby picked up an issue containing the same photo she'd seen of Blake and Natalie, with the caption about their upcoming engagement. She turned the magazine around and showed him, hoping her expression was pleasant, hiding the lump that had lodged in her throat.

Blake groaned, taking the magazine from her hands. "I remember that. That's the day Daveux practically accosted me."

"And your fiancée?" Abby bit her lip at her own catty remark. *Way to hide the feelings, Abigail.*

"She's *not* my fiancée. She was," Blake said, passing the photo back to her with an annoyed expression. He stared her square in the eyes. "But I called it off because it would have been the biggest mistake of my life."

Who was he trying to convince—her or himself?

"It's none of my business," Abby said.

Blake had just opened his mouth to reply when Mr. Bain walked into the reception area.

"Dr. Jamison! I hope you're here to say that you're finally agreeing to a cover story." Bain's voice was overbearingly loud and almost comical coming from such a small man. His suit was made of expensive material but in a very loud pattern, and his tie had been loosened at the neck with the top few buttons of his shirt open, revealing a thick gold chain.

"Not exactly." Blake stood and motioned to Abby. "This is Abigail Miller. We work together at the hospital."

"Ms. Miller, nice to meet you." Bain looked tense and his speech was hurried. "Well, then…if you're not here about a cover story, then what can I do for you today?"

"If we could speak somewhere privately?" Blake suggested politely.

Blake and Abby followed Bain down a long, narrow hallway lined with closet-size offices, most occupied by severely stressed-looking men and women busy typing away at their computers. At the end of the hallway, they entered a slightly larger office where they took seats around Bain's tiny desk. He had to remove a few stacks of papers so that they could all see each other. He sat back, glancing down at the screen of his smartphone as he waited for Blake to speak.

"First of all, I want to know how you got this story. And then how it got to a Dr. Dodd at Fairview Hospital." Blake handed over the magazine copy that he'd gotten from Dr. Dodd—the one with the short blurb about Hancock's death, which insinuated malpractice in the affair.

Bain took the copy from Blake. His stubby fingers reminded Abby of her attack at the hospital. She closed her eyes against the flash of images firing through her mind, but she couldn't stop them. The fat fingers closing around her arm. She could still feel the bruise on her flesh even now. And those cold gray eyes...

"I don't know who Dr. Dodd is and I certainly don't know how this got to anyone." Bain turned page after page of the magazine issue with an astonished look on his face. "This hasn't come out and I didn't authorize this blurb about you. I'm as stunned as you are, Dr. Jamison. In fact, I have the mock-up for this month's issue right here. It releases next week, so of course it's already been finalized, but you aren't in it. This page is completely different."

While Bain pulled the mock-up of the current issue up on his computer, Blake looked over at Abigail. "The missing piece?"

She nodded. "One of them."

Bain showed them the current issue, which—as he'd said—did not include the small but damaging paragraph about Blake, Hancock's death and Fairview Hospital.

"So, how could a doctor in Lancaster produce a magazine copy so convincing and with every other page of the issue exactly correct?" Abby asked.

"It had to come off our printer, I suppose? Or maybe someone here on staff?" Bain said. "But it's completely against policy. Staff members are not even allowed to discuss articles, let alone distribute early copies or, even worse, tampered copies. I want to know who is responsible for this. This is exactly the kind of employee that will sell me out to the *New Yorker* and put me out of business."

"Who usually writes these blurbs for you?" Blake asked.

"Freelance writers," Bain said. "There's one in particular that sort of comes and goes. A photojournalist. I can't think of his name. I haven't heard from him in weeks. I don't like him. He writes a good story but he always goes too far. The *NYW* is about showing successes in New York. Not this." He threw the phony magazine on the desk. "I'll do anything you need, Dr. Jamison, to find the person responsible. I intend to get to the bottom of this."

Abby leaned forward. "How about you start by calling Dr. Dodd and telling him what you just told us so that Dr. Jamison can get back to work at the hospital?"

Bain nodded. "Done. What else?"

"The name of the writer you're talking about…" Abby said. "It doesn't happen to be Daveux, does it?"

"Yes. That's it. Phillipe Daveux." Bain hit the top of the magazine copy with his hand. "This is exactly the sort of thing he likes to dig up. And if not him, one of the others in his little club, as we call it. You know they all hang together—that group of journalists and photographers."

Abby and Blake exchanged glances.

"So, it might be worth our while to speak to him or to this group," Blake said.

"I suppose. But I can assure you that copy will not be hitting the newsstands."

"I'd still like to know how he got the information, if he is the one responsible," Blake said. "Are you allowed to give us his contact information?"

"Daveux is not his real name. Let me check with Payroll."

Bain picked up his phone and called Payroll. Seconds later, Bain checked his computer. "Payroll is going to email the information.... Ah, here it is. Lyle Morris."

"Lyle Morris?"

"Right. Daveux is an alias," Bain explained. "You know, a pen name. These guys dig up dirt on people like you but they don't want you doing the same. They all use fake names to protect themselves and their families. So, do you want his info?"

Blake typed the address and phone number into his phone. They would have to work in another visit during their trip.

"Thank you, Mr. Bain. You've been extremely helpful."

"What do you say we grab a bite before we go see Dr. Miles? This is one of my favorites." Blake had the taxi stop in front of an elegant bistro.

"I'd say I thought you'd never ask. I'm famished. Also, we should probably let Langer know our additional plans, right?"

"We should."

Blake was immediately greeted by the maître d' of the little French restaurant, who made a little more fuss over him than was necessary. They sat, ordered and called Langer.

"Well, look who's back in town and doesn't call his friends?" A foursome of young men surrounded their table.

"How's that country-doctor thing working out for you?" another of the men asked.

Blake smiled with reserve. "Abby, meet my partners. This is Bill, Sam, Devin and Artie."

"Nice to meet you."

"Nice to meet you, too," the one named Artie said, making big eyes. "Are you the reason Jamison took off to the country?"

"I don't think so."

"Abby is a nurse at Fairview Hospital. We're here checking on a patient." Blake ignored their efforts to belittle his sabbatical.

"Kind of a long-distance house visit."

"Blake, you really need to look over all those files I sent you. The lawyer and business manager are tired of waiting."

"I'll get to it as soon as possible," Blake said.

The others nodded, but even Abby could feel their frustration with Blake. If only they knew what he'd been through over the past few days, but she imagined they had no idea.

"Well," one of them said as they moved away, "if you're here tonight, a group of us are meeting up at the club after work. You should both come."

"Thanks, but we're not staying." Blake shook his

head. "Like I said, we are here on hospital business and have to get back to Lancaster tonight."

His partners' faces expressed mixtures of bewilderment, concern and perhaps even some amusement.

When they had gone, Blake sat down again and placed his napkin in his lap. "Sorry about those guys. They aren't too on board with my sabbatical to Fairview."

Their sandwiches came quickly and Abby found that she was even hungrier than she'd thought. Getting some food into her system seemed to recharge her spirits, too. What did she care if Blake was a rich New York doctor with lots of rich, good-looking friends? They just needed to find out what had happened back at Fairview so they could both get on with their lives.

She took a long drink of water, thinking over all the events of the past few days.

"You asked me what I'll ask Daveux.... I guess the most important thing to get out of him is whether or not he knows how that information about Hancock's death got to the magazine."

"What?" Abby was still staring out the window, lost in her own review of the events, not listening. "I'm sorry. I was just thinking all that over. You know, we know why I'm a target. But why are you a target? Why does someone want you away from Fairview so badly? Maybe the information you need about your birth parents is at the hospital."

Blake scratched his head. "I hadn't thought about that. Maybe I should talk to Dr. Dodd?"

"Maybe..."

"Maybe?" Blake followed her eyes to the front desk, where the maître d' pointed a long-legged brunette dressed in a gorgeous black fitted suit toward them.

"Natalie?"

"Yes. I'd bet a million dollars one of my partners thought this would be funny."

Abby shrugged. "I'll just go powder my nose and give you a few minutes alone."

She started to stand but Blake grabbed her by the arm. He clamped his fingers on her tiny wrist and gently kept her from pulling away. Natalie was quickly approaching. Abby hated that her heart was beating so fast. She hoped Blake couldn't tell what she felt inside. That he mattered to her. And that she was so happy that this woman was no longer his fiancée. Of course, what, then, was Natalie to him? And why was she here hunting him down?

Chapter Seventeen

"Sit down, Abby." Blake looked at her with pleading brown eyes. "Please? You don't need to go powder anything. You need to stay right here. With me."

Blake tried to silently plead with Abby to stay in her seat.

"Please?"

Abby sat back in her seat with reluctance.

"There you are." Natalie stopped beside the table. Her eyes dropped down to where Blake held tight to Abigail's hand. Her perfectly toned skin blanched.

"I suppose Artie told you we were here?" he said.

"He said *you* were here with a colleague."

"Good old Artie."

"Hi, I'm Abigail Miller. I work at the hospital where Blake is on sabbatical." Abby wriggled her arm free and offered her hand to Natalie.

Natalie shook Abby's hand but not without giving her the up and down. Abby slyly contained a smile at Natalie's shallow behavior.

"So, here on business and you didn't even call?"

"Why would I call you, Natalie?"

"We have a lot to go over for the gala." She looked

behind her, grabbed an empty chair and made a place for herself at the table. "We could talk now, if Miss Miller doesn't mind?"

Abby shrugged. "Sure."

"I mind." Blake stood. He walked around Natalie and reached his arm around Abigail. "We have a two-o'clock appointment. I know this is short notice and I'm sorry for that, but I may not make it to the gala, Nat. You should ask someone else to introduce the keynote speaker."

"What?" She stood as they walked away. "What about the foundation? Your parents? What will every-one say? You have responsibilities, Blake. You can't just move to Tombouctou and think that everything you left behind will just take care of itself."

Blake stopped. He looked at Abigail. He'd felt more peace with her in a week and with a killer after them than he'd ever had in New York City with Natalie and everything in the world at his fingertips. And yet, Nata-lie was right. He had responsibilities. He owed it to his parents to run the foundation and continue their work. Was there a way he could do that without falling into the trap of his old life?

"Don't move," he said to Abby. "Stay right here. Promise me."

"And miss this? Are you kidding?" She smiled. But he knew Abby was uncomfortable and confused about his friendship with Natalie. If only he'd fully explained it before...

Blake sighed as he walked back to Natalie. "You're right, Natalie. I do want to slip from these responsi-bilities for a bit. In fact, I have to. I have some things I have to figure out and I'm asking you as a friend to try to understand that."

She looked over his shoulder at Abby. "Is she what you're trying to figure out?"

He glanced back at Abigail, too. "Look, Nat, just cover for me at the gala. After that, I'll get back to work with the foundation."

"Then you're coming back from Pennsylvania?" Natalie lit up.

"I don't know."

"Are you in love with her?" Natalie frowned disapprovingly. "She's so...plain."

"Goodbye, Nat. Thanks for taking care of the gala." Blake walked back to Abigail. "We need to hurry to Dr. Miles's office. It's not in this part of town."

He hailed a cab and followed Abby into it. "I'm sorry about all that back there."

"All what? I told you before it's none of my business." Abby looked him square in the eyes. She was either really put off with him or she meant exactly what she said. Either way, he didn't like it one bit. As soon as there was a chance, he was going to tell her the whole story, whether she wanted to hear it or not.

"You know, I haven't seen Langer since we went into the restaurant. Should we be worried?"

"No. He knows our agenda." They exited the cab in SoHo near St. John's Park and began to walk the three blocks east to Miles's office.

"Is that Langer?" Abby motioned toward a man standing outside of a deli just across the street.

"I can't tell—he has his head down. But he had this address, so that would make sense that he..."

"What?" Abby asked him. "You look concerned."

"I just thought I saw..." *Dr. Granger.* "Never mind. My eyes are playing tricks on me. You know, Abigail, you can ask me anything about my friends, including

Natalie. Or about my life in New York. I can't help but notice that you seem a little tense after lunch. I hope that wasn't because of the unexpected interruptions."

"I—I don't have any questions, Blake. I'm tense because we're in trouble and the detective assigned to escort us seems to be missing." She looked at him with a matter-of-fact expression.

Blake dropped his head as he opened the door to Dr. Miles's office. Apparently, she really didn't care about him or his life here. And what did it matter? He had to come back to New York, back to his practice and back to the foundation. He owed it to his parents, and besides, it was important, valuable work.

Even if it could never make him fully happy.

Abby pushed away all thoughts of Blake's offer to ask him questions about his life in New York. She'd seen plenty with her own two eyes. Now she just needed to figure this mystery out and get back to her clinic.

Dr. Miles's office was warm and cozy, painted brightly in shades of orange and yellow. Three women in their second or third trimesters sat in the waiting room, reading on Kindles and iPads. Abby felt comforted by the scene—finally, something familiar to her, when the rest of New York had seemed like a foreign planet. A young and attractive nurse escorted them to a small office. They sat opposite the desk and Dr. Miles joined them in less than a minute. He was a big, whiteheaded and white-bearded man, jovial and handsome. He could have played Santa Claus at Macy's without even applying any makeup. He even had a deep, jolly chuckle and a twinkle in his eye. All he lacked was the red suit. It made him seem familiar and Abby couldn't help but think that she must have met him before.

"Dr. Miles," Blake said after introducing the two of them. "I understand that about thirty years ago you were working in Lancaster County?"

His eyes opened wide but his smile never faltered. "That's right. I wasn't there for long. Just my first year out of medical school."

"Do you remember delivering babies for any Amish families?"

"Well, yes. Yes, I do. Many."

"Were any of those babies put up for adoption that you know of?"

He chuckled again and smiled wider. "That was a long time ago, son. But I don't remember any. Of course, I'm not so sure I'd know about an adoption. I just went in and delivered the baby. I worked nights on call. I hardly knew the patients. I never saw the families after the babies were born. I wasn't the main doctor. Just his night watchman, so to speak."

"So, who was the main obstetrician for the practice?" Abby asked.

Dr. Miles dropped his smile for a nanosecond, recovering his cheery disposition with another one of his chuckles. "It was a large practice. There were many others. I don't remember all their names. So, why all the questions about my early career? I guess I misunderstood why you needed to see me. What exactly is this all about?"

Blake cleared his throat. "We work at Fairview Hospital in Lancaster and we're trying to straighten up some incomplete birth files. Your name or your signature is on many of these incomplete records. I know it was a long time ago, but we were just hoping you might remember if some of the babies you delivered ended up going out for adoption. Several of these birth records you signed have Jane and John Doe listed as the parents."

Once more, Dr. Miles's eyes flickered and his jovial Santa Claus demeanor slipped away. This time, a sense of evil flashed across his face. Abby closed her eyes. Could it be? Could those gray Santa Claus eyes be the same ones that delivered a lethal injection to her arm? The voice sounded like the one she'd heard in that hallway—but was her mind playing tricks on her, making her think she was hearing similarities that weren't actually there? Abby's fingers tightened around the arms of her chair as she tried to remain calm.

"Did the hospital send you here?" Dr. Miles asked, his composure now completely returned.

"No, sir. This is more of a personal quest."

"I see. Well, I may be able to help you." He stood and pulled a buzzing pager from his waist. He turned his head away from them and Abby could no longer double-check his face for comparison with the doctor she'd walked in on in the closed-off wing of Fairview.

"Stay here," he said. "I have some old files stacked away in storage. I'll be right back." He slipped out, shutting the door to his office behind him.

Blake was so frustrated he didn't notice her shaking and still, seated in her chair. "Well, that was a waste of time. I'm afraid we aren't going to get anything from Daveux, either. And this whole trip will have been useless."

"Check the door," she said.

"What?" Blake turned to her and lifted an eyebrow. "Abby, what's the matter? You're shaking from head to toe."

"Dr. Miles, I think he's the same doctor I—I saw... I think he's the same doctor that—"

Blake put a hand on her trembling shoulder. "Shh."

"Try the door."

Blake put his hand on the knob. It wouldn't turn. "He locked us in?"

"He locked us in. Of course he locked us in. He's a killer!"

"Hold on," Blake said, pulling a credit card from his wallet.

"You really think that will work?" Abby asked.

"I hope so." Blake inserted the card through the crack between the door and the door frame. He pulled it down and wiggled the doorknob. Abby held her breath.

Click!

It worked. Blake pushed the door open, grabbed Abby by the hand and raced out of the room. At the end of the hallway was a fire-exit stairwell. They ran for it and dashed out of the hallway as fast as they could. With his free hand, Blake dialed Detective Langer. "We're coming out of the building. Pick us up!"

Chapter Eighteen

"Whew! That was close."

A few minutes later, they were safe inside an unmarked police vehicle and talking on the phone to Agent Day.

"It was him. I'm sure of it." Abby clutched the phone in her shaking hands. "Dr. Miles, he was the man with Hancock in the empty wing of Fairview. He's the one who killed Hancock and then tried to kill me. He hid it at first with his phony smiles and jovial attitude, but the second he became angry, his eyes gave him away."

"Okay. Okay." Blake could hear Day's voice over the line loud and clear. "I'll get our people on that angle. He wasn't even on our radar but we will definitely look into it ASAP. We've been so busy focusing on the doctors at the hospital and Granger that we hadn't—"

"Tell her that Miles may have worked at Fairview at one time—or at least that he worked for people who worked at the hospital. He said so himself. That would have been thirty years ago, but he'd still know his way around the building."

Abby nodded and passed on the information. After a few more of Day's questions, she disconnected and put the phone away. Langer was taking them to the address for Phillipe Daveux, aka Lyle Morris—their last visit of the day.

"Are you sure you're up for this visit to Mr. Morris?" Blake asked. "I'm sure you could sit with Langer while I go to the apartment."

"No way. I want to go with you. I want to see this guy who prints lies and tries to ruin other people's lives."

The drive to the apartment was a long one, all the way to the Upper West Side. Even Blake was surprised to find that the address took them to a lovely brownstone not too far from Central Park.

"I suppose writing freelance articles is a pretty good living," Blake said. After a nod to Langer, he followed Abby up the front steps, joining her just as she rang the doorbell. Footsteps sounded up to the front door, which slowly cracked open but only as far as the chain lock would allow.

"Mrs. Morris?" Blake said.

"Who's asking?" The woman was a caramel blonde, midforties with large dark circles under her eyes as if she'd been sick for a long time. Her accent was thick, French, perhaps.

"I'm Abigail Miller and this is Dr. Blake Jamison." Abby stepped forward, thinking she might be a little less intimidating to the woman than Blake in his stiff, starched shirt. "We just came from *New York Way* magazine after talking to the managing editor, Mr. Bain. There's a really important article we'd like to discuss with Lyle Morris. We tried his cell phone and couldn't get an answer."

The woman let her words sink in. She looked at Blake. "You look familiar, *non?*"

"Yes," Blake said. "Your...husband? Mr. Morris has written a few articles about my family."

Mrs. Morris hesitated again, her eyes stuck on Blake. At length, she shut the door, unfastened the chain lock and reopened it. "I don't know what to tell you. Lyle left last week to follow a story. I haven't heard from him since. I thought he would be back by now. Maybe tomorrow he will be here. I don't know. If you want to leave your number, I can have him call you when he returns."

"This really can't wait." Blake pressed her. "You must have some way to get in touch with him. In case of an emergency?"

"I don't." She shrugged. "He doesn't like to be bothered while he's working. And we are all fine here, as you see."

Abby scratched her head, unable to understand the arrangement the Morrises seemed to have. "Do you know what sort of story he was working on? This is really important. Dr. Jamison's foundation for children with medical needs and his own career are at risk. If you can help us..."

"I only know that he was traveling." She tilted her head to the side. "So this story you want to talk to him about—it is about you, Dr. Jamison? I know about your foundation. My husband and I, of course, have great interest in it. Our oldest son was born with a birth defect. Your foundation funded a special operation for him that our insurance would not pay."

No wonder the man had devoted a webpage to Blake and his family and written so many articles about the foundation. He was personally invested in it.

"I would love to hear his story," Blake said.

Again, the woman hesitated, but then she stepped aside and motioned for them to come in.

They followed Mrs. Morris down a narrow hallway lined with amazing black-and-white photos in simple gray frames.

"Your husband took these?"

"Yes."

"He is very talented."

"But this work does not bring money. Everyone, they want a scandal. Everyone wants to read about someone else's dirt. I do not understand this. But I am not American."

"Well, I am American," said Abby. "And I don't understand it, either."

"Here. Have a seat. I'll look at Lyle's desk calendar. If there are any notes about where he might be, they would be there." Mrs. Morris gestured to a small brown couch.

The living space was cramped with overstuffed furniture and more framed black-and-white photos. "Are these your sons?"

"Yes. Freddy and Nate. They are at school." Mrs. Morris scooted behind the couch to a hidden alcove.

Abby continued to study the images of the boys that were hung all along the opposing wall. Blake, too, seemed fixated on a set of photographs—another series that was displayed neatly across the end table on his side of the sofa.

They could hear her riffling through files and papers on her husband's desk. "I don't see anything.... Wait... here is something...maybe..."

While Mrs. Morris spoke, Blake's hand reached back and took hold of Abby's wrist.

"I think I know where Lyle Morris is." He turned his head to her and spoke in the lowest whisper.

"Where?" Abby's eyes grew wide.

"In the morgue." Blake pulled one of the small photos off the side table and handed it to her.

Abby shivered as she recognized the round, bald-headed face of Nicolas Hancock. No wonder Mrs. Morris hadn't heard from her husband in several days.

He'd been murdered. And she had no idea....

Blake's head was swimming. Should they call Langer first? Tell Mrs. Morris and call in Agent Day? The look on Abby's face showed that she was considering a similar set of anxious thoughts. She'd gone pale when she'd seen the picture, and he was struck by how tired and strained she looked. But really, what else could he have expected? She was still shaking from the visit to Dr. Miles's office. Not to mention the burns on her arms had to be throbbing even with the ibuprofen he'd convinced her to take.

Mrs. Morris, still scavenging through her husband's desk in the alcove behind them, was obliviously content, thinking her dear husband would be home any minute with a million-dollar story. This was the worst part of being a doctor—the moment when you had to tell someone that it was time to give up hope.

"Oh...here. I found something," she said.

Blake pulled his eyes away from Abby and replaced the picture of Morris, aka Hancock, on the side table.

"It's about your family, Dr. Jamison." She scooted out from the desk and returned to the sitting area, handing him a fistful of crumpled papers. "I can't tell if it's old or new."

Blake took the papers, no longer interested in the

hospital story against him but only in how to talk to Mrs. Morris about her husband, who wasn't coming back home.

"Would you like a coffee, perhaps? Tea?" she offered. "I always take espresso this time of day. And my boys will be home soon. I'd like to introduce you to Nate, since he used your facility. I think he would like very much to meet you."

"Please," Abby said. "Some coffee would be very nice. Thank you."

Mrs. Morris disappeared around the corner. Abby let out a great sigh.

"What do we say?" she asked.

"I don't know. I guess we should notify Agent Day." Blake handed the papers from Morris's desk to Abby so that he could retrieve his cell phone.

"Or Langer. What if we're wrong?"

"Good point." Blake used his phone and took a picture of the portrait on the side table. He sent the picture to Langer. The accompanying text read:

Lyle Morris, aka Nicolas Hancock?

He looked to Abby for her approval. She nodded. He hit Send. Now they had time to look at the pages that Mrs. Morris had taken from her husband's desk. Abby straightened the papers on her lap and glanced down at the first sheet.

"This is all about you," she said.

They could hear Mrs. Morris making espresso in the next room. The high-pressure machine whistled and dishes clanged. Still, they spoke at a whisper.

"What do you mean it's all about me?" Blake said.

"Here." Abby handed him the first two pages that she'd already looked through.

Blake felt his hands begin to shake as he recognized the documents. "This is a copy of the file from my mother's lawyer. How would Nicolas Hancock, I mean Lyle Morris, get his hands on this?"

"It's about your adoption, isn't it?" Abby handed him the rest of the pages.

Blake nodded. He could feel his pulse racing as he scanned through the rest of the papers from Lyle Morris's desk. "Yes, it's all here. Copies of my mother's letter and the notes from the doctor. This is a copy of the birth record that I found in Lancaster."

"Wow. I guess we know why Hancock was killed. He was after the same information that you're after. It really is all connected."

"So, Dr. Miles maybe had something to do with my adoption and he was willing to kill to keep it a secret?"

Abby shrugged.

Blake saw his cell phone vibrate on the table. It was a response from Langer. The text read:

Yes. Morris is Hancock. FBI confirmed. Will be there in 20 with FBI agent.

Blake held the cell phone so that Abby could also read the text. Blake typed Okay and reset the phone on the coffee table but the question still remained—should they tell Mrs. Morris the truth before the FBI arrived?

"So, what do we do? Wait?" Abby asked.

There was no chance to respond to her question as Mrs. Morris entered the room holding a large tray with coffee and cookies, which she then placed on the coffee table. Taking the first cup and saucer for Blake, she poured a small espresso for him.

"Would you like sugar?"

"Please." Blake could hardly speak, thinking of what horrible news awaited this poor woman.

She did the same for Abby, then poured a cup for herself and took a seat across from them in a high wingbacked chair.

"We couldn't help but admire all of the photos," Abby said as she sipped her coffee.

"Oh," Mrs. Morris said. "These are just a few of the family, the boys, Lyle and me."

"Is this your husband?" Abby gestured to the photo on the table next to Blake.

"Yes, it was taken just last fall while we were on vacation in the Catskill Mountains. That was just after Nate's surgery. We were celebrating its success. I can't tell you how thankful we are for your foundation, Dr. Jamison."

Blake and Abby both squirmed uncomfortably at her praise.

"Did you find anything interesting in those papers from Lyle's desk?"

"Actually, we did. Somehow your husband has copies of some of my personal and private legal files. I didn't give them to him."

Mrs. Morris's expression darkened. "Are you sure? That doesn't sound like Lyle."

"Yes, I'm sure," Blake said. "In fact, these papers seem to be in high demand. The same ones were stolen last night from my hotel room."

"But that's impossible. Those papers have been here since last week. I'm sure of it. As I told you, my husband hasn't been home. He's working on a story, so these must have already been here before he left."

"Oh, we believe you, Mrs. Morris. We don't think your husband stole the papers from my hotel room. We think he's had them longer than that. Anyway, these are copies. Mine were originals."

"This isn't sounding very good," said Mrs. Morris. "I hope my husband isn't in any trouble. I said earlier that I don't hear from him sometimes when he's working on a story, but usually that's only a day. Maybe two at most. This has been five days."

"I'm afraid we do have bad news."

"The worst kind," Abby said, picking up where he'd left off. "There's an FBI agent and a Lancaster police detective on their way here to talk to you." Blake was just about to tell her about her husband's untimely death when two middle-school-aged boys came busting into the room with their backpacks. They stopped short when they saw that their mother had visitors.

"Bonjour, mes fils." She stood and kissed each of them on the cheek.

"Bonjour, Maman."

"I want to introduce you to Dr. Jamison. He runs the foundation where you had your surgery, Nate."

Blake stood and shook hands with both the boys. He introduced Abby and they passed a few pleasantries. Blake asked many questions about Nate's surgery, all the while feeling like a liar for not telling them about their loss. But at this point, he couldn't imagine telling them—not only that their father had died, but that he'd been murdered. They shouldn't have to hear it from a stranger, and their mother should have a chance to process the news before sharing it with her sons. After a few minutes, Mrs. Morris sent her boys to get a snack in the kitchen and start their homework.

"Have you met my dad?" Nate asked as he was leaving the room. "He's written a lot of articles about you and your foundation."

Blake swallowed down the lump that had formed in his throat. "I haven't had that pleasure."

After the boys had settled away from the living area, Mrs. Morris finished her espresso. Leaning over the coffee table, she spoke in a whisper. "I'm guessing Lyle must be in a lot of trouble if an FBI agent is coming over to the house."

At that moment, there was a knock at the front door. Detective Langer and the FBI agent had arrived. Mrs. Morris looked nervous as she stood and headed for the door. When she returned, she was crying hysterically. She looked up at Blake and Abby. "You already knew, didn't you?"

Blake dropped his head in shame. There was no way he could not feel some of the guilt at the loss of Lyle Morris.

He had no excuses to offer or justifications to share. He simply stammered out a few broken words of condolence, and then he and Abby quietly took their leave.

Chapter Nineteen

Abby and Blake were not allowed to return to Lancaster that night. The FBI put them up at the Waldorf Astoria in a large suite with Detective Langer as their guardian. Abby had never seen anything quite like the hotel as they sat on the fanciest sofa she'd ever seen and had a room-service dinner. Her first ever.

"Your trip to New York was pretty productive," Langer said. "We might never have figured out this ring of adoption scandals if it hadn't been for you two. There may still be some other people involved but the FBI is pretty certain they've got the three main players, Dr. Miles, Mr. Linton and Mr. Pooler."

"But I don't understand," said Abby. "How did it all piece together?"

"Well, first," said Detective Langer, "you recognized Dr. Miles as Hancock's—Morris's—murderer. We caught up with him at the Teterboro Airport in New Jersey. He was getting ready to leave the country after you came to his office and scared him. The FBI is certain after going through his home and office that they will have more than enough incriminating evidence to put him away for murder and kidnapping."

"Okay, I understand the murder charges—he killed Morris. But kidnapping? Who was kidnapped? Do you mean to tell me that he gave away a baby that wasn't really up for adoption?"

"Exactly," said Blake, who had gotten more of the details out of Langer while Abby had been freshening up. "He stole me and other Amish babies. He would deliver us, then whisk the baby away, apparently telling the family the infant had a terrible disease and needed special treatment. Later, he'd tell them the baby had died and had to be cremated because of risk of infection. He would then sell the baby to rich couples in New York for millions."

"And the lawyers helped make the connections?"

"Right. Linton and Pooler, who are brothers—which explains why I confused them. They all took a cut of the million-dollar adoptions. For thirty years they've been doing this—abusing the most unsuspecting people, the Amish, knowing that they would not be likely to question any doctor's authority."

"No wonder they didn't want anyone to find out about it."

"Where are Pooler and Linton?"

"That we don't know," said Langer. "But we will question Dr. Miles and get more answers over the next few days."

"Well, how did Mr. Morris fit into all of this?" asked Abby. "Why would Pooler give him the files about the adoptions if it incriminated him?"

"Morris knew too much. He had enough information about you and your family to know that you were adopted, and if he dug into it further, he probably discovered that the paperwork wasn't legit. We imagine Pooler tried to bribe him to keep quiet. And when he didn't agree, they—Dr. Miles—decided to eliminate him. Linton called him and convinced him to become a patient at Fairview Hospital under the pretense that he'd be able to access your adoption records. The files Pooler gave him were most likely the bait to convince him of their sincerity. Morris fell for the idea hook, line and sinker. Dr. Miles slipped in and—"

"Shot him full of epinephrine," said Abby. "But why was Blake's name on the hospital file?"

"Well, when you, Dr. Jamison, transferred to Fairview, they all saw embroiling you in the investigation as a way to distract you from looking up the truth, too."

"You mean they were trying to frame me for Hancock's death?"

"Sure. Something to keep you occupied and hopefully get you back to New York."

"And what about Dr. Granger? Granger had to know that I was adopted. Was he in on all of this, too?"

"We don't think so," Langer said. "We think Miles placed his name on the file as another lure to get you back to New York."

"Then why the phony files from Granger?"

"We think Pooler put him up to it as a favor," Langer said. "Which means there may be something else illegal going on over there. We'll look into that another day."

"Eliminate Morris and get Blake back to New York and all would have been fine, except that Miss Miller here cut through the middle of a closed-off wing of the hospital and ruined the whole plan."

"Yes, Abby. If it weren't for you," said Blake, "no one would have known that Hancock was injected. It would have looked like an ordinary cardiac arrest, and I'd have been questioned by the hospital for possible maltreatment of a patient."

"Now, the only question that remains is, who are your real parents?" Abby said.

Langer shook his head. "The FBI thinks that may be a mystery that's never solved. Between the fire and all the stolen and lost files, the chances of Blake finding his birth parents are not very good." There was a moment of silence as Blake and Abby processed this.

"Well, I think we should all get some rest." Langer stood and waited for Abby and Blake, who didn't move. He blushed, finally realizing that they wanted a moment alone. "After I make a few phone calls. Excuse me."

He slipped into one of the bedrooms.

"I can't believe it." Blake moved in close to her. "It's all over."

Abby shook her head. "I don't know. It still doesn't seem quite finished. If Dr. Miles has been in New York all these years, then how was he able to continue stealing Amish babies? And who grabbed little Stephen in Eli's stable and spoke Pennsylvania Dutch to him?"

"Relax." Blake reached for her hand. "Let the police worry about all that. We're safe for now."

Abby didn't feel safe, but maybe that was because of the man sitting next to her—the one she was falling in love with. She pulled her hand away. Blake Jamison was not for her. "Don't."

"Don't what? Abby, I know you feel this, too. I can see it in your eyes. Don't lie to me and tell me you feel nothing for me."

"This isn't what I want, Blake."

"You don't want...what? Love? A relationship with a man who cares about you? I could take care of you."

"I have to focus on my work. It's the way it has to be."

Blake stood from the sofa and walked away a few

feet, turning his back to her. She had hurt him and herself with her words, but he had to know that she was right. They might be attracted to each other, but nothing could ever come of it. They were too different. He knew it as well as she did.

He turned back to her, shaking his head. "Don't you understand? You would never have to work, Abby. Or you could work anywhere you wanted. I could build a clinic for you. Give you everything you ever wanted…"

"I made a promise—"

"To your father?"

"I made a promise to God and to myself. I won't break it. And if you really cared about me, you wouldn't ask me to."

He continued to shake his head as if he couldn't even believe what she was saying to him. "So, you choose work over love?"

"I'm choosing what will give me peace. You should do the same. Good night, Blake. I'm riding back in the morning with Detective Langer. You should stay here in New York. It's where you belong."

Abby got up and ran into her bedroom. She didn't look back as she shut the door behind her. She didn't want Blake to see the tears that might show him what she was really feeling inside.

Chapter Twenty

Abby awoke to the beautiful sounds of birds—larks, bluebirds and robins—singing outside her window. Happy songs of spring and love. It seemed as if the events of the week before had happened years ago. Morris's murder. The car accident. The fire. The trip to New York. Saying goodbye to Blake.

Had that been a mistake?

Abby had struggled all week with her parting words to him. She wished she'd been more honest about her response. She *did* have feelings for him. The fact that she couldn't stop thinking about him was proof of that. But he didn't know what he wanted and he certainly didn't understand what she wanted or needed. He'd come to Lancaster looking for parents, not a romance, and he'd certainly never had any intention of staying. He wasn't a part of her world and she wasn't a part of his.

Yes, she had done the right thing in leaving. Blake would be back in New York permanently now. Dr. Finley had returned early to resume his work in the E.R. Abby could once again concentrate on her clinic and her family. Like today, there was the big wedding at Lydia Yoder's farmhouse. Or rather, soon-to-be Lydia

Yoder—today she would marry Joseph Yoder. It was an unusual spring wedding, as most Amish weddings took place in November. The couple had been separated for a long time and requested a special date from the elders of the church.

Her father would be there. He might not like her choices, but today at least he would appreciate that she was wearing an Amish frock and upholding all the traditions that were allowed her under the circumstances.

The smell of roasted coffee brewing rose up to the bedroom from Hannah's kitchen. She'd been staying over at Eli and Hannah's since she'd returned from New York. The FBI had said that the case was wrapping up but she got the impression from Eli—whom she knew had been talking to his police friends behind her back—that it was still not safe for her to go home. But today she was putting all that behind her. She was with family, forgetting the past and moving forward.

"Hey, Abby, are you ready to come on down? There's someone here to see you." Her brother's voice boomed up the narrow stairwell.

Abby hesitated at the bedroom door. It was probably Detective Langer or Chief McClendon, neither of whom she wanted to see. She didn't really want to talk to them any more about the case. She just wanted to move forward.

"I'm coming," she said. "Just a minute."

Why did she feel so nervous? Was it seeing her father again? Abby let out a deep sigh, hoping to expel all her anxiety along with it. Then she prayed a short prayer of thanksgiving and faith for her future. *Oh, Lord, You give me all that is good. And from You I accept whatever You offer me from Your hand.*

Abby knew that all would be well. It just took patience. And then, mentally, spiritually and especially emotionally, it would all make sense again.

Or not...

Abby paused halfway down the stairs. It was not Chief McClendon. Nor Detective Langer.

It was Dr. Blake Jamison at the bottom of the stairs. But why? What was he doing back in Willow Trace? Dressed in a suit and tie, he looked as if he planned to go to the wedding, too. His hair was combed back and he wore a grand smile on his face. He had never looked more handsome. Abby walked slowly down the rest of the staircase. She wondered what he thought of her dressed in her traditional *Kapp,* frock and apron.

"You promised me a ride in your buggy. Remember?"

Blake wanted to savor every moment of their buggy ride. He wanted to memorize every detail, from the azure blue of Abby's frock, complementing her regal eyes, to the ivory creams of her skin, the peach blush of her lips and the golden tendrils of hair, which peeked out from under her pinned-on prayer *Kapp.*

He loved the feel of the buggy, the slow movement of the vehicle rocking back and forth. The steady beat of her gelding Blue-jeans as his hooves clip-clopped across the asphalt matched the even rhythm of Blake's heartbeat. The fresh air he breathed in gave him hope. Part of him wanted to gush out every feeling he had. But his common sense told him that to touch Abby's heart, to fix the damage he'd done, he had to move slowly—slow and steady, like the trot of her brown-and-white horse.

It hadn't taken Blake more than twenty-four hours to realize that he'd said all the wrong things to Abby that night after Dr. Miles had been arrested. He only hoped she hadn't been saying no to *him,* just no to his stupid offers of buying her things and taking her places. That wasn't what Abby wanted. Abby had everything she wanted right here in Lancaster. And so did he, away from the fuss and nonsense of New York that he was more than ready to leave behind. He just hoped that when he moved back here as he planned that she would let him be a part of her life.

"How did you get invited to the Yoder wedding?" She eyed him curiously as she held on to the reins of her horse.

"It's a long story." He smiled, not sure how much to reveal.

"Well, how about the short version?" Her tone told him he still had a ways to go in coaxing her to a softer mood and winning her heart.

"I had to come back to get my things from the bed-and-breakfast. While I was there, the Youngers…well, they convinced me to stay the night. Some of the wedding party was staying at the bed-and-breakfast and they…"

"Invited you to the wedding? Just like that?" Her suspicious look told him she wasn't completely buying his story.

"Hey, you wanted the short version."

"Fair enough."

"I wanted my buggy ride," he said. "And I wanted to see you."

Abby looked away. "Don't. I don't want to go through that again. Let's just enjoy the day."

But I've changed… . The words were silent on his lips. *Everything has changed.* His cell buzzed in his coat pocket, killing his hopeful thoughts. Ugh. He'd forgotten to turn it off. "Sorry. Look. I'm turning it off. Not even looking to see who it is."

He pulled the phone out, turned it off and threw it into the backseat of the buggy.

"That's a smart thing to do," she said. "No one wants a cell phone to go off during a wedding."

"Especially an Amish wedding, right?"

She smiled and, for a second, all felt right with his world. If only Abby would give him another chance. He would make her see that he did understand her.

"Don't worry. There will be a lot of *Englisch* guests at this wedding. You won't be the only one. Joseph has a lot of *Englisch* clients for his beautiful furniture and I think many of them will be there today."

"So how does it work?"

"You all, the *Englisch,* will be seated on one side, with the Amish men and all the women on the other side."

"Oh, I'm used to bride's side/groom's side."

"If I'd known you were coming," Abby said, "I wouldn't have worn the traditional dress. Then I could have sat with you and explained the ceremony."

While Blake liked the idea of sitting next to Abby at the wedding, he wouldn't have wanted to miss seeing her in the traditional Amish dress. "You've never looked more beautiful. The last week has been so hard."

He tried to take her hand, but she shook her head with an expression of regret.

"Don't. I really just want to enjoy the day. Okay?"

Blake wanted to enjoy the day, too, and in his opinion, holding her hand and talking about the future would make the day quite agreeable. Too bad she didn't feel the same way.

Abby tapped her horse with the reins and Blue-jeans pulled them up a great hill. "This is Holly Hill. It's a beautiful farm. My favorite in all of Willow Trace.

Joseph works for my father, who'll be conducting the ceremony."

Abby parked the buggy along with all the others. There was a long, long line of them up and down the hill and many cars, too. She directed Blake toward her brother and off she went with the women. He wondered how long it would be before he'd be able to talk to her again. He already missed her.

The ceremony was brief, only a few words said by her father. Then there was a great meal, more like a feast. The men were seated first in rows and rows of tables and benches lined up in front of the farmhouse. The women served them. Abby was among them. She was busy but he was able to catch her eye a few times. When the meal was over, Blake followed the men to the stable area, where there was much talk and laughter and games. Eli must have read his long expression.

"The women eat inside. They will be out soon." He patted him on the back. "Give her time, Blake. She's a stubborn girl. But she's a smart one, too, and the way she's been moping around here over the last week? Well, I think you two have some things you need to iron out."

"I just hope she'll listen."

It was another hour before the women began to trickle out of the farmhouse kitchen. But Abby was not among them. Blake was starting to lose hope, especially when he saw Hannah bringing a large slice of cake to her husband.

"Is Abigail still inside?" he asked the couple.

Eli looked around, then shrugged. "I suppose she's still helping."

He looked down the long line of buggies. Blake didn't know much about horses but Abby's was a paint, so he was patched with white and brown. He was pretty easy to spot—and he wasn't there.

"Can you ask Hannah? Looks to me like her buggy is gone."

Eli flipped his head toward the line of buggies. "What?"

"Blue-jeans. He was just there between the two chestnuts."

"Yes, he's gone." Eli looked concerned. "The buggy is still there. Someone's unhitched Blue-jeans.... Hannah," he called to his wife, "have you seen Abigail?"

"She was inside a minute ago. Should I go back and look?"

"Yeah, we haven't seen her. And Blue-jeans is missing."

Blake could feel the panic rising through his veins.

Hannah jogged over. "Oh, wait. I remember now. She got a phone call while we were doing dishes."

"A phone call?"

"I assumed she was talking with a patient. That's what it sounded like. But it was noisy in there. You know, all those women talking at the same time."

Blake and Eli exchanged glances.

"She's gone to deliver a baby," Blake said. "I'm sure of it."

"Why wouldn't she tell one of us?" Eli said, his voice a mixture of worry and frustration—the same things Blake was feeling himself.

"I don't have a good feeling about this." Blake turned to Hannah. "Who is close to delivering? Do you know?"

"Francis Cook and...um," Hannah stuttered, "Becka. Becka Esche."

Blake looked at Eli. "Tell me how to get to the Esches' home."

* * *

Abby had been helping in the kitchen when her phone buzzed against her hip. While Blake had left his phone in the buggy, she had not. It was too close to Becka's delivery date and she couldn't risk missing her call.

She slipped the phone out of hiding and answered. The other women shot her some disapproving looks, but they would understand soon enough. Still, Hannah raced over, worried that Abby had upset Lydia's mother with her phone call.

"What are you doing?" Hannah said. "Put that away or the ladies are going to kick you out of here for good."

"Becka is due any minute," Abby explained. "I had no choice."

She slipped out the back door of the kitchen. "Hello."

"This is Becka Esche. I know you are at the wedding. But it's time." Becka's voice sounded strange.

"I'll be there as soon as I can. Where is Jonas?"

Becka moaned. "I—I don't know."

"What? You're alone?"

There was a lot of hesitation before Becka answered, "Yes, I'm alone. Hurry, Abigail." Becka cried out as if a labor pain had passed over. At the end of it there was a quick whisper. "Don't come."

"What? Becka, you sound..."

Then the line went dead. Abby paused for a second, anxiety filling her every fiber. *Don't come? Why would Becka say that?* Perhaps she'd meant the baby? Perhaps she was in a lot of pain. It was only natural she'd be scared after losing her first child just after delivery.

After Abigail hung up her cell phone, she raced toward her buggy, berating herself for giving in to Blake's stupid request for a buggy ride. Right now she needed a car.

Abby looked out over the fields surrounding the

Stoltz farm. Where were the men? She wanted to tell Blake and Eli where she was going. But she didn't see them anywhere. They were probably all gone to the other side of the barn to play a game. In any case, there was no time for her to waste searching. Blake would only want to come with her, which Becka and Jonas wouldn't want. She wasn't too sure she did, either. In any case, Hannah knew what had happened. She'd been standing there when the cell phone rang along with ten other women who all knew Becka Esche was about to deliver. Any one of those women could tell the boys what had happened and they would figure out where she was…if they even noticed she was gone.

Abby arrived at her buggy and chucked her cell phone into the front seat. Becka's panicked voice rang through her ears. The buggy might be too slow, she thought. So Abby unhitched Blue-jeans. She would ride him to the Esches'. Cutting across the Lapps' and the Youngers' fields, she would be there in no time.

"I don't like this," said Blake.

"How long ago did she receive that phone call?" Eli asked his wife.

"A while." Hannah shrugged and Blake realized she had no watch. Whatever figure she came up with would be pure conjecture.

"Like 'twenty minutes' a while or like 'over an hour'?" Eli placed a hand on Hannah's shoulder. "I didn't tell you this because I didn't want you to worry. But the FBI is still looking for Anthony Linton and Pooler."

"What?" Hannah's expression darkened. "Why didn't you tell me? Abigail is still in danger, isn't she?"

"I didn't know this, either," Blake said.

"You were in New York," Eli explained. "The FBI had you under surveillance. They didn't want you or Abby to know because they want Linton and Pooler to think it's safe to come out."

"Then someone is watching Abby now?"

"I don't know. At first, they were certain that Linton had left the country with Pooler. But now they aren't so sure. There are phone calls back to someone in the States. So they think Linton or someone is still here. In Lancaster."

"Linton?"

"I guess."

"I have a really bad feeling about Abby's taking off like this." Blake's pulse was already rising when he followed Eli's pointed finger, which directed everyone's eyes across the grassy field to an approaching white truck.

"That's Chief McClendon," said Eli.

"And he's headed right for us." Blake shook his head. Abby was in trouble. He could feel it.

"I hate to interrupt the wedding—" McClendon spoke quickly "—but there didn't seem to be any other way to get in touch with you."

Blake felt his pockets before remembering he'd left his cell phone in the buggy. "Why? What's happened?"

"More like what's happening." McClendon looked through the wedding guests. "Where is Abigail? She needs to hear this, too."

"We aren't sure," said Blake. "It seems she went to deliver a baby without telling anyone. On horseback. I doubt she has her phone."

McClendon frowned and swallowed hard. Blake did not like the look on the chief's face.

"What is it?" he asked. "Why did you come to the wedding?"

"The FBI found Pooler and Linton. They were both on Grand Cayman. But Dr. Dodd was not with them."

"Dr. Dodd? What's he got to do with anything?" Blake said, thinking about the overly efficient administrator of Fairview.

"Everything. He has everything to do with this—he was the brains behind the whole concept. He started the whole affair of stealing and selling Amish babies and has continued it for over thirty years. He's a very dangerous man and the FBI thinks he's still inside of Lancaster County. He was brought up Amish, so he knows how to blend in, play the part, disappear and fool others."

"Wow. That explains a lot. And where better to hide in Lancaster County than among the Amish?" said Eli. "Come on. Let's go find Abigail and hunt down this baby-stealing monster."

Blake was already halfway to Chief McClendon's truck, where he saw Detective Langer already seated at the wheel.

"Where are we going?" said McClendon.

"To Becka Esche's."

Abby was really sorry that she wasn't wearing a pair of pants. Blue-jeans was a great horse to ride, but not bareback and not in her Amish frock. She hadn't done this since she and Hannah were little girls. And just like back then, her prayer *Kapp* dropped to the ground and her hair danced around her shoulders with the beat of the horse's gait. But after she got over the initial discomfort, muscle memory kicked in. So, once the gelding settled into a steady canter, Abby was able to join the horse's rhythm and think about what lay ahead.

Becka had gained very little weight during her pregnancy. What little bit she had eaten never seemed to stay down. Abby had never felt that Becka's pregnancy had been healthy and she had begged her—as she did all her patients—to see a licensed gynecologist at least once. But Becka and her husband, Jonas, had refused. With most of her Amish patients, the idea of a gynecologist did not sit well and was considered an unnecessary modern practice. But that was not the whole story with Jonas and Becka. They had actually been to the hospital with their first pregnancy. The baby had been born with a rare disease and died within hours of delivery. After that, nothing would convince either of them to return to a hospital or an *Englisch* doctor. And Abby could hardly blame them after such a bad experience. In fact, she thought it quite possible that stress and anxiety were the reasons for Becka's difficult pregnancy.

Thinking of Jonas, it was odd he wasn't at home with Becka. Jonas knew Becka was near term, and after what had happened last time, what could possibly have kept him from his wife? Abby could not imagine. As she rode up on their little cottage, she looked around. The place seemed eerily quiet. No dogs? No Jonas waiting at the door for her?

"Jonas?"

Abby saw their buggies parked by the paddock. Their three horses grazed in a small field next to the house. Abby dismounted, pulled off the bit and reins, and steered Blue-jeans into the field with the other horses. Jonas must be inside with Becka, she thought. He couldn't be far. All of his horses were there and Jonas was a carpenter. He and Becka didn't have a big farm or lots of animals to tend to over a big spread of land. Even from the farthest edge of their property, he should have heard her approaching. So why hadn't he come up to the door to greet her and take her horse?

The muscles in her neck tensed. Something wasn't right. She moved faster toward the house.

"Becka? Jonas?"

A woman's cry of pain pierced the still air. It was Becka. Was the baby already coming?

Please, Lord, please, let Becka and the baby be healthy.

Almost running now, Abby entered the house. Becka was on her back on the hardwood floor, a blanket thrown over her legs and lap. Her lips and face were gray with pain. Jonas stroked her hair. His eyes were closed as he whispered up prayers in a rotelike fashion.

Becka opened her tearstained eyes and tried to focus on Abby. "I told you not to come."

Abby stopped fast as she understood why Becka was on the floor, why Jonas was praying, why Becka had told her not to come.

Across the room, seated in a comfortable upholstered chair, was Dr. Dodd. He had a large handgun aimed at the Esche couple and a big creepy smile for her.

"We've been waiting for you," he said. A disgusting snarl slid across his face and he laughed. "You, Miss Miller, are going to deliver your last baby. But not here."

He stood, waving his gun around, as he walked toward the couple, holding the gun over Becka's head. "Pick her up and put her in the car," he ordered Jonas.

"What?" Abby knew why he wanted them to move. He knew as well as she did that others would join them soon. That didn't make the idea any less insane. "You can't move her in this condition. You're a doctor. You know this. Look at her. She's in agony and in labor."

"Of course she's in labor. I gave her a huge dose of Pitocin, too. Should speed things up. I don't have a whole lot of time. I need that baby."

"I have no idea what you're talking about," Abby said. "But you will be putting the baby and the mother at risk if you move them."

"I'm holding a gun. You are all at risk." He laughed.

Good point. Abby sighed. She was not going to win this fight, but she would do whatever she had to do to keep Becka and her baby alive.

Jonas didn't wait any longer. He scooped his struggling wife into his arms and stood.

"You." Dodd pointed the gun at Abby. "You're driving. My car is around back. I think you'll recognize it."

Abby glanced out the back door, which was wide-open. Parked behind the house was the same black sedan that had run her off the road last week. One by one, they filed out of the house and into the car. Dodd pointed his gun at one head and then at another, reminding them that obeying was their only option if they wanted to stay alive—for now.

"There's Blue-jeans!" Blake saw Abby's horse, happily grazing in the small paddock next to the tiny home that Eli had directed them to. Fortunately, it was not too far from the Holly Hill Farmhouse. But still, they had no idea how much time had passed since Abby had arrived. Blake shivered. Abby could have fallen into Dodd's hands over an hour ago.

Langer parked the Lancaster County Police truck in front of the house. Blake and Eli leaped from the vehicle.

"You go inside." Eli ran as he spoke, holding the spare handgun he'd taken from McClendon. He let his black felt hat fall to the ground behind him. "I'm going to cover the perimeter. Make sure no one goes anywhere."

McClendon and Langer radioed in their location and followed close behind.

Blake flew through the front door and into the tiny living space. He stopped short over a pool of blood covering a small area in the center of the hardwood floor. A white-and-yellow quilt had been thrown to the side. It was also stained with fresh blood. The rest of the house was as neat as a pin but empty. Completely empty.

"They're not here." Blake exited the Esches' home through the open back door, meeting up with Eli, who'd just circled around the outside. "But there is blood on the floor. If that's Becka's blood then there could be complications, unless she's already delivered."

"She didn't deliver yet. Dodd wants her baby. If the labor was over, he and the child would be gone and everyone else would be here."

"He moved a woman in labor?"

"Probably at gunpoint. I don't see Abby going along with it any other way."

"You're right."

"Tire marks right here." Eli pointed at the muddy ground. "These are fresh. It rained during the night. If they're in a car, they could be anywhere. It could take days to find them. If he lets them live…"

Days? Lets them live? More panic washed over Blake. He shook his head, clearing his thoughts. "Abby told me about Becka's pregnancy—that she had problems last time delivering the placenta. Maybe Abby convinced everyone to go to the hospital?"

McClendon and Detective Langer caught up with them after combing through the house behind Blake. "Unlikely. Eli's right. They are going to be hard to find."

Blake couldn't accept that. "Dodd wants that baby. He won't risk sabotaging the delivery. I don't think he'll go far."

"I'll send units to the hospital," McClendon said. "But that sounds risky for Dodd. Too many people—people who would recognize him."

Blake thought hard. Where else could they go with proper medical facilities for the delivery? Somewhere close by... "Abby's clinic?"

McClendon looked to Eli. Eli nodded. "Certainly worth a look."

The four men raced back to McClendon's police car and headed toward Abby's cottage, hoping they had guessed correctly and praying that they wouldn't arrive too late.

Jonas helped Abby place his wife on the examination table of her clinic.

"The same London family wants a sibling," said Dodd. "I've already chartered a flight to London for this afternoon."

"The same family?" Abby's brain took a second but then the whole affair made sense to her. "Becka's first baby didn't die, did it? You stole it and sold it. And now you want this one, too."

Thankfully, Dodd was so obsessed with getting the Esches' child she'd been able to convince him that he'd have the infant in less than ten minutes and that she'd needed a decent delivery setting immediately. She'd been bluffing, of course. She hadn't even examined her patient. She'd had no idea how long it would take. But now that they were in her clinic, she realized that she had not been far from the truth. Becka's baby was well on its way. Abby cleaned herself up and began coaching Becka through the labor. Jonas helped, too, making Becka as comfortable as possible.

It didn't take long—not even ten minutes. But for those very few minutes, Abby had been able to forget about the gun pointed at the back of her head and concentrate on the miracle of birth, on the comfort of her patient and on the safe delivery of the Esches' child.

"It's a girl." She delivered the infant into the arms of her father, then cut the umbilical cord. Jonas was crying. Becka looked gray and in more pain than Abby thought she had ever seen in any mother. She didn't seem to even understand that the baby had come.

"She's healthy," Abby told Becka. "Everything is going to be fine."

And that was what Abby had thought until the second she cut the cord. It retracted.

That wasn't supposed to happen.

Becka tucked up into a ball, hardly able to endure the pain. It was happening again. Her placenta was still attached. Just like last time when they'd been in the hospital and Dodd had stolen their first baby. At least then another doctor had been there to take the necessary measures to save Becka. Dodd was her only hope. Delivering an attached placenta was tricky, dangerous and if not done correctly could cause infection and death.

"Dr. Dodd, you have to help her. Her placenta is attached." Abby turned to the crazed doctor.

"I don't have to do anything." Dodd moved forward. He shoved Abby to the ground and put a bullet through her stomach. "Like I said. This was your last delivery."

Abby fell back to the floor. She grabbed at her midsection. Gritting her teeth, she pressed down on the hole before it had even begun to bleed. She could do nothing but watch as Dodd grabbed the baby from Jonas's arms.

He was too focused on the infant to even notice that his carelessly aimed shot hadn't hit any vital organs. There was still a chance that blood loss could finish her, but if she was able to get treatment in time, she'd survive. She was careful not to draw his attention in her direction, or he might notice. If he fired a second, more fatal shot, she wouldn't be able to help Becka.

"I don't have to worry about you. You won't fight back," he said to Jonas and then he was gone. Abby could hear the tires of his car crunching over the gravel as he sped out of her driveway, taking the Esches' child with him.

Abby closed her eyes as the pain receptors from her abdomen reached her brain and told it she'd been shot.

Please, Lord, she prayed, *please. I need Your hands and Your strength.*

Somehow, she was going to get up off that floor and she was going to do whatever she could to save Becka Esche. And she was going to pray that the FBI was right behind Dodd on its way to recover the Esche baby—and that the paramedics would make it to her clinic soon, for Becka's sake…and for her own.

"I don't see anyone there." Blake's heart sank to his stomach as McClendon's squad car pulled up in front of Abby's cottage and clinic.

"No, look!" Eli put a hand on his shoulder. "The front door is open. Someone has been here."

Detective Langer drew his pistol and led the way into Abby's house. Blake and Eli followed close behind.

None of them were prepared for what they saw as they entered the clinic.

"He's gone." Abby's voice was weak as she sat next to her patient holding a set of delivery forceps. "He took the baby with him. You have to find him."

"You've been hurt!" Blake rushed forward, only half hearing Abby's words. He pulled her hand away from her waist. "You've been shot."

"Forget…that. I'm…fine." She turned his attention toward Becka Esche as she struggled to breathe and speak. "She needs…help. The afterbirth…"

"Please, you're a doctor, aren't you?" An Amish-dressed man stood next to Abby's patient. He was so calm and quiet Blake had hardly noticed him there. He must be Mr. Esche. "I've been praying that you would come and save my Becka."

Blake's head swirled. He looked back at Abby, hesitating. She'd been shot. She was bleeding and hadn't stopped to bandage the wound. Already she had lost a lot of blood as she'd clearly been trying to use every bit of her energy to save her patient.

She wasn't fine.

Every bit of Blake's will told him to check Abby and her wound. To save her, to save the woman he'd come back to Lancaster for. The woman he loved and he didn't want to live without.

She shook her head at him. "I can wait for the EMTs. She can't. She's already passed out."

Abby held out the forceps for him. Blake resigned himself to doing what Abby wanted.

He turned to the sink. "I need to scrub. Eli, you'll assist me. For starters, wash your hands. Grab that brown bottle over there and those strips of bandages."

With dripping but clean hands, Blake returned to the

exam table. He took the instrument from Abby. "Pour that over the ends," he said to Eli, nodding to the bottle of povidone-iodine, a topical antiseptic, that he held.

Eli did as he said, sterilizing the tool that he would try to save Becka Esche with.

"Now, pour that same stuff all over the front and back of your sister's wound and wrap it up as tightly as possible. I'm assuming Langer has already called the EMS?" Blake knew his voice sounded detached and unfeeling, when it was the furthest thing from the truth. Inside he was dying with a panic that he'd never felt before in his whole career—his whole life.

Eli did exactly what he was told. Abby moaned as he pulled the bandages tight around her abdomen. It seemed like forever before the EMS arrived. Forever, while he struggled to save Becka and watched Abby grow paler by the minute.

But EMS arrived at last and they swept away both Becka and Abby and raced off to Fairview without him. Now all he could do was wait and pray....

Chapter Twenty-One

Abby had been in surgery for what seemed like hours to Blake. He waited outside the operatory. He sat. He stood. He paced. Abby's father sat next to him. Her mother, too. And Eli and Hannah.

"How's that search for your birth parents going?" Bishop Miller asked.

Blake shook his head. "The FBI said it was a lost cause. That they'll never be able to track down all the families Dodd stole babies from."

Anyway, he didn't care about that. All he cared about was Abby.

"You care for my daughter, don't you?" Bishop Miller asked.

"I love her."

The bishop nodded his head. Other than that, there seemed to be no reaction to Blake's confession.

"Maybe you should know I plan to move here and hopefully court your daughter… I mean, if she'll agree to that."

Again, the bishop just nodded. "I've made my peace with it, son. Relax."

Eli had been on his cell. He tucked it away and

walked over to them. "They found the Esches' baby and arrested Dodd."

Blake felt a fraction of the tension inside him relax. At least the monster who had shot Abby would face charges for his crimes. "And how is Becka?"

"She's fine."

"Has she seen her baby?"

"Not yet," said Hannah. "She's in the NICU."

Everyone sat again as there wasn't much else to say, and they waited. At long last, the E.R. surgeon came out.

"We removed the bullet. Luckily, it managed to avoid any major organs. Due to the blood loss, she'll be here for a few more days. But she will make a full recovery. She can have visitors, too—one at a time."

Abby's father headed toward Recovery without looking back.

"Wait, *Dat*. Let Blake go first," Eli said.

"No." Blake smiled. "She will want to see her dad first."

He didn't know if that was true or not but he wanted the bishop to be satisfied, and now that he knew she was going to be fine, he could stand to wait another five minutes. Blake was so happy and so nervous about what he had to tell Abby or ask Abby—a few minutes more to gather his thoughts might be a good thing.

Abby was surprised to see her father as her first visitor.

"How are you feeling, Abigail?" Her father sat next to her bedside and patted her hand.

"I've been better." She started to laugh. "Oooh. That hurts."

"You just rest. I'll do the talking," her *dat* said.

"There's a line of people waiting to get in here to see you. So, I'll make it quick."

Abby wondered if Blake was one of those people. She thought she had seen him come into her clinic. She vaguely remembered handing him the forceps to help Becka. Then again, maybe it had all been a dream.

"*Dat,* if you're here to tell me I made the wrong decision again, then please don't."

"I just told you that I was going to do the talking. Be quiet and listen. Goodness, you're as stubborn as your *mamm.*" He cleared his throat and patted her hand again. "I didn't come here to talk to you about your decision. Well, I did. But…"

Abby held her breath—she did not want to hear her father's disapproval once more.

"I came to tell you that I've been wrong," he said. "I wanted you to join the church. I wanted you to marry an Amish man. I wanted you to give me lots of grand-babies and be a farmer's wife. Or a carpenter's wife. Or a miller's wife… So, I let you go to school. I let you go to college. I let you work at the hospital. I let you start the clinic, thinking all the time that any day you would get tired of the outside world and all the complications. That you would give it up and come back home. And then I realized that home is where each one of us finds peace with the Lord. And you have that. All this time, Abby, you are home. You have been home. I just couldn't see it."

Abby could feel the tears pouring down her cheeks as she watched her dad touch his heart with his hand. "You are home. You were meant to be a nurse. And I'm very proud of you."

"Thank you, *Dat.* Thank you for understanding. I love you so much."

"And I love you, too. And now I have some things to do and you have other people to see. Get some rest and get better." He kissed her forehead and turned and left the room.

Moments later, Blake entered Abby's room and approached her slowly. She couldn't blame him for being cautious after all the pushing away she'd done. She was surprised he was brave enough to come in.

"I hope those are happy tears?" he said.

"The happiest." She smiled. "You saved Becka. Thank you."

"*You* saved Becka. I just came in and helped her hang on until the EMS arrived."

He reached her bedside. She motioned for him to sit down where her father had been. "They found Dodd and the baby. She's fine. She's here and ready to meet you. In the latest news from Hannah just a minute ago, I heard that her name is going to be Abigail."

"Stop," Abby said. "I'm going to start crying again and it hurts."

"Okay. I'll stop. In any case, I really wanted to talk about something else."

Abby didn't want to hear again about how he was leaving and going back to New York. The past week had been bad enough. She didn't want to live it all over again. "Do we have to talk, Blake? I'm scared. I can't be what you need. Just hold my hand and be my friend while you're here. I know that's all we can have."

"Shh. I'm going to talk, Abby. And you? You're just going to have to listen to me. No interrupting. Okay?"

"Have you been talking to my *dat?*"

He ignored her comment and resumed his speech, which sounded a bit as if he'd rehearsed it. "I know I haven't known you very long. I know I haven't been in

Lancaster very long. But I know what right is, Abby. I know what peace of mind is. And I know what home feels like. This is my home. Not New York. Not the private practice. Not the big apartment and the cover stories. *Right* is my being here. That's home for me—being with you. It's what I want and it's where I'm going to be."

"What?" Was she dreaming? Was she hearing him correctly? "What about your practice? Your foundations? Natalie? New York?"

"My partners are buying me out. I'm going to work here at Fairview. Natalie is engaged to Artie. Remember Artie? And I've taken up a permanent room at the bed-and-breakfast. You can't get rid of me. I'm here to stay. I love it here. And I love you."

"What about the foundation? What about finding your birth parents?" *Did he just say that he loves me?*

"I'm moving the foundation to Lancaster. And I gave up finding my birth parents. I thought I was coming here for that and I guess that is what brought me. But that wasn't what I was looking for, Abby. I was looking for you. I just didn't know it."

Abby felt frozen in the wonderful dream. She'd just had a bullet removed but she couldn't feel any pain. There was nothing but happiness inside.

"Abby? Did you hear me? I'm falling in love with you." He leaned over and kissed her softly on the lips.

"Oh, I hear you, Blake. I hear you." More happy tears fell from her eyes. "Kiss me again."

"I would…but I have something I need to know first," he teased her.

"Fair enough."

"I heard you were never going to consider marriage.

Ever. Is that true? Or is that up for negotiation? Because that might make a difference in how I kiss you..."

Abby felt the smile burst over her face. This was it. This was the man she was going to spend the rest of her life with. As a nurse, helping others and being so in love she thought she would burst.

"Are doctors allowed to marry their patients?" She lifted her eyes playfully.

Blake smiled. He knew her answer. "Well, this doctor plans to marry his patient—his one very stubborn, Amish-born, beautiful, wonderful, favorite patient. What do you say, Abigail Miller? Marry me?"

"Yes, Blake. I'll marry you. I love you so much."

He leaned in again and sealed her answer with another kiss.

* * * * *

WE HOPE YOU
ENJOYED THESE
LOVE INSPIRED®
AND
LOVE INSPIRED®
SUSPENSE
BOOKS.

Whether you prefer heartwarming contemporary romance or heart-pounding suspense, Love Inspired® books has it all!

Look for 6 new titles available every month from both Love Inspired® and Love Inspired® Suspense.

Love Inspired®

www.LoveInspired.com

Save $1.00

on the purchase of any
Love Inspired®,
Love Inspired® Suspense or
Love Inspired® Historical book.

Available wherever books are sold, including most bookstores, supermarkets, drugstores and discount stores.

Save $1.00

on the purchase of any Love Inspired®, Love Inspired® Suspense or Love Inspired® Historical book.

Coupon valid until January 31, 2017. Redeemable at participating retail outlets in the U.S. and Canada only. Limit one coupon per customer.

Canadian Retailers: Harlequin Enterprises Limited will pay the face value of this coupon plus 10.25¢ if submitted by customer for this product only. Any other use constitutes fraud. Coupon is nonassignable. Void if taxed, prohibited or restricted by law. Consumer must pay any government taxes. Void if copied. Inmar Promotional Services ("IPS") customers submit coupons and proof of sales to Harlequin Enterprises Limited, P.O. Box 3000, Saint John, NB E2L 4L3, Canada. Non-IPS retailer—for reimbursement submit coupons and proof of sales directly to Harlequin Enterprises Limited, Retail Marketing Department, 225 Duncan Mill Rd., Don Mills, ON M3B 3K9, Canada.

U.S. Retailers: Harlequin Enterprises Limited will pay the face value of this coupon plus 8¢ if submitted by customer for this product only. Any other use constitutes fraud. Coupon is nonassignable. Void if taxed, prohibited or restricted by law. Consumer must pay any government taxes. Void if copied. For reimbursement submit coupons and proof of sales directly to Harlequin Enterprises Limited, P.O. Box 880478, El Paso, TX 88588-0478, U.S.A. Cash value 1/100 cents.

® and ™ are trademarks owned and used by the trademark owner and/or its licensee.

© 2016 Harlequin Enterprises Limited

LIINCICOUPO916

SPECIAL EXCERPT FROM

*When Macy Swanson must suddenly raise her young
nephew, help comes in the form of single rancher and
boys ranch volunteer Tanner Barstow. Can he help her
see she's mom—and rural Texas—material?*

Read on for a sneak preview of the first book in the
LONE STAR COWBOY LEAGUE: BOYS RANCH
miniseries, THE RANCHER'S TEXAS MATCH
by Brenda Minton.

She leaned back in the seat and covered her face with her
hands. "I am angry. I'm mad because I don't know what to
do for Colby. And the person I always went to for advice
is gone. Grant is gone. I think Colby and I were both in
a delusional state, thinking they would come home. But
they're not. I'm not getting my brother, my best friend,
back. Colby isn't getting his parents back. And it isn't
fair. It isn't fair that I had to—"

Her eyes closed, and she shook her head.

"Macy?"

She pinched the bridge of her nose. "No. I'm not going
to say that. I lost a job and gave up an apartment. Colby
lost his parents. What I lost doesn't amount to anything. I
lost things I don't miss."

"I think you're wrong. I think you miss your life.
There's nothing wrong with that. Accept it, or it'll eat
you up."

Tanner pulled up to her house.

"I miss my life." She said it on a sigh. "I wouldn't be anywhere else. But I have to admit, there are days I wonder if Colby would be better off with someone else, with anyone but me. But I'm his family. We have each other."

"Yes, and in the end, that matters."

"But…" She bit down on her lip and glanced away from him, not finishing.

"But what?"

"What if I'm not a mom? What if I can't do this?" She looked young sitting next to him, her green eyes troubled.

"I'm guessing that even a mom who planned on having a child would still question if she could do it."

She reached for the door. "Thank you for letting me talk about Colby."

"Anytime." He said it, and then he realized the door that had opened.

She laughed. "Don't worry. I won't be calling at midnight to talk about my feelings."

"If you did, I'd answer."

She stood on tiptoe and touched his cheek to bring it down to her level. When she kissed him, he felt floored by the unexpected gesture. Macy had soft hair, soft gestures and a soft heart. She was easy to like. He guessed if a man wasn't careful, he'd find himself falling a little in love with her.

Don't miss
THE RANCHER'S TEXAS MATCH by Brenda Minton,
available October 2016 wherever
Love Inspired® books and ebooks are sold.

www.LoveInspired.com

*When a mysterious stranger washes up in her town with
no memory of his past, Deputy Sheriff Audrey Martin
must keep him safe from the men trying to kill him.*

Read on for an excerpt from
IDENTITY UNKNOWN,
the exciting conclusion to
NORTHERN BORDER PATROL.

Deputy Sheriff Audrey Martin sang along with the
Christmas carol playing on the patrol-car radio. The radio
crackled and buzzed before the sheriff's department
dispatcher, Ophelia Leighton, came on the line. "Unit
one, do you copy?"

Thumbing the answer button, Audrey replied, "Yes,
Dispatch, I copy."

"Uh, there's a reported sighting of a—"

The radio crackled and popped. In the background,
Audrey heard Ophelia talking, then the deep timbre of
the sheriff's voice. "Uh, sorry about that." Ophelia came
back on the line. "We're getting mixed reports, but
bottom line there's something washed up on the shore of
the Pine Street beach."

"Something?" Audrey shifted the car into Drive and
took off toward the north side of town. "What kind of
something?"

"Well, one report said a beached whale," Ophelia
came back with. "Another said dead shark. But a couple
people called in to say a drowned fisherman."

Her heart cramped with sorrow for the father she'd lost so many years ago to the sea.

She brought her vehicle to a halt in the cul-de-sac next to an early-model pickup truck where a small group of gawkers stood, and she climbed out.

"Audrey." Clem Previs rushed forward to grip her sleeve, his veined hand nearly blue from the cold. "Shouldn't you wait for the sheriff?"

Pressing her lips together, she covered Clem's hand with hers. "Clem, I can handle this," she assured him.

About ten yards down the beach, a man dressed from head to toe in black and wearing a mask that obscured his face struggled to drag something toward the water's edge.

Audrey narrowed her gaze. Her pulse raced. Amid a tangle of seaweed and debris, she could make out the dark outline of a large body. She shivered with dread. That certainly wasn't a fish, whale or shark. Definitely human. And from the size, she judged the body to be male.

And someone was intent on returning the man to the ocean.

Don't miss
IDENTITY UNKNOWN by Terri Reed,
available wherever
Love Inspired® Suspense books and ebooks are sold.

www.LoveInspired.com